ALICE; OR, THE MYSTERIES

EDWARD BULWER LYTTON

WILDSIDE PRESS

www.wildsidepress.com

ALICE; OR, THE MYSTERIES

BOOK I.

Σὲ τὰν ἐναυλίοις ὑπὸ δενδροκόμοις
. . . ἀναβοάσω. — EURIPIDES : *Hel.* 1. 1116.

"Thee, hid the bowering vales amidst, I call."

CHAPTER I.

WHO art thou, fair one, who usurp'st the place
Of Blanch, the lady of the matchless grace ? — LAMB.

IT was towards the evening of a day in early April that two
ladies were seated by the open windows of a cottage in Devonshire. The lawn before them was gay with evergreens, relieved by the first few flowers and fresh turf of the reviving
spring; and at a distance, through an opening amongst the
trees, the sea, blue and tranquil, bounded the view, and contrasted the more confined and home-like features of the scene.
It was a spot remote, sequestered, shut out from the business
and pleasures of the world; as such it suited the tastes and
character of the owner.

That owner was the younger of the ladies seated by the
window. You would scarcely have guessed, from her appearance, that she was more than seven or eight and twenty,
though she exceeded by four or five years that critical boundary in the life of beauty. Her form was slight and delicate
in its proportions, nor was her countenance the less lovely
because, from its gentleness and repose (not unmixed with a
certain sadness) the coarse and the gay might have thought it

1

wanting in expression. For there is a stillness in the aspect
of those who have felt deeply, which deceives the common
eye, — as rivers are often alike tranquil and profound, in proportion as they are remote from the springs which agitated
and swelled the commencement of their course, and by which
their waters are still, though invisibly, supplied.

The elder lady, the guest of her companion, was past
seventy; her gray hair was drawn back from the forehead,
and gathered under a stiff cap of quaker-like simplicity; while
her dress, rich but plain, and of no very modern fashion,
served to increase the venerable appearance of one who
seemed not ashamed of years.

"My dear Mrs. Leslie," said the lady of the house, after a
thoughtful pause in the conversation that had been carried on
for the last hour, "it is very true; perhaps I was to blame in
coming to this place; I ought not to have been so selfish."

"No, my dear friend," returned Mrs. Leslie, gently; "selfish is a word that can never be applied to you; you acted as
became you, — agreeably to your own instinctive sense of what
is best when at your age, — independent in fortune and rank,
and still so lovely, — you resigned all that would have
attracted others, and devoted yourself, in retirement, to a
life of quiet and unknown benevolence. You are in your
sphere in this village, — humble though it be, — consoling,
relieving, healing the wretched, the destitute, the infirm; and
teaching your Evelyn insensibly to imitate your modest and
Christian virtues." The good old lady spoke warmly, and
with tears in her eyes; her companion placed her hand in
Mrs. Leslie's.

"You cannot make me vain," said she, with a sweet and
melancholy smile. "I remember what I was when you first
gave shelter to the poor, desolate wanderer and her fatherless
child; and I, who was then so poor and destitute, what should
I be, if I was deaf to the poverty and sorrows of others, —
others, too, who are better than I am. But now Evelyn, as
you say, is growing up; the time approaches when she must
decide on accepting or rejecting Lord Vargrave. And yet in
this village how can she compare him with others; how can

she form a choice? What you say is very true; and yet I did
not think of it sufficiently. What shall I do? I am only
anxious, dear girl, to act so as may be best for her own
happiness."

"Of that I am sure," returned Mrs. Leslie; "and yet I
know not how to advise. On one hand, so much is due to
the wishes of your late husband, in every point of view,
that if Lord Vargrave be worthy of Evelyn's esteem and
affection, it would be most desirable that she should prefer
him to all others. But if he be what I hear he is considered
in the world, — an artful, scheming, almost heartless man,
of ambitious and hard pursuits, — I tremble to think how
completely the happiness of Evelyn's whole life may be
thrown away. She certainly is not in love with him, and
yet I fear she is one whose nature is but too susceptible of
affection. She ought now to see others, — to know her own
mind, and not to be hurried, blindfold and inexperienced, into
a step that decides existence. This is a duty we owe to her,
— nay, even to the late Lord Vargrave, anxious as he was for
the marriage. His aim was surely her happiness, and he
would not have insisted upon means that time and circumstances might show to be contrary to the end he had in view."

"You are right," replied Lady Vargrave. "When my poor
husband lay on his bed of death, just before he summoned his
nephew to receive his last blessing, he said to me, 'Providence can counteract all our schemes. If ever it should be
for Evelyn's real happiness that my wish for her marriage
with Lumley Ferrers should not be fulfilled, to you I must
leave the right to decide on what I cannot foresee. All I ask
is that no obstacle shall be thrown in the way of my wish;
and that the child shall be trained up to consider Lumley as
her future husband.' Among his papers was a letter addressed
to me to the same effect; and, indeed, in other respects that
letter left more to my judgment than I had any right to
expect. Oh, I am often unhappy to think that he did not
marry one who would have deserved his affection! and — but
regret is useless now."

"I wish you could really feel so," said Mrs. Leslie; "for

regret of another kind still seems to haunt you; and I do not think you have yet forgotten your early sorrows."

"Ah, how can I?" said Lady Vargrave, with a quivering lip.

At that instant, a light shadow darkened the sunny lawn in front of the casements, and a sweet, gay young voice was heard singing at a little distance; a moment more, and a beautiful girl, in the first bloom of youth, bounded lightly along the grass, and halted opposite the friends.

It was a remarkable contrast, — the repose and quiet of the two persons we have described, the age and gray hairs of one, the resigned and melancholy gentleness written on the features of the other — with the springing step and laughing eyes and radiant bloom of the new comer! As she stood with the setting sun glowing full upon her rich fair hair, her happy countenance and elastic form, it was a vision almost too bright for this weary earth, — a thing of light and bliss, that the joyous Greek might have placed among the forms of Heaven, and worshipped as an Aurora or a Hebe.

"Oh, how can you stay indoors this beautiful evening? Come, dearest Mrs. Leslie; come, Mother, dear Mother, you know you promised you would, — you said I was to call you; see, it will rain no more, and the shower has left the myrtles and the violet-bank so fresh."

"My dear Evelyn," said Mrs. Leslie, with a smile, "I am not so young as you."

"No; but you are just as gay when you are in good spirits — and who can be out of spirits in such weather? Let me call for your chair; let me wheel you — I am sure I can. Down, Sultan; so you have found me out, have you, sir? Be quiet, sir, down!"

This last exhortation was addressed to a splendid dog of the Newfoundland breed, who now contrived wholly to occupy Evelyn's attention.

The two friends looked at this beautiful girl, as with all the grace of youth she shared while she rebuked the exuberant hilarity of her huge playmate; and the elder of the two seemed the most to sympathize with her mirth. Both gazed

EVELYN AND SULTAN.

with fond affection upon an object dear to both. But some memory or association touched Lady Vargrave, and she sighed as she gazed.

CHAPTER II.

Is stormy life preferred to this serene ? — YOUNG : *Satires.*

AND the windows were closed in, and night had succeeded to evening, and the little party at the cottage were grouped together. Mrs. Leslie was quietly seated at her tambour-frame; Lady Vargrave, leaning her cheek on her hand, seemed absorbed in a volume before her, but her eyes were not on the page; Evelyn was busily employed in turning over the contents of a parcel of books and music which had just been brought from the lodge where the London coach had deposited it.

"Oh, dear Mamma!" cried Evelyn, "I am so glad; there is something you will like, — some of the poetry that touched you so much set to music."

Evelyn brought the songs to her mother, who roused herself from her revery, and looked at them with interest.

"It is very strange," said she, "that I should be so affected by all that is written by this person: I, too" (she added, tenderly stroking down Evelyn's luxuriant tresses), "who am not so fond of reading as you are!"

"You are reading one of his books now," said Evelyn, glancing over the open page on the table. "Ah, that beautiful passage upon ' Our First Impressions.' Yet I do not like you, dear Mother, to read his books; they always seem to make you sad."

"There is a charm to me in their thoughts, their manner of expression," said Lady Vargrave, "which sets me thinking, which reminds me of — of an early friend, whom I could fancy I hear talking while I read. It was so from the first time I opened by accident a book of his years ago."

"Who is this author that pleases you so much?" asked Mrs. Leslie, with some surprise; for Lady Vargrave had usually little pleasure in reading even the greatest and most popular masterpieces of modern genius.

"Maltravers," answered Evelyn; "and I think I almost share my mother's enthusiasm."

"Maltravers!" repeated Mrs. Leslie. "He is, perhaps, a dangerous writer for one so young. At your age, dear girl, you have naturally romance and feeling enough of your own without seeking them in books."

"But, dear madam," said Evelyn, standing up for her favourite, "his writings do not consist of romance and feeling only; they are not exaggerated, they are so simple, so truthful."·

"Did you ever meet him?" asked Lady Vargrave.

"Yes," returned Mrs. Leslie, "once, when he was a gay, fair-haired boy. His father resided in the next county, and we met at a country-house. Mr. Maltravers himself has an estate near my daughter in B——shire, but he does not live on it; he has been some years abroad, — a strange character!"

"Why does he write no more?" said Evelyn; "I have read his works so often, and know his poetry so well by heart, that I should look forward to something new from him as an event."

"I have heard, my dear, that he has withdrawn much from the world and its objects, — that he has lived greatly in the East. The death of a lady to whom he was to have been married is said to have unsettled and changed his character. Since that event he has not returned to England. Lord Vargrave can tell you more of him than I."

·"Lord Vargrave thinks of nothing that is not always before the world," said Evelyn.

"I am sure you wrong him," said Mrs. Leslie, looking up and fixing her eyes on Evelyn's countenance; "for *you* are not before the world."

Evelyn slightly — very slightly — pouted her pretty lip, but made no answer. She took up the music, and seating herself at the piano, practised the airs. Lady Vargrave listened with emotion; and as Evelyn in a voice exquisitely sweet, though not powerful, sang the words, her mother turned away her face, and half unconsciously, a few tears stole silently down her cheek.

When Evelyn ceased, herself affected, — for the lines were impressed with a wild and melancholy depth of feeling, — she came again to her mother's side, and seeing her emotion, kissed away the tears from the pensive eyes.   Her own gayety left her; she drew a stool to her mother's feet, and nestling to her, and clasping her hand, did not leave that place till they retired to rest.

And the lady blessed Evelyn, and felt that, if bereaved, she was not alone.

CHAPTER III.

But come, thou Goddess, fair and free,
In heaven yclept Euphrosyne !

.   .   .   .   :   .

To hear the lark begin his flight,
And, singing, startle the dull night. — *L'Allegro.*

But come, thou Goddess, sage and holy,
Come, divinest Melancholy !

.   .   .   .   .   .

There held in holy passion still,
Forget thyself to marble. — *Il Penseroso.*

THE early morn of early spring — what associations of freshness and hope in that single sentence!   And there — a little after sunrise — there was Evelyn, fresh and hopeful as the morning itself, bounding with the light step of a light heart over the lawn.   Alone, alone! no governess, with a pinched nose and a sharp voice, to curb her graceful movements, and tell her how young ladies ought to walk.   How silently morning stole over the earth!   It was as if youth had

the day and the world to itself.   The shutters of the cottage
were still closed, and Evelyn cast a glance upward, to assure
herself that her mother, who also rose betimes, was not yet
stirring.   So she tripped along, singing from very glee, to
secure a companion, and let out Sultan; and a few moments
afterwards, they were scouring over the grass, and descending
the rude steps that wound down the cliff to the smooth sea-
sands.   Evelyn was still a child at heart, yet somewhat more
than a child in mind.   In the majesty of —

" That hollow, sounding, and mysterious main," —

in the silence broken but by the murmur of the billows, in
the solitude relieved but by the boats of the early fishermen,
she felt those deep and tranquillizing influences which belong
to the Religion of Nature.   Unconsciously to herself, her
sweet face grew more thoughtful, and her step more slow.
What a complex thing is education!   How many circumstances, that have no connection with books and tutors, contribute to the rearing of the human mind!   The earth and the
sky and the ocean were among the teachers of Evelyn Cameron; and beneath her simplicity of thought was daily filled,
from the turns of invisible spirits, the fountain of the poetry
of feeling.

This was the hour when Evelyn most sensibly felt how
little our real life is chronicled by external events, — how
much we live a second and a higher life in our meditations
and dreams.   Brought up, not more by precept than example,
in the faith which unites creature and Creator, this was the
hour in which thought itself had something of the holiness of
prayer; and if (turning from dreams divine to earlier visions)
this also was the hour in which the heart painted and peopled
its own fairyland below, of the two ideal worlds that stretch
beyond the inch of time on which we stand, Imagination is
perhaps holier than Memory.

So now, as the day crept on, Evelyn returned in a more
sober mood, and then she joined her mother and Mrs. Leslie
at breakfast; and then the household cares — such as they

were — devolved upon her, heiress though she was; and, that
duty done, once more the straw hat and Sultan were in requisition; and opening a little gate at the back of the cottage,
she took the path along the village churchyard that led to the
house of the old curate. The burial-ground itself was surrounded and shut in with a belt of trees. Save the small
time-discoloured church and the roofs of the cottage and the
minister's house, no building — not even a cotter's hut — was
visible there. Beneath a dark and single yew-tree in the
centre of the ground was placed a rude seat; opposite to this
seat was a grave, distinguished from the rest by a slight palisade. As the young Evelyn passed slowly by this spot, a
glove on the long damp grass beside the yew-tree caught her
eye. She took it up and sighed, — it was her mother's. She
sighed, for she thought of the soft melancholy on that mother's
face which her caresses and her mirth never could wholly
chase away. She wondered why that melancholy was so fixed
a habit, for the young ever wonder why the experienced should
be sad.

And now Evelyn had passed the churchyard, and was on the
green turf before the minister's quaint, old-fashioned house.

The old man himself was at work in his garden; but he
threw down his hoe as he saw Evelyn, and came cheerfully
up to greet her.

It was easy to see how dear she was to him.

"So you are come for your daily lesson, my young pupil?"

"Yes; but Tasso can wait if the — "

"If the tutor wants to play truant; no, my child; and,
indeed, the lesson must be longer than usual to-day, for I
fear I shall have to leave you to-morrow for some days."

"Leave us! why? — leave Brook-Green — impossible!"

"Not at all impossible; for we have now a new vicar, and I
must turn courtier in my old age, and ask him to leave me
with my flock. He is at Weymouth, and has written to me to
visit him there. So, Miss Evelyn, I must give you a holiday
task to learn while I am away."

Evelyn brushed the tears from her eyes — for when the
heart is full of affection the eyes easily run over — and clung

mournfully to the old man, as she gave utterance to all her half-childish, half-womanly grief at the thought of parting so soon with him. And what, too, could her mother do without him; and why could he not write to the vicar instead of going to him?

The curate, who was childless and a bachelor, was not insensible to the fondness of his beautiful pupil, and perhaps he himself was a little more *distrait* than usual that morning, or else Evelyn was peculiarly inattentive; for certain it is that she reaped very little benefit from the lesson.

Yet he was an admirable teacher, that old man! Aware of Evelyn's quick, susceptible, and rather fanciful character of mind, he had sought less to curb than to refine and elevate her imagination. Himself of no ordinary abilities, which leisure had allowed him to cultivate, his piety was too large and cheerful to exclude literature — Heaven's best gift — from the pale of religion. And under his care Evelyn's mind had been duly stored with the treasures of modern genius, and her judgment strengthened by the criticisms of a graceful and generous taste.

In that sequestered hamlet, the young heiress had been trained to adorn her future station; to appreciate the arts and elegances that distinguish (no matter what the rank) the refined from the low, better than if she had been brought up under the hundred-handed Briareus of fashionable education. Lady Vargrave, indeed, like most persons of modest pretensions and imperfect cultivation, was rather inclined to overrate the advantages to be derived from book-knowledge; and she was never better pleased than when she saw Evelyn opening the monthly parcel from London, and delightedly poring over volumes which Lady Vargrave innocently believed to be reservoirs of inexhaustible wisdom.

But this day Evelyn would not read, and the golden verses of Tasso lost their music to her ear. So the curate gave up the lecture, and placed a little programme of studies to be conned during his absence in her reluctant hand; and Sultan, who had been wistfully licking his paws for the last half-hour, sprang up and caracoled once more into the garden; and the old priest and the young woman left the works of man for those of Nature.

"Do not fear, I will take such care of your garden while you are away," said Evelyn; "and you must write and let us know what day you are to come back."

"My dear Evelyn, you are born to spoil every one — from Sultan to Aubrey."

"And to be spoilt too, don't forget that," cried Evelyn, laughingly shaking back her ringlets. "And now, before you go, will you tell me, as you are so wise, what I can do to make — to make — my mother love me?"

Evelyn's voice faltered as she spoke the last words, and Aubrey looked surprised and moved.

"Your mother love you, my dear Evelyn! What do you mean, — does she not love you?"

"Ah, not as I love her. She is kind and gentle, I know, for she is so to all; but she does not confide in me, she does not trust me; she has some sorrow at heart which I am never allowed to learn and soothe. Why does she avoid all mention of her early days? She never talks to me as if *she*, too, had once a mother! Why am I never to speak of her first marriage, of my father? Why does she look reproachfully at me, and shun me — yes, shun me, for days together — if — if I attempt to draw her to the past? Is there a secret? If so, am I not old enough to know it?"

Evelyn spoke quickly and nervously, and with quivering lips. Aubrey took her hand, and pressing it, said, after a little pause, —

"Evelyn, this is the first time you have ever thus spoken to me. Has anything chanced to arouse your — shall I call it curiosity, or shall I call it the mortified pride of affection?"

"And you, too, are harsh; you blame me! No, it is true that I have not thus spoken to you before; but I have long, long thought with grief that I was insufficient to my mother's happiness, — I who love her so dearly. And now, since Mrs. Leslie has been here, I find her conversing with this comparative stranger so much more confidentially than with me. When I come in unexpectedly, they cease their conference, as if I were not worthy to share it; and — and oh, if I could but make you understand that all I desire is that my mother should love me and know me and trust me — "

"Evelyn," said the curate, coldly, "you love your mother, and justly; a kinder and a gentler heart than hers does not beat in a human breast. Her first wish in life is for your happiness and welfare. You ask for confidence, but why not confide in her; why not believe her actuated by the best and the tenderest motives; why not leave it to her discretion to reveal to you any secret grief, if such there be, that preys upon her; why add to that grief by any selfish indulgence of over-susceptibility in yourself? My dear pupil, you are yet almost a child; and they who have sorrowed may well be reluctant to sadden with a melancholy confidence those to whom sorrow is yet unknown. This much, at least, I may tell you, — for this much she does not seek to conceal, — that Lady Vargrave was early inured to trials from which you, more happy, have been saved. She speaks not to you of her relations, for she has none left on earth. And after her marriage with your benefactor, Evelyn, perhaps it seemed to her a matter of principle to banish all vain regret, all remembrance if possible, of an earlier tie."

"My poor, poor mother! Oh, yes, you are right; forgive me. She yet mourns, perhaps, my father, whom I never saw, whom I feel, as it were, tacitly forbid to name, — you did not know him?"

"Him! — whom?"

"My father, my mother's first husband."

"No."

"But I am sure I could not have loved him so well as my benefactor, my real and second father, who is now dead and gone. Oh, how well I remember *him*, — how fondly!" Here Evelyn stopped and burst into tears.

"You do right to remember him thus; to love and revere his memory, — a father indeed he was to you. But now, Evelyn, my own dear child, hear me. Respect the silent heart of your mother; let her not think that her misfortunes, whatever they may be, can cast a shadow over you, — you, her last hope and blessing. Rather than seek to open the old wounds, suffer them to heal, as they must, beneath the influences of religion and time; and wait the hour when without, perhaps, too keen a grief, your mother can go back with you into the past."

"I will, I will! Oh, how wicked, how ungracious I have been! It was but an excess of love, believe it, dear Mr. Aubrey, believe it."

"I do believe it, my poor Evelyn; and now I know that I may trust in you. Come, dry those bright eyes, or they will think I have been a hard taskmaster, and let us go to the cottage."

They walked slowly and silently across the humble garden into the churchyard, and there, by the old yew-tree, they saw Lady Vargrave. Evelyn, fearful that the traces of her tears were yet visible, drew back; and Aubrey, aware of what passed within her, said, —

"Shall I join your mother, and tell her of my approaching departure? And perhaps in the meanwhile you will call at our poor pensioner's in the village, — Dame Newman is so anxious to see you; we will join you there soon."

Evelyn smiled her thanks, and kissing her hand to her mother with seeming gayety, turned back and passed through the glebe into the little village. Aubrey joined Lady Vargrave, and drew her arm in his.

Meanwhile Evelyn thoughtfully pursued her way. Her heart was full, and of self-reproach. Her mother had, then, known cause for sorrow; and perhaps her reserve was but occasioned by her reluctance to pain her child. Oh, how doubly anxious would Evelyn be hereafter to soothe, to comfort, to wean that dear mother from the past! Though in this girl's character there was something of the impetuosity and thoughtlessness of her years, it was noble as well as soft; and now the woman's trustfulness conquered all the woman's curiosity.

She entered the cottage of the old bedridden crone whom Aubrey had referred to. It was as a gleam of sunshine, — that sweet comforting face; and here, seated by the old woman's side, with the Book of the Poor upon her lap, Evelyn was found by Lady Vargrave. It was curious to observe the different impressions upon the cottagers made by the mother and daughter. Both were beloved with almost equal enthusiasm; but with the first the poor felt more at home. They could talk to her more at ease: she understood them so much more quickly; they had no need to beat about the bush to tell the little peevish complaints that they were half-ashamed to utter to Evelyn. What seemed so light to the young, cheerful beauty, the mother listened to with so grave and sweet a patience. When all went right, they rejoiced to see Evelyn; but in their little difficulties and sorrows nobody was like "my good Lady!"

So Dame Newman, the moment she saw the pale countenance and graceful shape of Lady Vargrave at the threshold, uttered an exclamation of delight. Now she could let out all that she did not like to trouble the young lady with; now she could complain of east winds, and rheumatiz, and the parish officers, and the bad tea they sold poor people at Mr. Hart's shop, and the ungrateful grandson who was so well to do and who forgot he had a grandmother alive!

---◆---

CHAPTER IV.

TOWARDS the end of the week we received a card from the town ladies.
Vicar of Wakefield.

THE curate was gone, and the lessons suspended; otherwise — as like each to each as sunshine or cloud permitted — day followed day in the calm retreat of Brook-Green, — when, one morning, Mrs. Leslie, with a letter in her hand, sought Lady Vargrave, who was busied in tending the flowers of a small conservatory which she had added to the cottage, when, from various motives, and one in especial powerful and mysterious, she exchanged for so sequestered a home the luxurious villa bequeathed to her by her husband.

To flowers — those charming children of Nature, in which our age can take the same tranquil pleasure as our youth — Lady Vargrave devoted much of her monotonous and unchequered time. She seemed to love them almost as living things; and her memory associated them with hours as bright and as fleeting as themselves.

"My dear friend," said Mrs. Leslie, "I have news for you. My daughter, Mrs. Merton, who has been in Cornwall on a visit to her husband's mother, writes me word that she will visit us on her road home to the Rectory in B——shire. She will not put you much out of the way," added Mrs. Leslie, smiling, "for Mr. Merton will not accompany her; she only brings her daughter Caroline, a lively, handsome, intelligent girl, who will be enchanted with Evelyn. All you will regret is, that she comes to terminate my visit, and take me away with her. If you can forgive that offence, you will have nothing else to pardon."

Lady Vargrave replied with her usual simple kindness; but she was evidently nervous at the visit of a stranger (for she had never yet seen Mrs. Merton), and still more distressed at the thought of losing Mrs. Leslie a week or two sooner than had been anticipated. However, Mrs. Leslie hastened to reassure her. Mrs. Merton was so quiet and good-natured, the wife of a country clergyman with simple tastes; and after all, Mrs. Leslie's visit might last as long, if Lady Vargrave would be contented to extend her hospitality to Mrs. Merton and Caroline.

When the visit was announced to Evelyn, her young heart was susceptible only of pleasure and curiosity. She had no friend of her own age; she was sure she should like the grandchild of her dear Mrs. Leslie.

Evelyn, who had learned betimes, from the affectionate solicitude of her nature, to relieve her mother of such few domestic cares as a home so quiet, with an establishment so regular, could afford, gayly busied herself in a thousand little preparations. She filled the rooms of the visitors with flowers (not dreaming that any one could fancy them unwholesome), and spread the tables with her own favourite books, and had the little cottage piano in her own dressing-room removed into Caroline's — Caroline must be fond of music. She had some doubts of transferring a cage with two canaries into Caroline's room also; but when she approached the cage with that intention, the birds chirped so merrily, and seemed so glad to see her, and so expectant of sugar, that her heart smote her for her meditated desertion and ingratitude. No, she could not give up the canaries; but the glass bowl with the goldfish — oh, that would look so pretty on its stand just by the casement; and the fish — dull things! — would not miss her.

The morning, the noon, the probable hour of the important arrival came at last; and after having three times within the last half-hour visited the rooms, and settled and unsettled and settled again everything before arranged, Evelyn retired to her own room to consult her wardrobe, and Margaret, — once her nurse, now her abigail. Alas! the wardrobe of the destined Lady Vargrave — the betrothed of a rising statesman, a new and now an ostentatious peer; the heiress of the wealthy Templeton — was one that many a tradesman's daughter would have disdained. Evelyn visited so little; the clergyman of the place, and two old maids who lived most respectably on a hundred and eighty pounds a year, in a cottage, with one maidservant, two cats, and a footboy, bounded the circle of her acquaintance. Her mother was so indifferent to dress; she herself had found so many other ways of spending money! — but Evelyn was not now more philosophical than others of her age. She turned from muslin to muslin — from the coloured to the white, from the white to the coloured — with pretty anxiety and sorrowful suspense. At last she decided on the newest, and when it was on, and the single rose set in the lustrous and beautiful hair, Carson herself could not have added a charm. Happy age! Who wants the arts of the milliner at seventeen?

"And here, miss; here's the fine necklace Lord Vargrave brought down when my lord came last; it will look so grand!"

The emeralds glittered in their case; Evelyn looked at them irresolutely; then, *as* she looked, a shade came over her forehead, and she sighed, and closed the lid.

"No, Margaret, I do not want it; take it away."

"Oh, dear, miss! what would my lord say if he were down! And they are so beautiful! they will look so fine! Deary me, how they sparkle! But you will wear much finer when you are my lady."

"I hear Mamma's bell; go, Margaret, she wants you."

Left alone, the young beauty sank down abstractedly, and though the looking-glass was opposite, it did not arrest her eye; she forgot her wardrobe, her muslin dress, her fears, and her guests.

"Ah," she thought, "what a weight of dread I feel *here* when I think of Lord Vargrave and this fatal engagement; and every day I feel it more and more. To leave my dear, dear mother, the dear cottage — oh! I never can. I used to like him when I was a child; now I shudder at his name. Why is this? He is kind; he condescends to seek to please. It was the wish of my poor father, — for father he really was to me; and yet — oh that he had left me poor and free!"

At this part of Evelyn's meditation the unusual sound of wheels was heard on the gravel; she started up, wiped the tears from her eyes, and hurried down to welcome the expected guests.

———◆———

CHAPTER V.

Tell me, Sophy, my dear, what do you think of our new visitors ?
Vicar of Wakefield.

Mrs. Merton and her daughter were already in the middle drawing-room, seated on either side of Mrs. Leslie, — the former a woman of quiet and pleasing exterior, her face still handsome, and if not intelligent, at least expressive of sober

2

good-nature and habitual content; the latter a fine dark-eyed girl, of decided countenance, and what is termed a showy style of beauty, — tall, self-possessed, and dressed plainly indeed, but after the approved fashion. The rich bonnet of the large shape then worn; the Chantilly veil; the gay French *Cachemire;* the full sleeves, at that time the unnatural rage; the expensive yet unassuming *robe de soie;* the perfect *chaussure;* the air of society, the easy manner, the tranquil but scrutinizing gaze, — all startled, discomposed, and half-frightened Evelyn.

Miss Merton herself, if more at her ease, was equally surprised by the beauty and unconscious grace of the young fairy before her, and rose to greet her with a well-bred cordiality, which at once made a conquest of Evelyn's heart.

Mrs. Merton kissed her cheek, and smiled kindly on her, but said little. It was easy to see that she was a less conversable and more homely person than Caroline.

When Evelyn conducted them to their rooms, the mother and daughter detected at a glance the care that had provided for their comforts; and something eager and expectant in Evelyn's eyes taught the good-nature of the one and the good breeding of the other to reward their young hostess by various little exclamations of pleasure and satisfaction.

"Dear, how nice! What a pretty writing-desk!" said one — "And the pretty goldfish!" said the other — "And the piano, too, so well placed;" and Caroline's fair fingers ran rapidly over the keys. Evelyn retired, covered with smiles and blushes. And then Mrs. Merton permitted herself to say to the well-dressed abigail, —

"Do take away those flowers, they make me quite faint."

"And how low the room is, — so confined!" said Caroline, when the lady's lady withdrew with the condemned flowers. "And I see no Pysche. However, the poor people have done their best."

"Sweet person, Lady Vargrave!" said Mrs. Merton, — "so interesting, so beautiful; and how youthful in appearance!"

"No *tournure* — not much the manner of the world," said Caroline.

"No; but something better."

'Hem!" said Caroline. "The girl is very pretty, though too small."

"Such a smile, such eyes, — she is irresistible! and what a fortune! She will be a charming friend for you, Caroline."

"Yes, she may be useful, if she marry Lord Vargrave; or, indeed, if she make any brilliant match. What sort of a man is Lord Vargrave?"

"I never saw him; they say, most fascinating."

"Well, she is very happy," said Caroline, with a sigh.

CHAPTER VI.

Two lovely damsels cheer my lonely walk. — LAMB: *Album Verses.*

AFTER dinner there was still light enough for the young people to stroll through the garden. Mrs. Merton, who was afraid of the damp, preferred staying within; and she was so quiet, and made herself so much at home, that Lady Vargrave, to use Mrs. Leslie's phrase, was not the least "put out" by her. Besides, she talked of Evelyn, and that was a theme very dear to Lady Vargrave, who was both fond and proud of Evelyn.

"This is very pretty indeed, — the view of the sea quite lovely!" said Caroline. "You draw?"

"Yes, a little."

"From Nature?"

"Oh, yes."

"What, in Indian ink?"

"Yes; and water-colours."

"Oh! Why, who could have taught you in this little village; or, indeed, in this most primitive county?"

"We did not come to Brook-Green till I was nearly fifteen. My dear mother, though very anxious to leave our villa at

Fulham, would not do so on my account, while masters could be of service to me; and as I knew she had set her heart on this place, I worked doubly hard."

"Then she knew this place before?"

"Yes; she had been here many years ago, and took the place after my poor father's death, — I always call the late Lord Vargrave my father. She used to come here regularly once a year without me; and when she returned, I thought her even more melancholy than before."

"What makes the charm of the place to Lady Vargrave?" asked Caroline, with some interest.

"I don't know; unless it be its extreme quiet, or some early association."

"And who is your nearest neighbour?"

"Mr. Aubrey, the curate. It is so unlucky, he is gone from home for a short time. You can't think how kind and pleas‑ ant he is, — the most amiable old man in the world; just such a man as Bernardin St. Pierre would have loved to describe."

"Agreeable, no doubt, but dull — good curates generally are."

"Dull? not the least; cheerful even to playfulness, and full of information. He has been so good to me about books; indeed, I have learned a great deal from him." .

"I dare say he is an admirable judge of sermons."

."But Mr. Aubrey is not severe," persisted Evelyn, earn‑ estly; "he is very fond of Italian literature, for instance; we are reading Tasso together."

"Oh! pity he is old — I think you said he was old. Per‑ haps there is a son, the image of the sire?"

"Oh, no," said Evelyn, laughing innocently; "Mr. Aubrey never married."

"And where does the old gentleman live?"

"Come a little this way; there, you can just see the roof of his house, close by the church."

"I see; it is *tant soit peu triste* to have the church so near you."

"*Do* you think so? Ah, but you have not seen it; it is the prettiest church in the county; and the little burial‑ground —

so quiet, so shut in; I feel better every time I pass it. Some places breathe of religion."

"You are poetical, my dear little friend."

Evelyn, who *had* poetry in her nature, and therefore sometimes it broke out in her simple language, coloured and felt half-ashamed.

"It is a favourite walk with my mother," said she, apologetically; "she often spends hours there alone: and so, perhaps, I think it a prettier spot than others may. It does not seem to me to have anything of gloom in it; when I die, I should like to be buried there."

Caroline laughed slightly. "That is a strange wish; but perhaps you have been crossed in love?"

"I!—oh, you are laughing at me!"

"You do not remember Mr. Cameron, your real father, I suppose?"

"No; I believe he died before I was born."

"Cameron is a Scotch name: to what tribe of Camerons do you belong?"

"I don't know," said Evelyn, rather embarrassed; "indeed I know nothing of my father's or mother's family. It is very odd, but I don't think we have any relations. You know when I am of age that I am to take the name of Templeton."

"Ah, the name goes with the fortune; I understand. Dear Evelyn, how rich you will be! I do so wish I were rich!"

"And I that I were poor," said Evelyn, with an altered tone and expression of countenance.

"Strange girl! what can you mean?"

Evelyn said nothing, and Caroline examined her curiously.

"These notions come from living so much out of the world, my dear Evelyn. How you must long to see more of life!"

"I! not in the least. I should never like to leave this place, —I could live and die here."

"You will think otherwise when you are Lady Vargrave. Why do you look so grave? Do you not love Lord Vargrave?"

"What a question!" said Evelyn, turning away her head, and forcing a laugh.

"It is no matter whether you do or not: it is a brilliant

position. He has rank, reputation, high office; all he wants
is money, and that you will give him. Alas! I have no prospect so bright. I have no fortune, and I fear my face will
never buy a title, an opera-box, and a house in Grosvenor
Square. I wish I were the future Lady Vargrave."

"I am sure I wish you were," said Evelyn, with great
naïveté; "you would suit Lord Vargrave better than I
should."

Caroline laughed.

"Why do you think so?"

"Oh, his way of thinking is like yours; he never says anything I can sympathize with."

"A pretty compliment to me! Depend upon it, my dear,
you will sympathize with me when you have seen as much of
the world. But Lord Vargrave — is he too old?"

"No, I don't think of his age; and indeed he looks younger
than he is."

"Is he handsome?"

"He is what may be called handsome, — you would think
so."

"Well, if he comes here, I will do my best to win him from
you; so look to yourself."

"Oh, I should be so grateful; I should like him so much,
if he would fall in love with you!"

"I fear there is no chance of that."

"But how," said Evelyn, hesitatingly, after a pause, —
"how is it that you have seen so much more of the world
than I have? I thought Mr. Merton lived a great deal in the
country."

"Yes, but my uncle, Sir John Merton, is member for the
county; my grandmother on my father's side — Lady Elizabeth, who has Tregony Castle (which we have just left) for her
jointure-house — goes to town almost every season, and I have
spent three seasons with her. She is a charming old woman,
— quite the *grand dame.* I am sorry to say she remains in
Cornwall this year. She has not been very well; the physicians forbid late hours and London; but even in the country
we are very gay. My uncle lives near us, and though a wid-

ower, has his house full when down at Merton Park; and
Papa, too, is rich, very hospitable and popular, and will, I
hope, be a bishop one of these days — not at all like a mere
country parson; and so, somehow or other, I have learned to
be ambitious, — we are an ambitious family on Papa's side.
But, alas! I have not your cards to play. Young, beautiful,
and an heiress! Ah, what prospects! You should make
your mamma take you to town."

"To town! she would be wretched at the very idea. Oh,
you don't know us."

"I can't help fancying, Miss Evelyn," said Caroline, archly,
"that you are not so blind to Lord Vargrave's perfections and
so indifferent to London, only from the pretty innocent way
of thinking, that so prettily and innocently you express. I
dare say, if the truth were known, there is some handsome
young rector, besides the old curate, who plays the flute, and
preaches sentimental sermons in white kid gloves."

Evelyn laughed merrily, — so merrily that Caroline's suspicions vanished. They continued to walk and talk thus till
the night came on, and then they went in; and Evelyn showed
Caroline her drawings, which astonished that young lady, who
was a good judge of accomplishments. Evelyn's performance
on the piano astonished her yet more; but Caroline consoled
herself on this point, for her voice was more powerful, and
she sang French songs with much more spirit. Caroline
showed talent in all she undertook; but Evelyn, despite her
simplicity, had genius, though as yet scarcely developed, for
she had quickness, emotion, susceptibility, imagination. And
the difference between talent and genius lies rather in the
heart than the head.

CHAPTER VII.

Dost thou feel
The solemn whispering influence of the scene
Oppressing thy young heart, that thou dost draw
More closely to my side ? — F. HEMANS : *Wood Walk and Hymn.*

CAROLINE and Evelyn, as was natural, became great friends.
They were not kindred to each other in disposition; but they
were thrown together, and friendship thus forced upon both.
Unsuspecting and sanguine, it was natural to Evelyn to admire; and Caroline was, to her inexperience, a brilliant and
imposing novelty. Sometimes Miss Merton's worldliness of
thought shocked Evelyn; but then Caroline had a way with
her as if she were not in earnest, — as if she were merely
indulging an inclination towards irony; nor was she without
a certain vein of sentiment that persons a little hackneyed in
the world and young ladies a little disappointed that they are
not wives instead of maids, easily acquire. Trite as this vein
of sentiment was, poor Evelyn thought it beautiful and most
feeling. Then, Caroline was clever, entertaining, cordial,
with all that superficial superiority that a girl of twenty-
three who knows London readily exercises over a country girl
of seventeen. On the other hand, Caroline was kind and affectionate towards her. The clergyman's daughter felt that she
could not be always superior, even in fashion, to the wealthy
heiress.

One evening, as Mrs. Leslie and Mrs. Merton sat under the
veranda of the cottage, without their hostess, who had gone
alone into the village, and the young ladies were confidentially
conversing on the lawn, Mrs. Leslie said rather abruptly, "Is
not Evelyn a delightful creature? How unconscious of her
beauty; how simple, and yet so naturally gifted!"

"I have never seen one who interested me more," said Mrs.
Merton, settling her *pélerine;* "she is extremely pretty."

"I am so anxious about her," resumed Mrs. Leslie, thoughtfully. "You know the wish of the late Lord Vargrave that she should marry his nephew, the present lord, when she reaches the age of eighteen. She only wants nine or ten months of that time; she has seen nothing of the world: she is not fit to decide for herself; and Lady Vargrave, the best of human creatures, is still herself almost too inexperienced in the world to be a guide for one so young placed in such peculiar circumstances, and of prospects so brilliant. Lady Vargrave at heart is a child still, and will be so even when as old as I am."

"It is very true," said Mrs. Merton. "Don't you fear that the girls will catch cold? The dew is falling, and the grass must be wet."

"I have thought," continued Mrs. Leslie, without heeding the latter part of Mrs. Merton's speech, "that it would be a kind thing to invite Evelyn to stay with you a few months at the Rectory. To be sure, it is not like London; but you see a great deal of the world. The society at your house is well selected, and at times even brilliant; she will meet young people of her own age, and young people fashion and form each other."

"I was thinking myself that I should like to invite her," said Mrs. Merton; "I will consult Caroline."

"Caroline, I am sure, would be delighted; the difficulty lies rather in Evelyn herself."

"You surprise me! she must be moped to death here."

"But will she leave her mother?"

"Why, Caroline often leaves me," said Mrs. Merton.

Mrs. Leslie was silent, and Evelyn and her new friend now joined the mother and daughter.

"I have been trying to persuade Evelyn to pay us a little visit," said Caroline; "she could accompany us so nicely; and if she is still strange with us, dear grandmamma goes too, — I am sure we can make her at home."

"How odd!" said Mrs. Merton; "we were just saying the same thing. My dear Miss Cameron, we should be so happy to have you."

"And I should be so happy to go, if Mamma would but go too."

As she spoke, the moon, just risen, showed the form of Lady Vargrave slowly approaching the house. By the light, her features seemed more pale than usual; and her slight and delicate form, with its gliding motion and noiseless step, had in it something almost ethereal and unearthly.

Evelyn turned and saw her, and her heart smote her. Her mother, so wedded to the dear cottage — and had this gay stranger rendered that dear cottage less attractive, — she who had said she could live and die in its humble precincts? Abruptly she left her new friend, hastened to her mother, and threw her arms fondly round her.

"You are pale; you have over-fatigued yourself. Where have you been? Why did you not take me with you?"

Lady Vargrave pressed Evelyn's hand affectionately.

"You care for me too much," said she. "I am but a dull companion for you; I was so glad to see you happy with one better suited to your gay spirits. What can we do when she leaves us?"

"Ah, I want no companion but my own, own mother. And have I not Sultan, too?" added Evelyn, smiling away the tear that had started to her eyes.

CHAPTER VIII.

FRIEND after friend departs;
  Who hath not lost a friend?
There is no union here of hearts
  That finds not here an end. — J. MONTGOMERY.

THAT night Mrs. Leslie sought Lady Vargrave in her own room. As she entered gently she observed that, late as the hour was, Lady Vargrave was stationed by the open window, and seemed intently gazing on the scene below. Mrs. Leslie

reached her side unperceived. The moonlight was exceedingly bright; and just beyond the garden, from which it was
separated but by a slight fence, lay the solitary churchyard
of the hamlet, with the slender spire of the holy edifice rising
high and tapering into the shining air. It was a calm and
tranquillizing scene; and so intent was Lady Vargrave's
abstracted gaze, that Mrs. Leslie was unwilling to disturb
her revery.

At length Lady Vargrave turned; and there was that
patient and pathetic resignation written in her countenance
which belongs to those whom the world can deceive no more,
and who have fixed their hearts in the life beyond.

Mrs. Leslie, whatever she thought or felt, said nothing,
except in kindly remonstrance on the indiscretion of braving
the night air. The window was closed; they sat down to
confer.

Mrs. Leslie repeated the invitation given to Evelyn, and
urged the advisability of accepting it. "It is cruel to separate you," said she; "I feel it acutely. Why not, then, come
with Evelyn? You shake your head: why always avoid society? So young, yet you give yourself too much to the past!"

Lady Vargrave rose, and walked to a cabinet at the end of
the room; she unlocked it, and beckoned to Mrs. Leslie to
approach. In a drawer lay carefully folded articles of female
dress, — rude, homely, ragged, — the dress of a peasant girl.

"Do these remind you of your first charity to me?" she
said touchingly: "they tell me that I have nothing to do
with the world in which you and yours, and Evelyn herself,
should move."

"Too tender conscience! — your errors were but those of
circumstances, of youth; — how have they been redeemed!
none even suspect them. Your past history is known but to
the good old Aubrey and myself. No breath, even of rumour,
tarnishes the name of Lady Vargrave."

"Mrs. Leslie," said Lady Vargrave, reclosing the cabinet,
and again seating herself, "my world lies around me; I cannot quit it. If I were of use to Evelyn, then indeed I would
sacrifice, brave all; but I only cloud her spirits. I have no

advice to give her, no instruction to bestow. When she was a child I could watch over her; when she was sick, I could nurse her; but now she requires an adviser, a guide; and I feel too sensibly that this task is beyond my powers. I, a guide to youth and innocence, — *I!* No, I have nothing to offer her, dear child! but my love and my prayers. Let your daughter take her, then, — watch over her, guide, advise her. For me — unkind, ungrateful as it may seem — were she but happy, I could well bear to be alone!"

"But she — how will she, who loves you so, submit to this separation?"

"It will not be long; and," added Lady Vargrave, with a serious, yet sweet smile, "she had better be prepared for that separation which must come at last. As year by year I out-live my last hope, — that of once more beholding *him*, — I feel that life becomes feebler and feebler, and I look more on that quiet churchyard as a home to which I am soon return-ing. At all events, Evelyn will be called upon to form new ties that must estrange her from me; let her wean herself from one so useless to her, to all the world, — now, and by degrees."

"Speak not thus," said Mrs. Leslie, strongly affected; "you have many years of happiness yet in store for you. The more you recede from youth, the fairer life will become to you."

"God is good to me," said the lady, raising her meek eyes; "and I have already found it so. I am contented."

CHAPTER IX.

THE greater part of them seemed to be charmed with his presence.
MACKENZIE : *The Man of the World.*

IT was with the greatest difficulty that Evelyn could at last be persuaded to consent to the separation from her mother; she wept bitterly at the thought. But Lady Vargrave, though

touched, was firm, and her firmness was of that soft, imploring character which Evelyn never could resist. The visit
was to last some months, it is true, but she would return to
the cottage; she would escape, too — and this, perhaps, unconsciously reconciled her more than aught else — the period-
ical visit of Lord Vargrave. At the end of July, when the
parliamentary session at that unreformed era usually expired,
he always came to Brook-Green for a month. His last visits
had been most unwelcome to Evelyn, and this next visit she
dreaded more than she had any of the former ones. It is
strange, — the repugnance with which she regarded the suit
of her affianced! — she, whose heart was yet virgin; who had
never seen any one who, in form, manner, and powers to
please, could be compared to the gay Lord Vargrave. And
yet a sense of honour, of what was due to her dead benefactor,
her more than father, — all combated that repugnance, and
left her uncertain what course to pursue, uncalculating as to
the future. In the happy elasticity of her spirits, and with
a carelessness almost approaching to levity, which, to say
truth, was natural to her, she did not often recall the solemn
engagement that must soon be ratified or annulled; but when
that thought did occur, it saddened her for hours, and left her
listless and despondent. The visit to Mrs. Merton was, then,
finally arranged, the day of departure fixed, when, one morning, came the following letter from Lord Vargrave himself: —

To the LADY VARGRAVE, *etc.*

MY DEAR FRIEND, — I find that we have a week's holiday in our do-
nothing Chamber, and the weather is so delightful, that I long to share
its enjoyment with those I love best. You will, therefore, see me almost
as soon as you receive this ; that is, I shall be with you at dinner on the
same day. What can I say to Evelyn ? Will you, dearest Lady
Vargrave, make her accept all the homage which, when uttered by me,
she seems half inclined to reject ?

In haste, most affectionately yours,

VARGRAVE.

HAMILTON PLACE, *April* 30, 18—.

This letter was by no means welcome, either to Mrs. Leslie
or to Evelyn. The former feared that Lord Vargrave would

disapprove of a visit, the real objects of which could scarcely be owned to him; the latter was reminded of all she desired to forget. But Lady Vargrave herself rather rejoiced at the thought of Lumley's arrival. Hitherto, in the spirit of her passive and gentle character, she had taken the engagement between Evelyn and Lord Vargrave almost as a matter of course. The will and wish of her late husband operated most powerfully on her mind; and while Evelyn was yet in child-hood, Lumley's visits had ever been acceptable, and the play-ful girl liked the gay and good-humoured lord, who brought her all sorts of presents, and appeared as fond of dogs as her-self. But Evelyn's recent change of manner, her frequent fits of dejection and thought, once pointed out to Lady Vargrave by Mrs. Leslie, aroused all the affectionate and maternal anx-iety of the former. She was resolved to watch, to examine, to scrutinize, not only Evelyn's reception of Vargrave, but, as far as she could, the manner and disposition of Vargrave him-self. She felt how solemn a trust was the happiness of a whole life; and she had that romance of heart, learned from Nature, not in books, which made her believe that there could be no happiness in a marriage without love.

The whole family party were on the lawn, when, an hour earlier than he was expected, the travelling carriage of Lord Vargrave was whirled along the narrow sweep that conducted from the lodge to the house. Vargrave, as he saw the party, kissed his hand from the window; and leaping from the car-riage, when it stopped at the porch, hastened to meet his hostess.

"My dear Lady Vargrave, I am so glad to see you! You are looking charmingly; and Evelyn? — oh, there she is; the dear coquette, how lovely she is! how she has improved! But who [sinking his voice], who are those ladies?"

"Guests of ours, — Mrs. Leslie, whom you have often heard us speak of, but never met — "

"Yes; and the others?"

"Her daughter and grandchild."

"I shall be delighted to know them."

A more popular manner than Lord Vargrave's it is impos-

sible to conceive. Frank and prepossessing, even when the
poor and reckless Mr. Ferrers, without rank or reputation, his
smile, the tone of his voice, his familiar courtesy, — apparently so inartificial and approaching almost to a boyish
bluntness of good-humour, — were irresistible in the rising
statesman and favoured courtier.

Mrs. Merton was enchanted with him; Caroline thought
him, at the first glance, the most fascinating person she had
ever seen; even Mrs. Leslie, more grave, cautious, and penetrating, was almost equally pleased with the first impression;
and it was not till, in his occasional silence, his features settled into their natural expression that she fancied she detected
in the quick suspicious eye and the close compression of the
lips the tokens of that wily, astute, and worldly character,
which, in proportion as he had risen in his career, even his
own party reluctantly and mysteriously assigned to one of
their most prominent leaders.

When Vargrave took Evelyn's hand, and raised it with
meaning gallantry to his lips, the girl first blushed deeply,
and then turned pale as death; nor did the colour thus chased
away soon return to the transparent cheek. Not noticing
signs which might bear a twofold interpretation, Lumley,
who seemed in high spirits, rattled away on a thousand matters, — praising the view, the weather, the journey, throwing
out a joke here and a compliment there, and completing his
conquest over Mrs. Merton and Caroline.

"You have left London in the very height of its gayety,
Lord Vargrave," said Caroline, as they sat conversing after
dinner.

"True, Miss Merton; but the country is in the height of its
gayety too."

"Are you so fond of the country, then?"

"By fits and starts; my passion for it comes in with the
early strawberries, and goes out with the hautboys. I lead so
artificial a life; but then I hope it is a useful one. I want
nothing but a home to make it a happy one."

"What is the latest news? — dear London! I am so sorry
Grandmamma, Lady Elizabeth, is not going there this year,

so I am compelled to rusticate. Is Lady Jane D—— to be married at last?"

"Commend me to a young lady's idea of news, — always marriage! Lady Jane D——! yes, she is to be married, as you say — *at last!* While she was a beauty, our cold sex was shy of her; but she has now faded into plainness, — the proper colour for a wife."

"Complimentary!"

"Indeed it is — for you beautiful women we love too much for our own happiness — heigho! — and a prudent marriage means friendly indifference, not rapture and despair. But give me beauty and love; I never was prudent: it is not my weakness."

Though Caroline was his sole supporter in this dialogue, Lord Vargrave's eyes attempted to converse with Evelyn, who was unusually silent and abstracted. Suddenly Lord Vargrave seemed aware that he was scarcely general enough in his talk for his hearers. He addressed himself to Mrs. Leslie, and glided back, as it were, into a former generation. He spoke of persons gone and things forgotten; he made the subject interesting even to the young, by a succession of various and sparkling anecdotes. No one could be more agreeable; even Evelyn now listened to him with pleasure, for to all women wit and intellect have their charm. But still there was a cold and sharp levity in the tone of the man of the world that prevented the charm sinking below the surface. To Mrs. Leslie, he seemed unconsciously to betray a laxity of principle; to Evelyn, a want of sentiment and heart. Lady Vargrave, who did not understand a character of this description, listened attentively, and said to herself, "Evelyn may admire, but I fear she cannot love him." Still, time passed quickly in Lumley's presence, and Caroline thought she had never spent so pleasant an evening.

When Lord Vargrave retired to his room, he threw himself in his chair, and yawned with exceeding fervour. His servant arranged his dressing-robe, and placed his portfolios and letter-boxes on the table.

"What o'clock is it?" said Lumley.

"Very early, my lord; only eleven."

"The devil! The country air is wonderfully exhausting. I am very sleepy; you may go."

"This little girl," said Lumley, stretching himself, "is preternaturally shy. I must neglect her no longer — yet it is surely all safe? She has grown monstrous pretty; but the other girl is more amusing, more to my taste, and a much easier conquest, I fancy. Her great dark eyes seem full of admiration for my lordship. Sensible young woman! she may be useful in piquing Evelyn."

CHAPTER X.

Julio. Wilt thou have him? — *The Maid in the Mill.*

LORD VARGRAVE heard the next morning, with secret distaste and displeasure, of Evelyn's intended visit to the Mertons. He could scarcely make any open objection to it; but he did not refrain from many insinuations as to its impropriety.

"My dear friend," said he to Lady Vargrave, "it is scarcely right in you (pardon me for saying it) to commit Evelyn to the care of comparative strangers. Mrs. Leslie, indeed, you know; but Mrs. Merton, you allow, you have now seen for the first time. A most respectable person doubtless; but still, recollect how young Evelyn is, how rich; what a prize to any younger sons in the Merton family (if such there be). Miss Merton herself is a shrewd, worldly girl; and if she were of our sex would make a capital fortune-hunter. Don't think my fear is selfish; I do not speak for myself. If I were Evelyn's brother, I should be yet more earnest in my remonstrance."

"But, Lord Vargrave, poor Evelyn is dull here; my spirits infect hers. She ought to mix more with those of her own age, to see more of the world before — before — "

"Before her marriage with me? Forgive me, but is not

that my affair? If I am contented, nay, charmed with her innocence, if I prefer it to all the arts which society could teach her, surely you would be acquitted for leaving her in the beautiful simplicity that makes her chief fascination? She will see enough of the world as Lady Vargrave."

"But if she should resolve never to be Lady Vargrave — ?"

Lumley started, bit his lip, and frowned. Lady Vargrave had never before seen on his countenance the dark expression it now wore. He recollected and recovered himself, as he observed her eye fixed upon him, and said, with a constrained smile, —

"Can you anticipate an event so fatal to my happiness, so unforeseen, so opposed to all my poor uncle's wishes, as Evelyn's rejection of a suit pursued for years, and so solemnly sanctioned in her very childhood?"

"She must decide for herself," said Lady Vargrave. "Your uncle carefully distinguished between a wish and a command. Her heart is as yet untouched. If she can love you, may you deserve her affection."

"It shall be my study to do so. But why this departure from your roof just when we ought to see most of each other? It cannot be that you would separate us?"

"I fear, Lord Vargrave, that if Evelyn were to remain here, she would decide against you. I fear if you press her now, such now may be her premature decision. Perhaps this arises from too fond an attachment for her home; perhaps even a short absence from her home — from me — may more reconcile her to a permanent separation."

Vargrave could say no more, for here they were joined by Caroline and Mrs. Merton; but his manner was changed, nor could he recover the gayety of the previous night.

When, however, he found time for meditation, he contrived to reconcile himself to the intended visit. He felt that it was easy to secure the friendship of the whole of the Merton family; and that friendship might be more useful to him than the neutral part adopted by Lady Vargrave. He should, of course, be invited to the rectory; it was much nearer London than Lady Vargrave's cottage, he could more often escape

from public cares to superintend his private interest. A country neighbourhood, particularly at that season of the year, was
not likely to abound in very dangerous rivals. Evelyn would,
he saw, be surrounded by a *worldly* family, and he thought
that an advantage; it might serve to dissipate Evelyn's
romantic tendencies, and make her sensible of the pleasures
of the London life, the official rank, the gay society that her
union with him would offer as an equivalent for her fortune.
In short, as was his wont, he strove to make the best of the
new turn affairs had taken. Though guardian to Miss Cameron, and one of the trustees for the fortune she was to receive
on attaining her majority, he had not the right to dictate as to
her residence. The late lord's will had expressly and pointedly corroborated the natural and lawful authority of Lady
Vargrave in all matters connected with Evelyn's education
and home. It may be as well, in this place, to add, that to
Vargrave and the co-trustee, Mr. Gustavus Douce, a banker
of repute and eminence, the testator left large discretionary
powers as to the investment of the fortune. He had stated it
as his wish that from one hundred and twenty to one hundred
and thirty thousand pounds should be invested in the purchase of a landed estate; but he had left it to the discretion
of the trustees to increase that sum, even to the amount of the
whole capital, should an estate of adequate importance be in
the market, while the selection of time and purchase was un-
reservedly confided to the trustees. Vargrave had hitherto
objected to every purchase in the market, — not that he was
insensible to the importance and consideration of landed property, but because, till he himself became the legal receiver of
the income, he thought it less trouble to suffer the money to
lie in the Funds, than to be pestered with all the onerous
details in the management of an estate that might never be
his. He, however, with no less ardour than his deceased relative, looked forward to the time when the title of Vargrave
should be based upon the venerable foundation of feudal
manors and seignorial acres.

"Why did you not tell me Lord Vargrave was so charming?" said Caroline to Evelyn, as the two girls were saunter-

ing, in familiar *tête-à-tête*, along the gardens. "You will be very happy with such a companion."

Evelyn made no answer for a few moments, and then, turning abruptly round to Caroline, and stopping short, she said, with a kind of tearful eagerness, "Dear Caroline, you are so wise, so kind too; advise me, tell me what is best. I am very unhappy."

Miss Merton was moved and surprised by Evelyn's earnestness.

"But what is it, my poor Evelyn," said she; "why are you unhappy? — you whose fate seems to me so enviable."

"I cannot love Lord Vargrave; I recoil from the idea of marrying him. Ought I not fairly to tell him so? Ought I not to say that I cannot fulfil the wish that — oh, there's the thought which leaves me so irresolute! — His uncle bequeathed to me — me who have no claim of relationship — the fortune that should have been Lord Vargrave's, in the belief that my hand would restore it to him. It is almost a fraud to refuse him. Am I not to be pitied?"

"But why can you not love Lord Vargrave? If past the *première jeunesse*, he is still handsome. He is more than handsome, — he has the air of rank, an eye that fascinates, a smile that wins, the manners that please, the abilities that command, the world! Handsome, clever, admired, distinguished — what can woman desire more in her lover, her husband? Have you ever formed some fancy, some ideal of the one you could love, and how does Lord Vargrave fall short of the vision?"

"Have I ever formed an ideal? — oh, yes!" said Evelyn, with a beautiful enthusiasm that lighted up her eyes, blushed in her cheek, and heaved her bosom beneath its robe; "something that in loving I could also revere, — a mind that would elevate my own; a heart that could sympathize with my weakness, my follies, my romance, if you will; and in which I could treasure my whole soul."

"You paint a schoolmaster, not a lover!" said Caroline, "You do not care, then, whether this hero be handsome or young?"

"Oh, yes, he should be both," said Evelyn, innocently; "and yet," she added, after a pause, and with an infantine playfulness of manner and countenance, "I know you will laugh at me, but I think I could be in love with more than one at the same time!"

"A common case, but a rare confession!"

"Yes; for if I might ask for the youth and outward advantages that please the eye, I could also love with a yet deeper love that which would speak to my imagination, — Intellect, Genius, Fame! Ah, these have an immortal youth and imperishable beauty of their own!"

"You are a very strange girl."

"But we are on a very strange subject — it is all an enigma!" said Evelyn, shaking her wise little head with a pretty gravity, half mock, half real. "Ah, if Lord Vargrave should love you — and you — oh, you *would* love him, and then I should be free, and so happy!"

They were then on the lawn in sight of the cottage windows, and Lumley, lifting his eyes from the newspaper, which had just arrived and been seized with all a politician's avidity, saw them in the distance. He threw down the paper, mused a moment or two, then took up his hat and joined them; but before he did so, he surveyed himself in the glass. "I think I look young enough still," thought he.

"Two cherries on one stalk," said Lumley, gayly: "by the by, it is not a complimentary simile. What young lady would be like a cherry? — such an uninteresting, common, charity-boy sort of fruit. For my part, I always associate cherries with the image of a young gentleman in corduroys and a skeleton jacket, with one pocket full of marbles, and the other full of worms for fishing, with three-halfpence in the left paw, and two cherries on one stalk (Helena and Hermia) in the right."

"How droll you are!" said Caroline, laughing.

"Much obliged to you, and don't envy your discrimination, ' Melancholy marks me for its own.' You ladies, — ah, yours is the life for gay spirits and light hearts; to us are left business and politics, law, physic, and murder, by way of pro-

fessions; abuse, nicknamed fame; and the privilege of seeing
how universal a thing, among the great and the wealthy, is
that pleasant vice, beggary, — which privilege is proudly
entitled 'patronage and power.' Are we the things to be
gay, —'droll,' as you say? Oh, no, all our spirits are forced,
believe me. Miss Cameron, did you ever know that wretched
species of hysterical affection called 'forced spirits'? Never,
I am sure; your ingenuous smile, your laughing eyes, are the
index to a happy and a sanguine heart."

"And what of me?" asked Caroline, quickly, and with a
slight blush.

"You, Miss Merton? Ah, I have not yet read your character, — a fair page, but an unknown letter. You, however,
have seen the world, and know that we must occasionally
wear a mask." Lord Vargrave sighed as he spoke, and
relapsed into sudden silence; then looking up, his eyes encountered Caroline's, which were fixed upon him. Their gaze
flattered him; Caroline turned away, and busied herself with
a rose-bush. Lumley gathered one of the flowers, and presented it to her. Evelyn was a few steps in advance.

"There is no thorn in this rose," said he; "may the offering
be an omen. You are now Evelyn's friend, oh, be mine; she
is to be your guest. Do not scorn to plead for me."

"Can *you* want a pleader?" said Caroline, with a slight
tremor in her voice.

"Charming Miss Merton, love is diffident and fearful; but
it must now find a voice, to which may Evelyn benignly listen.
What I leave unsaid — would that my new friend's eloquence
could supply."

He bowed slightly, and joined Evelyn. Caroline understood the hint, and returned alone and thoughtfully to the
house.

"Miss Cameron — Evelyn — ah, still let me call you so,
as in the happy and more familiar days of your childhood, I wish you could read my heart at this moment.
You are about to leave your home; new scenes will surround, new faces smile on you; dare I hope that I may still
be remembered?"

He attempted to take her hand as he spoke; Evelyn with drew it gently.

"Ah, my lord," said she, in a very low voice, "if remembrance were all that you asked of me --"

"It is all, — favourable remembrance, remembrance of the love of the past, remembrance of the bond to come."

Evelyn shivered. "It is better to speak openly," said she. "Let me throw myself on your generosity. I am not insensible to your brilliant qualities, to the honour of your attachment; but — but — as the time approaches in which you will call for my decision, let me now say, that I cannot feel for you — those — those sentiments, without which you could not desire our union, — without which it were but a wrong to both of us to form it. Nay, listen to me. I grieve bitterly at the tenor of your too generous uncle's will; can I not atone to you? Willingly would I sacrifice the fortune that, indeed, ought to be yours; accept it, and remain my friend."

"Cruel Evelyn! and can you suppose that it is your fortune I seek? It is yourself. Heaven is my witness, that, had you no dowry but your hand and heart, it were treasure enough to me. You think you cannot love me. Evelyn, you do not yet know yourself. Alas! your retirement in this distant village, my own unceasing avocations, which chain me, like a slave, to the galley-oar of politics and power, have kept us separate. You do not know me. I am willing to hazard the experiment of that knowledge. To devote my life to you, to make you partaker of my ambition, my career, to raise you to the highest eminence in the matronage of England, to transfer pride from myself to you, to love and to honour and to prize you, — all this will be my boast; and all this will win love for me at last. Fear not, Evelyn, — fear not for your happiness; with me you shall know no sorrow. Affection at home, splendour abroad, await you. I have passed the rough and arduous part of my career; sunshine lies on the summit to which I climb. No station in England is too high for me to aspire to, — prospects, how bright with you, how dark without you! Ah, Evelyn! be this hand mine — the heart shall follow!"

Vargrave's words were artful and eloquent; the *words* were calculated to win their way, but the manner, the tone of voice, wanted earnestness and truth. This was his defect; this characterized all his attempts to seduce or to lead others, in public or in private life. He had no heart, no deep passion, in what he undertook. He could impress you with the conviction of his ability, and leave the conviction imperfect, because he could not convince you that he was sincere. That best gift of mental power — *earnestness* — was wanting to him; and Lord Vargrave's deficiency of heart was the true cause why he was not a great man. Still, Evelyn was affected by his words; she suffered the hand he now once more took to remain passively in his, and said timidly, " Why, with sentiments so generous and confiding, why do you love me, who cannot return your affection worthily? No, Lord Vargrave; there are many who must see you with juster eyes than mine, — many fairer, and even wealthier. Indeed, indeed, it cannot be. Do not be offended, but think that the fortune left to me was on one condition I cannot, ought not to fulfil. Failing that condition, in equity and honour it reverts to you."

"Talk not thus, I implore you, Evelyn; do not imagine me the worldly calculator that my enemies deem me. But, to remove at once from your mind the possibility of such a compromise between your honour and repugnance — repugnance! have I lived to say that word? — know that your fortune is not at your own disposal. Save the small forfeit that awaits your non-compliance with my uncle's dying prayer, the whole is settled peremptorily on yourself and your children; it is entailed, — you cannot alienate it. Thus, then, your generosity can never be evinced but to him on whom you bestow your hand. Ah, let me recall that melancholy scene. Your benefactor on his death-bed, your mother kneeling by his side, your hand clasped in mine, and those lips, with their latest breath, uttering at once a blessing and a command."

"Ah, cease, cease, my lord! " said Evelyn, sobbing.

"No; bid me not cease before you tell me you will be mine. Beloved Evelyn, I may hope, — you will not resolve against me?"

"No," said Evelyn, raising her eyes and struggling for composure; "I feel too well what should be my duty; I will endeavor to perform it. Ask me no more now. I will struggle to answer you as you wish hereafter."

Lord Vargrave, resolved to push to the utmost the advantage he had gained, was about to reply when he heard a step behind him; and turning round, quickly and discomposed, beheld a venerable form approaching them. The occasion was lost: Evelyn also turned; and seeing who was the intruder, sprang towards him almost with a cry of joy.

The new comer was a man who had passed his seventieth year; but his old age was green, his step light, and on his healthful and benignant countenance time had left but few furrows. He was clothed in black; and his locks, which were white as snow, escaped from the broad hat, and almost touched his shoulders.

The old man smiled upon Evelyn, and kissed her forehead fondly. He then turned to Lord Vargrave, who, recovering his customary self-possession, advanced to meet him with extended hand.

"My dear Mr. Aubrey, this is a welcome surprise. I heard you were not at the vicarage, or I would have called on you."

"Your lordship honours me," replied the curate. "For the first time for thirty years I have been thus long absent from my cure; but I am now returned, I hope, to end my days among my flock."

"And what," asked Vargrave, — "what — if the question be not presumptuous — occasioned your unwilling absence?"

"My lord," replied the old man, with a gentle smile, "a new vicar has been appointed. I went to him, to proffer an humble prayer that I might remain amongst those whom I regarded as my children. I have buried one generation, I have married another, I have baptized a third."

"You should have had the vicarage itself; you should be better provided for, my dear Mr. Aubrey; I will speak to the Lord Chancellor."

Five times before had Lord Vargrave uttered the same promise, and the curate smiled to hear the familiar words.

"The vicarage, my lord, is a family living, and is now vested in a young man who requires wealth more than I do. He has been kind to me, and re-established me among my flock; I would not leave them for a bishopric. My child," continued the curate, addressing Evelyn with great affection, "you are surely unwell, — you are paler than when I left you."

Evelyn clung fondly to his arm, and smiled — her old gay smile — as she replied to him. They took the way towards the house.

The curate remained with them for an hour. There was a mingled sweetness and dignity in his manner which had in it something of the primitive character we poetically ascribe to the pastors of the Church. Lady Vargrave seemed to vie with Evelyn which should love him the most. When he retired to his home, which was not many yards distant from the cottage, Evelyn, pleading a headache, sought her chamber, and Lumley, to soothe his mortification, turned to Caroline, who had seated herself by his side. Her conversation amused him, and her evident admiration flattered. While Lady Vargrave absented herself, in motherly anxiety, to attend on Evelyn, while Mrs. Leslie was occupied at her frame, and Mrs. Merton looked on, and talked indolently to the old lady of rheumatism and sermons, of children's complaints and servants' misdemeanours, — the conversation between Lord Vargrave and Caroline, at first gay and animated, grew gradually more sentimental and subdued; their voices took a lower tone, and Caroline sometimes turned away her head and blushed.

CHAPTER XI.

THERE stands the Messenger of Truth — there stands
The Legate of the skies. — COWPER.

FROM that night Lumley found no opportunity for private conversation with Evelyn; she evidently shunned to meet with him alone. She was ever with her mother or Mrs. Leslie or the good curate, who spent much of his time at the cottage; for the old man had neither wife nor children, he was alone at home, he had learned to make his home with the widow and her daughter. With them he was an object of the tenderest affection, of the deepest veneration. Their love delighted him, and he returned it with the fondness of a parent and the benevolence of a pastor. He was a rare character, that village priest!

Born of humble parentage, Edward Aubrey had early displayed abilities which attracted the notice of a wealthy proprietor, who was not displeased to affect the patron. Young Aubrey was sent to school, and thence to college as a sizar: he obtained several prizes, and took a high degree. Aubrey was not without the ambition and the passions of youth: he went into the world, ardent, inexperienced, and without a guide. He drew back before errors grew into crimes, or folly became a habit. It was nature and affection that reclaimed and saved him from either alternative, — fame or ruin. His widowed mother was suddenly stricken with disease. Blind and bedridden, her whole dependence was on her only son. This affliction called forth a new character in Edward Aubrey. This mother had stripped herself of so many comforts to provide for him, — he devoted his youth to her in return. She was now old and imbecile. With the mingled selfishness and sentiment of age, she would not come to London, — she would not move from the village where her husband lay buried, where her youth had been spent. In this village the able and ambitious young man buried his hopes and his talents; by degrees the quiet and tranquillity of the country life became dear to him. As steps in a ladder, so piety leads to piety, and religion grew to him a habit. He took orders and entered the Church. A disappointment in love ensued; it left on his mind and heart a sober and resigned melancholy, which at length mellowed into content. His profession and its sweet duties became more and more dear to him; in the hopes of the next world he forgot the ambition of the present. He did not seek to shine, —

"More skilled to raise the wretched than to rise."

His own birth made the poor his brothers, and their dispositions and wants familiar to him. His own early errors made him tolerant to the faults of others, — few men are charitable who remember not that they have sinned. In our faults lie the germs of virtues. Thus gradually and serenely had worn away his life — obscure but useful, calm but active, — a man whom "the great prizes" of the Church might have rendered an ambitious schemer, to whom a modest confidence gave the true pastoral power, — to conquer the world within himself, and to sympathize with the wants of others. Yes, he was a rare character, that village priest!

CHAPTER XII.

Tout notre raisonnement se réduit à céder au sentiment.[1] — Pascal.

Lord Vargrave, who had no desire to remain alone with the widow when the guests were gone, arranged his departure for the same day as that fixed for Mrs. Merton's; and as their road lay together for several miles, it was settled that they should all dine at ——, whence Lord Vargrave would proceed to London. Failing to procure a second chance-interview with

[1] "All our reasoning reduces itself to yielding to sentiment."

Evelyn, and afraid to demand a formal one — for he felt the insecurity of the ground he stood on — Lord Vargrave, irritated and somewhat mortified, sought, as was his habit, whatever amusement was in his reach.   In the conversation of Caroline Merton — shrewd, worldly, and ambitious — he found the sort of plaything that he desired.   They were thrown much together; but to Vargrave, at least, there appeared no danger in the intercourse; and perhaps his chief object was to pique Evelyn, as well as to gratify his own spleen.

It was the evening before Evelyn's departure; the little party had been for the last hour dispersed; Mrs. Merton was in her own room, making to herself gratuitous and unnecessary occupation in seeing her woman *pack up*.   It was just the kind of task that delighted her.   To sit in a large chair and see somebody else at work — to say languidly, "Don't crumple that scarf, Jane; and where shall we put Miss Caroline's blue bonnet?" — gave her a very comfortable notion of her own importance and habits of business, — a sort of title to be the superintendent of a family and the wife of a rector. Caroline had disappeared, so had Lord Vargrave; but the first was supposed to be with Evelyn, the second, employed in writing letters, — at least, it was so when they had been last observed.   Mrs. Leslie was alone in the drawing-room, and absorbed in anxious and benevolent thoughts on the critical situation of her young favourite, about to enter an age and a world the perils of which Mrs. Leslie had not forgotten.

It was at this time that Evelyn, forgetful of Lord Vargrave and his suit, of every one, of everything but the grief of the approaching departure, found herself alone in a little arbour that had been built upon the cliff to command the view of the sea below.   That day she had been restless, perturbed; she had visited every spot consecrated by youthful recollections; she had clung with fond regret to every place in which she had held sweet converse with her mother.   Of a disposition singularly warm and affectionate, she had often, in her secret heart, pined for a more yearning and enthusiastic love than it seemed in the subdued nature of Lady Vargrave to bestow

In the affection of the latter, gentle and never fluctuating as it was, there seemed to her a something wanting, which she could not define. She had watched that beloved face all the morning. She had hoped to see the tender eyes fixed upon her, and hear the meek voice exclaim, "I cannot part with my child!" All the gay pictures which the light-hearted Caroline drew of the scenes she was to enter had vanished away — now that the hour approached when her mother was to be left alone. Why was she to go? It seemed to her an unnecessary cruelty.

As she thus sat, she did not observe that Mr. Aubrey, who had seen her at a distance, was now bending his way to her; and not till he had entered the arbour, and taken her hand, did she waken from those reveries in which youth, the Dreamer and the Desirer, so morbidly indulges.

"Tears, my child?" said the curate. "Nay, be not ashamed of them; they become you in this hour. How we shall miss you! and you, too, will not forget us?"

"Forget you! Ah, no, indeed! But why should I leave you? Why will you not speak to my mother, implore her to let me remain? We were so happy till these strangers came. We did not think there was any other world, — *here* there is world enough for me!"

"My poor Evelyn," said Mr. Aubrey, gently, "I have spoken to your mother and to Mrs. Leslie; they have confided to me all the reasons for your departure, and I cannot but subscribe to their justice. You do not want many months of the age when you will be called upon to decide whether Lord Vargrave shall be your husband. Your mother shrinks from the responsibility of influencing your decision; and here, my child, inexperienced, and having seen so little of others, how can you know your own heart?"

"But, oh, Mr. Aubrey," said Evelyn, with an earnestness that overcame embarrassment, "have I a choice left to me? Can I be ungrateful, disobedient to him who was a father to me? Ought I not to sacrifice my own happiness? And how willingly would I do so, if my mother would smile on me approvingly!"

"My child," said the curate, gravely, "an old man is a bad judge of the affairs of youth; yet in this matter, I think your duty plain. Do not resolutely set yourself against Lord Vargrave's claim; do not persuade yourself that you must be unhappy in a union with him. Compose your mind, think seriously upon the choice before you, refuse all decision at the present moment; wait until the appointed time arrives, or, at least, more nearly approaches. Meanwhile, I understand that Lord Vargrave is to be a frequent visitor at Mrs. Merton's; there you will see him with others, his character will show itself. Study his principles, his disposition; examine whether he is one whom you can esteem and render happy: there may be a love without enthusiasm, and yet sufficient for domestic felicity, and for the employment of the affections. You will insensibly, too, learn from other parts of his character which he does not exhibit to us. If the result of time and examination be that you can cheerfully obey the late lord's dying wish, unquestionably it will be the happier decision. If not, if you still shrink from vows at which your heart now rebels, as unquestionably you may, with an acquitted conscience, become free. The best of us are imperfect judges of the happiness of others. In the woe or weal of a whole life, we must decide for ourselves. Your benefactor could not mean you to be wretched; and if he now, with eyes purified from all worldly mists, look down upon you, his spirit will approve your choice; for when we quit the world, all worldly ambition dies with us. What now to the immortal soul can be the title and the rank which on earth, with the desires of earth, your benefactor hoped to secure to his adopted child? This is my advice. Look on the bright side of things, and wait calmly for the hour when Lord Vargrave can demand your decision."

The words of the priest, which well defined her duty, inexpressibly soothed and comforted Evelyn; and the advice upon other and higher matters, which the good man pressed upon a mind so softened at that hour to receive religious impressions, was received with gratitude and respect. Subsequently their conversation fell upon Lady Vargrave, — a theme dear to both of them. The old man was greatly touched by the poor girl's unselfish anxiety for her mother's comfort, by her fears that she might be missed, in those little attentions which filial love alone can render; he was almost yet more touched when, with a less disinterested feeling, Evelyn added mournfully, —

"Yet why, after all, should I fancy she will so miss me? Ah, though I will not *dare* complain of it, I feel still that she does not love me as I love her."

"Evelyn," said the curate, with mild reproach, "have I not said that your mother has known sorrow? And though sorrow does not annihilate affection, it subdues its expression, and moderates its outward signs."

Evelyn sighed, and said no more.

As the good old man and his young friend returned to the cottage, Lord Vargrave and Caroline approached them, emerging from an opposite part of the grounds. The former hastened to Evelyn with his usual gayety and frank address; and there was so much charm in the manner of a man, whom *apparently* the world and its cares had never rendered artificial or reserved, that the curate himself was impressed by it. He thought that Evelyn might be happy with one amiable enough for a companion and wise enough for a guide. But old as he was, he had loved, and he knew that there are instincts in the heart which defy all our calculations.

While Lumley was conversing, the little gate that made the communication between the gardens and the neighbouring churchyard, through which was the nearest access to the village, creaked on its hinges, and the quiet and solitary figure of Lady Vargrave threw its shadow over the grass.

CHAPTER XIII.

AND I can listen to thee yet,
Can lie upon the plain;
And listen till I do beget
That golden time again. — WORDSWORTH.

IT was past midnight — hostess and guests had retired to repose — when Lady Vargrave's door opened gently. The lady herself was kneeling at the foot of the bed; the moonlight came through the half-drawn curtains of the casement, and by its ray her pale, calm features looked paler, and yet more hushed.

Evelyn, for she was the intruder, paused at the threshold till her mother rose from her devotions, and then she threw herself on Lady Vargrave's breast, sobbing as if her heart would break. Hers were the wild, generous, irresistible emotions of youth. Lady Vargrave, perhaps, had known them once; at least, she could sympathize with them now.

She strained her child to her bosom; she stroked back her hair, and kissed her fondly, and spoke to her soothingly.

"Mother," sobbed Evelyn, "I could not sleep, I could not rest. Bless me again, kiss me again; tell me that you love me — you cannot love me as I do you; but tell me that I am dear to you; tell me you will regret me, but not too much; tell me —" Here Evelyn paused, and could say no more.

"My best, my kindest Evelyn," said Lady Vargrave, "there is nothing on earth I love like you. Do not fancy I am ungrateful."

"Why do you say ungrateful? — your own child, — your only child!" And Evelyn covered her mother's face and hands with passionate tears and kisses.

At that moment, certain it is that Lady Vargrave's heart reproached her with not having, indeed, loved this sweet girl as she deserved. True, no mother was more mild, more atten-

4

tive, more fostering, more anxious for a daughter's welfare
but Evelyn was right. The gushing fondness, the mysterious
entering into every subtle thought and feeling, which should
have characterized the love of such a mother to such a child,
had been to outward appearance wanting. Even in this pres·
ent parting there had been a prudence, an exercise of reason·
ing, that savoured more of duty than love. Lady Vargrave
felt all this with remorse; she gave way to emotions new to
her, — at least to exhibit; she wept with Evelyn, and returned her caresses with almost equal fervour. Perhaps, too,
she thought at that moment of what love that warm nature
was susceptible; and she trembled for her future fate. It
was as a full reconciliation — that mournful hour — between
feelings on either side, which something mysterious seemed
to have checked before; and that last night the mother and
the child did not separate, — the same couch contained them:
and when, worn out with some emotions which she could not
reveal, Lady Vargrave fell into the sleep of exhaustion, Evelyn's arm was round her, and Evelyn's eyes watched her with
pious and anxious love as the gray morning dawned.

She left her mother still sleeping, when the sun rose, and
went silently down into the dear room below, and again busied
herself in a thousand little provident cares, which she wondered she had forgot before.

The carriages were at the door before the party had assembled at the melancholy breakfast-table. Lord Vargrave was
the last to appear.

"I have been like all cowards," said he, seating himself, —
"anxious to defer an evil as long as possible; a bad policy,
for it increases the worst of all pains, — that of suspense."

Mrs. Merton had undertaken the duties that appertain to
the "hissing urn." "You prefer coffee, Lord Vargrave?
Caroline, my dear — "

Caroline passed the cup to Lord Vargrave, who looked at
her hand as he took it — there was a ring on one of those
slender fingers never observed there before. Their eyes met,
and Caroline coloured. Lord Vargrave turned to Evelyn,
who, pale as death, but tearless and speechless, sat beside her

mother; he attempted in vain to draw her into conversation. Evelyn, who desired to restrain her feelings, would not trust herself to speak.

Mrs. Merton, ever undisturbed and placid, continued to talk on: to offer congratulations on the weather, — it was such a lovely day; and they should be off so early; it would be so well arranged, — they should be in such good time to dine at ——, and then go three stages after dinner; the moon would be up.

"But," said Lord Vargrave, "as I am to go with you as far as ——, where our roads separate, I hope I am not condemned to go alone, with my red box, two old newspapers, and the blue devils. Have pity on me."

"Perhaps you will take Grandmamma, then?" whispered Caroline, archly.

Lumley shrugged his shoulders, and replied in the same tone, —

"Yes, — provided you keep to the proverb, ' Les extrêmes se touchent,' and the lovely grandchild accompany the venerable grandmamma."

"What would Evelyn say?" retorted Caroline.

Lumley sighed, and made no answer.

Mrs. Merton, who had hung fire while her daughter was carrying on this "aside," now put in, —

"Suppose I and Caroline take your *britzka*, and you go in our old coach with Evelyn and Mrs. Leslie?"

Lumley looked delightedly at the speaker, and then glanced at Evelyn; but Mrs. Leslie said very gravely, "No, *we* shall feel too much in leaving this dear place to be gay companions for Lord Vargrave. We shall all meet at dinner; or," she added, after a pause, "if this be uncourteous to Lord Vargrave, suppose Evelyn and myself take his carriage, and he accompanies you?"

"Agreed," said Mrs. Merton, quietly; "and now I will just go and see about the strawberry-plants and slips — it was so kind in you, dear Lady Vargrave, to think of them."

An hour had elapsed, and Evelyn was gone! She had left her maiden home, she had wept her last farewell on her mother's bosom, the sound of the carriage-wheels had died away; but still Lady Vargrave lingered on the threshold, still she gazed on the spot where the last glimpse of Evelyn had been caught. A sense of dreariness and solitude passed into her soul: the very sunlight, the spring, the songs of the birds, made loneliness more desolate.

Mechanically, at last, she moved away, and with slow steps and downcast eyes passed through the favourite walk that led into the quiet burial-ground. The gate closed upon her, and now the lawn, the gardens, the haunts of Evelyn, were solitary as the desert itself; but the daisy opened to the sun, and the bee murmured along the blossoms, not the less blithely for the absence of all human life. In the bosom of Nature there beats no heart for man!

BOOK II.

— ἔτος ἦλθε, περιπλομένων ἐνιαυτῶν
Τῷ οἱ ἐπεκλώσατο θεοὶ, οἰκόνδε νέεσθαι,
Εἰς Ἰθάκην, οὐδ' ἔνθα πεφυγμένος ἦεν ἀέθλων.
HOMER: *Od.* lib. i, 16.

" The hour arrived — years having rolled away —
When his return the Gods no more delay.
Lo! Ithaca the Fates award; and there
New trials meet the Wanderer."

CHAPTER I.

THERE is continual spring and harvest here —
Continual, both meeting at one time;
For both the boughs do laughing blossoms bear,
And with fresh colours deck the wanton prime;
And eke at once the heavy trees they climb,
Which seem to labour under their fruit's load.
SPENSER: *The Garden of Adonis.*

Vis boni
In ipsa inesset forma.[1] — TERENCE.

BEAUTY, thou art twice blessed; thou blessest the gazer and the possessor; often at once the effect and the cause of goodness! A sweet disposition, a lovely soul, an affectionate nature, will speak in the eyes, the lips, the brow, and become the cause of beauty. On the other hand, they who have a gift that commands love, a key that opens all hearts, are ordinarily inclined to look with happy eyes upon the world, — to be cheerful and serene, to hope and to confide. There is more wisdom than the vulgar dream of in our admiration of a fair face.

[1] " Even in beauty there exists the power of virtue."

Evelyn Cameron was beautiful, — a beauty that came from the heart, and went to the heart; a beauty, the very spirit of which was love! Love smiled on her dimpled lips, it reposed on her open brow, it played in the profuse and careless ringlets of darkest yet sunniest auburn, which a breeze could lift from her delicate and virgin cheek; Love, in all its tenderness, in all its kindness, its unsuspecting truth, — Love coloured every thought, murmured in her low melodious voice, in all its symmetry and glorious womanhood. Love swelled the swan-like neck, and moulded the rounded limb.

She was just the kind of person that takes the judgment by storm: whether gay or grave, there was so charming and irresistible a grace about her. She seemed born, not only to captivate the giddy, but to turn the heads of the sage. Roxalana was nothing to her. How, in the obscure hamlet of Brook-Green, she had learned all the arts of pleasing it is impossible to say. In her arch smile, the pretty toss of her head, the half shyness, half freedom, of her winning ways, it was as if Nature had made her to delight one heart, and torment all others.

Without being learned, the mind of Evelyn was cultivated and well informed. Her heart, perhaps, helped to instruct her understanding; for by a kind of intuition she could appreciate all that was beautiful and elevated. Her unvitiated and guileless taste had a logic of its own: no schoolman had ever a quicker penetration into truth, no critic ever more readily detected the meretricious and the false. The book that Evelyn could admire was sure to be stamped with the impress of the noble, the lovely, or the true!

But Evelyn had faults, — the faults of her age; or, rather, she had tendencies that might conduce to error. She was of so generous a nature that the very thought of sacrificing herself for another had a charm. She ever acted from impulse, — impulses pure and good, but often rash and imprudent. She was yielding to weakness, persuaded into anything, so sensitive, that even a cold look from one moderately liked cut her to the heart; and by the sympathy that accompanies sensitiveness, no pain to her was so great as the thought of giving pain to another. Hence it was that Vargrave might form reasonable hopes of his ultimate success. It was a dangerous constitution for happiness! How many chances must combine to preserve to the mid-day of characters like this the sunshine of their dawn! The butterfly that seems the child of the summer and the flowers — what wind will not chill its mirth, what touch will not brush away its hues?

CHAPTER II.

THESE, on a general survey, are the modes
Of pulpit oratory which agree
With no unlettered audience. — POLWHELE.

MRS. LESLIE had returned from her visit to the rectory to her own home, and Evelyn had now been some weeks at Mrs. Merton's. As was natural, she had grown in some measure reconciled and resigned to her change of abode. In fact, no sooner did she pass Mrs. Merton's threshold, than, for the first time, she was made aware of her consequence in life.

The Rev. Mr. Merton was a man of the nicest perception in all things appertaining to worldly consideration. The second son of a very wealthy baronet (who was the first commoner of his county) and of the daughter of a rich and highly-descended peer, Mr. Merton had been brought near enough to rank and power to appreciate all their advantages. In early life he had been something of a "tuft-hunter;" but as his understanding was good and his passions not very strong, he had soon perceived that that vessel of clay, a young man with a moderate fortune, cannot long sail down the same stream with the metal vessels of rich earls and extravagant dandies. Besides, he was destined for the Church — because there was one of the finest livings in England in the family. He therefore took orders at six-and-twenty; married Mrs. Leslie's daughter who had thirty thousand pounds: and settled at the

rectory of Merton, within a mile of the family seat. He became a very respectable and extremely popular man. He was
singularly hospitable, and built a new wing — containing a
large dining-room and six capital bed-rooms — to the rectory,
which had now much more the appearance of a country villa
than a country parsonage. His brother, succeeding to the
estates, and residing chiefly in the neighbourhood, became,
like his father before him, member for the county, and was
one of the country gentlemen most looked up to in the House
of Commons. A sensible and frequent, though uncommonly
prosy speaker, singularly independent (for he had a clear
fourteen thousand pounds a year, and did not desire office),
and valuing himself on not being a party man, so that his
vote on critical questions was often a matter of great doubt,
and, therefore, of great moment, Sir John Merton gave considerable importance to the Rev. Charles Merton. The latter
kept up all the more select of his old London acquaintances;
and few country houses, at certain seasons of the year, were
filled more aristocratically than the pleasant rectory-house.
Mr. Merton, indeed, contrived to make the Hall a reservoir
for the parsonage, and periodically drafted off the *élite* of the
visitors at the former to spend a few days at the latter. This
was the more easily done, as his brother was a widower, and
his conversation was all of one sort, — the state of the nation
and the agricultural interest. Mr. Merton was upon very
friendly terms with his brother, looked after the property in
the absence of Sir John, kept up the family interest, was an
excellent electioneerer, a good speaker at a pinch, an able
magistrate, — a man, in short, most useful in the county; on
the whole, he was more popular than his brother, and almost
as much looked up to — perhaps, because he was much less
ostentatious. He had very good taste, had the Rev. Charles
Merton! — his table plentiful, but plain — his manners affable
to the low, though agreeably sycophantic to the high; and
there was nothing about him that ever wounded self-love. To
add to the attractions of his house, his wife, simple and good-
tempered, could talk with anybody, take off the bores, and
leave people to be comfortable in their own way: while he

had a large family of fine children of all ages, that had long
given easy and constant excuse under the name of "little
children's parties," for getting up an impromptu dance or a
gypsy dinner, — enlivening the neighbourhood, in short.
Caroline was the eldest; then came a son, attached to a
foreign ministry, and another, who, though only nineteen,
was a private secretary to one of our Indian satraps. The
acquaintance of these young gentlemen, thus engaged, it was
therefore Evelyn's misfortune to lose the advantage of culti-
vating, — a loss which both Mr. and Mrs. Merton assured her
was very much to be regretted. But to make up to her for
such a privation there were two lovely little girls, one ten,
and the other seven years old, who fell in love with Evelyn at
first sight. Caroline was one of the beauties of the county,
clever and conversable, "drew young men," and set the fashion to young ladies, especially when she returned from spending the season with Lady Elizabeth.

It was a delightful family!

In person, Mr. Merton was of the middle height; fair, and
inclined to stoutness, with small features, beautiful teeth, and
great suavity of address. Mindful still of the time when he
had been "about town," he was very particular in his dress:
his black coat, neatly relieved in the evening by a white un-
derwaistcoat, and a shirt-front admirably plaited, with plain
studs of dark enamel, his well-cut trousers, and elaborately
polished shoes — he was good-humouredly vain of his feet
and hands — won for him the common praise of the dandies
(who occasionally honoured him with a visit to shoot his
game, and flirt with his daughter), "That old Merton was a
most gentlemanlike fellow — so d—d neat for a parson!"

Such, mentally, morally, and physically, was the Rev.
Charles Merton, rector of Merton, brother of Sir John, and
possessor of an income that, what with his rich living, his
wife's fortune, and his own, which was not inconsiderable,
amounted to between four and five thousand pounds a year,
which income, managed with judgment as well as liberality,
could not fail to secure to him all the good things of this
world, — the respect of his friends amongst the rest. Caro-

line was right when she told Evelyn that her papa was very
different from a mere country parson.

Now this gentleman could not fail to see all the claims that
Evelyn might fairly advance upon the esteem, nay, the veneration of himself and family: a young beauty, with a fortune
of about a quarter of a million, was a phenomenon that might
fairly be called celestial. Her pretensions were enhanced by
her engagement to Lord Vargrave, — an engagement which
might be broken; so that, as he interpreted it, the *worst* that
could happen to the young lady was to marry an able and
rising Minister of State, — a peer of the realm; but she was
perfectly free to marry a still greater man, if she could find
him; and who knows but what perhaps the *attaché*, if he could
get leave of absence? Mr. Merton was too sensible to pursue
that thought further for the present.

The good man was greatly shocked at the too familiar manner in which Mrs. Merton spoke to this high-fated heiress, at
Evelyn's travelling so far without her own maid, at her very
primitive wardrobe — poor, ill-used child! Mr. Merton was a
connoisseur in ladies' dress. It was quite painful to see that
the unfortunate girl had been so neglected. Lady Vargrave
must be a very strange person. He inquired compassionately
whether she was allowed any pocket money; and finding,
to his relief, that in that respect Miss Cameron was munifi-
cently supplied, he suggested that a proper abigail should be
immediately engaged; that proper orders to Madame Devy
should be immediately transmitted to London, with one of
Evelyn's dresses, as a pattern for nothing but length and
breadth. He almost stamped with vexation when he heard
that Evelyn had been placed in one of the neat little rooms
generally appropriated to young lady visitors.

"She is quite contented, my dear Mr. Merton; she is
so simple; she has not been brought up in the style you
think for."

"Mrs. Merton," said the rector, with great solemnity, "Miss
Cameron may know no better now; but what will she think of
us hereafter? It is my maxim to recollect what people will
be, and show them that respect which may leave pleasing im-

pressions when they have it in their power to show us civility
in return."

With many apologies, which quite overwhelmed poor Evelyn, she was transferred from the little chamber, with its
French bed and bamboo-coloured washhand-stand, to an apartment with a buhl wardrobe and a four-post bed with green
silk curtains, usually appropriated to the regular Christmas
visitant, the Dowager Countess of Chipperton. A pretty
morning room communicated with the sleeping apartment,
and thence a private staircase conducted into the gardens.
The whole family were duly impressed and re-impressed with
her importance. No queen could be made more of. Evelyn
mistook it all for pure kindness, and returned the hospitality
with an affection that extended to the whole family, but particularly to the two little girls, and a beautiful black spaniel.
Her dresses came down from London; her abigail arrived;
the buhl wardrobe was duly filled, — and Evelyn at last
learned that it is a fine thing to be rich. An account of all
these proceedings was forwarded to Lady Vargrave, in a long
and most complacent letter, by the rector himself. The
answer was short, but it contented the excellent clergyman;
for it approved of all he had done, and begged that Miss
Cameron might have everything that seemed proper to her
station.

By the same post came two letters to Evelyn herself, — one
from Lady Vargrave, one from the curate. They transported
her from the fine room and the buhl wardrobe to the cottage
and the lawn; and the fine abigail, when she came to dress
her young lady's hair, found her weeping.

It was a matter of great regret to the rector that it was that
time of year when — precisely because the country is most
beautiful — every one worth knowing is in town. Still, however, some stray guests found their way to the rectory for a
day or two, and still there were some aristocratic old families
in the neighbourhood, who never went up to London: so that
two days in the week the rector's wine flowed, the whist-
tables were set out, and the piano called into requisition.

Evelyn — the object of universal attention and admiration

— was put at her ease by her station itself; for good manners
come like an instinct to those on whom the world smiles.
Insensibly she acquired self-possession and the smoothness
of society; and if her child-like playfulness broke out from
all conventional restraint, it only made more charming and
brilliant the great heiress, whose delicate and fairy cast of
beauty so well became her graceful *abandon* of manner, and
who looked so unequivocally ladylike to the eyes that rested
on Madame Devy's blondes and satins.

Caroline was not so gay as she had been at the cottage.
Something seemed to weigh upon her spirits: she was often
moody and thoughtful. She was the only one in the family
not good-tempered; and her peevish replies to her parents,
when no visitor imposed a check on the family circle, incon-
ceivably pained Evelyn, and greatly contrasted the flow of
spirits which distinguished her when she found somebody
worth listening to. Still Evelyn — who, where she once
liked, found it difficult to withdraw regard — sought to over-
look Caroline's blemishes, and to persuade herself of a thousand good qualities below the surface; and her generous nature
found constant opportunity of venting itself in costly gifts,
selected from the London parcels, with which the officious
Mr. Merton relieved the monotony of the rectory. These
gifts Caroline could not refuse without paining her young
friend. She took them reluctantly, for, to do her justice,
Caroline, though ambitious, was not mean.

Thus time passed in the rectory, in gay variety and constant
entertainment; and all things combined to spoil the heiress,
if, indeed, goodness ever is spoiled by kindness and prosperity. Is it to the frost or to the sunshine that the flower opens
its petals, or the fruit ripens from the blossom?

CHAPTER III.

Rod. How sweet these solitary places are !

Ped. What strange musick
Was that we heard afar off ?
Curio. We 've told you what he is, what time we 've sought him,
His nature and his name.
BEAUMONT AND FLETCHER : *The Pilgrim.*

ONE day, as the ladies were seated in Mrs. Merton's morn-ing-room, Evelyn, who had been stationed by the window hearing the little Cecilia go through the French verbs, and had just finished that agreeable task, exclaimed, —

"Do tell me to whom that old house belongs, with the picturesque gable-end and Gothic turrets, there, just peeping through the trees, — I have always forgot to ask you."

"Oh, my dear Miss Cameron," said Mrs. Merton, "that is Burleigh; have you not been there? How stupid in Caroline not to show it to you ! It is one of the lions of the place. It belongs to a man you have often heard of, — Mr. Maltravers."

"Indeed!" cried Evelyn; and she gazed with new interest on the gray melancholy pile, as the sunshine brought it into strong contrast with the dark pines around it. "And Mr. Maltravers himself — ? "

"Is still abroad, I believe; though I did hear the other day that he was shortly expected at Burleigh. It is a curious old place, though much neglected. I believe, indeed, it has not been furnished since the time of Charles the First. (Cissy, my love, don't stoop so.) Very gloomy, in my opinion; and not any fine room in the house, except the library, which was once a chapel. However, people come miles to see it."

"Will you go there to-day?" said Caroline, languidly; "it is a very pleasant walk through the glebe-land and the wood, — not above half a mile by the foot-path."

"I should like it so much."

"Yes," said Mrs. Merton, "and you had better go before he returns, — he is so strange. He does not allow it to be seen when he is down. But, indeed, he has only been once at the old place since he was of age. (Sophy, you will tear Miss Cameron's scarf to pieces; do be quiet, child.) That was before he was a great man; he was then very odd, saw no society, only dined once with us, though Mr. Merton paid him every attention. They show the room in which he wrote his books."

"I remember him very well, though I was then but a chiid," said Caroline, — "a handsome, thoughtful face."

"Did you think so, my dear? Fine eyes and teeth, cer- tainly, and a commanding figure, but nothing more."

"Well," said Caroline, "if you like to go, Evelyn, I am at your service."

"And — I — Evy, dear — I — may go," said Cecilia, cling- ing to Evelyn.

"And me, too," lisped Sophia, the youngest hope, — "there's such a pretty peacock."

"Oh, yes, they may go, Mrs. Merton, we'll take such care of them."

"Very well, my dear; Miss Cameron quite spoils you."

Evelyn tripped away to put on her bonnet, and the children ran after her, clapping their hands, — they could not bear to lose sight of her for a moment.

"Caroline," said Mrs. Merton, affectionately, "are you not well? You have seemed pale lately, and not in your usual spirits."

"Oh, yes, I'm well enough," answered Caroline, rather peevishly; "but this place is so dull now; very provoking that Lady Elizabeth does not go to London this year."

"My dear, it will be gayer, I hope, in July, when the races at Knaresdean begin; and Lord Vargrave has promised to come."

"Has Lord Vargrave written to you lately?"

"No, my dear."

"Very odd."

"Does Evelyn ever talk of him?"

"Not much," said Caroline, rising and quitting the room.

It was a most cheerful exhilarating day, — the close of sweet May; the hedges were white with blossoms; a light breeze rustled the young leaves; the butterflies had ventured forth, and the children chased them over the grass, as Evelyn and Caroline, who walked much too slow for her companion (Evelyn longed to run), followed them soberly towards Burleigh.

They passed the glebe-fields; and a little bridge, thrown over a brawling rivulet, conducted them into a wood.

"This stream," said Caroline, "forms the boundary between my uncle's estates and those of Mr. Maltravers. It must be very unpleasant to so proud a man as Mr. Maltravers is said to be, to have the land of another proprietor so near his house. He could hear my uncle's gun from his very drawing-room. However, Sir John takes care not to molest him. On the other side, the Burleigh estates extend for some miles; indeed, Mr. Maltravers is the next great proprietor to my uncle in this part of the county. Very strange that he does not marry! There, now you can see the house."

The mansion lay somewhat low, with hanging woods in the rear; and the old-fashioned fish-ponds gleaming in the sunshine and overshadowed by gigantic trees increased the venerable stillness of its aspect. Ivy and innumerable creepers covered one side of the house; and long weeds cumbered the deserted road.

"It is sadly neglected," said Caroline; "and was so, even in the last owner's life. Mr. Maltravers inherits the place from his mother's uncle. We may as well enter the house by the private way. The front entrance is kept locked up."

Winding by a path that conducted into a flower-garden, divided from the park by a ha-ha, over which a plank and a small gate, rusting off its hinges, were placed, Caroline led the way towards the building. At this point of view it presented a large bay window that by a flight of four steps led into the garden. On one side rose a square, narrow turret, surmounted by a gilt dome and quaint weathercock, below the architrave of which was a sun-dial, set in the stonework, and

another dial stood in the garden, with the common and beau
tiful motto, —

" Non numero horas, nisi serenas ! " [1]

On the other side of the bay window a huge buttress cast its
mass of shadow.   There was something in the appearance of
the whole place that invited to contemplation and repose, —
something almost monastic.   The gayety of the teeming
spring-time could not divest the spot of a certain sadness, not
displeasing, however, whether to the young, to whom there is
a luxury in the vague sentiment of melancholy, or to those
who, having known real griefs, seek for an anodyne in meditation and memory.   The low lead-coloured door, set deep in the
turret, was locked, and the bell beside it broken.   Caroline
turned impatiently away.   "We must go round to the other
side," said she, "and try to make the deaf old man hear us."

"Oh, Carry!" cried Cecilia, "the great window is open;"
and she ran up the steps.

"That is lucky," said Caroline; and the rest followed
Cecilia.

Evelyn now stood within the library of which Mrs. Merton
had spoken.   It was a large room, about fifty feet in length,
and proportionably wide; somewhat dark, for the light came
only from the one large window through which they entered;
and though the window rose to the cornice of the ceiling, and
took up one side of the apartment, the daylight was subdued
by the heaviness of the stonework in which the narrow panes
were set, and by the glass stained with armorial bearings in
the upper part of the casement.   The bookcases, too, were of
the dark oak which so much absorbs the light; and the gild-
ing, formerly meant to relieve them, was discoloured by time.

The room was almost disproportionably lofty; the ceiling,
elaborately coved, and richly carved with grotesque masks,
preserved the Gothic character of the age in which it had
been devoted to a religious purpose.   Two fireplaces, with
high chimney-pieces of oak, in which were inserted two portraits, broke the symmetry of the tall bookcases.   In one of

---

[1] " I number not the hours, unless sunny."

these fireplaces were half-burnt logs; and a huge armchair, with a small reading-desk beside it, seemed to bespeak the recent occupation of the room. On the fourth side, opposite the window, the wall was covered with faded tapestry, representing the meeting of Solomon and the Queen of Sheba; the arras was nailed over doors on either hand, — the chinks between the door and the wall serving, in one instance, to cut off in the middle his wise majesty, who was making a low bow; while in the other it took the ground from under the wanton queen, just as she was descending from her chariot.

Near the window stood a grand piano, the only modern article in the room, save one of the portraits, presently to be described. On all this Evelyn gazed silently and devoutly: she had naturally that reverence for genius which is common to the enthusiastic and young; and there is, even to the dullest, a certain interest in the homes of those who have implanted within us a new thought. But here there was, she imagined, a rare and singular harmony between the place and the mental characteristics of the owner. She fancied she now better understood the shadowy and metaphysical repose of thought that had distinguished the earlier writings of Maltravers, — the writings composed or planned in this still retreat.

But what particularly caught her attention was one of the two portraits that adorned the mantelpieces. The further one was attired in the rich and fanciful armour of the time of Elizabeth; the head bare, the helmet on a table on which the hand rested. It was a handsome and striking countenance; and an inscription announced it to be a Digby, an ancestor of Maltravers.

But the other was a beautiful girl of about eighteen, in the now almost antiquated dress of forty years ago. The features were delicate, but the colours somewhat faded, and there was something mournful in the expression. A silk curtain, drawn on one side, seemed to denote how carefully it was prized by the possessor.

Evelyn turned for explanation to her cicerone.

"This is the second time I have seen that picture," said

Caroline; "for it is only by great entreaty and as a mysterious favour that the old housekeeper draws aside the veil.
Some touch of sentiment in Maltravers makes him regard it
as sacred. It is the picture of his mother before she married;
she died in giving him birth."

Evelyn sighed; how well she understood the sentiment
which seemed to Caroline so eccentric! The countenance
fascinated her; the eye seemed to follow her as she turned.

"As a proper pendant to this picture," said Caroline, "he
ought to have dismissed the effigies of yon warlike gentleman,
and replaced it by one of poor Lady Florence Lascelles, for
whose loss he is said to have quitted his country: but, perhaps, it was the loss of her fortune."

"How can you say so? — fie!" cried Evelyn, with a burst
of generous indignation.

"Ah, my dear, you heiresses have a fellow-feeling with
each other! Nevertheless, clever men are less sentimental
than we deem them. Heigho! this quiet room gives me the
spleen, I fancy."

"Dearest Evy," whispered Cecilia, "I think you have a
look of that pretty picture, only you are much prettier. Do
take off your bonnet; your hair just falls down like hers."

Evelyn shook her head gravely; but the spoiled child hastily
untied the ribbons and snatched away the hat, and Evelyn's
sunny ringlets fell down in beautiful disorder. There was no
resemblance between Evelyn and the portrait, except in the
colour of the hair, and the careless fashion it now by chance
assumed. Yet Evelyn was pleased to think that a likeness
did exist, though Caroline declared it was a most unflattering
compliment.

"I don't wonder," said the latter, changing the theme, —
"I don't wonder Mr. Maltravers lives so little in this 'Castle
Dull;' yet it might be much improved. French windows and
plate-glass, for instance; and if those lumbering bookshelves
and horrid old chimney-pieces were removed and the ceiling
painted white and gold like that in my uncle's saloon, and a
rich, lively paper, instead of the tapestry, it would really
make a very fine ballroom."

"Let us have a dance here now," cried Cecilia. "Come, stand up, Sophy;" and the children began to practise a waltz step, tumbling over each other, and laughing in full glee.

"Hush, hush!" said Evelyn, softly. She had never before checked the children's mirth, and she could not tell why she did so now.

"I suppose the old butler has been entertaining the bailiff here," said Caroline, pointing to the remains of the fire.

"And is this the room he chiefly inhabited, — the room that you say they show as his?"

"No; that tapestry door to the right leads into a little study where he wrote." So saying, Caroline tried to open the door, but it was locked from within. She then opened the other door, which showed a long wainscoted passage, hung with rusty pikes, and a few breastplates of the time of the Parliamentary Wars. "This leads to the main body of the house," said Caroline, "from which the room we are now in and the little study are completely detached, having, as you know, been the chapel in popish times. I have heard that Sir Kenelm Digby, an ancestral connection of the present owner, first converted them into their present use, and, in return, built the village church on the other side of the park."

Sir Kenelm Digby, the old cavalier philosopher! — a new name of interest to consecrate the place! Evelyn could have lingered all day in the room; and perhaps as an excuse for a longer sojourn, hastened to the piano — it was open — she ran her fairy fingers over the keys, and the sound from the untuned and neglected instrument thrilled wild and spiritlike through the melancholy chamber.

"Oh, do sing us something, Evy," cried Cecilia, running up to, and drawing a chair to, the instrument.

"Do, Evelyn," said Caroline, languidly; "it will serve to bring one of the servants to us, and save us a journey to the offices."

It was just what Evelyn wished. Some verses, which her mother especially loved, verses written by Maltravers upon returning after absence to his own home, had rushed into her mind as she had touched the keys. They were appropriate to the place, and had been beautifully set to music. So the children hushed themselves, and nestled at her feet; and after a little prelude, keeping the accompaniment under, that the spoiled instrument might not mar the sweet words and sweeter voice, she began the song.

Meanwhile in the adjoining room, the little study which Caroline had spoken of, sat the owner of the house! He had returned suddenly and unexpectedly the previous night. The old steward was in attendance at the moment, full of apolo-gies, congratulations, and gossip; and Maltravers, grown a stern and haughty man, was already impatiently turning away, when he heard the sudden sound of the children's laughter and loud voices in the room beyond. Maltravers frowned.

"What impertinence is this?" said he in a tone that, though very calm, made the steward quake in his shoes.

"I don't know, really, your honour; there be so many grand folks come to see the house in the fine weather, that — "

"And you permit your master's house to be a raree-show? You do well, sir."

"If your honour were more amongst us, there might be more discipline like," said the steward, stoutly; "but no one in my time has cared so little for the old place as those it belongs to."

"Fewer words with me, sir," said Maltravers, haughtily; "and now go and inform those people that I am returned, and wish for no guests but those I invite myself."

"Sir!"

"Do you not hear me? Say that if it so please them, these old ruins are my property, and are not to be jobbed out to the insolence of public curiosity. Go, sir."

"But — I beg pardon, your honour — if they be great folks?"

"Great folks! — great! Ay, there it is. Why, if they be great folks, they have great houses of their own, Mr. Justis."

The steward stared. "Perhaps, your honour," he put in, deprecatingly, "they be Mr. Merton's family: they come very often when the London gentlemen are with them."

"Merton! — oh, the cringing parson. Harkye! one word
more with me, sir, and you quit my service to-morrow."

Mr. Justis lifted his eyes and hands to heaven; but there
was something in his master's voice and look which checked
reply, and he turned slowly to the door — when a voice of
such heavenly sweetness was heard without that it arrested
his own step and made the stern Maltravers start in his seat.
He held up his hand to the steward to delay his errand, and
listened, charmed and spell-bound. His own words came on
his ear, — words long unfamiliar to him, and at first but imperfectly remembered; words connected with the early and
virgin years of poetry and aspiration; words that were as the
ghosts of thoughts now far too gentle for his altered soul. He
bowed down his head, and the dark shade left his brow.

The song ceased. Maltravers moved with a sigh, and his
eyes rested on the form of the steward with his hand on the
door.

"Shall I give your honour's message?" said Mr. Justis,
gravely.

"No; take care for the future; leave me now."

Mr. Justis made one leg, and then, well pleased, took to
both.

"Well," thought he, as he departed, "how foreign parts do
spoil a gentleman! so mild as he was once! I must botch up
the accounts, I see, — the squire has grown sharp."

As Evelyn concluded her song, she — whose charm in singing was that she sang from the heart — was so touched by the
melancholy music of the air and words, that her voice faltered, and the last line died inaudibly on her lips.

The children sprang up and kissed her.

"Oh," cried Cecilia, "there is the beautiful peacock!"
And there, indeed, on the steps without — perhaps attracted
by the music — stood the picturesque bird. The children ran
out to greet their old favourite, who was extremely tame; and
presently Cecilia returned.

"Oh, Carry! do see what beautiful horses are coming up
the park!"

Caroline, who was a good rider, and fond of horses, and

whose curiosity was always aroused by things connected with show and station, suffered the little girl to draw her into the garden. Two grooms, each mounted on a horse of the pure Arabian breed, and each leading another, swathed and bandaged, were riding slowly up the road; and Caroline was so attracted by the novel appearance of the animals in a place so deserted that she followed the children towards them, to learn who could possibly be their enviable owner. Evelyn, forgotten for the moment, remained alone. She was pleased at being so, and once more turned to the picture which had so attracted her before. The mild eyes fixed on her, with an expression that recalled to her mind her own mother.

"And," thought she, as she gazed, "this fair creature did not live to know the fame of her son, to rejoice in his success, or to soothe his grief. And he, that son, a disappointed and solitary exile in distant lands, while strangers stand within his deserted hall!"

The images she had conjured up moved and absorbed her; and she continued to stand before the picture, gazing upward with moistened eyes. It was a beautiful vision as she thus stood, with her delicate bloom, her luxuriant hair (for the hat was not yet replaced), her elastic form, so full of youth and health and hope, — the living form beside the faded canvas of the dead, once youthful, tender, lovely as herself! Evelyn turned away with a sigh; the sigh was re-echoed yet more deeply. She started: the door that led to the study was opened, and in the aperture was the figure of a man in the prime of life. His hair, still luxuriant as in his earliest youth, though darkened by the suns of the East, curled over a forehead of majestic expanse. The high and proud features, that well became a stature above the ordinary standard; the pale but bronzed complexion; the large eyes of deepest blue, shaded by dark brows and lashes; and more than all, that expression at once of passion and repose which characterizes the old Italian portraits, and seems to denote the inscrutable power that experience imparts to intellect, constituted an *ensemble* which, if not faultlessly handsome, was eminently striking, and formed at once to interest and command. It was a face, once seen, never to be forgotten; it was a face that had long, half unconsciously, haunted Evelyn's young dreams; it was a face she had seen before, though, then younger and milder and fairer, it wore a different aspect.

Evelyn stood rooted to the spot, feeling herself blush to her very temples, — an enchanting picture of bashful confusion and innocent alarm.

"Do not let me regret my return," said the stranger, approaching after a short pause, and with much gentleness in his voice and smile; "and think that the owner is doomed to scare away the fair spirits that haunted the spot in his absence."

"The owner!" repeated Evelyn, almost inaudibly, and in increased embarrassment; "are you then the — the — "

"Yes," courteously interrupted the stranger, seeing her confusion, "my name is Maltravers; and I am to blame for not having informed you of my sudden return, or for now trespassing on your presence. But you see my excuse;" and he pointed to the instrument. "You have the magic that draws even the serpent from his hole. But you are not alone?"

"Oh, no! no, indeed! Miss Merton is with me. I know not where she is gone. I will seek her."

"Miss Merton! You are not then one of that family?"

"No, only a guest. I will find her; she must apologize for us. We were not aware that you were here, — indeed we were not."

"That is a cruel excuse," said Maltravers, smiling at her eagerness: and the smile and the look reminded her yet more forcibly of the time when he had carried her in his arms and soothed her suffering and praised her courage and pressed the kiss almost of a lover on her hand. At that thought she blushed yet more deeply, and yet more eagerly turned to escape.

Maltravers did not seek to detain her, but silently followed her steps. She had scarcely gained the window, before little Cecilia scampered in, crying, —

"Only think! Mr. Maltravers has come back, and brought such beautiful horses!"

Cecilia stopped abruptly, as she caught sight of the stranger; and the next moment Caroline herself appeared. Her worldly experience and quick sense saw immediately what had chanced; and she hastened to apologize to Maltravers, and congratulate him on his return, with an ease that astonished poor Evelyn, and by no means seemed appreciated by Maltravers himself. He replied with brief and haughty courtesy.

"My father," continued Caroline, "will be so glad to hear you are come back. He will hasten to pay you his respects, and apologize for his truants. But I have not formally introduced you to my fellow-offender. My dear, let me present to you one whom Fame has already made known to you; Mr. Maltravers, Miss Cameron, step-daughter," she added in a lower voice, "to the late Lord Vargrave."

At the first part of this introduction Maltravers frowned; at the last he forgot all displeasure.

"Is it possible? I *thought* I had seen you before, but in a dream. Ah, then we are not quite strangers!"

Evelyn's eye met his, and though she coloured and strove to look grave, a half smile brought out the dimples that played round her arch lips.

"But you do not remember me?" added Maltravers.

"Oh, yes!" exclaimed Evelyn, with a sudden impulse; and then checked herself.

Caroline came to her friend's relief.

"What is this? You surprise me; where did you ever see Mr. Maltravers before?"

"I can answer that question, Miss Merton. When Miss Cameron was but a child, as high as my little friend here, an accident on the road procured me her acquaintance; and the sweetness and fortitude she then displayed left an impression on me not worn out even to this day. And thus we meet again," added Maltravers, in a muttered voice, as to himself. "How strange a thing life is!"

"Well," said Miss Merton, "we must intrude on you no more, — you have so much to do. I am so sorry Sir John is not down to welcome you; but I hope we shall be good neighbours. *Au revoir!*"

And, fancying herself most charming, Caroline bowed, smiled, and walked off with her train. Maltravers paused irresolute. If Evelyn had looked back, he would have accompanied them home; but Evelyn did not look back, — and he stayed.

Miss Merton rallied her young friend unmercifully, as they walked homeward, and she extracted a very brief and imperfect history of the adventure that had formed the first acquaintance, and of the interview by which it had been renewed. But Evelyn did not heed her; and the moment they arrived at the rectory, she hastened to shut herself in her room, and write the account of her adventure to her mother. How often, in her girlish reveries, had she thought of that incident, that stranger! And now, by such a chance, and after so many years, to meet the Unknown by his own hearth! and that Unknown to be Maltravers! It was as if a dream had come true. While she was yet musing — and the letter not yet begun — she heard the sound of joy-bells in the distance. At once she divined the cause; it was the welcome of the wanderer to his solitary home!

CHAPTER IV.

Mais en connaissant votre condition naturelle, usez des moyens qui lui sont propres, et ne prétendez pas régner par une autre voie que par celle qui vous fait roi.[1] — Pascal.

In the heart as in the ocean, the great tides ebb and flow. The waves which had once urged on the spirit of Ernest Maltravers to the rocks and shoals of active life had long since receded back upon the calm depths, and left the strand bare. With a melancholy and disappointed mind, he had

[1] "But in understanding your natural condition, use the means which are proper to it; and pretend not to govern by any other way than by that which constitutes you governor."

quitted the land of his birth; and new scenes, strange and wild, had risen before his wandering gaze. Wearied with civilization, and sated with many of the triumphs for which civilized men drudge and toil, and disquiet themselves in vain, he had plunged amongst hordes, scarce redeemed from primeval barbarism. The adventures through which he had passed, and in which life itself could only be preserved by wary vigilance and ready energies, had forced him, for a while, from the indulgence of morbid contemplations. His heart, indeed, had been left inactive; but his intellect and his physical powers had been kept in hourly exercise. He returned to the world of his equals with a mind laden with the treasures of a various and vast experience, and with much of the same gloomy moral as that which, on emerging from the Catacombs, assured the restless speculations of Rasselas of the vanity of human life and the folly of moral aspirations.

Ernest Maltravers, never a faultless or completed character, falling short in practice of his own capacities, moral and intellectual, from his very desire to overpass the limits of the Great and Good, was seemingly as far as heretofore from the grand secret of life. It was not so in reality; his mind had acquired what before it wanted, — *hardness ;* and we are nearer to true virtue and true happiness when we demand too little from men than when we exact too much.

Nevertheless, partly from the strange life that had thrown him amongst men whom safety itself made it necessary to command despotically, partly from the habit of power and disdain of the world, his nature was incrusted with a stern imperiousness of manner, often approaching to the harsh and morose, though beneath it lurked generosity and benevolence.

Many of his younger feelings, more amiable and complex, had settled into one predominant quality, which more or less had always characterized him, — Pride! Self-esteem made inactive, and Ambition made discontented, usually engender haughtiness. In Maltravers this quality, which, properly controlled and duly softened, is the essence and life of honour, was carried to a vice. He was perfectly conscious of its excess, but he cherished it as a virtue. Pride had served to

console him in sorrow, and therefore it was a friend; it had
supported him when disgusted with fraud, or in resistance to
violence, and therefore it was a champion and a fortress.   It
was a pride of a peculiar sort: it attached itself to no one
point in especial, — not to talent, knowledge, mental gifts,
still less to the vulgar commonplaces of birth and fortune; it
rather resulted from a supreme and wholesale contempt of all
other men, and all their objects, — of ambition, of glory, of
the hard business of life.   His favourite virtue was fortitude;
it was on this that he now mainly valued himself.   He was
proud of his struggles against others, prouder still of conquests over his own passions.   He looked upon FATE as the
arch enemy against whose attacks we should ever prepare.
He fancied that against fate he had thoroughly schooled himself.   In the arrogance of his heart he said, "I can defy the
future."   He believed in the boast of the vain old sage, —
"I am a world to myself!"   In the wild career through which
his later manhood had passed, it is true that he had not carried his philosophy into a rejection of the ordinary world.
The shock occasioned by the death of Florence yielded gradually to time and change; and he had passed from the deserts
of Africa and the East to the brilliant cities of Europe.   But
neither his heart nor his reason had ever again been enslaved
by his passions.   Never again had he known the softness of
affection.   Had he done so, the ice had been thawed, and the
fountain had flowed once more into the great deeps.   He had
returned to England, — he scarce knew wherefore, or with
what intent, certainly not with any idea of entering again
upon the occupations of active life; it was, perhaps, only the
weariness of foreign scenes and unfamiliar tongues, and the
vague, unsettled desire of change, that brought him back to
the fatherland.   But he did not allow so unphilosophical a
cause to himself: and, what was strange, he would not allow
one much more amiable, and which was, perhaps, the truer
cause, — the increasing age and infirmities of his old guardian, Cleveland, who prayed him affectionately to return.
Maltravers did not like to believe that his heart was still so
kind.   Singular form of pride!   No, he rather sought to per-

suade himself that he intended to sell Burleigh, to arrange his affairs finally, and then quit forever his native land. To prove to himself that this was the case, he had intended at Dover to hurry at once to Burleigh, and merely write to Cleveland that he was returned to England. But his heart would not suffer him to enjoy this cruel luxury of self-mortification, and his horses' heads were turned to Richmond when within a stage of London. He had spent two days with the good old man, and those two days had so warmed and softened his feelings that he was quite appalled at his own dereliction from fixed principles! However, he went before Cleveland had time to discover that he was changed; and the old man had promised to visit him shortly.

This, then, was the state of Ernest Maltravers at the age of thirty-six, — an age in which frame and mind are in their fullest perfection; an age in which men begin most keenly to feel that they are citizens. With all his energies braced and strengthened; with his mind stored with profusest gifts; in the vigour of a constitution to which a hardy life had imparted a second and fresher youth; so trained by stern experience as to redeem with an easy effort all the deficiencies and faults which had once resulted from too sensitive an imagination and too high a standard for human actions; formed to render to his race the most brilliant and durable service, and to secure to himself the happiness which results from sobered fancy, a generous heart, and an approving conscience, — here was Ernest Maltravers, backed, too, by the appliances and gifts of birth and fortune, perversely shutting up genius, life, and soul in their own thorny leaves, and refusing to serve the fools and rascals who were formed from the same clay, and gifted by the same God. Morbid and morose philosophy, begot by a proud spirit on a lonely heart!

CHAPTER V.

Let such amongst us as are willing to be children again, if it be only for
an hour, resign ourselves to the sweet enchantment that steals upon the spirit
when it indulges in the memory of early and innocent enjoyment.

D. L. Richardson.

At dinner, Caroline's lively recital of their adventures was
received with much interest, not only by the Merton family,
but by some of the neighbouring gentry who shared the rector's hospitality. The sudden return of any proprietor to his
old hereditary seat after a prolonged absence makes some sensation in a provincial neighbourhood. In this case, where
the proprietor was still young, unmarried, celebrated, and
handsome, the sensation was of course proportionably increased. Caroline and Evelyn were beset by questions, to
which the former alone gave any distinct reply. Caroline's
account was, on the whole, gracious and favourable, and
seemed complimentary to all but Evelyn, who thought that
Caroline was a very indifferent portrait-painter.

It seldom happens that a man is a prophet in his own
neighbourhood; but Maltravers had been so little in the
county, and in his former visit his life had been so secluded,
that he was regarded as a stranger. He had neither outshone
the establishments nor interfered with the sporting of his fel-
low-squires; and on the whole, they made just allowance for
his habits of distant reserve. Time, and his retirement from
the busy scene, long enough to cause him to be missed, not
long enough for new favourites to supply his place, had
greatly served to mellow and consolidate his reputation, and
his country was proud to claim him. Thus (though Maltravers would not have believed it had an angel told him) he
was not spoken ill of behind his back: a thousand little anecdotes of his personal habits, of his generosity, independence
of spirit, and eccentricity were told. Evelyn listened in **rapt**

delight to all; she had never passed so pleasant an evening; and she smiled almost gratefully on the rector, who was a man that always followed the stream, when he said with benign affability, "We must really show our distinguished neighbour every attention, — we must be indulgent to his little oddities. His politics are not mine, to be sure; but a man who has a stake in the country has a right to his own opinion, that was always my maxim, — thank Heaven, I am a very moderate man. We must draw him amongst us; it will be our own fault, I am sure, if he is not quite domesticated at the rectory."

"With such attraction, — yes," said the thin curate, timidly bowing to the ladies.

"It would be a nice match for Miss Caroline," whispered an old lady; Caroline overheard, and pouted her pretty lip.

The whist-tables were now set out, the music began, and Maltravers was left in peace.

The next day Mr. Merton rode his pony over to Burleigh. Maltravers was not at home. He left his card, and a note of friendly respect, begging Mr. Maltravers to waive ceremony, and dine with them the next day. Somewhat to the surprise of the rector, he found that the active spirit of Maltravers was already at work. The long-deserted grounds were filled with labourers; the carpenters were busy at the fences; the house looked alive and stirring; the grooms were exercising the horses in the park, — all betokened the return of the absentee. This seemed to denote that Maltravers had come to reside; and the rector thought of Caroline, and was pleased at the notion.

The next day was Cecilia's birthday, — and birthdays were kept at Merton Rectory; the neighbouring children were invited. They were to dine on the lawn, in a large marquee, and to dance in the evening. The hothouses yielded their early strawberries, and the cows, decorated with blue ribbons, were to give syllabubs. The polite Caroline was not greatly fascinated by pleasure of this kind; she graciously appeared at dinner, kissed the prettiest of the children, helped them to soup, and then, having done her duty, retired to her room to write letters. The children were not sorry, for they were a little afraid of the grand Caroline; and they laughed much more loudly, and made much more noise, when she was gone — and the cake and strawberries appeared.

Evelyn was in her element; she had, as a child, mixed so little with children, she had so often yearned for playmates, she was still so childlike. Besides, she was so fond of Cecilia, she had looked forward with innocent delight to the day; and a week before had taken the carriage to the neighbouring town to return with a carefully concealed basket of toys, — dolls, sashes, and picture-books. But somehow or other, she did not feel so childlike as usual that morning; her heart was away from the pleasure before her, and her smile was at first languid. But in children's mirth there is something so con tagious to those who love children; and now, as the party scattered themselves on the grass, and Evelyn opened the basket, and bade them with much gravity keep quiet, and be good children, she was the happiest of the whole group. But she knew how to give pleasure: and the basket was presented to Cecilia, that the little queen of the day might enjoy the luxury of being generous; and to prevent jealousy, the notable expedient of a lottery was suggested.

"Then Evy shall be Fortune!" cried Cecilia; "nobody will be sorry to get anything from Evy, — and if any one is dis contented Evy sha'n't kiss her."

Mrs. Merton, whose motherly heart was completely won by Evelyn's kindness to the children, forgot all her husband's lectures, and willingly ticketed the prizes, and wrote the numbers of the lots on slips of paper carefully folded. A large old Indian jar was dragged from the drawing-room and constituted the fated urn; the tickets were deposited therein, and Cecilia was tying the handkerchief round Evelyn's eyes, — while Fortune struggled archly not to be as blind as she ought to be, — and the children, seated in a circle, were in full joy and expectation when there was a sudden pause. The laughter stopped; so did Cissy's little hands. What could it be? Evelyn slipped the bandage, and her eyes rested on Maltravers!

"Well, really, my dear Miss Cameron," said the rector, who was by the side of the intruder, and who, indeed, had just brought him to the spot, "I don't know what these little folks will do to you next."

"I ought rather to be their victim," said Maltravers, good-humouredly; "the fairies always punish us grown-up mortals for trespassing on their revels."

While he spoke, his eyes — those eyes, the most eloquent in the world — dwelt on Evelyn (as, to cover her blushes, she took Cecilia in her arms, and appeared to attend to nothing else) with a look of such admiration and delight as a mortal might well be supposed to cast on some beautiful fairy.

Sophy, a very bold child, ran up to him. "How do, sir?" she lisped, putting up her face to be kissed; "how's the pretty peacock?"

This opportune audacity served at once to renew the charm that had been broken, — to unite the stranger with the children. Here was acquaintance claimed and allowed in an instant. The next moment Maltravers was one of the circle, on the turf with the rest, as gay, and almost as noisy, — that hard, proud man, so disdainful of the trifles of the world!

"But the gentleman must have a prize, too," said Sophy, proud of her tall new friend. "What's your other name; why do you have such a long, hard name?"

"Call me Ernest," said Maltravers.

"Why don't we begin?" cried the children.

"Evy, come, be a good child, miss," said Sophy, as Evelyn, vexed and ashamed, and half ready to cry, resisted the bandage.

Mr. Merton interposed his authority; but the children clamoured, and Evelyn hastily yielded. It was Fortune's duty to draw the tickets from the urn, and give them to each claimant whose name was called; when it came to the turn of Maltravers, the bandage did not conceal the blush and smile of the enchanting goddess, and the hand of the aspirant thrilled as it touched hers.

The children burst into screams of laughter when Cecilia gravely awarded to Maltravers the worst prize in the lot, — a

blue riobon, — which Sophy, however, greedily insisted on
having; but Maltravers would not yield it.

Maltravers remained all day at the rectory, and shared in
the ball, — yes, he danced with Evelyn — he, Maltravers, who
had never been known to dance since he was twenty-two!
The ice was fairly broken, — Maltravers was at home with
the Mertons. And when he took his solitary walk to his solitary house — over the little bridge, and through the shadowy
wood — astonished, perhaps, with himself, every one of the
guests, from the oldest to the youngest, pronounced him
delightful. Caroline, perhaps, might have been piqued some
months ago that he did not dance with *her;* but now, her
heart — such as it was — felt preoccupied.

CHAPTER VI.

L'ESPRIT de l'homme est plus pénétrant que conséquent, et embrasse plus
qu'il ne peut lier.[1] — VAUVENARGUES.

AND now Maltravers was constantly with the Merton family;
there was no need of excuse for familiarity on his part. Mr.
Merton, charmed to find his advances not rejected, thrust intimacy upon him.

One day they spent the afternoon at Burleigh, and Evelyn
and Caroline finished their survey of the house, — tapestry,
and armour, pictures and all. This led to a visit to the
Arabian horses. Caroline observed that she was very fond
of riding, and went into ecstasies with one of the animals, —
the one, of course, with the longest tail. The next day the
horse was in the stables at the rectory, and a gallant epistle
apologized for the costly gift.

Mr. Merton demurred, but Caroline always had her own
way; and so the horse remained (no doubt, in much amaze-

---

[1] "The spirit of man is more penetrating than logical, and gathers more
than it can garner."

ment and disdain) with the parson's pony, and the brown
carriage horses.   The gift naturally conduced to parties on
horseback — it was cruel entirely to separate the Arab from
his friends — and how was Evelyn to be left behind? —
Evelyn, who had never yet ridden anything more spirited
than an old pony!   A beautiful little horse belonging to an
elderly lady, now growing too stout to ride, was to be sold
hard by.   Maltravers discovered the treasure, and apprised
Mr. Merton of it — he was too delicate to affect liberality to
the rich heiress.   The horse was bought; nothing could go
quieter; Evelyn was not at all afraid.   They made two or
three little excursions.   Sometimes only Mr. Merton and
Maltravers accompanied the young ladies, sometimes the
party was more numerous.   Maltravers appeared to pay
equal attention to Caroline and her friend; still Evelyn's
inexperience in equestrian matters was an excuse for his
being ever by her side.   They had a thousand opportunities
to converse; and Evelyn now felt more at home with him;
her gentle gayety, her fanciful yet chastened intellect, found
a voice.   Maltravers was not slow to discover that beneath
her simplicity there lurked sense, judgment, and imagination.   Insensibly his own conversation took a higher flight.
With the freedom which his mature years and reputation
gave him, he mingled eloquent instruction with lighter and
more trifling subjects; he directed her earnest and docile
mind, not only to new fields of written knowledge, but to
many of the secrets of Nature, subtle or sublime.   He had a
wide range of scientific as well as literary lore; the stars, the
flowers, the phenomena of the physical world, afforded themes
on which he descanted with the fervent love of a poet and the
easy knowledge of a sage.

  Mr. Merton, observing that little or nothing of sentiment
mingled with their familiar intercourse, felt perfectly at ease;
and knowing that Maltravers had been intimate with Lumley,
he naturally concluded that he was aware of the engagement
between Evelyn and his friend.   Meanwhile Maltravers appeared unconscious that such a being as Lord Vargrave
existed.

It is not to be wondered at that the daily presence, the delicate flattery of attention from a man like Maltravers, should strongly impress the imagination, if not the heart, of a susceptible girl. Already prepossessed in his favour, and wholly unaccustomed to a society which combined so many attractions, Evelyn regarded him with unspeakable veneration; to the darker shades in his character she was blind, — to her, indeed, they did not appear. True that once or twice in mixed society his disdainful and imperious temper broke hastily and harshly forth. To folly, to pretension, to presumption, he showed but slight forbearance. The impatient smile, the biting sarcasm, the cold repulse, that might gall, yet could scarce be openly resented, betrayed that he was one who affected to free himself from the polished restraints of social intercourse. He had once been too scrupulous in not wounding vanity; he was now too indifferent to it. But if sometimes this unamiable trait of character, as displayed to others, chilled or startled Evelyn, the contrast of his manner towards herself was a flattery too delicious not to efface all other recollections. To her ear his voice always softened its tone; to her capacity of mind ever bent as by sympathy, not condescension; to her — the young, the timid, the half-informed — to her alone he did not disdain to exhibit all the stores of his knowledge, all the best and brightest colours of his mind. She modestly wondered at so strange a preference. Perhaps a sudden and blunt compliment which Maltravers once addressed to her may explain it. One day, when she had conversed more freely and more fully than usual, he broke in upon her with this abrupt exclamation, —

"Miss Cameron, you must have associated from your childhood with beautiful minds. I see already that from the world, vile as it is, you have nothing of contagion to fear. I have heard you talk on the most various matters, on many of which your knowledge is imperfect; but you have never uttered one mean idea, or one false sentiment. Truth seems intuitive to you."

It was indeed this singular purity of heart which made to the world-wearied man the chief charm in Evelyn Cameron.

From this purity came, as from the heart of a poet, a thousand new and heaven-taught thoughts which had in them a wisdom of their own, — thoughts that often brought the stern listener back to youth, and reconciled him with life. The wise Maltravers learned more from Evelyn than Evelyn did from Maltravers.

There was, however, another trait — deeper than that of temper — in Maltravers, and which was, unlike the latter, more manifest to her than to others, — his contempt for all the things her young and fresh enthusiasm had been taught to prize, the fame that endeared and hallowed him to her eyes, the excitement of ambition, and its rewards. He spoke with such bitter disdain of great names and great deeds. "Children of a larger growth they were," said he, one day, in answer to her defence of the luminaries of their kind, "allured by baubles as poor as the rattle and the doll's house. How many have been made great, as the word is, by their vices! Paltry craft won command to Themistocles; to escape his duns, the profligate Cæsar heads an army, and achieves his laurels; Brutus, the aristocrat, stabs his patron, that patricians might again trample on plebeians, and that posterity might talk of *him*. The love of posthumous fame — what is it but as puerile a passion for notoriety as that which made a Frenchman I once knew lay out two thousand pounds in sugar-plums? To be talked of — how poor a desire! Does it matter whether it be by the gossips of this age or the next? Some men are urged on to fame by poverty — that is an excuse for their trouble; but there is no more nobleness in the motive than in that which makes yon poor ploughman sweat in the eye of Phœbus. In fact, the larger part of eminent men, instead of being inspired by any lofty desire to benefit their species or enrich the human mind, have acted or composed, without any definite object beyond the satisfying a restless appetite for excitement, or indulging the dreams of a selfish glory. And when nobler aspirations have fired them, it has too often been but to wild fanaticism and sanguinary crime. What dupes of glory ever were animated by a deeper faith, a higher ambition, than the frantic followers of

Mahomet, — taught to believe that it was virtue to ravage the earth, and that they sprang from the battle-field into Paradise? Religion and liberty, love of country, what splendid motives to action! Lo, the results, when the motives are keen, the action once commenced! Behold the Inquisition, the Days of Terror, the Council of Ten, and the Dungeons of Venice!"

Evelyn was scarcely fit to wrestle with these melancholy fallacies; but her instinct of truth suggested an answer.

"What would society be if all men thought as you do, and acted up to the theory? No literature, no art, no glory, no patriotism, no virtue, no civilization! You analyze men's motives — how can you be sure you judge rightly? Look to the results, — our benefit, our enlightenment! If the results be great, Ambition is a virtue, no matter what motive awakened it. Is it not so?"

Evelyn spoke blushingly and timidly. Maltravers, despite his own tenets, was delighted with her reply.

"You reason well," said he, with a smile. "But how are we sure that the results are such as you depict them? Civilization, enlightenment, — they are vague terms, hollow sounds. Never fear that the world will reason as I do. Action will never be stagnant while there are such things as gold and power. The vessel will move on — let the galley-slaves have it to themselves. What I have seen of life convinces me that progress is not always improvement. Civilization has evils unknown to the savage state; and *vice versa*. Men in all states seem to have much the same proportion of happiness. We judge others with eyes accustomed to dwell on our own circumstances. I have seen the slave, whom we commiserate, enjoy his holiday with a rapture unknown to the grave freeman. I have seen that slave made free, and enriched by the benevolence of his master; and he has been gay no more. The masses of men in all countries are much the same. If there are greater comforts in the hardy North, Providence bestows a fertile earth and a glorious heaven, and a mind susceptible to enjoyment as flowers to light, on the voluptuous indulgence of the Italian, or the contented apathy of the

Hindoo. In the mighty organization of good and evil, what can we vain individuals effect? They who labour most, how doubtful is their reputation! Who shall say whether Voltaire or Napoleon, Cromwell or Cæsar, Walpole or Pitt, has done most good or most evil? It is a question casuists may dispute on. Some of us think that poets have been the delight and the lights of men; another school of philosophy has treated them as the corrupters of the species, — panderers to the false glory of war, to the effeminacies of taste, to the pampering of the passions above the reason. Nay, even those who have effected inventions that change the face of the earth — the printing-press, gunpowder, the steam-engine, — men hailed as benefactors by the unthinking herd, or the would-be sages, — have introduced ills unknown before, adulterating and often counterbalancing the good. Each new improvement in machinery deprives hundreds of food. Civilization is the eternal sacrifice of one generation to the next. An awful sense of the impotence of human agencies has crushed down the sublime aspirations for mankind which I once indulged. For myself, I float on the great waters, without pilot or rudder, and trust passively to the winds, that are the breath of God."

This conversation left a deep impression upon Evelyn; it inspired her with a new interest in one in whom so many noble qualities lay dulled and torpid, by the indulgence of a self-sophistry, which, girl as she was, she felt wholly unworthy of his powers. And it was this error in Maltravers that, levelling his superiority, brought him nearer to her heart. Ah, if she could restore him to his race! It was a dangerous desire, but it intoxicated and absorbed her.

Oh, how sweetly were those fair evenings spent, — the evenings of happy June! And then, as Maltravers suffered the children to tease him into talk about the wonders he had seen in the regions far away, how did the soft and social hues of his character unfold themselves! There is in all real genius so much latent playfulness of nature it almost seems as if genius never could grow old. The inscriptions that youth writes upon the tablets of an imaginative mind are, indeed, never wholly obliterated, — they are as an invisible writing which gradually becomes clear in the light and warmth. Bring genius familiarly with the young, and it is as young as they are. Evelyn did not yet, therefore, observe the disparity of *years* between herself and Maltravers. But the disparity of knowledge and power served for the present to interdict to her that sweet feeling of equality in commune, without which love is rarely a very intense affection in women. It is not so with men. But by degrees she grew more and more familiar with her stern friend; and in that familiarity there was perilous fascination to Maltravers. She could laugh him at any moment out of his most moody reveries; contradict with a pretty wilfulness his most favourite dogmas; nay, even scold him, with bewitching gravity, if he was not always at the command of her wishes — or caprice. At this time it seemed certain that Maltravers would fall in love with Evelyn; but it rested on more doubtful probabilities whether Evelyn would fall in love with him.

CHAPTER VII.

CONTRAHE vela,
Et te littoribus cymba propinqua vehat.[1] — SENECA.

"HAS not Miss Cameron a beautiful countenance?" said Mr. Merton to Maltravers, as Evelyn, unconscious of the compliment, sat at a little distance, bending down her eyes to Sophy, who was weaving daisy-chains on a stool at her knee, and whom she was telling not to talk loud, — for Merton had been giving Maltravers some useful information respecting the management of his estate; and Evelyn was already interested in all that could interest her friend. She had one excellent thing in woman, had Evelyn Cameron: despite her sunny cheerfulness of temper she was *quiet*; and she had

[1] "Furl your sails, and let the next boat carry you to the shore."

insensibly acquired, under the roof of her musing and silent mother, the habit of never disturbing others. What a blessed secret is that in the intercourse of domestic life!

"Has not Miss Cameron a beautiful countenance?"

Maltravers started at the question, — it was a literal translation of his own thought at that moment. He checked the enthusiasm that rose to his lip, and calmly re-echoed the word, —

"Beautiful indeed!"

"And so sweet-tempered and unaffected; she has been admirably brought up. I believe Lady Vargrave is a most exemplary woman. Miss Cameron will, indeed, be a treasure to her betrothed husband. He is to be envied."

"Her betrothed husband!" said Maltravers, turning very pale.

"Yes; Lord Vargrave. Did you not know that she was engaged to him from her childhood? It was the wish, nay, command, of the late lord, who bequeathed her his vast fortune, if not on that condition, at least on that understanding. Did you never hear of this before?"

While Mr. Merton spoke, a sudden recollection returned to Maltravers. He *had* heard Lumley himself refer to the engagement, but it had been in the sick chamber of Florence, — little heeded at the time, and swept from his mind by a thousand after-thoughts and scenes. Mr. Merton continued, —

"We expect Lord Vargrave down soon. He is an ardent lover, I conclude; but public life chains him so much to London. He made an admirable speech in the Lords last night; at least, our party appear to think so. They are to be married when Miss Cameron attains the age of eighteen."

Accustomed to endurance, and skilled in the proud art of concealing emotion, Maltravers betrayed to the eye of Mr. Merton no symptom of surprise or dismay at this intelligence. If the rector had conceived any previous suspicion that Maltravers was touched beyond mere admiration for beauty, the suspicion would have vanished as he heard his guest coldly reply, —

"I trust Lord Vargrave may deserve his happiness. But, to return to Mr. Justis; you corroborate my own opinion of that smooth-spoken gentleman."

The conversation flowed back to business. At last, Maltravers rose to depart.

"Will you not dine with us to-day?" said the hospitable rector.

"Many thanks, — no; I have much business to attend to at home for some days to come."

"Kiss Sophy, Mr. Ernest, — Sophy very good girl to-day. Let the pretty butterfly go, because Evy said it was cruel to put it in a card-box; kiss Sophy."

Maltravers took the child (whose heart he had completely won) in his arms, and kissed her tenderly; then advancing to Evelyn, he held out his hand, while his eyes were fixed upon her with an expression of deep and mournful interest, which she could not understand.

"God bless you, Miss Cameron," he said, and his lip quivered.

Days passed, and they saw no more of Maltravers. He excused himself on pretence, now of business, now of other engagements, from all the invitations of the rector. Mr. Merton unsuspectingly accepted the excuse; for he knew that Maltravers was necessarily much occupied.

His arrival had now spread throughout the country; and such of his equals as were still in B——shire hastened to offer congratulations, and press hospitality. Perhaps it was the desire to make his excuses to Merton valid which prompted the master of Burleigh to yield to the other invitations that crowded on him. But this was not all, — Maltravers acquired in the neighbourhood the reputation of a man of business. Mr. Justis was abruptly dismissed; with the help of the bailiff Maltravers became his own steward. His parting address to this personage was characteristic of the mingled harshness and justice of Maltravers.

"Sir," said he, as they closed their accounts, "I discharge you because you are a rascal, — there can be no dispute about that; you have plundered your owner, yet you have ground his tenants, and neglected the poor. My villages are filled with paupers, my rent-roll is reduced a fourth; and yet, while some of my tenants appear to pay nominal rents (why, you best know), others are screwed up higher than any man's in the country. You are a rogue, Mr. Justis, — your own account-books show it; and if I send them to a lawyer, you would have to refund a sum that I could apply very advantageously to the rectification of your blunders."

"I hope, sir," said the steward, conscience-stricken and appalled, — "I hope you will not ruin me; indeed, indeed, if I was called upon to refund, I should go to jail."

"Make yourself easy, sir. It is just that I should suffer as well as you. My neglect of my own duties tempted you to roguery. You were honest under the vigilant eye of Mr. Cleveland. Retire with your gains: if you are quite hardened, no punishment can touch you; if you are not, it is punishment enough to stand there gray-headed, with one foot in the grave, and hear yourself called a rogue, and know that you cannot defend yourself, — go!"

Maltravers next occupied himself in all the affairs that a mismanaged estate brought upon him. He got rid of some tenants, he made new arrangements with others; he called labour into requisition by a variety of improvements; he paid minute attention to the poor, not in the weakness of careless and indiscriminate charity, by which popularity is so cheaply purchased, and independence so easily degraded, — no, his main care was to stimulate industry and raise hope. The ambition and emulation that he so vainly denied in himself, he found his most useful levers in the humble labourers whose characters he had studied, whose condition he sought to make themselves desire to elevate. Unconsciously his whole practice began to refute his theories. The abuses of the old Poor-Laws were rife in his neighbourhood; his quick penetration, and perhaps his imperious habits of decision, suggested to him many of the best provisions of the law now called into operation; but he was too wise to be the Philosopher Square of a system. He did not attempt too much; and he recognized one principle, which, as yet, the administrators of the new Poor-Laws have not sufficiently discovered. One main object of the new code was, by curbing public charity, to task the activity of individual benevolence. If the proprietor or the clergyman find under his own eye isolated instances of severity, oppression, or hardship in a general and salutary law, instead of railing against the law, he ought to attend to the individual instances; and private benevolence ought to keep the balance of the scales even, and be the makeweight wherever there is a just deficiency of national charity.[1] It was this which, in the modified and discreet regulations that he sought to establish on his estates, Maltravers especially and pointedly attended to. Age, infirmity, temporary distress, unmerited destitution, found him a steady, watchful, indefatigable friend. In these labours, commenced with extraordinary promptitude, and the energy of a single purpose and stern mind, Maltravers was necessarily brought into contact with the neighbouring magistrates and gentry. He was combating evils and advancing objects in which all were interested; and his vigorous sense, and his past parliamentary reputation, joined with the respect which in provinces always attaches to ancient birth, won unexpected and general favour to his views. At the rectory they heard of him constantly, not only through occasional visitors, but through Mr. Merton, who was ever thrown in his way; but he continued to keep himself aloof from the house. Every one (Mr. Merton excepted) missed him, — even Caroline, whose able though worldly mind could appreciate his conversation; the children mourned for their playmate, who was so much more affable than their own stiff-neckclothed brothers; and Evelyn was at least more serious and thoughtful than she had ever been before, and the talk of others seemed to her wearisome, trite, and dull.

Was Maltravers happy in his new pursuits? His state of

[1] The object of parochial reform is not that of economy alone; not merely to reduce poor-rates. The ratepayer ought to remember that the more he wrests from the gripe of the sturdy mendicant, the more he ought to bestow on undeserved distress. Without the mitigations of private virtue, every law that benevolists could make would be harsh.

mind at that time it is not easy to read.   His masculine spirit
and haughty temper were wrestling hard against a feeling that
had been fast ripening into passion; but at night, in his solitary and cheerless home, a vision, too exquisite to indulge,
would force itself upon him, till he started from the revery,
and said to his rebellious heart: "A few more years, and thou
wilt be still.   What in this brief life is a pang more or less?
Better to have nothing to care for, so wilt thou defraud Fate,
thy deceitful foe!   Be contented that thou art alone!"

Fortunate was it, then, for Maltravers, that he was in his
native land, not in climes where excitement is in the pursuit
of pleasure rather than in the exercise of duties.   In the hardy
air of the liberal England, he was already, though unknown
to himself, bracing and ennobling his dispositions and desires.
It is the boast of this island that the slave whose foot touches
the soil is free.   The boast may be enlarged.   Where so much
is left to the people, where the life of civilization, not locked
up in the tyranny of Central Despotism, spreads, vivifying,
restless, ardent, through every vein of the healthful body, the
most distant province, the obscurest village, has claims on
our exertions, our duties, and forces us into energy and citi-
zenship.   The spirit of liberty, that strikes the chain from
the slave, binds the freeman to his brother.   This is the Religion of Freedom.   And hence it is that the stormy struggles of
free States have been blessed with results of Virtue, of Wisdom, and of Genius by Him who bade us love one another, —
not only that love in itself is excellent, but that from love,
which in its widest sense is but the spiritual term for liberty,
whatever is worthiest of our solemn nature has its birth.

BOOK III.

Τραχέα λειαίνει, παύει κόρον.
Fx. SOLON : *Eleg.*

"Harsh things he mitigates, and pride subdues."

CHAPTER I.

YOU still are what you were, sir !

. . . With most quick agility could turn
And return; make knots and undo them,
Give forked counsel. — *Volpone, or the Fox.*

BEFORE a large table, covered with parliamentary papers, sat Lumley Lord Vargrave. His complexion, though still healthy, had faded from the freshness of hue which distinguished him in youth. His features, always sharp, had grown yet more angular: his brows seemed to project more broodingly over his eyes, which, though of undiminished brightness, were sunk deep in their sockets, and had lost much of their quick restlessness. The character of his mind had begun to stamp itself on the physiognomy, especially on the mouth when in repose. It was a face striking for acute intelligence, for concentrated energy; but there was a something written in it which said, "BEWARE!" It would have inspired any one who had mixed much amongst men with a vague suspicion and distrust.

Lumley had been always careful, though plain, in dress; but there was now a more evident attention bestowed on his person than he had ever manifested in youth, — while there was something of the Roman's celebrated foppery in the skill with which his hair was arranged on his high forehead, so as either to conceal or relieve a partial baldness at the temples. Perhaps, too, from the possession of high station, or the habit of living only amongst the great, there was a certain dignity insensibly diffused over his whole person that was not noticeable in his earlier years, when a certain *ton de garnison* was blended with his ease of manners. Yet, even now, dignity was not his prevalent characteristic; and in ordinary occasions, or mixed society, he still found a familiar frankness a more useful species of simulation. At the time we now treat of, Lord Vargrave was leaning his cheek on one hand, while the other rested idly on the papers methodically arranged before him. He appeared to have suspended his labours, and to be occupied in thought. It was, in truth, a critical period in the career of Lord Vargrave.

From the date of his accession to the peerage, the rise of Lumley Ferrers had been less rapid and progressive than he himself could have foreseen. At first, all was sunshine before him; he had contrived to make himself useful to his party; he had also made himself personally popular. To the ease and cordiality of his happy address, he added the seemingly careless candour so often mistaken for honesty; while, as there was nothing showy or brilliant in his abilities or oratory — nothing that aspired far above the pretensions of others, and aroused envy by mortifying self-love — he created but little jealousy even amongst the rivals before whom he obtained precedence. For some time, therefore, he went smoothly on, continuing to rise in the estimation of his party, and commanding a certain respect from the neutral public, by acknowledged and eminent talents in the details of business; for his quickness of penetration, and a logical habit of mind, enabled him to grapple with and generalize the minutiæ of official labour or of legislative enactments with a masterly success. But as the road became clearer to his steps, his ambition became more evident and daring. Naturally dictatorial and presumptuous, his early suppleness to superiors was now exchanged for a self-willed pertinacity, which often displeased the more haughty leaders of his party, and often

wounded the more vain. His pretensions were scanned with
eyes more jealous and less tolerant than at first. Proud
aristocrats began to recollect that a mushroom peerage was
supported but by a scanty fortune; the men of more dazzling
genius began to sneer at the red-tape minister as a mere official manager of details; he lost much of the personal popularity which had been one secret of his power. But what
principally injured him in the eyes of his party and the public
were certain ambiguous and obscure circumstances connected
with a short period when himself and his associates were
thrown out of office. At this time, it was noticeable that the
journals of the Government that succeeded were peculiarly
polite to Lord Vargrave, while they covered all his coadjutors
with obloquy: and it was more than suspected that secret
negotiations between himself and the new ministry were
going on, when suddenly the latter broke up, and Lord
Vargrave's proper party were reinstated. The vague suspicions that attached to Vargrave were somewhat strengthened
in the opinion of the public by the fact that he was at first
left out of the restored administration; and when subsequently, after a speech which showed that he could be
mischievous if not propitiated, he was readmitted, it was
precisely to the same office he had held before, — an office
which did not admit him into the Cabinet. Lumley, burning with resentment, longed to decline the offer; but, alas!
he was poor, and, what was worse, in debt; "his poverty, but
not his will, consented." He was reinstated; but though prodigiously improved as a debater, he felt that he had not
advanced as a public man. His ambition inflamed by his
discontent, he had, since his return to office, strained every
nerve to strengthen his position. He met the sarcasms on
his poverty by greatly increasing his expenditure, and by
advertising everywhere his engagement to an heiress whose
fortune, great as it was, he easily contrived to magnify. As
his old house in Great George Street — well fitted for the
bustling commoner — was no longer suited to the official and
fashionable peer, he had, on his accession to the title, exchanged that respectable residence for a large mansion in

Hamilton Place; and his sober dinners were succeeded by splendid banquets. Naturally, he had no taste for such things; his mind was too nervous, and his temper too hard, to take pleasure in luxury or ostentation. But now, as ever he *acted upon a system*. Living in a country governed by the mightiest and wealthiest aristocracy in the world, which, from the first class almost to the lowest, ostentation pervades, — the very backbone and marrow of society, — he felt that to fall far short of his rivals in display was to give them an advantage which he could not compensate either by the power of his connections or the surpassing loftiness of his character and genius. Playing for a great game, and with his eyes open to all the consequences, he cared not for involving his private fortunes in a lottery in which a great prize might be drawn. To do Vargrave justice, money with him had never been an object, but a means; he was grasping, but not avaricious. If men much richer than Lord Vargrave find State distinctions very expensive, and often ruinous, it is not to be supposed that his salary, joined to so moderate a private fortune, could support the style in which he lived. His income was already deeply mortgaged, and debt accumulated upon debt. Nor had this man, so eminent for the management of public business, any of that talent which springs from *justice*, and makes its possessor a skilful manager of his own affairs. Perpetually absorbed in intrigues and schemes, he was too much engaged in cheating others on a large scale to have time to prevent being himself cheated on a small one. He never looked into bills till he was compelled to pay them; and he never calculated the amount of an expense that seemed the least necessary to his purposes. But still Lord Vargrave relied upon his marriage with the wealthy Evelyn to relieve him from all his embarrassments; and if a doubt of the realization of that vision ever occurred to him, still public life had splendid prizes. Nay, should he fail with Miss Cameron, he even thought that, by good management, he might ultimately make it worth while to his colleagues to purchase his absence with the gorgeous bribe of the Governor-Generalship of India.

As oratory is an art in which practice and the dignity of station produce marvellous improvement, so Lumley had of late made effects in the House of Lords of which he had once been judged incapable. It is true that no practice and no station can give men qualities in which they are wholly deficient; but these advantages can bring out in the best light all the qualities they *do* possess. The glow of a generous imagination, the grasp of a profound statesmanship, the enthusiasm of a noble nature,—these no practice could educe from the eloquence of Lumley Lord Vargrave, for he had them not; but bold wit, fluent and vigorous sentences, effective arrangement of parliamentary logic, readiness of retort, plausibility of manner, aided by a delivery peculiar for self-possession and ease, a clear and ringing voice (to the only fault of which, shrillness without passion, the ear of the audience had grown accustomed), and a coun⁺enance impressive from its courageous intelligence, — all these had raised the promising speaker into the matured excellence of a nervous and formid- able debater.   But precisely as he rose in the display of his talents, did he awaken envies and enmities hitherto dormant. And it must be added that, with all his craft and coldness, Lord Vargrave was often a very dangerous and mischievous speaker for the interests of his party.   His colleagues had often cause to tremble when he rose: nay, even when the cheers of his own faction shook the old tapestried walls.   A man who has no sympathy with the public must commit many and fatal indiscretions when the public, as well as his audi- ence, is to be his judge.   Lord Vargrave's utter incapacity to comprehend political morality, his contempt for all the objects of social benevolence, frequently led him into the avowal of doctrines, which, if they did not startle the men of the world whom he addressed (smoothed away, as such doctrines were, by speciousness of manner and delivery), created deep disgust in those even of his own politics who read their naked exposi- tion in the daily papers.   Never did Lord Vargrave utter one of those generous sentiments which, no matter whether pro- pounded by Radical or Tory, sink deep into the heart of the people, and do lasting service to the cause they adorn.   But no man defended an abuse, however glaring, with a more vigorous championship, or hurled defiance upon a popular demand with a more courageous scorn. In some times, when the anti-popular principle is strong, such a leader may be useful; but at the moment of which we treat he was a most equivocal auxiliary. A considerable proportion of the ministers, headed by the premier himself, a man of wise views and unimpeachable honour, had learned to view Lord Vargrave with dislike and distrust. They might have sought to get rid of him; but he was not one whom slight mortifications could induce to retire of his own accord, nor was the sarcastic and bold debater a person whose resentment and opposition could be despised. Lord Vargrave, moreover, had secured a party of his own, — a party more formidable than himself. He went largely into society; he was the special favourite of the female diplomats, whose voices at that time were powerful suffrages, and with whom, by a thousand links of gallantry and intrigue, the agreeable and courteous minister formed a close alliance. All that *salons* could do for him was done. Added to this, he was personally liked by his royal master; and the Court gave him their golden opinions; while the poorer, the corrupter, and the more bigoted portion of the ministry regarded him with avowed admiration.

In the House of Commons, too, and in the bureaucracy, he had no inconsiderable strength; for Lumley never contracted the habits of personal abruptness and discourtesy common to men in power who wish to keep applicants aloof. He was bland and conciliating to all men of ranks; his intellect and self-complacency raised him far above the petty jealousies that great men feel for rising men. Did any tyro earn the smallest distinction in parliament, no man sought his acquaintance so eagerly as Lord Vargrave; no man complimented, encouraged, "brought on" the new aspirants of his party with so hearty a good will.

Such a minister could not fail of having devoted followers among the able, the ambitious, and the vain. It must also be confessed that Lord Vargrave neglected no baser and less justifiable means to cement his power by placing it on the sure rock of self-interest. No jobbing was too gross for him. He was shamefully corrupt in the disposition of his patronage;

and no rebuffs, no taunts from his official brethren, could restrain him from urging the claims of any of his creatures upon the public purse. His followers regarded this charitable selfishness as the stanchness and zeal of friendship; and the ambition of hundreds was wound up in the ambition of the unprincipled minister.

But besides the notoriety of his public corruption, Lord Vargrave was secretly suspected by some of personal dishonesty, — suspected of selling his State information to stockjobbers, of having pecuniary interests in some of the claims he urged with so obstinate a pertinacity. And though there was not the smallest evidence of such utter abandonment of honour, though it was probably but a calumnious whisper, yet the mere suspicion of such practices served to sharpen the aversion of his enemies, and justify the disgust of his rivals.

In this position now stood Lord Vargrave: supported by interested, but able and powerful partisans; hated in the country, feared by some of those with whom he served, despised by others, looked up to by the rest. It was a situation that less daunted than delighted him; for it seemed to render necessary and excuse the habits of scheming and manœuvre which were so genial to his crafty and plotting temper. Like an ancient Greek, his spirit loved intrigue for intrigue's sake. Had it led to no end, it would still have been sweet to him as a means. He rejoiced to surround himself with the most complicated webs and meshes; to sit in the centre of a million plots. He cared not how rash and wild some of them were. He relied on his own ingenuity, promptitude, and habitual good fortune to make every spring he handled conducive to the purpose of the machine — SELF.

His last visit to Lady Vargrave, and his conversation with Evelyn, had left on his mind much dissatisfaction and fear. In the earlier years of his intercourse with Evelyn, his good humour, gallantry, and presents had not failed to attach the child to the agreeable and liberal visitor she had been taught to regard as a relation. It was only as she grew up to womanhood, and learned to comprehend the nature of the tie between them, that she shrank from his familiarity; and then only had

he learned to doubt of the fulfilment of his uncle's wish. The
last visit had increased this doubt to a painful apprehension.
He saw that he was not loved; he saw that it required great
address, and the absence of happier rivals, to secure to him
the hand of Evelyn; and he cursed the duties and the schemes
which necessarily kept him from her side. He had thought
of persuading Lady Vargrave to let her come to London,
where he could be ever at hand; and as the season was now
set in, his representations on this head would appear sensible
and just. But then again this was to incur greater dangers
than those he would avoid. London! — a beauty and an heiress, in her first *début* in London! What formidable admirers
would flock around her! Vargrave shuddered to think of the
gay, handsome, well-dressed, seductive young *élégans*, who
might seem, to a girl of seventeen, suitors far more fascinating than the middle-aged politician. This was perilous; nor
was this all: Lord Vargrave knew that in London — gaudy,
babbling, and remorseless London — all that he could most
wish to conceal from the young lady would be dragged to day.
He had been the lover, not of one, but of a dozen women, for
whom he did not care three straws, but whose favour had
served to strengthen him in society, or whose influence made
up for his own want of hereditary political connections. The
manner in which he contrived to shake off these various
Ariadnes, whenever it was advisable, was not the least striking proof of his diplomatic abilities. He never left them
enemies. According to his own solution of the mystery, he
took care never to play the gallant with Dulcineas under a
certain age. "Middle-aged women," he was wont to say, "are
very little different from middle-aged men; they see things
sensibly, and take things coolly." Now Evelyn could not be
three weeks, perhaps three days, in London, without learning
of one or the other of these *liaisons*. What an excuse, if she
sought one, to break with him! Altogether, Lord Vargrave
was sorely perplexed, but not despondent. Evelyn's fortune
was more than ever necessary to him, and Evelyn he was
resolved to obtain since to that fortune she was an indispensa-
ble appendage.

CHAPTER II.

You shall be Horace, and Tibullus I. — POPE.

LORD VARGRAVE was disturbed from his revery by the entrance of the Earl of Saxingham.

"You are welcome!" said Lumley, "welcome! — the very man I wished to see."

Lord Saxingham, who was scarcely altered since we met with him in the last series of this work, except that he had grown somewhat paler and thinner, and that his hair had changed from iron-gray to snow-white, threw himself in the armchair beside Lumley, and replied, —

"Vargrave, it is really unpleasant, our finding ourselves always thus controlled by our own partisans. I do not understand this new-fangled policy, this squaring of measures to please the Opposition, and throwing sops to that many-headed monster called Public Opinion. I am sure it will end most mischievously."

"I am satisfied of it," returned Lord Vargrave. "All vigour and union seem to have left us; and if they carry the —— question against us, I know not what is to be done."

"For my part, I shall resign," said Lord Saxingham, doggedly; "it is the only alternative left to men of honour."

"You are wrong; I know another alternative."

"What is that?"

"Make a Cabinet of our own. Look ye, my dear lord; you have been ill-used; your high character, your long experience, are treated with contempt. It is an affront to you — the situation you hold. You, Privy Seal! — you ought to be Premier; ay, and, if you are ruled by me, Premier you shall be yet."

Lord Saxingham coloured, and breathed hard.

"You have often hinted at this before, Lumley; but you are so partial, so friendly."

"Not at all. You saw the leading article in the ——
to-day? That will be followed up by two evening papers
within five hours of this time. We have strength with the
Press, with the Commons, with the Court, — only let us hold
fast together. This —— question, by which they hope to get
rid of us, shall destroy them. You shall be Prime Minister
before the year is over — by Heaven, you shall! — and then, I
suppose, *I* too may be admitted to the Cabinet!"

"But how? — how, Lumley? You are too rash, too
daring."

"It has not been my fault hitherto, — but boldness is
caution in our circumstances. If they throw us out now, I
see the inevitable march of events, — we shall be out for
years, perhaps for life. The Cabinet will recede more and
more from our principles, our party. Now is the time for a
determined stand; now can we make or mar ourselves. I
will not resign; the king is with us; our strength shall be
known. These haughty imbeciles shall fall into the trap they
have dug for us."

Lumley spoke warmly, and with the confidence of a mind
firmly assured of success. Lord Saxingham was moved;
bright visions flashed across him, — the premiership, a dukedom. Yet he was old and childless, and his honours would
die with the last lord of Saxingham!

"See," continued Lumley, "I have calculated our resources
as accurately as an electioneering agent would cast up the list
of voters. In the Press, I have secured —— and ——, and
in the Commons we have the subtle ——, and the vigour of
——, and the popular name of ——, and all the boroughs of
——; in the Cabinet we have ——, and at Court you know
our strength. Let us choose our moment; a sudden *coup*, an
interview with the king, statement of our conscientious scruples to this atrocious measure. I know the vain, stiff mind
of the premier; *he* will lose temper, he will tender his resignation; to his astonishment, it will be accepted. You will
be sent for; we will dissolve parliament; we will strain every
nerve in the elections; we shall succeed, I know we shall.
But be silent in the meanwhile, be cautious: let not a word

escape you, let them think us beaten; lull suspicion asleep; let us lament our weakness, and hint, only hint at our resignation, but with assurances of continued support. I know how to blind them, if you leave it to me."

The weak mind of the old earl was as a puppet in the hands of his bold kinsman. He feared one moment, hoped another; now his ambition was flattered, now his sense of honour was alarmed. There was something in Lumley's intrigue to oust the government with which he served that had an appearance of cunning and baseness, of which Lord Saxingham, whose personal character was high, by no means approved. But Vargrave talked him over with consummate address, and when they parted, the earl carried his head two inches higher, — he was preparing himself for his rise in life.

"That is well! that is well!" said Lumley, rubbing his hands when he was left alone: "the old driveller will be my *locum tenens*, till years and renown enable me to become his successor. Meanwhile, I shall be really what he will be in name."

Here Lord Vargrave's well-fed servant, now advanced to the dignity of own gentleman and house-steward, entered the room with a letter; it had a portentous look; it was wafered, the paper was blue, the hand clerklike, there was no envelope; it bore its infernal origin on the face of it, — IT WAS A DUN'S.

Lumley opened the epistle with an impatient pshaw! The man, a silversmith (Lumley's plate was much admired!) had applied for years in vain; the amount was large, and execution was threatened! An execution! — it is a trifle to a rich man; but no trifle to one suspected of being poor, one straining at that very moment at so high an object, one to whom public opinion was so necessary, one who knew that nothing but his title, and scarcely that, saved him from the reputation of an adventurer! He must again have recourse to the money-lenders, — his small estate was long since too deeply mortgaged to afford new security. Usury, usury, again! — he knew its price, and he sighed — but what was to be done?

"It is but for a few months, a few months, and Evelyn .nust be mine. Saxingham has already lent me what he can;

but he is embarrassed.   This d—d office, what a tax it is! and
the rascals say we are too well paid!   I, too, who could live
happy in a garret, if this purse-proud England would but
allow one to exist within one's income.   My fellow-trustee,
the banker, my uncle's old correspondent — ah, well thought
of!   He knows the conditions of the will; he knows that, at
the worst, I must have thirty thousand pounds, if I live a few
months longer.   I will go to him."

CHAPTER III.

ANIMUM nunc hoc celerem, nunc dividit illuc.[1] — VIRGIL.

THE late Mr. Templeton had been a banker in a provincial
town, which was the centre of great commercial and agricultural activity and enterprise.   He had made the bulk of his
fortune in the happy days of paper currency and war.   Besides his country bank he had a considerable share in a metropolitan one of some eminence.   At the time of his marriage
with the present Lady Vargrave he retired altogether from
business, and never returned to the place in which his wealth
had been amassed.   He had still kept up a familiar acquaintance with the principal and senior partner of the metropolitan
bank I have referred to; for he was a man who always loved
to talk about money matters with those who understood them.
This gentleman, Mr. Gustavus Douce, had been named, with
Lumley, joint trustee to Evelyn's fortune.   They had full
powers to invest it in whatever stock seemed most safe or
advantageous.   The trustees appeared well chosen, as one,
being destined to share the fortune, would have the deepest
interest in its security; and the other, from his habits and
profession, would be a most excellent adviser.

Of Mr. Douce, Lord Vargrave had seen but little; they

---

[1] "Now this, now that, distracts the active mind."

were not thrown together. But Lord Vargrave, who thought every rich man might, some time or other, become a desirable acquaintance, regularly asked him once every year to dinner; and twice in return he had dined with Mr. Douce, in one of the most splendid villas, and off some of the most splendid plate it had ever been his fortune to witness and to envy! — so that the little favour he was about to ask was but a slight return for Lord Vargrave's condescension.

He found the banker in his private sanctum, his carriage at the door; for it was just four o'clock, an hour in which Mr. Douce regularly departed to Caserta, as his aforesaid villa was somewhat affectedly styled.

Mr. Douce was a small man, a nervous man; he did not seem quite master of his own limbs: when he bowed he seemed to be making you a present of his legs; when he sat down, he twitched first on one side, then on the other, thrust his hands into his pockets, then took them out, and looked at them, as if in astonishment, then seized upon a pen, by which they were luckily provided with incessant occupation. Meanwhile, there was what might fairly be called a constant play of countenance: first he smiled, then looked grave; now raised his eyebrows, till they rose like rainbows, to the horizon of his pale, straw-coloured hair; and next darted them down, like an avalanche, over the twinkling, restless, fluttering, little blue eyes, which then became almost invisible. Mr. Douce had, in fact, all the appearance of a painfully shy man, which was the more strange, as he had the reputation of enterprise, and even audacity, in the business of his profession, and was fond of the society of the great.

"I have called on you, my dear sir," said Lord Vargrave, after the preliminary salutations, "to ask a little favour, which, if the least inconvenient, have no hesitation in refusing. You know how I am situated with regard to my ward, Miss Cameron; in a few months I hope she will be Lady Vargrave."

Mr. Douce showed three small teeth, which were all that, in the front of his mouth, fate had left him; and then, as if alarmed at the indelicacy of a smile upon such a subject, pushed back his chair, and twitched up his blotting-paper-coloured trousers.

"Yes, in a few months I hope she will be Lady Vargrave; and you know then, Mr. Douce, that I shall be in no want of money."

"I hope — that is to say, I am sure, — that — I trust that never will be the ca-ca-case with your lordship," put in Mr. Douce, with timid hesitation. Mr. Douce, in addition to his other good qualities, stammered much in the delivery of his sentences.

"You are very kind, but it is the case just at present; I have great need of a few thousand pounds upon my personal security. My estate is already a little mortgaged, and I don't wish to encumber it more; besides, the loan would be merely temporary. You know that if at the age of eighteen Miss Cameron refuses me (a supposition out of the question, but in business we must calculate on improbabilities), I claim the forfeit she incurs, — thirty thousand pounds; you remember."

"Oh, yes — that — is — upon my word — I — I don't exactly — but — your lord — l-l-l-lord-lordship knows best — I have been so — so busy — I forget the exact — hem — hem!"

"If you just turn to the will you will see it is as I say. Now, could you conveniently place a few thousands to my account, just for a short time? But I see you don't like it. Never mind, I can get it elsewhere; only, as you were my poor uncle's friend — "

"Your lord — l-l-l-lordship is quite mistaken," said Mr. Douce, with trembling agitation; "upon my word, yes, a few thou-thou-thousands — to be sure — to be sure. Your lordship's banker is — is — "

"Drummond — disagreeable people — by no means obliging. I shall certainly change to your house when my accounts are better worth keeping."

"You do me great — great honour; I will just — step — step — step out for a moment — and — and speak to Mr. Dobs; — not but what you may depend on. — Excuse me! 'Morning Chron-chron-Chronicle,' my lord!"

Mr. Douce rose, as if by galvanism, and ran out of the

room, spinning round as he ran, to declare, again and again,
that he would not be gone a moment.

"Good little fellow, that — very like an electrified frog!"
murmured Vargrave, as he took up the "Morning Chronicle,"
so especially pointed out to his notice; and turning to the
leading article, read a very eloquent attack on himself.
Lumley was thick-skinned on such matters; he liked to
be attacked, — it showed that he was up in the world.

Presently Mr. Douce returned. To Lord Vargrave's amazement and delight, he was informed that £10,000 would be
immediately lodged with Messrs. Drummond. His bill of
promise to pay in three months — five per cent interest — was
quite sufficient. Three months was a short date; but the bill
could be renewed on the same terms, from quarter to quarter,
till quite convenient to his lordship to pay. "Would Lord
Vargrave do him the honour to dine with him at Caserta next
Monday?"

Lord Vargrave tried to affect apathy at his sudden accession
of ready money, but really it almost turned his head; he griped
both Mr. Douce's thin, little shivering hands, and was speechless with gratitude and ecstasy. The sum, which doubled the
utmost he expected, would relieve him from all his immediate
embarrassments. When he recovered his voice, he thanked
his dear Mr. Douce with a warmth that seemed to make the
little man shrink into a nutshell; and assured him that he
would dine with him every Monday in the year — if he was
asked! He then longed to depart; but he thought, justly,
that to go as soon as he had got what he wanted would look
selfish. Accordingly, he reseated himself, and so did Mr.
Douce, and the conversation turned upon politics and news;
but Mr. Douce, who seemed to regard all things with a commercial eye, contrived, Vargrave hardly knew how, to veer
round from the change in the French ministry to the state of
the English money-market.

"It really is, indeed, my lord — I say it, I am sure, with
concern, a very bad ti-ti-ti-ti-time for men in business, —
indeed, for all men; such poor interest in the English fu-fun-
funds, and yet speculations are so unsound. I recommended

my friend Sir Giles Grimsby to — to invest some money in
the American canals; a most rare res-res-respons-reponsi-
bility, I may say, for me; I am cautious in — in recommend-
ing — but Sir Giles was an old friend, — con-con-connection,
I may say; but most providentially, all turned out — that is
— fell out — as I was sure it would, — thirty per cent, — and
the value of the sh-sh-sh-shares doubled. But such things
are very rare, — quite godsends, I may say!"

"Well, Mr. Douce, whenever I have money to lay out, I
must come and consult you."

"I shall be most happy at all times to — to advise your
lordship; but it is not a thing I 'm very fond of. There 's
Miss Cameron's fortune quite l-l-locked up, — three per cents
and exchequer bills; why, it might have been a mil-mil-mill-
ion by this ti-ti-time, if the good old gentleman — I beg pardon — old — old nobleman, my poor dear friend, had been
now alive!"

"Indeed!" said Lumley, greedily, and pricking up his
ears; "he was a good manager, my uncle!"

"None better, none better. I may say a genius for busi —
hem — hem! Miss Cameron a young woman of bus-bus-busi-
ness, my lord?"

"Not much of that, I fear. A million, did you say?"

"At least! — indeed, at least — money so scarce, speculation so sure in America; great people the Americans, rising
people, gi-gi-giants — giants!"

"I am wasting your whole morning, — too bad in me," said
Vargrave, as the clock struck five; "the Lords meet this evening, — important business; once more a thousand thanks to
you; good day."

"A very good day to you, my lord; don't mention it; glad
at any time to ser-ser-serve you," said Mr. Douce, fidgeting,
curveting, and prancing round Lord Vargrave, as the latter
walked through the outer office to the carriage.

"Not a step more; you will catch cold. Good-by — on
Monday, then, seven o'clock. The House of Lords."

And Lumley threw himself back in his carriage in high
spirits.

CHAPTER IV.

OUBLIÉ de Tullie, et bravé du Sénat.[1]
VOLTAIRE : *Brutus*, Act ii. sc. 1.

IN the Lords that evening the discussion was animated and prolonged, — it was the last party debate of the session. The astute Opposition did not neglect to bring prominently, though incidentally, forward the question on which it was whispered that there existed some growing difference in the Cabinet. Lord Vargrave rose late. His temper was excited by the good fortune of his day's negotiation; he felt himself of more importance than usual, as a needy man is apt to do when he has got a large sum at his banker's; moreover, he was exasperated by some personal allusions to himself, which had been delivered by a dignified old lord who dated his family from the ark, and was as rich as Crœsus. Accordingly, Vargrave spoke with more than his usual vigour. His first sentences were welcomed with loud cheers; he warmed, he grew vehement, he uttered the most positive and unalterable sentiments upon the question alluded to, he greatly transgressed the discretion which the heads of his party were desirous to maintain, — instead of conciliating without compromising, he irritated, galled, *and* compromised. The angry cheers of the opposite party were loudly re-echoed by the cheers of the more hot-headed on his own side. The premier and some of his colleagues observed, however, a moody silence. The premier once took a note, and then reseated himself, and drew his hat more closely over his brows. It was an ominous sign for Lumley; but he was looking the Opposition in the face, and did not observe it. He sat down in triumph; he had made a most effective and a most mischievous speech, — a combination extremely common. The leader of the Opposition replied

---

[1] " Forgotten by Tully and bullied by the Senate."

to him with bitter calmness; and when citing some of his
sharp sentences, he turned to the premier, and asked, "Are
these opinions those also of the noble lord? I call for a
reply, — I have a right to demand a reply," Lumley was startled to hear the tone in which his chief uttered the compre-
hensive and significant "*Hear, hear!*"

At midnight the premier wound up the debate; his speech
was short, and characterized by moderation. He came to
the question put to him. The House was hushed, — you
might have heard a pin drop; the Commoners behind the
throne pressed forward with anxiety and eagerness on their
countenances.

"I am called upon," said the minister, "to declare if those
sentiments, uttered by my noble friend, are mine also, as the
chief adviser of the Crown. My lords, in the heat of debate
every word is not to be scrupulously weighed, and rigidly
interpreted." ("Hear, hear," ironically from the Opposition,
approvingly from the Treasury benches.) "My noble friend
will doubtless be anxious to explain what he intended to say.
I hope, nay, I doubt not, that his explanation will be satisfactory to the noble lord, to the House, and to the country; but
since I am called upon for a distinct reply to a distinct inter-
rogatory, I will say at once, that if those sentiments be rightly
interpreted by the noble lord who spoke last, those sentiments
are not mine, and will never animate the conduct of any cabinet of which I am a member." (Long-continued cheering
from the Opposition.) "At the same time, I am convinced
that my noble friend's meaning has not been rightly construed; and till I hear from himself to the contrary, I will
venture to state what I think he designed to convey to your
lordships." Here the premier, with a tact that nobody could
be duped by, but every one could admire, stripped Lord
Vargrave's unlucky sentences of every syllable that could
give offence to any one; and left the pointed epigrams
and vehement denunciations a most harmless arrangement
of commonplace.

The House was much excited; there was a call for Lord
Vargrave, and Lord Vargrave promptly rose. It was one of

those dilemmas out of which Lumley was just the man to
extricate himself with address.   There was so much manly
frankness in his manner, there was so much crafty subtlety
in his mind!   He complained, with proud and honest bitterness, of the construction that had been forced upon his words
by the Opposition.   "If," he added (and no man knew better
the rhetorical effect of the *tu quoque* form of argument), — "if
every sentence uttered by the noble lord opposite in his zeal
for liberty had, in days now gone by, been construed with
equal rigour, or perverted with equal ingenuity, that noble
lord had long since been prosecuted as an incendiary, perhaps
executed as a traitor!"   Vehement cheers from the ministerial
benches; cries of "Order!" from the Opposition.   A military
lord rose to order, and appealed to the Woolsack.

Lumley sat down as if chafed at the interruption; he had
produced the effect he had desired, — he had changed the public question at issue into a private quarrel; a new excitement
was created; dust was thrown into the eyes of the House.
Several speakers rose to accommodate matters; and after half-
an-hour of public time had been properly wasted, the noble
lord on the one side and the noble lord on the other duly
explained, paid each other the highest possible compliments,
and Lumley was left to conclude his vindication, which now
seemed a comparatively flat matter after the late explosion.
He completed his task so as to satisfy, apparently, all parties
— for all parties were now tired of the thing, and wanted to
go to bed.   But the next morning there were whispers about
the town, articles in the different papers, evidently by authority, rejoicings among the Opposition, and a general feeling
that though the Government might keep together that session,
its dissensions would break out before the next meeting of
parliament.

As Lumley was wrapping himself in his cloak after this
stormy debate, the Marquess of Raby — a peer of large possessions, and one who entirely agreed with Lumley's views —
came up to him, and proposed that they should go home together in Lord Raby's carriage.   Vargrave willingly consented, and dismissed his own servants.

"You did that admirably, my dear Vargrave!" said Lord Raby, when they were seated in the carriage. "I quite coincide in all your sentiments; I declare my blood boiled when I heard —— [the premier] appear half inclined to throw you over. Your hit upon ·—— was first-rate, — he will not get over it for a month; and you extricated yourself well."

"I am glad you approve my conduct, — it comforts me," said Vargrave, feelingly; "at the same time I see all the conse· quences; but I can brave all for the sake of character and conscience."

"I feel just as you do!" replied Lord Raby, with some warmth; "and if I thought that —— meant to yield to this question, I should certainly oppose his administration."

Vargrave shook his head, and held his tongue, which gave Lord Raby a high idea of his discretion.

After a few more observations on political matters, Lord Raby invited Lumley to pay him a visit at his country-seat.

"I am going to Knaresdean next Monday; you know we have races in the park, and really they are sometimes good sport; at all events, it is a very pretty sight. There will be nothing in the Lords now, — the recess is just at hand; and if you can spare the time, Lady Raby and myself will be delighted to see you."

"You may be sure, my dear lord, I cannot refuse your invi· tation; indeed, I intended to visit your county next week. You know, perhaps, a Mr. Merton."

"Charles Merton? — to be sure; most respectable man, cap· ital fellow, the best parson in the county, — no cant, but thor· oughly orthodox; he certainly keeps in his brother, who, though a very active member, is what I call a waverer on certain questions. Have you known Merton long?"

"I don't know him at all as yet; my acquaintance is with his wife and daughter, — a very fine girl, by the by. My ward, Miss Cameron, is staying with them."

"Miss Cameron! Cameron — ah, I understand. I think I have heard that — But gossip does not always tell the truth!"

Lumley smiled significantly, and the carriage now stopped at his door.

"Perhaps you will take a seat in our carriage on Monday?" said Lord Raby.

"Monday? Unhappily I am engaged; but on Tuesday your lordship may expect me."

"Very well; the races begin on Wednesday: we shall have a full house. Good-night."

CHAPTER V.

HOMUNCULI quanti sunt, cum recogito.[1] — PLAUTUS.

IT is obvious that for many reasons we must be brief upon the political intrigue in which the scheming spirit of Lord Vargrave was employed. It would, indeed, be scarcely possible to preserve the necessary medium between too plain a revelation and too complex a disguise. It suffices, therefore, very shortly to repeat what the reader has already gathered from what has gone before; namely, that the question at issue was one which has happened often enough in all governments, — one on which the Cabinet was divided, and in which the weaker party was endeavouring to out-trick the stronger.

The malcontents, foreseeing that sooner or later the head of the gathering must break, were again divided among themselves whether to resign, or to stay in and strive to force a resignation on their dissentient colleagues. The richer and the more honest were for the former course; the poorer and the more dependent for the latter. We have seen that the latter policy was that espoused and recommended by Vargrave, who, though not in the Cabinet, always contrived somehow or other to worm out its secrets. At the same time he by no means rejected the other string to his bow. If it were possible so to arrange and to strengthen his faction, that, by the *coup d'état* of a sudden resignation in a formidable body, the whole Government might be broken up,

[1] "When I reflect, how great your little men are in their own consideration!"

and a new one formed from among the resignees, it would obviously be the best plan. But then Lord Vargrave was doubtful of his own strength, and fearful to play into the hands of his colleagues, who might be able to stand even better without himself and his allies, and by conciliating the Opposition take a step onward in political movement, — which might leave Vargrave placeless and powerless for years to come.

He repented his own rashness in the recent debate, which was, indeed, a premature boldness that had sprung out of momentary excitement — for the craftiest orator must be indiscreet sometimes. He spent the next few days in alter-nately seeking to explain away to one party, and to sound, unite, and consolidate the other. His attempts in the one quarter were received by the premier with the cold politeness of an offended but careful statesman, who believed just as much as he chose, and preferred taking his own opportunity for a breach with a subordinate to risking any imprudence by the gratification of resentment. In the last quarter, the penetrating adventurer saw that his ground was more insecure than he had anticipated. He perceived in dismay and secret rage that many of those most loud in his favour while he was with the Government would desert him the soonest if thrown out. Liked as a subordinate minister, he was viewed with very different eyes the moment it was a question whether, instead of cheering his sentiments, men should trust them-selves to his guidance. Some did not wish to displease the Government; others did not seek to weaken but to correct them. One of his stanchest allies in the Commons was a can-didate for a peerage; another suddenly remembered that he was second cousin to the premier. Some laughed at the idea of a puppet premier in Lord Saxingham; others insinuated to Vargrave that he himself was not precisely of that standing in the country which would command respect to a new party, of which, if not the head, he would be the mouthpiece. For themselves they knew, admired, and trusted him; but those d—d country gentlemen — and the dull public!

Alarmed, wearied, and disgusted, the schemer saw himself

reduced to submission, for the present at least; and more than ever he felt the necessity of Evelyn's fortune to fall back upon, if the chance of the cards should rob him of his salary. He was glad to escape for a breathing-while from the vexations and harassments that beset him, and looked forward with the eager interest of a sanguine and elastic mind — always escaping from one scheme to another — to his excursion into B——shire.

At the villa of Mr. Douce, Lord Vargrave met a young nobleman who had just succeeded to a property not only large and unencumbered, but of a nature to give him importance in the eyes of politicians. Situated in a very small county, the estates of Lord Doltimore secured to his nomination at least one of the representatives, while a little village at the back of his pleasure-grounds constituted a borough, and returned two members to parliament. Lord Doltimore, just returned from the Continent, had not even taken his seat in the Lords; and though his family connections, such as they were — and they were not very high, and by no means in the fashion — were ministerial, his own opinions were as yet unrevealed.

To this young nobleman Lord Vargrave was singularly attentive. He was well formed to attract men younger than himself, and he eminently succeeded in his designs upon Lord Doltimore's affection.

His lordship was a small, pale man, with a very limited share of understanding, supercilious in manner, elaborate in dress, not ill-natured *au fond,* and with much of the English gentleman in his disposition, — that is, he was honourable in his ideas and actions, whenever his natural dulness and neglected education enabled him clearly to perceive (through the midst of prejudices, the delusions of others, and the false lights of the dissipated society in which he had lived) what was right and what wrong. But his leading characteristics were vanity and conceit. He had lived much with younger sons, cleverer than himself, who borrowed his money, sold him their horses, and won from him at cards. In return they gave him all that species of flattery which young men *can* give with so hearty an appearance of cordial admiration. "You certainly have the best horses in Paris. You are really a devilish good fellow, Doltimore. Oh, do you know, Dolti-more, what little Désiré says of you? You have certainly turned the girl's head."

This sort of adulation from one sex was not corrected by any great acerbity from the other. Lord Doltimore at the age of twenty-two was a very good *parti ;* and, whatever his other deficiencies, he had sense enough to perceive that he received much greater attention — whether from opera-dancers in search of a friend, or virtuous young ladies in search of a husband — than any of the companions, good-looking though many of them were, with whom he had habitually lived.

"You will not long remain in town now the season is over?" said Vargrave, as after dinner he found himself, by the departure of the ladies, next to Lord Doltimore.

"No, indeed; even in the season I don't much like London. Paris has rather spoiled me for any other place."

"Paris is certainly very charming; the ease of French life has a fascination that our formal ostentation wants. Nevertheless, to a man like you, London must have many attractions."

"Why, I have a good many friends here; but still, after Ascot, it rather bores me."

"Have you any horses on the turf?"

"Not yet; but Legard (you know Legard, perhaps, — a very good fellow) is anxious that I should try my luck. I was very fortunate in the races at Paris — you know we have established racing there. The French take to it quite naturally."

"Ah, indeed! It is so long since I have been in Paris — most exciting amusement! *À propos* of races, I am going down to Lord Raby's to-morrow; I think I saw in one of the morning papers that you had very largely backed a horse entered at Knaresdean."

"Yes, Thunderer — I think of buying Thunderer. Legard — Colonel Legard (he was in the Guards, but he sold out) —

is a good judge, and recommends the purchase. How very odd that you too should be going to Knaresdean!"

"Odd, indeed, but most lucky! We can go together, if you are not better engaged."

Lord Doltimore coloured and hesitated. On the one hand he was a little afraid of being alone with so clever a man; on the other hand, it was an honour, — it was something for him to talk of to Legard. Nevertheless, the shyness got the better of the vanity. He excused himself; he feared he was engaged to take down Legard.

Lumley smiled, and changed the conversation; and so agreeable did he make himself, that when the party broke up, and Lumley had just shaken hands with his host, Doltimore came to him, and said in a little confusion, —

"I think I can put off Legard — if — if you —"

"That's delightful! What time shall we start? — need not get down much before dinner — one o'clock?"

"Oh, yes! not too long before dinner; one o'clock will be a little too early."

"Two then. Where are you staying?"

"At Fenton's."

"I will call for you. Good-night! I long to see Thunderer!"

CHAPTER VI.

LA santé de l'âme n'est pas plus assurée que celle du corps; et quoique l'on paraisse éloigné des passions, on n'est pas moins en danger de s'y laisser emporter que de tomber malade quand on se porte bien.[1] — LA ROCHEFOUCAULD.

IN spite of the efforts of Maltravers to shun all occasions of meeting Evelyn, they were necessarily sometimes thrown together in the round of provincial hospitalities; and cer-

[1] "The health of the soul is not more sure than that of the body; and although we may appear free from passions, there is not the less danger of their attack than of falling sick at the moment we are well."

tainly, if either Mr. Merton or Caroline (the shrewder observer of the two) had ever formed any suspicion that Evelyn had made a conquest of Maltravers, his manner at such times effectually removed it.

Maltravers was a man to feel deeply, but no longer a boy to yield to every tempting impulse. I have said that FORTI-TUDE was his favourite virtue, but fortitude is the virtue of great and rare occasions; there was another, equally hard-favoured and unshowy, which he took as the staple of active and every-day duties, and that virtue was JUSTICE. Now, in earlier life, he had been enamoured of the conventional Florimel that we call HONOUR, — a shifting and shadowy phantom, that is but the reflex of the opinion of the time and clime. But justice has in it something permanent and solid; and out of justice arises the real not the false honour.

"Honour!" said Maltravers, — "honour is to justice as the flower to the plant, — its efflorescence, its bloom, its consum-mation! But honour that does not spring from justice is but a piece of painted rag, an artificial rose, which the men-milliners of society would palm upon us as more natural than the true."

This principle of justice Maltravers sought to carry out in all things — not, perhaps, with constant success; for what practice can always embody theory? — but still, at least his endeavour at success was constant. This, perhaps, it was which had ever kept him from the excesses to which exuber-ant and liberal natures are prone, from the extravagances of pseudo-genius.

"No man, for instance," he was wont to say, "can be em-barrassed in his own circumstances, and not cause embarrass-ment to others. Without economy, who can be just? And what are charity, generosity, but the poetry and the beauty of justice?"

No man ever asked Maltravers twice for a just debt; and no man ever once asked him to fulfil a promise. You felt that, come what would, you might rely upon his word. To him might have been applied the witty eulogium passed by Johnson upon a certain nobleman: "If he had promised you an acorn, and the acorn season failed in England, he would have sent to Norway for one!" .

It was not, therefore, the mere Norman and chivalrous spirit of honour, which he had worshipped in youth as a part of the Beautiful and the Becoming, but which in youth had yielded to temptation, as a *sentiment* ever must yield to a passion, but it was the more hard, stubborn, and reflective *principle*, which was the later growth of deeper and nobler wisdom, that regulated the conduct of Maltravers in this crisis of his life. Certain it is, that he had never but once loved as he loved Evelyn; and yet that he never yielded so little to the passion.

"If engaged to another," thought he, "that engagement it is not for a third person to attempt to dissolve. I am the last to form a right judgment of the strength or weakness of the bonds which unite her to Vargrave, for my emotions would prejudice me despite myself. I may fancy that her betrothed is not worthy of her, — but that is for her to de-cide. While the bond lasts, who can be justified in tempting her to break it?"

Agreeably to these notions, which the world may, perhaps, consider overstrained, whenever Maltravers met Evelyn, he intrenched himself in a rigid and almost a chilling formality. How difficult this was with one so simple and ingenuous! Poor Evelyn! she thought she had offended him; she longed to ask him her offence, — perhaps, in her desire to rouse his genius into exertion, she had touched some secret sore, some latent wound of the memory? She recalled all their conver-sations again and again. Ah, why could they not be re-newed? Upon her fancy and her thoughts Maltravers had made an impression not to be obliterated. She wrote more frequently than ever to Lady Vargrave, and the name of Maltravers was found in every page of her correspondence.

One evening, at the house of a neighbour, Miss Cameron (with the Mertons) entered the room almost in the same instant as Maltravers. The party was small, and so few had yet arrived that it was impossible for Maltravers, without marked rudeness, to avoid his friends from the rectory; and

Mrs. Merton, placing herself next to Evelyn, graciously motioned to Maltravers to occupy the third vacant seat on the sofa, of which she filled the centre.

"We grudge all your improvements, Mr. Maltravers, since they cost us your society. But we know that our dull circle must seem tame to one who has seen so much. However, we expect to offer you an inducement soon in Lord Vargrave. What a lively, agreeable person he is!"

Maltravers raised his eyes to Evelyn, calmly and penetratingly, at the latter part of this speech. He observed that she turned pale, and sighed involuntarily.

"He had great spirits when I knew him," said he; "and he had then less cause to make him happy."

Mrs. Merton smiled, and turned rather pointedly towards Evelyn.

Maltravers continued, "I never met the late lord. He had none of the vivacity of his nephew, I believe."

"I have heard that he was very severe," said Mrs. Merton, lifting her glass towards a party that had just entered.

"Severe!" exclaimed Evelyn. "Ah, if you could have known him! the kindest, the most indulgent — no one ever loved me as he did." She paused, for she felt her lip quiver.

"I beg your pardon, my dear," said Mrs. Merton, coolly. Mrs. Merton had no idea of the pain inflicted by *treading upon a feeling*. Maltravers was touched, and Mrs. Merton went on. "No wonder he was kind to you, Evelyn, — a brute would be that; but he was generally considered a stern man."

"I never saw a stern look, I never heard a harsh word; nay, I do not remember that he ever even used the word ' command,' " said Evelyn, almost angrily.

Mrs. Merton was about to reply, when suddenly seeing a lady whose little girl had been ill of the measles, her motherly thoughts flowed into a new channel, and she fluttered away in that sympathy which unites all the heads of a growing family. Evelyn and Maltravers were left alone.

"You do not remember your father, I believe?" said Maltravers.

"No father but Lord Vargrave; while he lived, I never knew the loss of one."

"Does your mother resemble you?"

"Ah, I wish I could think so; it is the sweetest countenance!"

"Have you no picture of her?"

"None; she would never consent to sit."

"Your father was a Cameron; I have known some of that name."

"No relation of ours: my mother says we have none living."

"And have we no chance of seeing Lady Vargrave in B——shire?"

"She never leaves home; but I hope to return soon to Brook-Green."

Maltravers sighed, and the conversation took a new turn.

"I have to thank you for the books you so kindly sent; I ought to have returned them ere this," said Evelyn.

"I have no use for them. Poetry has lost its charm for me, — especially that species of poetry which unites with the method and symmetry something of the coldness of Art. How did you like Alfieri?"

"His language is a kind of Spartan French," answered Evelyn, in one of those happy expressions which every now and then showed the quickness of her natural talent.

"Yes," said Maltravers, smiling, "the criticism is acute. Poor Alfieri! in his wild life and his stormy passions he threw out all the redundance of his genius; and his poetry is but the representative of his thoughts, not his emotions. Happier the man of genius who lives upon his reason, and wastes feeling only on his verse!"

"You do not think that we *waste* feeling upon human beings?" said Evelyn, with a pretty laugh.

"Ask me that question when you have reached my years, and can look upon fields on which you have lavished your warmest hopes, your noblest aspirations, your tenderest affections, and see the soil all profitless and barren. 'Set not your heart on the things of earth,' saith the Preacher."

Evelyn was affected by the tone, the words, and the melancholy countenance of the speaker. "You, of all men, ought not to think thus," said she, with a sweet eagerness; "you who have done so much to awaken and to soften the heart in others; you — who —" she stopped short, and added, more gravely. "Ah, Mr. Maltravers, I cannot reason with you, but I can hope you will refute your own philosophy."

"Were your wish fulfilled," answered Maltravers, almost with sternness, and with an expression of great pain in his compressed lips, "I should have to thank you for much misery." He rose abruptly, and turned away.

"How have I offended him?" thought Evelyn, sorrowfully; "I never speak but to wound him. What *have* I done?"

She could have wished, in her simple kindness, to follow him, and make peace; but he was now in a coterie of strangers; and shortly afterwards he left the room, and she did not see him again for weeks.

———•———

CHAPTER VII.

NIHIL est aliud magnum quam multa minuta.[1] — VETUS. AUCTOR.

AN anxious event disturbed the smooth current of cheerful life at Merton Rectory. One morning when Evelyn came down, she missed little Sophy, who had contrived to establish for herself the undisputed privilege of a stool beside Miss Cameron at breakfast. Mrs. Merton appeared with a graver face than usual. Sophy was unwell, was feverish; the scarlet fever had been in the neighbourhood. Mrs. Merton was very uneasy.

"It is the more unlucky, Caroline," added the mother, turning to Miss Merton, "because to-morrow, you know, we were to have spent a few days at Knaresdean to see the races. If poor Sophy does not get better, I fear you and Miss Cameron must go without me. I can send to Mrs. Hare to be your chaperon; she would be delighted."

———

[1] "There is nothing so great as the collection of the minute."

"Poor Sophy!" said Caroline; "I am very sorry to hear she is unwell; but I think Taylor would take great care of her; you surely need not stay, unless she is much worse."

Mrs. Merton, who, tame as she seemed, was a fond and attentive mother, shook her head and said nothing; but Sophy was much worse before noon. The doctor was sent for, and pronounced it to be the scarlet fever.

It was now necessary to guard against the infection. Caroline had had the complaint, and she willingly shared in her mother's watch of love for two or three hours. Mrs. Merton gave up the party. Mrs. Hare (the wife of a rich squire in the neighbourhood) was written to, and that lady willingly agreed to take charge of Caroline and her friend.

Sophy had been left asleep. When Mrs. Merton returned to her bed, she found Evelyn quietly stationed there. This alarmed her, for Evelyn had never had the scarlet fever, and had been forbidden the sick-room. But poor little Sophy had waked and querulously asked for her dear Evy; and Evy, who had been hovering round the room, heard the inquiry from the garrulous nurse, and come in she would; and the child gazed at her so beseechingly, when Mrs. Merton entered, and said so piteously, "Don't take Evy away," that Evelyn stoutly declared that she was not the least afraid of infection, and stay she must. Nay, her share in the nursing would be the more necessary since Caroline was to go to Knaresdean the next day.

"But you go too, my dear Miss Cameron?"

"Indeed I could not. I don't care for races, I never wished to go, I would much sooner have stayed; and I am sure Sophy will not get well without me,— will you, dear?"

"Oh, yes, yes; if I'm to keep you from the nice races, I should be worse if I thought that."

"But I don't like the nice races, Sophy, as your sister Carry does; she must go, — they can't do without her; but nobody knows me, so I shall not be missed."

"I can't hear of such a thing," said Mrs. Merton, with tears in her eyes; and Evelyn said no more then. But the next morning Sophy was still worse, and the mother was too anxious and too sad to think more of ceremony and politeness, so Evelyn stayed.

A momentary pang shot across Evelyn's breast when all was settled; but she suppressed the sigh which accompanied the thought that she had lost the only opportunity she might have for weeks of seeing Maltravers. To that chance she had indeed looked forward with interest and timid pleasure. The chance was lost; but why should it vex her,— what was he to her?

Caroline's heart smote her, as she came into the room in her lilac bonnet and new dress; and little Sophy, turning on her eyes which, though languid, still expressed a child's pleasure at the sight of finery, exclaimed, "How nice and pretty you look, Carry! Do take Evy with you,— Evy looks pretty too!"

Caroline kissed the child in silence, and paused irresolute; glanced at her dress, and then at Evelyn, who smiled on her without a thought of envy; and she had half a mind to stay too, when her mother entered with a letter from Lord Vargrave. It was short: he should be at the Knaresdean races, hoped to meet them there, and accompany them home. This information re-decided Caroline, while it rewarded Evelyn. In a few minutes more, Mrs. Hare arrived; and Caroline, glad to escape, perhaps, her own compunction, hurried into the carriage, with a hasty "God bless you all! Don't fret — I'm sure she will be well to-morrow; and mind, Evelyn, you don't catch the fever!" Mr. Merton looked grave and sighed, as he handed her into the carriage; but when, seated there, she turned round and kissed her hand at him, she looked so handsome and distinguished, that a sentiment of paternal pride smoothed down his vexation at her want of feeling. He himself gave up the visit; but a little time after, when Sophy fell into a tranquil sleep, he thought he might venture to canter across the country to the race-ground, and return to dinner.

Days — nay, a whole week passed, the races were over, but Caroline had not returned. Meanwhile, Sophy's fever left

her; she could quit her bed, her room; she could come down-
stairs now, and the family was happy. It is astonishing how
the least ailment in those little things stops the wheels of
domestic life! Evelyn fortunately had not caught the fever:
she was pale, and somewhat reduced by fatigue and confinement; but she was amply repaid by the mother's swimming
look of quiet gratitude, the father's pressure of the hand,
Sophy's recovery, and her own good heart. They had heard
twice from Caroline, putting off her return: Lady Raby was
so kind, she could not get away till the party broke up; she
was so glad to hear such an account of Sophy.

Lord Vargrave had not yet arrived at the rectory to stay;
but he had twice ridden over, and remained there some hours.
He exerted himself to the utmost to please Evelyn; and she
— who, deceived by his manners, and influenced by the recollections of long and familiar acquaintance, was blinded to his
real character — reproached herself more bitterly than ever
for her repugnance to his suit and her ungrateful hesitation
to obey the wishes of her stepfather.

To the Mertons, Lumley spoke with good-natured praise of
Caroline; she was so much admired; she was the beauty at
Knaresdean. A certain young friend of his, Lord Doltimore, was evidently smitten. The parents thought much
over the ideas conjured up by that last sentence.

One morning, the garrulous Mrs. Hare, the gossip of the
neighbourhood, called at the rectory; she had returned, two
days before, from Knaresdean; and she, too, had her tale to
tell of Caroline's conquests.

"I assure you, my dear Mrs. Merton, if we had not all
known that his heart was pre-occupied, we should have
thought that Lord Vargrave was her warmest admirer. Most
charming man, Lord Vargrave! but as for Lord Doltimore, it
was quite a flirtation. Excuse *me;* no scandal, you know,
ha, ha! a fine young man, but stiff and reserved, — not the
fascination of Lord Vargrave."

"Does Lord Raby return to town, or is he now at Knaresdean for the autumn?"

"He goes on Friday, I believe: very few of the guests are

left now. Lady A. and Lord B., and Lord Vargrave and your daughter, and Mr. Legard and Lord Doltimore, and Mrs. and the Misses Cipher; all the rest went the same day I did."

"Indeed!" said Mrs. Merton, in some surprise.

"Ah, I read your thoughts: you wonder that Miss Caroline has not come back, — is not that it? But perhaps Lord Doltimore — ha, ha!— no scandal now — do excuse *me!*"

"Was Mr. Maltravers at Knaresdean?" asked Mrs. Merton, anxious to change the subject, and unprepared with any other question. Evelyn was cutting out a paper horse for Sophy, who — all her high spirits flown — was lying on the sofa, and wistfully following her fairy fingers. "Naughty Evy, you have cut off the horse's head!"

"Mr. Maltravers? No, I think not; no, he was not there. Lord Raby asked him pointedly to come, and was, I know, much disappointed that he did not. But *à propos* of Mr. Maltravers: I met him not a quarter of an hour ago, this morning, as I was coming to you. You know we have leave to come through his park, and as I was in the park at the time, I stopped the carriage to speak to him. I told him that I was coming here, and that you had had the scarlet fever in the house, which was the reason you had not gone to the races; and he turned quite pale, and seemed so alarmed. I said we were all afraid that Miss Cameron should catch it; and, excuse me — ah, ah! — no scandal, I hope — but — "

"Mr. Maltravers," said the butler, throwing open the door.

Maltravers entered with a quick and even a hurried step. He stopped short when he saw Evelyn; and his whole countenance was instantly lightened up by a joyous expression, which as suddenly died away.

"This is kind, indeed," said Mrs. Merton; "it is so long since we have seen you."

"I have been very much occupied," muttered Maltravers, almost inaudibly, and seated himself next Evelyn. "I only just heard — that — that you had sickness in the house. Miss Cameron, you look pale — you — you have not suffered, I hope?"

"No, I am quite well," said Evelyn, with a smile; and she felt happy that her friend was kind to her once more.

"It's only me, Mr. Ernest," said Sophy, "you have for-got me."

Maltravers hastened to vindicate himself from the charge, and Sophy and he were soon made excellent friends again.

Mrs. Hare, whom surprise at this sudden meeting had hitherto silenced, and who longed to shape into elegant peri-phrasis the common adage, "Talk of," etc., now once more opened her budget. She tattled on, first to one, then to the other, then to all, till she had tattled herself out of breath; and then the orthodox half-hour was expired, and the bell was rung, and the carriage ordered, and Mrs. Hare rose to depart.

"Do just come to the door, Mrs. Merton," said she, "and look at my pony-phaeton, it is so pretty; Lady Raby admires it so much; you ought to have just such another." As she spoke, she favoured Mrs. Merton with a significant glance, that said, as plainly as glance could say, "I have something to communicate." Mrs. Merton took the hint, and followed the good lady out of the room.

"Do you know, my dear Mrs. Merton," said Mrs. Hare, in a whisper, when they were safe in the billiard-room, that in-terposed between the apartment they had left and the hall; "do you know whether Lord Vargrave and Mr. Maltravers are very good friends?"

"No, indeed; why do you ask?"

"Oh, because when I was speaking to Lord Vargrave about him, he shook his head; and really I don't remember what his lordship said, but he seemed to speak as if there was a little soreness. And then he inquired very anxiously if Mr. Maltravers was much at the rectory, and looked discomposed when he found you were such near neighbours. You'll excuse *me*, you know — ha, ha! but we're such old friends! — and if Lord Vargrave is coming to stay here, it might be unpleasant to meet — you'll excuse *me*. I took the liberty to tell him he need not be jealous of Mr. Maltravers — ha, ha! — not a mar-rying man at all. But I did think Miss Caroline was the attraction — you'll excuse me — no scandal — ha, ha! But, after all, Lord Doltimore must be the man. Well, good morning, I thought I'd just give you this hint. Is not the phaeton pretty? Kind compliments to Mr. Merton."

And the lady drove off.

During this confabulation, Maltravers and Evelyn were left alone with Sophy. Maltravers had continued to lean over the child, and appeared listening to her prattle; while Evelyn, having risen to shake hands with Mrs. Hare, did not reseat herself, but went to the window, and busied herself with a flowerstand in the recess.

"Oh, very fine, Mr. Ernest," said Sophy (always pronouncing that proper name as if it ended in *th*), "you care very much for us to stay away so long, — don't he, Evy? I 've a great mind not to speak to you, sir, that I have!'

"That would be too heavy a punishment, Miss Sophy, — only, luckily, it would punish yourself; you could not live without talking — talk — talk — talk!"

"But I might never have talked more, Mr. Ernest, if Mamma and pretty Evy had not been so kind to me; " and the child shook her head mournfully, as if she had *pitié de soi-même*. But you won't stay away so long again, will you? Sophy play to-morrow; come to-morrow, and swing Sophy; no nice swinging since you 've been gone."

While Sophy spoke Evelyn turned half round, as if to hear Maltravers answer; he hesitated, and Evelyn spoke.

"You must not tease Mr. Maltravers so; Mr. Maltravers has too much to do to come to us."

Now this was a very pettish speech in Evelyn, and her cheek glowed while she spoke; but an arch, provoking smile was on her lips.

"It can be a privation only to me, Miss Cameron," said Maltravers, rising, and attempting in vain to resist the impulse that drew him towards the window. The reproach in her tone and words at once pained and delighted him; and then this scene, the suffering child, brought back to him his first interview with Evelyn herself. He forgot, for the moment, the lapse of time, the new ties she had formed, his own resolutions.

"That is a bad compliment to us," answered Evelyn, in-
genuously; "do you think we are so little worthy your society
as not to value it? But, perhaps" (she added, sinking her
voice) "perhaps you have been offended — perhaps I — I —
said — something that — that hurt you!"

"You!" repeated Maltravers, with emotion.

Sophy, who had been attentively listening, here put in,
"Shake hands and make it up with Evy — you've been quar-
relling, naughty Ernest!"

Evelyn laughed, and tossed back her sunny ringlets. "I
think Sophy is right," said she, with enchanting simplicity; "let us make it up," and she held out her hand to
Maltravers.

Maltravers pressed the fair hand to his lips. "Alas!" said
he, affected with various feelings which gave a tremor to his
deep voice, "your only fault is that your society makes me
discontented with my solitary home; and as solitude must be
my fate in life, I seek to inure myself to it betimes."

Here — whether opportunely or not, it is for the reader to
decide — Mrs. Merton returned to the room.

She apologized for her absence, talked of Mrs. Hare and
the little Master Hares, — fine boys, but noisy; and then she
asked Maltravers if he had seen Lord Vargrave since his lordship had been in the county. Maltravers replied, with coldness, that he had not had that honour. that Vargrave had
called on him in his way from the rectory the other day, but
that he was from home, and that he had not seen him for
some years.

"He is a person of most prepossessing manners," said Mrs.
Merton.

"Certainly, — most prepossessing."

"And very clever."

"He has great talents."

"He seems most amiable."

Maltravers bowed, and glanced towards Evelyn, whose
face, however, was turned from him.

The turn the conversation had taken was painful to the
visitor, and he rose to depart.

"Perhaps," said Mrs. Merton, "you will meet Lord Vargrave at dinner to-morrow; he will stay with us a few days,
— as long as he can be spared."

Maltravers meet Lord Vargrave! the happy Vargrave, the
betrothed to Evelyn! Maltravers witness the familiar rights,
the enchanting privileges, accorded to another! and that other
one whom he could not believe worthy of Evelyn! He writhed
at the picture the invitation conjured up.

"You are very kind, my dear Mrs. Merton, but I expect a
visitor at Burleigh, — an old and dear friend, Mr. Cleveland."

"Mr. Cleveland! — we shall be delighted to see him too.
We knew him many years ago, during your minority, when
he used to visit Burleigh two or three times a year."

"He is changed since then; he is often an invalid. I fear
I cannot answer for him; but he will call as soon as he
arrives, and apologize for himself."

Maltravers then hastily took his departure. He would not
trust himself to do more than bow distantly to Evelyn; she
looked at him reproachfully. So, then, it was really premeditated and resolved upon — his absence from the rectory;
and why? She was grieved, she was offended — but more
grieved than offended, — perhaps because esteem, interest,
admiration, are more tolerant and charitable than love.

———◆———

CHAPTER VIII.

Arethusa. 'T is well, my lord, your courting of ladies.

Claremont. Sure this lady has a good turn done her against her will.

PHILASTER.

IN the breakfast-room at Knaresdean, the same day, and
almost at the same hour, in which occurred the scene and
conversation at the rectory recorded in our last chapter, sat
Lord Vargrave and Caroline alone. The party had dispersed, as was usual, at noon. They heard at a distance

the sounds of the billiard-balls. Lord Doltimore was playing with Colonel Legard, one of the best players in Europe, but who, fortunately for Doltimore, had of late made it a rule never to play for money. Mrs. and the Misses Cipher, and most of the guests, were in the billiard-room looking on. Lady Raby was writing letters, and Lord Raby riding over his home farm. Caroline and Lumley had been for some time in close and earnest conversation. Miss Merton was seated in a large armchair, much moved, with her handkerchief to her eyes. Lord Vargrave, with his back to the chimney-piece, was bending down and speaking in a very low voice, while his quick eye glanced, ever and anon, from the lady's countenance to the windows, to the doors, to be prepared against any interruption.

"No, my dear friend," said he, "believe me that I am sincere. My feelings for you are, indeed, such as no words can paint."

"Then why — "

"Why wish you wedded to another; why wed another myself? Caroline, I have often before explained to you that we are in this the victims of an inevitable fate. It is absolutely necessary that I should wed Miss Cameron. I never deceived you from the first. I should have loved her, — my heart would have accompanied my hand, but for your too seductive beauty, your superior mind! — yes, Caroline, your mind attracted me more than your beauty. Your mind seemed kindred to my own, — inspired with the proper and wise ambition which regards the fools of the world as puppets, as counters, as chessmen. For myself, a very angel from heaven could not make me give up the great game of life, yield to my enemies, slip from the ladder, unravel the web I have woven! Share my heart, my friendship, my schemes! this is the true and dignified affection that should exist between minds like ours; all the rest is the prejudice of children."

"Vargrave, I am ambitious, worldly: I own it; but I could give up all for you!"

"You think so, for you do not know the sacrifice. You see me now apparently rich, in power, courted; and this fate you are willing to share; and this fate you *should* share, were it the real one I could bestow on you. But reverse the medal. Deprived of office, fortune gone, debts pressing, destitution notorious, the ridicule of embarrassments, the disrepute attached to poverty and defeated ambition, an exile in some foreign town on the poor pension to which alone I should be entitled, a mendicant on the public purse, and that, too, so eaten into by demands and debts, that there is not a grocer in the next market-town who would envy the income of the retired minister! Retire, fallen, despised, in the prime of life, in the zenith of my hopes! Suppose that I could bear this for myself, could I bear it for you? *You*, born to be the ornament of courts! And you — could you see me thus — life embittered, career lost — and feel, generous as you are, that your love had entailed on me, on us both, on our children, this miserable lot! Impossible, Caroline! we are too wise for such romance. It is not because we love too little, but because our love is worthy of each other, that we disdain to make love a curse! We cannot wrestle against the world, but we may shake hands with it, and worm the miser out of its treasures. My heart must be ever yours; my hand must be Miss Cameron's. Money I must have, — my whole career depends on it. It is literally with me the highwayman's choice, — money or life."

Vargrave paused, and took Caroline's hand.

"I cannot reason with you," said she; "you know the strange empire you have obtained over me, and, certainly, in spite of all that has passed (and Caroline turned pale) I could bear anything rather than that you should hereafter reproach me for selfish disregard of your interests, — your just ambition."

"My noble friend! I do not say that I shall not feel a deep and sharp pang at seeing you wed another; but I shall be consoled by the thought that I have assisted to procure for you a station worthier of your merits than that which I can offer. Lord Doltimore is rich, — you will teach him to employ his riches well; he is weak, — your intellect will govern him; he is in love, — your beauty will suffice to preserve his regard. Ah, we shall be dear friends to the last!"

More — but to the same effect — did this able and crafty villain continue to address to Caroline, whom he alternately soothed, irritated, flattered, and revolted.   Love him she certainly did, as far as love in her could extend; but perhaps his rank, his reputation, had served to win her affection; and, not knowing his embarrassments, she had encouraged a worldly hope that if Evelyn should reject his hand it might be offered to her.   Under this impression she had trifled, she had coquetted, she had played with the serpent till it had coiled around her; and she could not escape its fascination and its folds.   She was sincere, — she could have resigned much for Lord Vargrave; but his picture startled and appalled her.   For difficulties in a palace she might be prepared; perhaps even for some privations in a *cottage ornée*, — but certainly not for penury in a lodging-house!   She listened by degrees with more attention to Vargrave's description of the power and homage that would be hers if she could secure Lord Doltimore she listened, and was in part consoled.   But the thought of Evelyn again crossed her; and perhaps with natural jealousy was mingled some compunction at the fate to which Lord Vargrave thus coldly appeared to condemn one so lovely and so innocent.

"But do not, Vargrave," she said, "do not be too sanguine, Evelyn may reject you.   She does not see you with my eyes; it is only a sense of honour that, as yet, forbids her openly to refuse the fulfilment of an engagement from which I know that she shrinks; and if she does refuse, and you be free, — and I another's — "

"Even in that case," interrupted Vargrave, "I must turn to the Golden Idol; my rank and name must buy me an heiress, if not so endowed as Evelyn, wealthy enough, at least, to take from my wheels the drag-chain of disreputable debt. But Evelyn — I will not doubt of her! her heart is still unoccupied!"

"True; as yet her affections are not engaged."

"And this Maltravers — she is romantic, I fancy — did he seem captivated by her beauty or her fortune?"

"No, indeed, I think not; he has been very little with us

of late. He talked to her more as to a child, — there is a disparity of years."

"I am many years older than Maltravers," muttered Vargrave, moodily.

"You — but your *manner* is livelier, and, therefore,
younger!"

"Fair flatterer! Maltravers does not love me I fear his
report of my character — "

"I never heard him speak of you, Vargrave, and I will do
Evelyn the justice to say, that precisely as she does not love
she esteems and respects you."

"Esteems! respects! these are the feelings for a prudent
Hymen," said Vargrave, with a smile. "But, hark! I don't
hear the billiard-balls; they may find us here, — we had better
separate."

Lord Vargrave lounged into the billiard-room. The young
men had just finished playing, and were about to visit Thunderer, who had won the race, and was now the property of
Lord Doltimore.

Vargrave accompanied them to the stables; and after concealing his ignorance of horseflesh as well as he could, beneath
a profusion of compliments on fore-hand, hind-quarters, breeding, bone, substance, and famous points, he contrived to draw
Doltimore into the courtyard, while Colonel Legard remained
in converse high with the head groom.

"Doltimore, I leave Knaresdean to-morrow; you go to
London, I suppose? Will you take a little packet for me to
the Home Office?"

"Certainly, when I go; but I think of staying a few days
with Legard's uncle — the old admiral; he has a hunting-
box in the neighbourhood, and has asked us both over."

"Oh, I can detect the attraction; but certainly it is a fair one,
— the handsomest girl in the county; pity she has no money."

"I don't care for money," said Lord Doltimore, colouring,
and settling his chin in his neckcloth; "but you are mistaken; I have no thoughts that way. Miss Merton is a very
fine girl; but I doubt much if she cares for me. I would

never marry any woman who was not very much in love with me.'' And Lord Doltimore laughed rather foolishly.

"You are more modest than clear-sighted," said Vargrave, smiling; "but mark my words, — I predict that the beauty of next season will be a certain Caroline Lady Doltimore."

The conversation dropped.

"I think that will be settled well," said Vargrave to him-self, as he was dressing for dinner. "Caroline will manage Doltimore, and I shall manage one vote in the Lords and three in the Commons. I have already talked him into proper poli-tics, a trifle all this, to be sure. but I had nothing else to amuse me, and one must never lose an occasion. Besides, Doltimore is rich, and rich friends are always useful. I have Caroline, too, in my power, and she may be of service with respect to this Evelyn, who, instead of loving, I half hate: she has crossed my path, robbed me of wealth; and now, if she does refuse me — but no, I will not think of *that !* "

----◆----

CHAPTER IX.

OUT of our reach the gods have laid
  Of time to come the event ;
And laugh to see the fools afraid
  Of what the knaves invent. — SEDLEY, *from Lycophron.*

THE next day Caroline returned to the rectory in Lady Raby's carriage; and two hours after her arrival came Lord Vargrave. Mr. Merton had secured the principal persons in the neighbourhood to meet a guest so distinguished, and Lord Vargrave, bent on shining in the eyes of Evelyn, charmed all with his affability and wit. Evelyn, he thought, seemed pale and dispirited. He pertinaciously devoted himself to her all the evening. Her ripening understanding was better able than heretofore to appreciate his abilities; yet, inwardly, she drew comparisons between his conversation and that of

Maltravers, not to the advantage of the former. There was much that amused but nothing that interested in Lord Vargrave's fluent ease. When he attempted sentiment, the vein was hard and hollow; he was only at home on worldly topics. Caroline's spirits were, as usual in society, high, but her laugh seemed forced, and her eye absent.

The next day, after breakfast, Lord Vargrave walked alone to Burleigh. As he crossed the copse that bordered the park, a large Persian greyhound sprang towards him, barking loudly; and, lifting his eyes, he perceived the form of a man walking slowly along one of the paths that intersected the wood. He recognized Maltravers. They had not till then encountered since their meeting a few weeks before Florence's death; and a pang of conscience came across the schemer's cold heart. Years rolled away from the past; he recalled the young, generous, ardent man, whom, ere the character or career of either had been developed, he had called his friend. He remembered their wild adventures and gay follies, in climes where they had been all in all to each other; and the beardless boy, whose heart and purse were ever open to him, and to whose very errors of youth and inexperienced passion he, the elder and the wiser, had led and tempted, rose before him in contrast to the grave and melancholy air of the baffled and solitary man, who now slowly approached him, — the man whose proud career he had served to thwart, whose heart his schemes had prematurely soured, whose best years had been consumed in exile, — a sacrifice to the grave which a selfish and dishonourable villany had prepared! Cesarini, the inmate of a mad-house, Florence in her shroud, — such were the visions the sight of Maltravers conjured up. And to the soul which the unwonted and momentary remorse awakened, a boding voice whispered, "And thinkest thou that thy schemes shall prosper, and thy aspirations succeed?" For the first time in his life, perhaps, the unimaginative Vargrave felt the mystery of a presentiment of warning and of evil.

The two men met, and with an emotion which seemed that of honest and real feeling, Lumley silently held out his hand, and half turned away his head.

"Lord Vargrave!" said Maltravers, with an equal agitation, "it is long since we have encountered."

"Long, — very long," answered Lumley, striving hard to regain his self-possession; "years have changed us both; but I trust it has still left in you, as it has in me, the remembrance of our old friendship."

Maltravers was silent, and Lord Vargrave continued, —

"You do not answer me, Maltravers. Can political differences, opposite pursuits, or the mere lapse of time, have sufficed to create an irrevocable gulf between us? Why may we not be friends again?"

"Friends!" echoed Maltravers; "at our age that word is not so lightly spoken, that tie is not so unthinkingly formed, as when we were younger men."

"But may not the old tie be renewed?"

"Our ways in life are different; and were I to scan your motives and career with the scrutinizing eyes of friendship, it might only serve to separate us yet more. I am sick of the great juggle of ambition, and I have no sympathy left for those who creep into the pint-bottle, or swallow the naked sword."

"If you despise the exhibition, why, then, let us laugh at it together, for I am as cynical as yourself."

"Ah," said Maltravers with a smile, half mournful, half bitter, "but are you not one of the Impostors?"

"Who ought better to judge of the Eleusiniana than one of the Initiated? But seriously, why on earth should political differences part private friendship? Thank Heaven! such has never been my maxim."

"If the differences be the result of honest convictions on either side, — no; but are you honest, Lumley?"

"Faith, I have got into the habit of thinking so; and habit's a second nature. However, I dare say we shall yet meet in the arena, so I must not betray my weak points. How is it, Maltravers, that they see so little of you at the rectory? You are a great favourite there. Have you any living that Charley Merton could hold with his own? You shake your head. And what think you of Miss Cameron, my intended?"

"You speak lightly. Perhaps you — "

"Feel deeply, — you were going to say. I do. In the hand of my ward, Evelyn Cameron, I trust to obtain at once the domestic happiness to which I have as yet been a stranger, and the wealth necessary to my career."

Lord Vargrave continued, after a short pause, "Though my avocations have separated us so much, I have no doubt of her steady affection, — and, I may add, of her sense of honour. She alone can repair to me what else had been injustice in my uncle." He then proceeded to repeat the moral obligations which the late lord had imposed on Evelyn, — obligations that he greatly magnified. Maltravers listened attentively, and said little.

"And these obligations being fairly considered," added Vargrave, with a smile, "I think, even had I rivals, that they could scarcely in honour attempt to break an existing engagement."

"Not while the engagement lasted," answered Maltravers; "not till one or the other had declined to fulfil it, and therefore left both free: but I trust it will be an alliance in which all but affection will be forgotten; that of honour alone would be but a harsh tie."

"Assuredly," said Vargrave; and, as if satisfied with what had passed, he turned the conversation, — praised Burleigh, spoke of county matters, resumed his habitual gayety, though it was somewhat subdued, and promising to call again soon, he at last took his leave.

Maltravers pursued his solitary rambles, and his commune with himself was stern and searching.

"And so," thought he, "this prize is reserved for Vargrave! Why should I deem him unworthy of the treasure? May he not be worthier, at all events, than this soured temper and erring heart? And he is assured too of her affection! Why this jealous pang? Why can the fountain within never be exhausted? Why, through so many scenes and sufferings, have I still retained the vain madness of my youth, — the haunting susceptibility to love? This is my latest folly."

BOOK IV.

Γυναικὸς οὐδὲ χρῆμ' ἀνὴρ ληίζεται
'Εσθλῆς ἄμεινον. — SIMONIDES.

"A virtuous woman is man's greatest pride."

CHAPTER I.

ABROAD uneasy, nor content at home.
.   .   .   .   .
And Wisdom shows the ill without the cure.
HAMMOND : Elegies.

Two or three days after the interview between Lord Vargrave and Maltravers, the solitude of Burleigh was relieved
by the arrival of Mr. Cleveland. The good old gentleman,
when free from attacks of the gout, which were now somewhat more frequent than formerly, was the same cheerful and
intelligent person as ever. Amiable, urbane, accomplished,
and benevolent, there was just enough worldliness in Cleveland's nature to make his views sensible as far as they went,
but to bound their scope. Everything he said was so rational;
and yet, to an imaginative person, his conversation was unsatisfactory, and his philosophy somewhat chilling.

"I cannot say how pleased and surprised I am at your care
of the fine old place," said he to Maltravers, as, leaning on
his cane and his ci-devant pupil's arm, he loitered observantly
through the grounds; "I see everywhere the presence of the
Master."

And certainly the praise was deserved. The gardens were
now in order, the dilapidated fences were repaired, the weeds
no longer encumbered the walks. Nature was just assisted

and relieved by Art, without being oppressed by too officious a service from her handmaid. In the house itself some suitable and appropriate repairs and decorations — with such articles of furniture as combined modern comfort with the ancient and picturesque shapes of a former fashion — had redeemed the mansion from all appearance of dreariness and neglect; while still was left to its quaint halls and chambers the character which belonged to their architecture and associations. It was surprising how much a little exercise of simple taste had effected.

"I am glad you approve what I have done," said Maltravers. "I know not how it was, but the desolation of the place when I returned to it reproached me. We contract friendship with places as with human beings, and fancy they have claims upon us; at least, that is my weakness."

"And an amiable one it is, too, — I share it. As for me, I look upon Temple Grove as a fond husband upon a fair wife. I am always anxious to adorn it, and as proud of its beauty as if it could understand and thank me for my partial admiration. When I leave you I intend going to Paris, for the purpose of attending a sale of the pictures and effects of M. de ——. These auctions are to me what a jeweller's shop is to a lover; but then, Ernest, I am an old bachelor."

"And I, too, am an Arcadian," said Maltravers, with a smile.

"Ah, but you are not too old for repentance. Burleigh now requires nothing but a mistress."

"Perhaps it may soon receive that addition. I am yet undecided whether I shall sell it."

"Sell it! sell Burleigh! — the last memorial of your mother's ancestry! the classic retreat of the graceful Digbys! Sell Burleigh!"

"I had almost resolved to do so when I came hither; then I forswore the intention: now again I sometimes sorrowfully return to the idea."

"And in Heaven's name, why?"

"My old restlessness returns. Busy myself as I will here, I find the range of action monotonous and confined. I began

too soon to draw around me the large circumference of literature and action; and the small provincial sphere seems to me
a sad going back in life. Perhaps I should not feel this, were
my home less lonely; but as it is — no, the wanderer's ban is
on me, and I again turn towards the lands of excitement and
adventure."

"I understand this, Ernest; but why is your home so solitary? You are still at the age in which wise and congenial
unions are the most frequently formed; your temper is domestic; your easy fortune and sobered ambition allow you to
choose without reference to worldly considerations. Look
round the world, and mix with the world again, and give
Burleigh the mistress it requires."

Maltravers shook his head, and sighed.

"I do not say," continued Cleveland, wrapped in the glowing interest of the theme, "that you should marry a mere girl,
but an amiable woman, who, like yourself, has seen something
of life, and knows how to reckon on its cares, and to be contented with its enjoyments."

"You have said enough," said Maltravers, impatiently;
"an experienced woman of the world, whose freshness of
hope and heart is gone! What a picture! No, to me there
is something inexpressibly beautiful in innocence and youth.
But you say justly, — my years are not those that would make
a union with youth desirable or well suited."

"I do *not* say that," said Cleveland, taking a pinch of snuff;
"but you should avoid great disparity of age, — not for the
sake of that disparity itself, but because with it is involved
discord of temper, pursuits. A *very* young woman, new to
the world, will not be contented with home alone; you are at
once too gentle to curb her wishes, and a little too stern and
reserved — pardon me for saying so — to be quite congenial to
very early and sanguine youth."

"It is true," said Maltravers, with a tone of voice that
showed he was struck with the remark; "but how have we
fallen on this subject? let us change it. I have no idea of
marriage, — the gloomy reminiscence of Florence Lascelles
chains me to the past."

"Poor Florence, she might once have suited you; but now you are older, and would require a calmer and more malleable temper."

"Peace, I implore you!"

The conversation was changed; and at noon Mr. Merton, who had heard of Cleveland's arrival, called at Burleigh to renew an old acquaintance. He invited them to pass the evening at the rectory; and Cleveland, hearing that whist was a regular amusement, accepted the invitation for his host and himself. But when the evening came, Maltravers pleaded indisposition, and Cleveland was obliged to go alone.

When the old gentleman returned about midnight, he found Maltravers awaiting him in the library; and Cleveland, having won fourteen points, was in a very gay, conversable humour.

"You perverse hermit!" said he, "talk of solitude, indeed, with so pleasant a family a hundred yards distant! You deserve to be solitary, — I have no patience with you. They complain bitterly of your desertion, and say you were, at first, the *enfant de la maison.*"

"So you like the Mertons? The clergyman is sensible, but commonplace."

"A very agreeable man, despite your cynical definition, and plays a very fair rubber. But Vargrave is a first-rate player."

"Vargrave is there still?"

"Yes, he breakfasts with us to-morrow, — he invited himself."

"Humph!"

"He played one rubber; the rest of the evening he devoted himself to the prettiest girl I ever saw, — Miss Cameron. What a sweet face! so modest, yet so intelligent! I talked with her a good deal during the deals in which I cut out. I almost lost my heart to her."

"So Lord Vargrave devoted himself to Miss Cameron?"

"To be sure, — you know they are to be married soon. Merton told me so. She is very rich. He is the luckiest fellow imaginable, that Vargrave! But he is much too old for her: she seems to think so too. I can't explain why I think it; but by her pretty reserved manner I saw that she tried to keep the gay minister at a distance: but it would not do. Now, if you were ten years younger, or Miss Cameron ten years older, you might have had some chance of cutting out your old friend."

"So you think I also am too old for a lover?"

"For a lover of a girl of seventeen, certainly. You seem touchy on the score of age, Ernest."

"Not I;" and Maltravers laughed.

"No? There was a young gentleman present, who, I think, Vargrave might really find a dangerous rival, — a Colonel Legard, — one of the handsomest men I ever saw in my life; just the style to turn a romantic young lady's head; a mixture of the wild and the thoroughbred; black curls, superb eyes, and the softest manners in the world. But, to be sure, he has lived all his life in the best society. Not so his friend, Lord Doltimore, who has a little too much of the green-room lounge and French *café* manner for my taste."

"Doltimore, Legard, names new to me; I never met them at the rectory."

"Possibly they are staying at Admiral Legard's, in the neighbourhood. Miss Merton made their acquaintance at Knaresdean. A good old lady — the most perfect Mrs. Grundy one would wish to meet with — who owns the monosyllabic appellation of Hare (and who, being my partner, trumped my king!) assured me that Lord Doltimore was desperately in love with Caroline Merton. By the way, now, there is a young lady of a proper age for you, — handsome and clever, too."

"You talk of antidotes to matrimony; and so Miss Cameron — "

"Oh, no more of Miss Cameron now, or I shall sit up all night; she has half turned my head. I can't help pitying her, — married to one so careless and worldly as Lord Vargrave, thrown so young into the whirl of London. Poor thing! she had better have fallen in love with Legard, — which I dare say she will do, after all. Well, good-night!"

CHAPTER II.

PASSION, as frequently is seen,
Subsiding, settles into spleen ;
Hence, as the plague of happy life,
I ran away from party strife. — MATTHEW GREEN.

Here nymphs from hollow oaks relate
The dark decrees and will of fate. — *Ibid.*

ACCORDING to his engagement, Vargrave breakfasted the next morning at Burleigh.   Maltravers at first struggled to return his familiar cordiality with equal graciousness. Condemning himself for former and unfounded suspicions, he wrestled against feelings which he could not or would not analyze, but which made Lumley an unwelcome visitor, and connected him with painful associations, whether of the present or the past.   But there were points on which the penetration of Maltravers served to justify his prepossessions.

The conversation, chiefly sustained by Cleveland and Vargrave, fell on public questions; and as one was opposed to the other, Vargrave's exposition of views and motives had in them so much of the self-seeking of the professional placeman, that they might well have offended any man tinged by the lofty mania of political Quixotism.   It was with a strange mixture of feelings that Maltravers listened : at one moment he proudly congratulated himself on having quitted a career where such opinions seemed so well to prosper : at another, his better and juster sentiments awoke the long-dormant combative faculty, and he almost longed for the turbulent but sublime arena, in which truths are vindicated and mankind advanced.

The interview did not serve for that renewal of intimacy which Vargrave appeared to seek, and Maltravers rejoiced when the placeman took his departure.

Lumley, who was about to pay a morning visit to Lord Doltimore, had borrowed Mr. Merton's stanhope, as being better adapted than any statelier vehicle to get rapidly through the cross-roads which led to Admiral Legard's house; and as he settled himself in the seat, with his servant by his side, he said laughingly, "I almost fancy myself naughty master Lumley again in this young-man-kind of two-wheeled cockle-boat: not dignified, but rapid, eh?"

And Lumley's face, as he spoke, had in it so much of frank gayety, and his manner was so simple, that Maltravers could with difficulty fancy him the same man who, five minutes before, had been uttering sentiments that might have become the oldest-hearted intriguer whom the hot-bed of ambition ever reared.

As soon as Lumley was gone, Maltravers left Cleveland alone to write letters (Cleveland was an exemplary and voluminous correspondent) and strolled with his dogs into the village. The effect which the presence of Maltravers produced among his peasantry was one that seldom failed to refresh and soothe his more bitter and disturbed thoughts. They had gradually (for the poor are quick-sighted) become sensible of his *justice*, — a finer quality than many that seem more amiable. They felt that his real object was to make them better and happier; and they had learned to see that the means he adopted generally advanced the end. Besides, if sometimes stern, he was never capricious or unreasonable; and then, too, he would listen patiently and advise kindly. They were a little in awe of him, but the awe only served to make them more industrious and orderly, — to stimulate the idle man, to reclaim the drunkard. He was one of the favourers of the small-allotment system, — not, indeed, as a panacea, but as one excellent stimulant to exertion and independence; and his chosen rewards for good conduct were in such comforts as served to awaken amongst those hitherto passive, dogged, and hopeless a desire to better and improve their condition. Somehow or other, without direct alms, the goodwife found that the little savings in the cracked teapot or the old stocking had greatly increased since the squire's

return, while her husband came home from his moderate cups
at the alehouse more sober and in better temper. Having
already saved something was a great reason why he should
save more. The new school, too, was so much better conducted than the old one; the children actually liked going
there; and now and then there were little village feasts
connected with the schoolroom; play and work were joint
associations.

And Maltravers looked into his cottages, and looked at the
allotment-ground; and it was pleasant to him to say to himself, "I am not altogether without use in life." But as he
pursued his lonely walk, and the glow of self-approval died
away with the scenes that called it forth, the cloud again settled on his brow; and again he felt that in solitude the passions feed upon the heart. As he thus walked along the green
lane, and the insect life of summer rustled audibly among the
shadowy hedges and along the thick grass that sprang up on
either side, he came suddenly upon a little group that arrested
all his attention.

It was a woman, clad in rags, bleeding, and seemingly
insensible, supported by the overseer of the parish and a
labourer.

"What is the matter?" asked Maltravers.

"A poor woman has been knocked down and run over by a
gentleman in a gig, your honour," replied the overseer. "He
stopped, half an hour ago, at my house to tell me that she
was lying on the road; and he has given me two sovereigns
for her, your honour. But, poor cretur! she was too heavy
for me to carry her, and I was forced to leave her and call
Tom to help me."

"The gentleman might have stayed to see what were the
consequences of his own act," muttered Maltravers, as he
examined the wound in the temple, whence the blood flowed
copiously.

"He said he was in a great hurry, your honour," said the
village official, overhearing Maltravers. "I think it was one
of the grand folks up at the parsonage; for I know it was Mr.
Merton's bay horse, — he is a hot 'un!"

"Does the poor woman live in the neighbourhood? Do you know her?" asked Maltravers, turning from the contemplation of this new instance of Vargrave's selfishness of character.

"No; the old body seems quite a stranger here, — a tramper, or beggar, I think, sir. But it won't be a settlement if we take her in; and we can carry her to the Chequers, up the village, your honour."

"What is the nearest house, — your own?"

"Yes; but we be so busy now!"

"She shall not go to your house, and be neglected; and as for the public-house, it is too noisy: we must move her to the Hall."

"Your honour!" ejaculated the overseer, opening his eyes.

"It is not very far; she is severely hurt. Get a hurdle, lay a mattress on it. Make haste, both of you; I will wait here till you return."

The poor woman was carefully placed on the grass by the road-side, and Maltravers supported her head, while the men hastened to obey his orders.

CHAPTER III.

Alse from that forked hill, the boasted seat
Of studious Peace and mild Philosophy,
Indignant murmurs mote be heard to threat. — West.

Mr. Cleveland wanted to enrich one of his letters with a quotation from Ariosto, which he but imperfectly remembered. He had seen the book he wished to refer to in the little study the day before; and he quitted the library to search for it.

As he was tumbling over some ·volumes that lay piled on the writing-table, he felt a student's curiosity to discover what now constituted his host's favourite reading. He was surprised to observe that the greater portion of the works that, by the doubled leaf and the pencilled reference, seemed most frequently consulted, were not of a literary nature, — they were chiefly scientific; and astronomy seemed the chosen science. He then remembered that he had heard Maltravers speaking to a builder, employed on the recent repairs, on the subject of an observatory. "This is very strange," thought Cleveland; "he gives up literature, the rewards of which are in his reach, and turns to science, at an age too late to discipline his mind to its austere training."

Alas! Cleveland did not understand that there are times in life when imaginative minds seek to numb and to blunt imagination. Still less did he feel that, when we perversely refuse to apply our active faculties to the catholic interests of the world, they turn morbidly into channels of research the least akin to their real genius. By the collision of minds alone does each mind discover what is its proper product: left to ourselves, our talents become but intellectual eccentricities.

Some scattered papers, in the handwriting of Maltravers. fell from one of the volumes. Of these, a few were but algebraical calculations, or short scientific suggestions, the value of which Mr. Cleveland's studies did not enable him to ascertain; but in others they were wild snatches of mournful and impassioned verse, which showed that the old vein of poetry still flowed, though no longer to the daylight. These verses Cleveland thought himself justified in glancing over; they seemed to portray a state of mind which deeply interested, and greatly saddened him. They expressed, indeed, a firm determination to bear up against both the memory and the fear of ill; but mysterious and hinted allusions here and there served to denote some recent and yet existent struggle, revealed by the heart only to the genius. In these partial and imperfect self-communings and confessions, there was the evidence of the pining affections, the wasted life, the desolate hearth of the lonely man. Yet so calm was Maltravers himself, even to his early friend, that Cleveland knew not what to think of the reality of the feelings painted. Had that fervid and romantic spirit been again awakened by a living

object? If so, where was the object found? The dates affixed
to the verses were most recent. But whom had Maltravers
seen? Cleveland's thoughts turned to Caroline Merton, to
Evelyn; but when he had spoken of both, nothing in the
countenance, the manner, of Maltravers had betrayed emotion. And once the heart of Maltravers had so readily betrayed itself! Cleveland knew not how pride, years, and
suffering school the features, and repress the outward signs
of what pass within. While thus engaged, the door of the
study opened abruptly, and the servant announced Mr.
Merton.

"A thousand pardons," said the courteous rector. "I fear
we disturb you; but Admiral Legard and Lord Doltimore,
who called on us this morning, were so anxious to see Burleigh, I thought I might take the liberty. We have come
over quite in a large party, — taken the place by storm. Mr.
Maltravers is out, I hear; but you will let us see the house.
My allies are already in the hall, examining the armour."

Cleveland, ever sociable and urbane, answered suitably, and
went with Mr. Merton into the hall, where Caroline, her little
sisters, Evelyn, Lord Doltimore, Admiral Legard, and his
nephew were assembled.

"Very proud to be my host's representative and your
guide," said Cleveland. "Your visit, Lord Doltimore, is
indeed an agreeable surprise. Lord Vargrave left us an
hour or so since to call on you at Admiral Legard's we
buy our pleasure with his disappointment."

"It is very unfortunate," said the admiral, a bluff, harsh-
looking old gentleman; "but we were not aware, till we saw
Mr. Merton, of the honour Lord Vargrave has done us. I
can't think how we missed him on the road."

"My dear uncle," said Colonel Legard, in a peculiarly sweet
and agreeable tone of voice, "you forget we came three miles
round by the high road; and Mr. Merton says that Lord Vargrave took the short cut by Langley End. My uncle, Mr.
Cleveland, never feels in safety upon land, unless the road is
as wide as the British Channel, and the horses go before the
wind at the rapid pace of two knots and a half an hour!"

"I just wish I had you at sea, Mr. Jackanapes," said the admiral, looking grimly at his handsome nephew, while he shook his cane at him.

The nephew smiled; and, falling back, conversed with Evelyn.

The party were now shown over the house; and Lord Dolti-more was loud in its praises. It was like a château he had once hired in Normandy, — it had a French character; those old chairs were in excellent taste, — quite the style of Francis the First.

"I know no man I respect more than Mr. Maltravers," quoth the admiral. "Since he has been amongst us this time, he has been a pattern to us country gentlemen. He would make an excellent colleague for Sir John. We really must get him to stand against that young puppy who is member of the House of Commons only because his father is a peer, and never votes more than twice a session."

Mr. Merton looked grave.

"I wish to Heaven you could persuade him to stay amongst you," said Cleveland. "He has half taken it into his head to part with Burleigh!"

"Part with Burleigh!" exclaimed Evelyn, turning abruptly from the handsome colonel, in whose conversation she had hitherto seemed absorbed.

"My very ejaculation when I heard him say so, my dear young lady."

"I wish he would," said Lord Doltimore hastily, and glan-cing towards Caroline. "I should much like to buy it. What do you think would be the purchase-money?"

"Don't talk so cold-bloodedly," said the admiral, letting the point of his cane fall with great emphasis on the floor. "I can't bear to see old families deserting their old places, — quite wicked. You buy Burleigh! have not you got a country-seat of your own, my lord? Go and live there, and take Mr. Maltravers for your model, — you could not have a better."

Lord Doltimore sneered, coloured, settled his neckcloth, and turning round to Colonel Legard, whispered, "Legard, your good uncle is a bore."

Legard looked a little offended, and made no reply.

"But," said Caroline, coming to the relief of her admirer, "if Mr. Maltravers will sell the place, surely he could not have a better successor."

"He sha' n't sell the place, ma'am, and that 's poz!" cried the admiral. "The whole county shall sign a round-robin to tell him it 's a shame; and if any one dares to buy it we 'll send him to Coventry."

Miss Merton laughed, but looked round the old wainscot walls with unusual interest; she thought it would be a fine thing to be Lady of Burleigh!

"And what is that picture so carefully covered up?" said the admiral, as they now stood in the library.

"The late Mrs. Maltravers, Ernest's mother," replied Cleveland, slowly. "He dislikes it to be shown — to strangers: the other is a Digby."

Evelyn looked towards the veiled portrait, and thought of her first interview with Maltravers; but the soft voice of Colonel Legard murmured in her ear, and her revery was broken.

Cleveland eyed the colonel, and muttered to himself, "Vargrave should keep a sharp look-out."

They had now finished their round of the show-apartments — which indeed had little but their antiquity and old portraits to recommend them — and were in a lobby at the back of the house, communicating with a courtyard, two sides of which were occupied with the stables. The sight of the stables reminded Caroline of the Arab horses; and at the word "horses" Lord Doltimore seized Legard's arm and carried him off to inspect the animals. Caroline, her father, and the admiral followed. Mr. Cleveland happened not to have on his walking-shoes; and the flagstones in the courtyard looked damp; and Mr. Cleveland, like most old bachelors, was prudently afraid of cold; so he excused himself, and stayed behind. He was talking to Evelyn about the Digbys, and full of anecdotes about Sir Kenelm at the moment the rest departed so abruptly; and Evelyn was interested, so she insisted on keeping him company.

The old gentleman was flattered; he thought it excellent breeding in Miss Cameron. The children ran out to renew acquaintance with the peacock, who, perched on an old stirrup-stone, was sunning his gay plumage in the noon-day.

"It is astonishing," said Cleveland, "how certain family features are transmitted from generation to generation! Maltravers has still the forehead and eyebrows of the Digbys, — that peculiar, brooding, thoughtful forehead, which you observed in the picture of Sir Kenelm. Once, too, he had much the same dreaming character of mind, but he has lost that, in some measure at least. He has fine qualities, Miss Cameron, — I have known him since he was born. I trust his career is not yet closed; could he but form ties that would bind him to England, I should indulge in higher expectations than I did even when the wild boy turned half the heads in Göttingen.

"But we were talking of family portraits: there is one in the entrance-hall, which perhaps you have not observed; it is half obliterated by damp and time, yet it is of a remarkable personage, connected with Maltravers by ancestral intermarriages, — Lord Falkland, the Falkland of Clarendon; a man weak in character, but made most interesting by history, — utterly unfitted for the severe ordeal of those stormy times; sighing for peace when his whole soul should have been in war; and repentant alike whether with the Parliament or the king, but still a personage of elegant and endearing associations; a student-soldier, with a high heart and a gallant spirit. Come and look at his features, — homely and worn, but with a characteristic air of refinement and melancholy thought."

Thus running on, the agreeable old gentleman drew Evelyn into the outer hall. Upon arriving there, through a small passage, which opened upon the hall, they were surprised to find the old housekeeper and another female servant standing by a rude kind of couch on which lay the form of the poor woman described in the last chapter. Maltravers and two other men were also there; and Maltravers himself was giving orders to his servants, while he leaned over the sufferer, who was now conscious both of pain and the service rendered to her. As Evelyn stopped abruptly, and in surprise, opposite and almost at the foot of the homely litter, the woman raised herself up on one arm, and gazed at her with a wild stare; then muttering some incoherent words which appeared to betoken delirium, she sank back, and was again insensible.

CHAPTER IV.

HENCE oft to win some stubborn maid,
    Still does the wanton god assume
The martial air, the gay cockade,
    The sword, the shoulder-knot, and plume.
                    MARRIOTT.

THE hall was cleared, the sufferer had been removed, and Maltravers was left alone with Cleveland and Evelyn.

He simply and shortly narrated the adventure of the morning; but he did not mention that Vargrave had been the cause of the injury his new guest had sustained. Now this event had served to make a mutual and kindred impression on Evelyn and Maltravers. The humanity of the latter, natural and commonplace as it was, was an endearing recollection to Evelyn, precisely as it showed that his cold theory of disdain towards the mass did not affect his actual conduct towards individuals. On the other hand, Maltravers had perhaps been yet more impressed with the prompt and ingenuous sympathy which Evelyn had testified towards the sufferer: it had so evidently been her first gracious and womanly impulse to hasten to the side of this humble stranger. In that impulse, Maltravers himself had been almost forgotten; and as the poor woman lay pale and lifeless, and the young Evelyn bent over her in beautiful compassion, Maltravers thought she had never seemed so lovely, so irresistible, — in fact, pity in woman is a great beautifier.

As Maltravers finished his short tale, Evelyn's eyes were fixed upon him with such frank and yet such soft approval,

that the look went straight to his heart. He quickly turned
away, and abruptly changed the conversation.

"But how long have you been here, Miss Cameron, — and
your companions?"

"We are again intruders; but this time it was not my
fault."

"No," said Cleveland, "for a wonder it was male, and not
lady-like curiosity that trespassed on Bluebeard's chamber.
But, however, to soften your resentment, know that Miss
Cameron has brought you a purchaser for Burleigh. Now,
then, we can test the sincerity of your wish to part with it.
I assure you, meanwhile, that Miss Cameron was as much
shocked at the idea as I was. Were you not?"

"But you surely have no intention of selling Burleigh?"
said Evelyn, anxiously.

"I fear I do not know my own mind."

"Well," said Cleveland, "here comes your tempter. Lord
Doltimore, let me introduce Mr. Maltravers."

Lord Doltimore bowed.

"Been admiring your horses, Mr. Maltravers. I never saw
anything so perfect as the black one; may I ask where you
bought him?"

"It was a present to me," answered Maltravers.

"A present?"

"Yes, from one who would not have sold that horse for a
king's ransom, — an old Arab chief, with whom I formed
a kind of friendship in the desert. A wound disabled him
from riding, and he bestowed the horse on me, with as much
solemn tenderness for the gift as if he had given me his
daughter in marriage."

"I think of travelling in the East," said Lord Doltimore,
with much gravity: "I suppose nothing will induce you to
sell the black horse?"

"Lord Doltimore!" said Maltravers, in a tone of lofty
surprise.

"I do not care for the price," continued the young nobleman, a little disconcerted.

"No; I never sell any horse that has once learned to know

me. I would as soon think of selling a friend. In the desert, one's horse is one's friend. I am almost an Arab myself in these matters."

"But talking of sale and barter reminds me of Burleigh," said Cleveland, maliciously. "Lord Doltimore is a universal buyer. He covets all your goods: he will take the house, if he can't have the stables."

"I only mean," said Lord Doltimore, rather peevishly, "that if you wish to part with Burleigh, I should like to have the option of purchase."

"I will remember it, if I determine to sell the place," answered Maltravers, smiling gravely; "at present I am undecided."

He turned away towards Evelyn as he spoke, and almost started to observe that she was joined by a stranger, whose approach he had not before noticed, — and that stranger a man of such remarkable personal advantages, that, had Maltravers been in Vargrave's position, he might reasonably have experienced a pang of jealous apprehension. Slightly above the common height; slender, yet strongly formed; set off by every advantage of dress, of air, of the nameless tone and pervading refinement that sometimes, though not always, springs from early and habitual intercourse with the most polished female society, — Colonel Legard, at the age of eight and twenty, had acquired a reputation for beauty almost as popular and as well known as that which men usually acquire by mental qualifications. Yet there was nothing effeminate in his countenance, the symmetrical features of which were made masculine and expressive by the rich olive of the complexion, and the close jetty curls of the Antinous-like hair.

They seemed, as they there stood — Evelyn and Legard — so well suited to each other in personal advantages, their different styles so happily contrasted; and Legard, at the moment, was regarding her with such respectful admiration, and whispering compliment to her in so subdued a tone, that the dullest observer might have ventured a prophecy by no means agreeable to the hopes of Lumley Lord Vargrave.

But a feeling or fear of this nature was not that which

occurred to Maltravers, or dictated his startled exclamation of surprise.

Legard looked up as he heard the exclamation, and saw Maltravers, whose back had hitherto been turned towards him. He, too, was evidently surprised, and seemingly confused; the colour mounted to his cheek, and then left it pale.

"Colonel Legard," said Cleveland, "a thousand apologies for my neglect: I really did not observe you enter, — you came round by the front door, I suppose. Let me make you acquainted with Mr. Maltravers."

Legard bowed low.

"We have met before," said he, in embarrassed accents: "at Venice, I think!"

Maltravers inclined his head rather stiffly at first, but then, as if moved by a second impulse, held out his hand cordially.

"Oh, Mr. Ernest, here you are!" cried Sophy, bounding into the hall, followed by Mr. Merton, the old admiral, Caroline, and Cecilia.

The interruption seemed welcome and opportune. The admiral, with blunt cordiality, expressed his pleasure at being made known to Mr. Maltravers.

The conversation grew general; refreshments were proffered and declined; the visit drew to its close.

It so happened that as the guests departed, Evelyn, from whose side the constant colonel had insensibly melted away, lingered last, — save, indeed, the admiral, who was discussing with Cleveland a new specific for the gout. And as Maltravers stood on the steps, Evelyn turned to him with all her beautiful *naïveté* of mingled timidity and kindness, and said, —

"And are we really never to see you again; never to hear again your tales of Egypt and Arabia, never to talk over Tasso and Dante? No books, no talk, no disputes, no quarrels? What have we done? I thought we had made it up, — and yet you are still unforgiving. Give me a good scold, and be friends!"

"Friends! you have no friend more anxious, more devoted than I am. Young, rich, fascinating as you are, you will

carve no impression on human hearts deeper than that you
have graven here! ''

Carried away by the charm of her childlike familiarity and
enchanting sweetness, Maltravers had said more than he
intended; yet his eyes, his emotion, said more than his
words.

Evelyn coloured deeply, and her whole manner changed.
However, she turned away, and saying, with a forced gayety,
" Well, then, you will not desert us; we shall see you once
more? " hurried down the steps to join her companions.

CHAPTER V.

SEE how the skilful lover spreads his toils. — STILLINGFLEET.

THE party had not long returned to the rectory, and the
admiral's carriage was ordered, when Lord Vargrave made
his appearance. He descanted with gay good-humour on his
long drive, the bad roads, and his disappointment at the *con-
tretemps* that awaited him; then, drawing aside Colonel
Legard, who seemed unusually silent and abstracted, he
said to him, —

" My dear colonel, my visit this morning was rather to you
than to Doltimore. I confess that I should like to see your
abilities enlisted on the side of the Government; and knowing that the post of Storekeeper to the Ordnance will be
vacant in a day or two by the promotion of Mr. ——, I wrote
to secure the refusal. To-day's post brings me the answer.
I offer the place to you; and I trust, before long, to procure
you also a seat in parliament. But you must start for London immediately."

A week ago, and Legard's utmost ambition would have been
amply gratified by this post; he now hesitated.

" My dear lord," said he, " I cannot say how grateful I
feel for your kindness; but — but — "

"Enough; no thanks, my dear Legard. Can you go to town to-morrow?"

"Indeed," said Legard, "I fear not; I must consult my uncle."

"I can answer for him; I sounded him before I wrote. Reflect! You are not rich, my dear Legard; it is an excellent opening: a seat in parliament, too! Why, what *can* be your reason for hesitation?"

There was something meaning and inquisitive in the tone of voice in which this question was put that brought the colour to the colonel's cheek. He knew not well what to reply; and he began, too, to think that he ought not to refuse the appointment. Nay, would his uncle, on whom he was dependent, consent to such a refusal? Lord Vargrave saw the irresolution, and proceeded. He spent ten minutes in combating every scruple, every objection: he placed all the advantages of the post, real or imaginary, in every conceivable point of view before the colonel's eyes; he sought to flatter, to wheedle, to coax, to weary him into accepting it; and he at length partially succeeded. The colonel petitioned for three days' consideration, which Vargrave reluctantly acceded to; and Legard then stepped into his uncle's carriage, with the air rather of a martyr than a maiden placeman.

"Aha!" said Vargrave, chuckling to himself as he took a turn in the grounds, "I have got rid of that handsome knave; and now I shall have Evelyn all to myself!"

CHAPTER VI.

I am forfeited to eternal disgrace if you do not commiserate.

Go to, then, raise, recover. — Ben Jonson : *Poetaster.*

The next morning Admiral Legard and his nephew were conversing in the little cabin consecrated by the name of the admiral's "own room."

"Yes," said the veteran, "it would be moonshine and madness not to accept Vargrave's offer; though one can see through such a millstone as that with half an eye. His lordship is jealous of such a fine, handsome young fellow as you are, — and very justly. But as long as he is under the same roof with Miss Cameron, you will have no opportunity to pay your court; when he goes, you can always manage to be in her neighbourhood; and then, you know — puppy that you are — her business will be very soon settled." And the admiral eyed the handsome colonel with grim fondness.

Legard sighed.

"Have you any commands at ——?" said he; "I am just going to canter over there before Doltimore is up."

"Sad lazy dog, your friend."   .

"I shall be back by twelve."

"What are you going to —— for?"

"Brookes, the farrier, has a little spaniel, — King Charles's breed. Miss Cameron is fond of dogs. I can send it to her, with my compliments, — it will be a sort of leave-taking."

"Sly rogue; ha, ha, ha! d—d sly; ha, ha!" and the admiral punched the slender waist of his nephew, and laughed till the tears ran down his cheeks.

"Good-by, sir."

"Stop, George; I forgot to ask you a question; you never told me you knew Mr. Maltravers. Why don't you cultivate his acquaintance?"

"We met at Venice accidentally. I did not know his name then; he left just as I arrived. As you say, I ought to cultivate his acquaintance."

"Fine character!"

"Very!" said Legard, with energy, as he abruptly quitted the room.

George Legard was an orphan. His father — the admiral's elder brother — had been a spendthrift man of fashion, with a tolerably large unentailed estate. He married a duke's daughter without a sixpence. Estates are troublesome, — Mr. Legard's was sold. On the purchase-money the happy pair lived for some years in great comfort, when Mr. Legard

died of a brain fever; and his disconsolate widow found herself alone in the world with a beautiful little curly-headed
boy, and an annuity of one thousand a year, for which her
settlement had been exchanged. All the rest of the fortune
was gone, — a discovery not made till Mr. Legard's death.
Lady Louisa did not long survive the loss of her husband and
her station in society; her income of course died with herself.
Her only child was brought up in the house of his grand-
father, the duke, till he was of age to hold the office of
king's page; thence, as is customary, he was promoted to a
commission in the Guards. To the munificent emoluments
of his pay, the ducal family liberally added an allowance of
two hundred a year; upon which income Cornet Legard contrived to get very handsomely in debt. The extraordinary
beauty of his person, his connections, and his manners obtained him all the celebrity that fashion can bestow; but
poverty is a bad thing. Luckily, at this time, his uncle the
admiral returned from sea, to settle for the rest of his life in
England.

Hitherto, the admiral had taken no notice of George. He
himself had married a merchant's daughter with a fair portion; and had been blessed with two children, who monopo-
lized all his affection. But there seemed some mortality in
the Legard family; in one year after returning to England
and settling in B——shire, the admiral found himself wife-
less and childless. He then turned to his orphan nephew;
and soon became fonder of him than he had ever been of his
own children. The admiral, though in easy circumstances,
was not wealthy; nevertheless, he advanced the money requisite for George's rise in the army, and doubled the allowance
bestowed by the duke. His grace heard of this generosity,
and discovered that he himself had a very large family growing up; that the marquess was going to be married, and
required an increase of income; that he had already behaved
most handsomely to his nephew; and the result of this discovery was that the duke withdrew the two hundred a year.
Legard, however, who looked on his uncle as an exhaustless
mine, went on breaking hearts and making debts — till one

morning he woke in the Bench. The admiral was hastily
summoned to London. He arrived; paid off the duns — a
kindness which seriously embarrassed him — swore, scolded,
and cried; and finally insisted that Legard should give up
that d—d coxcomb regiment, in which he was now captain,
retire on half-pay, and learn economy and a change of habits
on the Continent.

The admiral, a rough but good-natured man on the whole,
had two or three little peculiarities. In the first place, he
piqued himself on a sort of John Bull independence; was a
bit of a Radical (a strange anomaly in an admiral) — which
was owing, perhaps, to two or three young lords having been
put over his head in the earlier part of his career; and he
made it a point with his nephew (of whose affection he was
jealous) to break with those fine grand connections, who
plunged him into a sea of extravagance, and then never
threw him a rope to save him from drowning.

In the second place, without being stingy, the admiral had
a good deal of economy in his disposition. He was not a man
to allow his nephew to ruin him. He had an extraordinarily
old-fashioned horror of gambling, — a polite habit of George's;
and he declared positively that his nephew must, while a bachelor, learn to live upon seven hundred a year. Thirdly, the
admiral could be a very stern, stubborn, passionate old brute;
and when he coolly told George, "Harkye, you young puppy,
if you get into debt again — if you exceed the very handsome
allowance I make you — I shall just cut you off with a shilling," George was fully aware that his uncle was one who
would rigidly keep his word.

However, it was something to be out of debt, and one of
the handsomest men of his age; and George Legard, whose
rank in the Guards made him a colonel in the line, left England tolerably contented with the state of affairs.

Despite the foibles of his youth, George Legard had many
high and generous qualities. Society had done its best to
spoil a fine and candid disposition, with abilities far above
mediocrity; but society had only partially succeeded. Still,
unhappily, dissipation had grown a habit with him; all his

talents were of a nature that brought a ready return.   At his age, it was but natural that the praise of *salons* should retain all its sweetness.

In addition to those qualities which please the softer sex, Legard was a good whist player, superb at billiards, famous as a shot, unrivalled as a horseman, — in fact, an accomplished man, "who did everything so devilish well!" These accomplishments did not stand him in much stead in Italy; and, though with reluctance and remorse, he took again to gambling, — he really *had* nothing else to do.

In Venice there was, one year, established a society somewhat on the principle of the *salon* at Paris.   Some rich Venetians belonged to it; but it was chiefly for the convenience of foreigners, — French, English, and Austrians.   Here there was select gaming in one room, while another apartment served the purposes of a club.   Many who never played belonged to this society; but still they were not the *habitués*.

Legard played: he won at first, then he lost, then he won again; it was a pleasant excitement.   One night, after winning largely at *roulette*, he sat down to play *écarté* with a Frenchman of high rank.   Legard played well at this, as at all scientific games; he thought he should make a fortune out of the Frenchman.   The game excited much interest; the crowd gathered round the table; bets ran high; the vanity of Legard, as well as his interest, was implicated in the conflict.   It was soon evident that the Frenchman played as well as the Englishman.   The stakes, at first tolerably high, were doubled.   Legard betted freely.   Cards went against him; he lost much, lost all that he had, lost more than he had, lost several hundreds, which he promised to pay the next morning.   The table was broken up, the spectators separated.   Amongst the latter had been one Englishman, introduced into the club for the first time that night.   He had neither played nor betted, but had observed the game with a quiet and watchful interest.   This Englishman lodged at the same hotel as Legard.   He was at Venice only for a day; the promised sight of a file of English newspapers had drawn him to the club; the general excitement around had attracted him to the table; and once there, the spectacle of human emotions exercised its customary charm.

On ascending the stairs that conducted to his apartment, the Englishman heard a deep groan in a room the door of which was ajar. He paused, the sound was repeated; he gently pushed open the door and saw Legard seated by a table, while a glass on the opposite wall reflected his working and convulsed countenance, with his hands trembling visibly, as they took a brace of pistols from the case.

The Englishman recognized the loser at the club; and at once divined the act that his madness or his despair dictated. Legard twice took up one of the pistols, and twice laid it down irresolute; the third time he rose with a start, raised the weapon to his head, and the next moment it was wrenched from his grasp.

"Sit down, sir!" said the stranger, in a loud and commanding voice.

Legard, astonished and abashed, sank once more into his seat, and stared sullenly and half-unconsciously at his countryman.

"You have lost your money," said the Englishman, after calmly replacing the pistols in their case, which he locked, putting the key into his pocket; "and that is misfortune enough for one night. If you had won, and ruined your opponent, you would be excessively happy, and go to bed, thinking Good Luck (which is the representative of Providence) watched over you. For my part, I think you ought to be very thankful that you are not the winner."

"Sir," said Legard, recovering from his surprise, and beginning to feel resentment, "I do not understand this intrusion in my apartments. You have saved me, it is true, from death, — but life is a worse curse."

"Young man, no! moments in life are agony, but life itself is a blessing. Life is a mystery that defies all calculation. You can never say, ' To-day is wretched, therefore to-morrow must be the same!' And for the loss of a little gold you, in the full vigour of youth, with all the future before you, will dare to rush into the chances of eternity! You, who have never, perhaps, thought what eternity is! Yet," added the stranger, in a soft and melancholy voice, "you are young and beautiful, — perhaps the pride and hope of others! Have you no tie, no affection, no kindred; are you lord of yourself?"

Legard was moved by the tone of the stranger, as well as by the words.

"It is not the loss of money," said he, gloomily, — "it is the loss of honour. To-morrow I must go forth a shunned and despised man, — I, a gentleman and a soldier! They may insult me — and I have no reply!"

The Englishman seemed to muse, for his brow lowered, and he made no answer. Legard threw himself back, overcome with his own excitement, and wept like a child. The stranger, who imagined himself above the indulgence of emotion (vain man!), woke from his revery at this burst of passion. He gazed at first (I grieve to write) with a curl of the haughty lip that had in it contempt; but it passed quickly away; and the hard man remembered that he too had been young and weak, and his own errors greater perhaps than those of the one he had ventured to despise. He walked to and fro the room, still without speaking. At last he approached the gamester, and took his hand.

"What is your debt?" he asked gently.

"What matters it? — more than I can pay."

"If life is a trust, so is wealth: *you* have the first in charge for others, *I* may have the last. What is the debt?"

Legard started; it was a strong struggle between shame and hope. "If I could borrow it, I could repay it hereafter, — I know I could; I would not think of it otherwise."

"Very well, so be it, — I will lend you the money on one condition. Solemnly promise me, on your faith as a soldier and a gentleman, that you will not, for ten years to come — even if you grow rich, and can ruin others — touch card or dice-box. Promise me that you will shun all gaming for gain, under whatever disguise, whatever appellation. I will take your word as my bond."

Legard, overjoyed, and scarcely trusting his senses, gave the promise.

"Sleep then, to-night, in hope and assurance of the morrow," said the Englishman: "let this event be an omen to
you, that while there is a future there is no despair. One
word more, — I do not want your thanks! it is easy to be gen·
erous at the expense of justice. Perhaps I have been so now.
This sum, which is to save your life — a life you so little
value — might have blessed fifty human beings, — better men
than either the giver or receiver. What is given to error may
perhaps be a wrong to virtue. When you would ask others
to support a career of blind and selfish extravagance, pause
and think over the breadless lips this wasted gold would have
fed! the joyless hearts it would have comforted! You talk
of repaying me: if the occasion offer, do so; if not — if we
never meet again, and you have it in your power, pay it for
me to the Poor! And now, farewell."

"Stay, — give me the name of my preserver! Mine is — "

"Hush! what matter names? This is a sacrifice we have
both made to honour. You will sooner recover your self-
esteem (and without self-esteem there is neither faith nor
honour), when you think that your family, your connections,
are spared all association with your own error; that I may
hear them spoken of, that I may mix with them without
fancying that they owe me gratitude."

"Your own name then?" said Legard, deeply penetrated
with the delicate generosity of his benefactor.

"Tush!" muttered the stranger impatiently as he closed
the door.

The next morning when he awoke Legard saw upon the
table a small packet; it contained a sum that exceeded the
debt named.

On the envelope was written, "Remember the bond."

The stranger had already quitted Venice. He had not
travelled through the Italian cities under his own name, for
he had just returned from the solitudes of the East, and was
not yet hardened to the publicity of the gossip which in towns
haunted by his countrymen attended a well-known name; that
given to Legard by the innkeeper, mutilated by Italian pro·
nunciation, the young man had never heard before, and soon

forgot. He paid his debts, and he scrupulously kept his word. The adventure of that night went far, indeed, to reform and ennoble the mind and habits of George Legard. Time passed, and he never met his benefactor, till in the halls of Burleigh he recognized the stranger in Maltravers.

CHAPTER VII.

Why value, then, that strength of mind they boast,
As often varying, and as often lost ?
　　　　HAWKINS BROWNE (*translated by* SOAME JENYNS).

MALTRAVERS was lying at length, with his dogs around him, under a beech-tree that threw its arms over one of the calm still pieces of water that relieved the groves of Burleigh, when Colonel Legard spied him from the bridle-road which led through the park to the house. The colonel dismounted, threw the rein over his arm; and at the sound of the hoofs Maltravers turned, saw the visitor, and rose. He held out his hand to Legard, and immediately began talking of indifferent matters.

Legard was embarrassed; but his nature was not one to profit by the silence of a benefactor. "Mr. Maltravers," said he, with graceful emotion, "though you have not yet allowed me an opportunity to allude to it, do not think I am ungrateful for the service you rendered me."

Maltravers looked grave, but made no reply. Legard resumed, with a heightened colour, —

"I cannot say how I regret that it is not yet in my power to discharge my debt; but — "

"When it is, you will do so. Pray think no more of it. Are you going to the rectory?"

"No, not this morning; in fact, I leave B——shire to-morrow. Pleasant family, the Mertons."

"And Miss Cameron — "

"Is certainly beautiful, — and very rich. How could she ever think of marrying Lord Vargrave, so much older, — she who could have so many admirers? "

"Not, surely, while betrothed to another? "

This was a refinement which Legard, though an honourable man as men go, did not quite understand. "Oh," said he, "that was by some eccentric old relation, — her father-in-law, I think. Do you think she is bound by such an engagement? "

Maltravers made no reply, but amused himself by throwing a stick into the water, and sending one of his dogs after it.

Legard looked on, and his affectionate disposition yearned to make advances which something distant in the manner of Maltravers chilled and repelled.

When Legard was gone, Maltravers followed him with his eyes. "And this is the man whom Cleveland thinks Evelyn could love! I could forgive her marrying Vargrave. Independently of the conscientious feeling that may belong to the engagement, Vargrave has wit, talent, intellect; and this man has nothing but the skin of the panther. Was I wrong to save him? No. Every human life, I suppose, has its uses. But Evelyn — I could despise her if her heart was the fool of the eye! "

These comments were most unjust to Legard; but they were just of that kind of injustice which the man of talent often commits against the man of external advantages, and which the latter still more often retaliates on the man of talent. As Maltravers thus soliloquized, he was accosted by Mr. Cleveland.

"Come, Ernest, you must not cut these unfortunate Mertons any longer. If you continue to do so, do you know what Mrs. Hare and the world will say? "

"No — what? "

"That you have been refused by Miss Merton. "

"That *would* be a calumny! " said Ernest, smiling.

"Or that you are hopelessly in love with Miss Cameron. "

Maltravers started; his proud heart swelled; he pulled his hat over his brows, and said, after a short pause, —

"Well, Mrs. Hare and the world must not have it all their own way; and so, whenever you go to the rectory, take me with you."

———◆———

CHAPTER VIII.

THE more he strove
To advance his suit, the farther from her love.
DRYDEN: *Theodore and Honoria.*

THE line of conduct which Vargrave now adopted with regard to Evelyn was craftily conceived and carefully pursued. He did not hazard a single syllable which might draw on him a rejection of his claims; but at the same time no lover could be more constant, more devoted, in attentions. In the presence of others, there was an air of familiar intimacy that seemed to arrogate a right, which to her he scrupulously shunned to assert. Nothing could be more respectful, nay, more timid, than his language, or more calmly confident than his manner. Not having much vanity, nor any very acute self-conceit, he did not delude himself into the idea of winning Evelyn's affections; he rather sought to entangle her judgment, to weave around her web upon web, — not the less dangerous for being invisible. He took the compact as a matter of course, as something not to be broken by any possible chance; her hand was to be his as a right: it was her heart that he so anxiously sought to gain. But this distinction was so delicately drawn, and insisted upon so little in any tangible form, that, whatever Evelyn's wishes for an understanding, a much more experienced woman would have been at a loss to ripen one.

Evelyn longed to confide in Caroline, to consult her; but Caroline, though still kind, had grown distant. "I wish," said Evelyn, one night as she sat in Caroline's dressing-room, — "I wish that I knew what tone to take with Lord Vargrave.

I feel more and more convinced that a union between us is impossible; and yet, precisely because he does not press it, am I unable to tell him so. I wish you could undertake that task; you seem such friends with him."

"I!" said Caroline, changing countenance.

"Yes, you! Nay, do not blush, or I shall think you envy me. Could you not save us both from the pain that otherwise must come sooner or later?"

"Lord Vargrave would not thank me for such an act of friendship. Besides, Evelyn, consider, — it is scarcely possible to break off this engagement *now*."

"*Now!* and why now?" said Evelyn, astonished.

"The world believes it so implicitly. Observe, whoever sits next you rises if Lord Vargrave approaches; the neighbourhood talk of nothing else but your marriage; and your fate, Evelyn, is not pitied."

"I will leave this place! I will go back to the cottage! I cannot bear this!" said Evelyn, passionately wringing her hands.

"You do not love another, I am sure: not young Mr. Hare, with his green coat and straw-coloured whiskers; or Sir Henry Foxglove, with his how-d'ye-do like a view-halloo; perhaps, indeed, Colonel Legard, — he is handsome. What! do you blush at his name? No; you say 'not Legard:' who else is there?"

"You are cruel; you trifle with me!" said Evelyn, in tearful reproach; and she rose to go to her own room.

"My dear girl!" said Caroline, touched by her evident pain; "learn from me — if I may say so — that marriages are *not* made in heaven! Yours will be as fortunate as earth can bestow. A love-match is usually the least happy of all. Our foolish sex demand so much in love; and love, after all, is but one blessing among many. Wealth and rank remain when love is but a heap of ashes. For my part, I have chosen my destiny and my husband."

"Your husband!"

"Yes, you see him in Lord Doltimore. I dare say we shall be as happy as any amorous Corydon and Phyllis." But there was irony in Caroline's voice as she spoke; and she sighed heavily. Evelyn did not believe her serious; and the friends parted for the night.

"Mine is a strange fate!" said Caroline to herself; "I am asked by the man whom I love, and who professes to love me, to bestow myself on another, and to plead for him to a younger and fairer bride. Well, I will obey him in the first; the last is a bitterer task, and I cannot perform it earnestly. Yet Var-grave has a strange power over me; and when I look round the world, I see that he is right. In these most commonplace artifices, there is yet a wild majesty that charms and fasci-nates me. It is something to rule the world: and his and mine are natures formed to do so."

CHAPTER IX.

A SMOKE raised with the fume of sighs.
Romeo and Juliet.

IT is certain that Evelyn experienced for Maltravers senti-ments which, if not love, might easily be mistaken for it. But whether it were that master-passion, or merely its fanci-ful resemblance, — love in early youth and innocent natures, if of sudden growth, is long before it makes itself apparent. Evelyn had been prepared to feel an interest in her solitary neighbour. His mind, as developed in his works, had half formed her own. Her childish adventure with the stranger had never been forgotten. Her present knowledge of Mal-travers was an union of dangerous and often opposite associa-tions, — the Ideal and the Real.

Love, in its first dim and imperfect shape, is but imagina-tion concentrated on one object. It is a genius of the heart, resembling that of the intellect; it appeals to, it stirs up, it evokes, the sentiments and sympathies that lie most latent in our nature. Its sigh is the spirit that moves over the ocean, and arouses the Anadyomene into life. Therefore is it that

MIND produces affections deeper than those of external form; therefore it is that women are worshippers of glory, which is the palpable and visible representative of a genius whose operations they cannot always comprehend. Genius has so much in common with love, the imagination that animates one is so much the property of the other, that there is not a surer sign of the existence of genius than the love that it creates and bequeaths. It penetrates deeper than the reason, it binds a nobler captive than the fancy. As the sun upon the dial, it gives to the human heart both its shadow and its light. Nations are its worshippers and wooers; and Posterity learns from its oracles to dream, to aspire, to adore!

Had Maltravers declared the passion that consumed him, it is probable that it would soon have kindled a return. But his frequent absence, his sustained distance of manner, had served to repress the feelings that in a young and virgin heart rarely flow with much force until they are invited and aroused. *Le besoin d'aimer* in girls, is, perhaps, in itself powerful; but is fed by another want, *le besoin d'être aimé!* *If,* therefore. Evelyn at present felt love for Maltravers, the love had certainly not passed into the core of life: the tree had not so far struck its roots but what it might have borne transplanting. There was in her enough of the pride of sex to have recoiled from the thought of giving love to one who had not asked the treasure. Capable of attachment, more trustful and therefore, if less vehement, more beautiful and durable than that which had animated the brief tragedy of Florence Lascelles, she could not have been the unknown correspondent, or revealed the soul, because the features wore a mask.

It must also be allowed that, in some respects, Evelyn was too young and inexperienced thoroughly to appreciate all that was most truly lovable and attractive in Maltravers. At four and twenty she would, perhaps, have felt no fear mingled with her respect for him; but seventeen and six and thirty is a wide interval! She never felt that there was that difference in years until she had met Legard, and then at once she comprehended it. With Legard she had moved on equal terms; he was not too wise, too high for her every-day thoughts. He

less excited her imagination, less attracted her reverence.
But, somehow or other, that voice which proclaimed her
power, those eyes which never turned from hers, went nearer
to her heart. As Evelyn had once said to Caroline, "It was
a great enigma!" — her own feelings were a mystery to her;
and she reclined by the "Golden Waterfalls" without tracing
her likeness in the glass of the pool below.

Maltravers appeared again at the rectory. He joined their
parties by day, and his evenings were spent with them as of
old. In this I know not precisely what were his motives —
perhaps he did not know them himself. It might be that his
pride was roused; it might be that he could not endure the
notion that Lord Vargrave should guess his secret by an absence almost otherwise unaccountable, — he could not patiently
bear to give Vargrave that triumph; it might be that, in the
sternness of his self-esteem, he imagined he had already conquered all save affectionate interest in Evelyn's fate, and
trusted too vainly to his own strength; and it might be, also,
that he could not resist the temptation of seeing if Evelyn
were contented with her lot, and if Vargrave were worthy of
the blessing that awaited him. Whether one of these or all
united made him resolve to brave his danger, or whether, after
all, he yielded to a weakness, or consented to what — invited
by Evelyn herself — was almost a social necessity, the reader
and not the narrator shall decide.

Legard was gone; but Doltimore remained in the neighbourhood, having hired a hunting-box not far from Sir John
Merton's manors, over which he easily obtained permission
to sport. When he did not dine elsewhere, there was always
a place for him at the parson's hospitable board, — and that
place was generally next to Caroline. Mr. and Mrs. Merton
had given up all hope of Mr. Maltravers for their eldest
daughter; and, very strangely, this conviction came upon
their minds on the first day they made the acquaintance of
the young lord.

"My dear," said the rector, as he was winding up his
watch, preparatory to entering the connubial couch, — "my
dear, I don't think Mr. Maltravers is a marrying man."

"I was just going to make the same remark," said Mrs. Merton, drawing the clothes over her. "Lord Doltimore is a very fine young man, his estates unencumbered. I like him vastly, my love. He is evidently smitten with Caroline; so Lord Vargrave and Mrs. Hare said."

"Sensible, shrewd woman, Mrs. Hare. By the by, we'll send her a pineapple. Caroline was made to be a woman of rank!"

"Quite; so much self-possession!"

"And if Mr. Maltravers would sell or let Burleigh — "

"It would be so pleasant!"

"Had you not better give Caroline a hint?"

"My love, she is so sensible, let her go her own way."

"You are right, my dear Betsy; I shall always say that no one has more common-sense than you; you have brought up your children admirably!"

"Dear Charles!"

"It is coldish to-night, love," said the rector; and he put out the candle.

From that time, it was not the fault of Mr. and Mrs. Merton if Lord Doltimore did not find their house the pleasantest in the county.

One evening the rectory party were assembled together in the cheerful drawing-room. Cleveland, Mr. Merton, Sir John, and Lord Vargrave, reluctantly compelled to make up the fourth, were at the whist-table; Evelyn, Caroline, and Lord Doltimore were seated round the fire, and Mrs. Merton was working a footstool. The fire burned clear, the curtains were down, the children in bed: it was a family picture of elegant comfort.

Mr. Maltravers was announced.

"I am glad you are come at last," said Caroline, holding out her fair hand. "Mr. Cleveland could not answer for you. We are all disputing as to which mode of life is the happiest."

"And your opinion?" asked Maltravers, seating himself in the vacant chair, — it chanced to be next to Evelyn's.

"My opinion is decidedly in favour of London. A metro-

politan life, with its perpetual and graceful excitements, —
the best music, the best companions, the best things in short.
Provincial life is so dull, its pleasures so tiresome; to talk
over the last year's news, and wear out one's last year's
dresses, cultivate a conservatory, and play Pope Joan with a
young party, — dreadful! "

"I agree with Miss Merton," said Lord Doltimore, solemnly;
"not but what I like the country for three or four months in
the year, with good shooting and hunting, and a large house
properly filled, independent of one's own neighbourhood: but
if I am condemned to choose one place to live in, give me
Paris."

"Ah, Paris; I never was in Paris. I should so like to
travel!" said Caroline.

"But the inns abroad are so very bad," said Lord Doltimore;
"how people can rave about Italy, I can't think. I never suffered so much in my life as I did in Calabria; and at Venice
I was bit to death by mosquitoes. Nothing like Paris, I
assure you: don't you think so, Mr. Maltravers?"

"Perhaps I shall be able to answer you better in a short
time. I think of accompanying Mr. Cleveland to Paris!"

"Indeed!" said Caroline. "Well, I envy you; but is it a
sudden resolution?"

"Not very."

"Do you stay long?" asked Lord Doltimore.

"My stay is uncertain."

"And you won't let Burleigh in the meanwhile?"

"*Let* Burleigh? No; if it once pass from my hands it will
be forever!"

Maltravers spoke gravely, and the subject was changed.
Lord Doltimore challenged Caroline to chess.

They sat down, and Lord Doltimore arranged the pieces.

"Sensible man, Mr. Maltravers," said the young lord; "but
I don't hit it off with him: Vargrave is more agreeable.
Don't you think so?"

"Y—e—s."

"Lord Vargrave is very kind to me, — I never remember
any one being more so; got Legard that appointment solely

because it would please *me*, — very friendly fellow! I mean to put myself under his wing next session!"

"You could not do better, I'm sure," said Caroline; "he is so much looked up to; I dare say he will be prime minister one of these days."

"I take the bishop: — do you think so really? — you are rather a politician?"

"Oh, no; not much of that. But my father and my uncle are stanch politicians; gentlemen know so much more than ladies. We should always go by their opinions. I think I will take the queen's pawn — your politics are the same as Lord Vargrave's?"

"Yes, I fancy so: at least I shall leave my proxy with him. Glad you don't like politics, — great bore."

"Why, so young, so connected as you are — " Caroline stopped short, and made a wrong move.

"I wish we were going to Paris together, *we* should enjoy it so;" and Lord Doltimore's knight checked the tower and queen.

Caroline coughed, and stretched her hand quickly to move.

"Pardon me, you will lose the game if you do so!" and Doltimore placed his hand on hers, their eyes met, Caroline turned away, and Lord Doltimore settled his right collar.

"And is it true? are you really going to leave us?" said Evelyn, and she felt very sad. But still the sadness might not be that of love, — she had felt sad after Legard had gone.

"I do not think I shall long stay away," said Maltravers, trying to speak indifferently. "Burleigh has become more dear to me than it was in earlier youth; perhaps because I have made myself duties there: and in other places I am but an isolated and useless unit in the great mass."

"You! everywhere, you must have occupations and re-sources, — everywhere, you must find yourself not alone. But you will not go yet?"

"Not yet: no. [Evelyn's spirits rose.] Have you read the book I sent you?" (It was one of De Staël's.)

"Yes; but it disappoints me."

"And why? It is eloquent."

"But is it true? Is there so much melancholy in life? Are the affections so full of bitterness? For me, I am so happy when with those I love! When I am with my mother, the air seems more fragrant, the skies more blue: it is surely not affection, but the absence of it, that makes us melancholy."

"Perhaps so; but if we had never known affection, we might not miss it: and the brilliant Frenchwoman speaks from memory, while you speak from hope, — memory, which is the ghost of joy: yet surely, even in the indulgence of affection, there is at times a certain melancholy, a certain fear. Have you never felt it, even with — with your mother?"

"Ah, yes! when she suffered, or when I have thought she loved me less than I desired."

"That must have been an idle and vain thought. Your mother! does she resemble you?"

"I wish I could think so. Oh, if you knew her! I have longed so often that you were acquainted with each other! It was she who taught me to sing your songs."

"My dear Mrs. Hare, we may as well throw up our cards," said the keen clear voice of Lord Vargrave: "you have played most admirably, and I know that your last card will be the ace of trumps; still the luck is against us."

"No, no; pray play it out, my lord."

"Quite useless, ma'am," said Sir John, showing two hon-ours. "We have only the trick to make."

"Quite useless," echoed Lumley, tossing down his sover-eigns, and rising with a careless yawn.

"How d'ye do, Maltravers?"

Maltravers rose; and Vargrave turned to Evelyn, and addressed her in a whisper. The proud Maltravers walked away, and suppressed a sigh; a moment more, and he saw Lord Vargrave occupying the chair he had left vacant. He laid his hand on Cleveland's shoulder.

"The carriage is waiting, — are you ready?"

CHAPTER X.

Obscuris vera involvens.[1] — Virgil.

A day or two after the date of the last chapter, Evelyn and
Caroline were riding out with Lord Vargrave and Mr. Merton,
and on returning home they passed through the village of
Burleigh.

"Maltravers, I suppose, has an eye to the county one of
these days," said Lord Vargrave, who honestly fancied that a
man's eyes were always directed towards something for his
own interest or advancement; "otherwise he could not surely
take all this trouble about workhouses and paupers. Who
could ever have imagined my romantic friend would sink into
a country squire?"

"It is astonishing what talent and energy he throws into
everything he attempts," said the parson. "One could not,
indeed, have supposed that a man of genius could make a man
of business."

"Flattering to your humble servant — whom all the world
allow to be the last, and deny to be the first. But your
remark shows what a sad possession genius is: like the rest
of the world, you fancy that it cannot be of the least possible
use. If a man is called a genius, it means that he is to be
thrust out of all the good things in this life. He is not fit for
anything but a garret! Put a *genius* into office! make a *genius*
a bishop! or a lord chancellor! — the world would be turned
topsy turvy! You see that you are quite astonished that a
genius can be even a county magistrate, and know the difference between a spade and a poker! In fact, a genius is supposed to be the most ignorant, impracticable, good-for-nothing,
do-nothing sort of thing that ever walked upon two legs.
Well, when I began life I took excellent care that nobody
should take *me* for a genius; and it is only within the last

[1] " Wrapping truth in obscurity."

year or two that I ventured to emerge a little out of my shell.
I have not been the better for it; I was getting on faster while
I was merely a plodder.   The world is so fond of that droll
fable, the hare and the tortoise, — it really believes because
(I suppose the fable to be true!) a tortoise *once* beat a hare
that all tortoises are much better runners than hares possibly
can be.   Mediocre men have the monopoly of the loaves and
fishes; and even when talent does rise in life, it is a talent
which only differs from mediocrity by being more energetic
and bustling."

"You are bitter, Lord Vargrave," said Caroline, laughing;
"yet surely you have had no reason to complain of the non-
appreciation of talent?"

"Humph! if I had had a grain more talent I should have
been crushed by it.   There is a subtle allegory in the story of
the lean poet, who put *lead* in his pocket to prevent being
blown away!   'Mais à nos moutons,' — to return to Maltravers.   Let us suppose that he was merely clever, had not
had a particle of what is called genius, been merely a hard-
working able gentleman, of good character and fortune, he
might be half-way up the hill by this time; whereas now,
what is he?   Less before the public than he was at twenty-
eight, — a discontented anchorite, a meditative idler."

"No, not that," said Evelyn, warmly, and then checked
herself.

Lord Vargrave looked at her sharply; but his knowledge of
life told him that Legard was a much more dangerous rival
than Maltravers.   Now and then, it is true, a suspicion to
the contrary crossed him; but it did not take root and become
a serious apprehension.   Still, he did not quite like the tone
of voice in which Evelyn had put her abrupt negative, and
said, with a slight sneer, —

"If not that, what is he?"

"One who purchased by the noblest exertions the right to
be idle," said Evelyn with spirit; "and whom genius itself
will not suffer to be idle long."

"Besides," said Mr. Merton, "he has won a high reputation,
which he cannot lose merely by not seeking to increase it."

"Reputation! Oh, yes! we give men like that — men of genius — a large property in the clouds, in order to justify ourselves in pushing them out of our way below. But if they are contented with fame, why, they deserve their fate. Hang fame, — give me power."

"And is there no power in genius?" said Evelyn, with deepening fervour; "no power over the mind, and the heart, and the thought; no power over its own time, over posterity, over nations yet uncivilized, races yet unborn?"

This burst from one so simple and young as Evelyn seemed to Vargrave so surprising that he stared on her without saying a word.

"You will laugh at my championship," she added, with a blush and a smile; "but you provoked the encounter."

"And you have won the battle," said Vargrave, with prompt gallantry. "My charming ward, every day develops in you some new gift of nature!"

Caroline, with a movement of impatience, put her horse into a canter.

Just at this time, from a cross-road, emerged a horseman, — it was Maltravers. The party halted, salutations were exchanged.

"I suppose you have been enjoying the sweet business of squiredom," said Vargrave, gayly: "Atticus and his farm, — classical associations! Charming weather for the agriculturists, eh! What news about corn and barley? I suppose our English habit of talking on the weather arose when we were all a squirearchal farming, George-the-Third kind of people! Weather is really a serious matter to gentlemen who are interested in beans and vetches, wheat and hay. You hang your happiness upon the changes of the moon!"

"As you upon the smiles of a minister. The weather of a court is more capricious than that of the skies, — at least we are better husbandmen than you who sow the wind and reap the whirlwind."

"Well retorted: and really, when I look round, I am half inclined to envy you. Were I not Vargrave, I would be Maltravers."

It was, indeed, a scene that seemed quiet and serene, with the English union of the feudal and the pastoral life, — the village-green, with its trim scattered cottages; the fields and pastures that spread beyond; the turf of the park behind, broken by the shadows of the unequal grounds, with its mounds and hollows and venerable groves, from which rose the turrets of the old Hall, its mullion windows gleaming in the western sun; a scene that preached tranquillity and content, and might have been equally grateful to humble philosophy and hereditary pride.

"I never saw any place so peculiar in its character as Burleigh," said the rector; "the old seats left to us in England are chiefly those of our great nobles. It is so rare to see one that does not aspire beyond the residence of a private gentleman preserve all the relics of the Tudor age."

"I think," said Vargrave, turning to Evelyn, "that as by my uncle's will your fortune is to be laid out in the purchase of land, we could not find a better investment than Burleigh. So, whenever you are inclined to sell, Maltravers, I think we must outbid Doltimore. What say you, my fair ward?"

"Leave Burleigh in peace, I beseech you!" said Maltravers, angrily.

"That is said like a Digby," returned Vargrave. "*Allons!* — will you not come home with us?"

"I thank you, — not to-day."

"We meet at Lord Raby's next Thursday. It is a ball given almost wholly in honour of your return to Burleigh; we are all going, — it is my young cousin's *début* at Knaresdean. We have all an interest in her conquests."

Now, as Maltravers looked up to answer, he caught Evelyn's glance, and his voice faltered.

"Yes," he said, "we shall meet — once again. Adieu!" He wheeled round his horse, and they separated.

"I can bear this no more," said Maltravers to himself; "I overrated my strength. To see her thus, day after day, and to know her another's, to writhe beneath his calm, unconscious assertion of his rights! Happy Vargrave! — and yet, ah! will *she* be happy? Oh, could I think so!"

Thus soliloquizing, he suffered the rein to fall on the neck of his horse, which paced slowly home through the village, till it stopped — as if in the mechanism of custom — at the door of a cottage a stone's throw from the lodge. At this door, indeed, for several successive days, had Maltravers stopped regularly; it was now tenanted by the poor woman his introduction to whom has been before narrated. She had recovered from the immediate effects of the injury she had sustained; but her constitution, greatly broken by previous suffering and exhaustion, had received a mortal shock. She was hurt inwardly; and the surgeon informed Maltravers that she had not many months to live. He had placed her under the roof of one of his favourite cottagers, where she received all the assistance and alleviation that careful nursing and medical advice could give her.

This poor woman, whose name was Sarah Elton, interested Maltravers much. She had known better days: there was a certain propriety in her expressions which denoted an education superior to her circumstances; and what touched Maltravers most, she seemed far more to feel her husband's death than her own sufferings, — which, somehow or other, is not common with widows the other side of forty! We say that youth easily consoles itself for the robberies of the grave, — middle age is a still better self-comforter. When Mrs. Elton found herself installed in the cottage, she looked round, and burst into tears.

"And William is not here!" she said. "Friends — friends! if we had had but one such friend before he died!"

Maltravers was pleased that her first thought was rather that of sorrow for the dead than of gratitude for the living. Yet Mrs. Elton was grateful, — simply, honestly, deeply grateful; her manner, her voice, betokened it. And she seemed so glad when her benefactor called to speak kindly and inquire cordially, that Maltravers did so constantly; at first from a compassionate and at last from a selfish motive — for who is not pleased to give pleasure? And Maltravers had so few in the world to care for him, that perhaps he was flattered by the grateful respect of this humble stranger.

When his horse stopped, the cottager's daughter opened the door and courtesied, — it was an invitation to enter; and he threw his rein over the paling and walked into the cottage.

Mrs. Elton, who had been seated by the open casement, rose to receive him. But Maltravers made her sit down, and soon put her at her ease. The woman and her daughter who occupied the cottage retired into the garden, and Mrs. Elton, watching them withdraw, then exclaimed abruptly, —

"Oh, sir, I have so longed to see you this morning! I so long to make bold to ask you whether, indeed, I dreamed it — or did I, when you first took me to your house — did I see —" She stopped abruptly; and though she strove to suppress her emotion, it was too strong for her efforts, — she sank back on her chair, pale as death, and almost gasped for breath.

Maltravers waited in surprise for her recovery.

"I beg pardon, sir, — I was thinking of days long past; and — but I wished to ask whether, when I lay in your hall, almost insensible, any one besides yourself and your servants were present? — or was it " — added the woman, with a shudder — "was it the dead?"

"I remember," said Maltravers, much struck and interested in her question and manner, "that a lady was present."

"It is so! it is so!" cried the woman, half rising and clasping her hands. "And she passed by this cottage a little time ago; her veil was thrown aside as she turned that fair young face towards the cottage. Her name, sir, — oh, what is her name? It was the same — the same face that shone across me in that hour of pain! I did not dream! I was not mad!"

"Compose yourself; you could never, I think, have seen that lady before. Her name is Cameron."

"Cameron — Cameron!" The woman shook her head mournfully. "No; that name is strange to me. And her mother, sir, — she is dead?"

"No; her mother lives."

A shade came over the face of the sufferer; and she said, after a pause, —

"My eyes deceive me then, sir; and, indeed, I feel that my

head is touched, and I wander sometimes. But the likeness was so great; yet that young lady is even lovelier! "

"Likenesses are very deceitful and very capricious, and depend more on fancy than reality. One person discovers a likeness between faces most dissimilar, — a likeness invisible to others. But who does Miss Cameron resemble?"

"One now dead, sir; dead many years ago. But it is a long story, and one that lies heavy on my conscience. Some day or other, if you will give me leave, sir, I will unburden myself to you."

"If I can assist you in any way, command me. Meanwhile, have you no friends, no relations, no children, whom you would wish to see?"

"Children! — no, sir; I never had but one child of *my own*" (she laid an emphasis on the last words), "and that died in a foreign land."

"And no other relatives?"

"None, sir. My history is very short and simple. I was well brought up, — an only child. My father was a small farmer; he died when I was sixteen, and I went into service with a kind old lady and her daughter, who treated me more as a companion than a servant. I was a vain, giddy girl, then, sir. A young man, the son of a neighbouring farmer, courted me, and I was much attached to him; but neither of us had money, and his parents would not give their consent to our marrying. I was silly enough to think that, if William loved me, he should have braved all; and his prudence mortified me, so I married another whom I did not love. I was rightly punished, for he ill-used me and took to drinking; I returned to my old service to escape from him — for I was with child, and my life was in danger from his violence. He died suddenly, and in debt. And then, afterwards, a gentleman — a rich gentleman — to whom I rendered a service (do not misunderstand me, sir, if I say the service was one of which I repent), gave me money, and made me rich enough to marry my first lover; and William and I went to America. We lived many years in New York upon our little fortune comfortably; and I was a long while happy, for I had always

loved William dearly.   My first affliction was the death of
my child by my first husband; but I was soon roused from my
grief.   William schemed and speculated, as everybody does
in America, and so we lost all; and William was weakly and
could not work.   At length he got the place of steward on
board a vessel from New York to Liverpool, and I was taken
to assist in the cabin.   We wanted to come to London; I
thought my old benefactor might do something for us, though
he had never answered the letters I sent to him.   But poor
William fell ill on board, and died in sight of land."

Mrs. Elton wept bitterly, but with the subdued grief of one
to whom tears have been familiar; and when she recovered,
she soon brought her humble tale to an end.   She herself,
incapacitated from all work by sorrow and a breaking constitution, was left in the streets of Liverpool without other means
of subsistence than the charitable contributions of the passen-
gers and sailors on board the vessel.   With this sum she had
gone to London, where she found her old patron had been
long since dead, and she had no claims on his family.   She
had, on quitting England, left one relation settled in a town
in the North; thither she now repaired, to find her last hope
wrecked; the relation also was dead and gone.   Her money
was now spent, and she had begged her way along the road, or
through the lanes, she scarce knew whither, till the accident
which, in shortening her life, had raised up a friend for its
close.

"And such, sir," said she in conclusion, "such has been the
story of my life, except one part of it, which, if I get stronger,
I can tell better; but you will excuse that now."

"And are you comfortable and contented, my poor friend?
These people are kind to you?"

"Oh, so kind!   And every night we all pray for you, sir;
you ought to be happy, if the blessings of the poor can avail
the rich."

Maltravers remounted his horse, and sought his home; and
his heart was lighter than before he entered that cottage.   But
at evening Cleveland talked of Vargrave and Evelyn, and the

good fortune of the one, and the charms of the other; and the wound, so well concealed, bled afresh.

"I heard from De Montaigne the other day," said Ernest, just as they were retiring for the night, "and his letter decides my movements. If you will accept me, then, as a travelling companion, I will go with you to Paris. Have you made up your mind to leave Burleigh on Saturday?"

"Yes; that gives us a day to recover from Lord Raby's ball. I am so delighted at your offer! We need only stay a day or so in town. The excursion will do you good, — your spirits, my dear Ernest, seem more dejected than when you first returned to England. you live too much alone here; you will enjoy Burleigh more on your return. And perhaps then you will open the old house a little more to the neighbourhood, and to your friends. They expect it. you are looked to for the county."

"I have done with politics, and sicken but for peace."

"Pick up a wife in Paris, and you will then know that peace is an impossible possession," said the old bachelor, laughing.

BOOK V.

Νήπιοι· οὐδ' ἴσασιν ὅσῳ πλέον ἥμισυ παντὸς. — HESIOD : *Op. et Dies*, 40.

"FOOLS blind to truth ; nor know their erring soul
How much the half is better than the whole."

CHAPTER I.

Do as the Heavens have done ; forget your evil ;
With them, forgive yourself. — *The Winter's Tale.*

. . . The sweet'st companion that e'er man
Bred his hopes out of. — *Ibid.*

THE curate of Brook-Green was sitting outside his door.
The vicarage which he inhabited was a straggling, irregular,
but picturesque building, — humble enough to suit the means
of the curate, yet large enough to accommodate the vicar.
It had been built in an age when the *indigentes et pauperes* for
whom universities were founded supplied, more than they do
now, the fountains of the Christian ministry, when pastor
and flock were more on an equality.

From under a rude and arched porch, with an oaken settle
on either side for the poor visitor, the door opened at once
upon the old-fashioned parlour, — a homely but pleasant
room, with one wide but low cottage casement, beneath
which stood the dark shining table that supported the large
Bible in its green baize cover ; the Concordance, and the last
Sunday's sermon, in its jetty case. There by the fireplace
stood the bachelor's round elbow-chair, with a needlework
cushion at the back ; a walnut-tree bureau, another table or
two, half a dozen plain chairs, constituted the rest of the furniture, saving some two or three hundred volumes, ranged in

neat shelves on the clean wainscoted walls. There was another room, to which you ascended by two steps, communicating with this parlour, smaller but finer, and inhabited only
on festive days, when Lady Vargrave, or some other quiet
neighbour, came to drink tea with the good curate.

An old housekeeper and her grandson — a young fellow of
about two and twenty, who tended the garden, milked the
cow, and did in fact what he was wanted to do — composed
the establishment of the humble minister.

We have digressed from Mr. Aubrey himself.

The curate was seated, then, one fine summer morning, on
a bench at the left of his porch, screened from the sun by the
cool boughs of a chestnut-tree, the shadow of which half cov·
ered the little lawn that separated the precincts of the house
from those of silent Death and everlasting Hope; above the
irregular and moss-grown paling rose the village church; and,
through openings in the trees, beyond the burial-ground, partially gleamed the white walls of Lady Vargrave's cottage,
and were seen at a distance the sails on the —

" Mighty waters, rolling evermore."

The old man was calmly enjoying the beauty of the morning,
the freshness of the air, the warmth of the dancing beam, and
not least, perhaps, his own peaceful thoughts, — the sponta-
neous children of a contemplative spirit and a quiet conscience.   His was the age when we most sensitively enjoy
the mere sense of existence, — when the face of Nature and a
passive conviction of the benevolence of our Great Father suffice to create a serene and ineffable happiness, which rarely
visits us till we have done with the passions; till memories,
if more alive than heretofore, are yet mellowed in the hues
of time, and Faith softens into harmony all their asperities
and harshness; till nothing within us remains to cast a shadow
over the things without; and on the verge of life, the Angels
are nearer to us than of yore.   There is an old age which has
more youth of heart than youth itself!

As the old man thus sat, the little gate through which, on
Sabbath days, he was wont to pass from the humble mansion

to the house of God noiselessly opened, and Lady Vargrave appeared.

The curate rose when he perceived her; and the lady's fair features were lighted up with a gentle pleasure, as she pressed his hand and returned his salutation.

There was a peculiarity in Lady Vargrave's countenance which I have rarely seen in others. Her smile, which was singularly expressive, came less from the lip than from the eyes; it was almost as if the brow smiled; it was as the sudden and momentary vanishing of a light but melancholy cloud that usually rested upon the features, placid as they were.

They sat down on the rustic bench, and the sea-breeze wantoned amongst the quivering leaves of the chestnut-tree that overhung their seat.

"I have come, as usual, to consult my kind friend," said Lady Vargrave; "and, as usual also, it is about our absent Evelyn."

"Have you heard again from her, this morning?"

"Yes; and her letter increases the anxiety which your observation, so much deeper than mine, first awakened."

"Does she then write much of Lord Vargrave?"

"Not a great deal; but the little she does say, betrays how much she shrinks from the union my poor husband desired: more, indeed, than ever! But this is not all, nor the worst; for you know that the late lord had provided against that probability — he loved her so tenderly, his ambition for her only came from his affection; and the letter he left behind him pardons and releases her, if she revolts from the choice he himself preferred."

"Lord Vargrave is, perhaps, a generous, he certainly seems a candid, man, and he must be sensible that his uncle has already done all that justice required."

"I think so. But this, as I said, is not all; I have brought the letter to show you. It seems to me as you apprehended. This Mr. Maltravers has wound himself about her thoughts more than she herself imagines; you see how she dwells on all that concerns him, and how, after checking herself, she returns again and again to the same subject."

"The little gate opened, and Lady Vargrave appeared."

The curate put on his spectacles, and took the letter. It was a strange thing, that old gray-haired minister evincing such grave interest in the secrets of that young heart! But they who would take charge of the soul must never be too wise to regard the heart!

Lady Vargrave looked over his shoulder as he bent down to read, and at times placed her finger on such passages as she wished him to note. The old curate nodded as she did so; but neither spoke till the letter was concluded.

The curate then folded up the epistle, took off his spectacles, hemmed, and looked grave.

"Well," said Lady Vargrave, anxiously, "well?"

"My dear friend, the letter requires consideration. In the first place, it is clear to me that, in spite of Lord Vargrave's presence at the rectory, his lordship so manages matters that the poor child is unable of herself to bring that matter to a conclusion. And, indeed, to a mind so sensitively delicate and honourable, it is no easy task."

"Shall I write to Lord Vargrave?"

"Let us think of it. In the meanwhile, this Mr. Maltravers —"

"Ah, this Mr. Maltravers!"

"The child shows us more of her heart than she thinks of; and yet I myself am puzzled. If you observe, she has only once or twice spoken of the Colonel Legard whom she has made acquaintance with; while she treats at length of Mr. Maltravers, and confesses the effect he has produced on her mind. Yet, do you know, I more dread the caution respecting the first than all the candour that betrays the influence of the last? There is a great difference between first fancy and first love."

"Is there?" said the lady, abstractedly.

"Again, neither of us is acquainted with this singular man, — I mean Maltravers; his character, temper, and principles, of all of which Evelyn is too young, too guileless, to judge for herself. One thing, however, in her letter speaks in his favour."

"What is that?"

"He absents himself from her. This, if he has discovered her secret, or if he himself is sensible of too great a charm in her presence, would be the natural course that an honourable and a strong mind would pursue."

"What! — if he love her?"

"Yes; while he believes her hand is engaged to another."

"True! What shall be done — if Evelyn should love, and love in vain? Ah, it is the misery of a whole existence!"

"Perhaps she had better return to us," said Mr. Aubrey; "and yet, if already it be too late, and her affections are engaged, we should still remain in ignorance respecting the motives and mind of the object of her attachment; and he, too, might not know the true nature of the obstacle connected with Lord Vargrave's claims."

"Shall I, then, go to her? You know how I shrink from strangers; how I fear curiosity, doubts, and questions; how [and Lady Vargrave's voice faltered] — how unfitted I am for — for — " she stopped short, and a faint blush overspread her cheeks.

The curate understood her, and was moved.

"Dear friend," said he, "will you intrust this charge to myself? You know how Evelyn is endeared to me by certain recollections! Perhaps, better than you, I may be enabled silently to examine if this man be worthy of her, and one who could secure her happiness; perhaps, better than you I may ascertain the exact nature of her own feelings towards him; perhaps, too, better than you I may effect an understanding with Lord Vargrave."

"You are always my kindest friend," said the lady, with emotion; "how much I already owe you! what hopes beyond the grave! what — "

"Hush!" interrupted the curate, gently; "your own good heart and pure intentions have worked out your own atonement — may I hope also your own content? Let us return to our Evelyn. Poor child! how unlike this despondent letter to her gay light spirits when with us! We acted for the best; yet perhaps we did wrong to yield her up to strangers. And this Maltravers — with her enthusiasm and quick susceptibilities to genius, she was half prepared to imagine him all she depicts him to be. He must have a spell in his works that I have not discovered, for at times it seems to operate even on you."

"Because," said Lady Vargrave, "they remind me of *his* conversation, *his* habits of thought. If like *him* in other things, Evelyn may indeed be happy!"

"And if," said the curate, curiously, — "if now that you are free, you were ever to meet with *him* again, and his memory had been as faithful as yours; and if he offered the sole atonement in his power, for all that his early error cost you; if such a chance should happen in the vicissitudes of life, you would — "

The curate stopped short; for he was struck by the exceeding paleness of his friend's cheek, and the tremor of her delicate frame.

"If that were to happen," said she, in a very low voice, "if we were to meet again, and if he were — as you and Mrs. Leslie seem to think — poor, and, like myself, humbly born, if my fortune could assist him, if my love could still — changed, altered as I am — ah! do not talk of it — I cannot bear the thought of happiness! And yet, if before I die I *could* but see him again!" She clasped her hands fervently as she spoke, and the blush that overspread her face threw over it so much of bloom and freshness, that even Evelyn, at that moment, would scarcely have seemed more young. "Enough!" she added, after a little while, as the glow died away. "It is but a foolish hope; all earthly love is buried; and my heart is there!" — she pointed to the heavens, and both were silent.

CHAPTER II.

QUIBUS otio vel magnifice vel molliter, vivere copia era incerta pro certis malebant.[1] — SALLUST.

LORD RABY — one of the wealthiest and most splendid noblemen in England — was prouder, perhaps, of his provincial distinctions than the eminence of his rank or the fashion of his wife. The magnificent châteaux, the immense estates, of our English peers tend to preserve to us in spite of the freedom, bustle, and commercial grandeur of our people more of the Norman attributes of aristocracy than can be found in other countries. In his county, the great noble is a petty prince; his house is a court; his possessions and munificence are a boast to every proprietor in his district. They are as fond of talking of *the* earl's or *the* duke's movements and entertainments, as Dangeau was of the gossip of the Tuileries and Versailles.

Lord Raby, while affecting, as lieutenant of the county, to make no political distinctions between squire and squire — hospitable and affable to all — still, by that very absence of exclusiveness, gave a tone to the politics of the whole county; and converted many who had once thought differently on the respective virtues of Whigs and Tories. A great man never loses so much as when he exhibits intolerance, or parades the right of persecution.

"My tenants shall vote exactly as they please," said Lord Raby; and he was never known to have a tenant vote against his wishes! Keeping a vigilant eye on all the interests, and conciliating all the proprietors, in the county, he not only never lost a friend, but he kept together a body of partisans that constantly added to its numbers.

[1] " They who had the means to live at ease, either in splendour or in luxury, preferred the uncertainty of change to their natural security."

Sir John Merton's colleague, a young Lord Nelthorpe, who could not speak three sentences if you took away his hat, and who, constant at Almack's, was not only inaudible but invisible in parliament, had no chance of being re-elected. Lord Nelthorpe's father, the Earl of Mainwaring, was a new peer; and, next to Lord Raby, the richest nobleman in the county. Now, though they were much of the same politics, Lord Raby hated Lord Mainwaring. They were too near each other, — they clashed; they had the jealousy of rival princes!

Lord Raby was delighted at the notion of getting rid of Lord Nelthorpe, — it would be so sensible a blow to the Mainwaring interest. The party had been looking out for a new candidate, and Maltravers had been much talked of. It is true that, when in parliament some years before, the politics of Maltravers had differed from those of Lord Raby and his set. But Maltravers had of late taken no share in politics, had uttered no political opinions, was intimate with the electioneering Mertons, was supposed to be a discontented man, — and politicians believe in no discontent that is not political. Whispers were afloat that Maltravers had grown wise, and changed his views: some remarks of his, more theoretical than practical, were quoted in favour of this notion. Parties, too, had much changed since Maltravers had appeared on the busy scene, — new questions had arisen, and the old ones had died off.

Lord Raby and his party thought that, if Maltravers could be secured to them, no one would better suit their purpose. Political faction loves converts better even than consistent adherents. A man's rise in life generally dates from a well-timed *rat*. His high reputation, his provincial rank as the representative of the oldest commoner's family in the county, his age, which combined the energy of one period with the experience of another, — all united to accord Maltravers a preference over richer men. Lord Raby had been pointedly courteous and flattering to the master of Burleigh; and he now contrived it so, that the brilliant entertainment he was about to give might appear in compliment to a distinguished neighbour, returned to fix his residence on his patrimonial prop-

erty, while in reality it might serve an electioneering purpose,
— serve to introduce Maltravers to the county, as if under his
lordship's own wing, and minister to political uses that went
beyond the mere representation of the county.

Lord Vargrave had, during his stay at Merton Rectory, paid
several visits to Knaresdean, and held many private conversations with the marquess : the result of these conversations was
a close union of schemes and interests between the two noblemen.   Dissatisfied with the political conduct of government,
Lord Raby was also dissatisfied that, from various party reasons, a nobleman beneath himself in rank, and as he thought
in influence, had obtained a preference in a recent vacancy
among the Knights of the Garter.   And if Vargrave had a
talent in the world it was in discovering the weak points of
men whom he sought to gain, and making the vanities of
others conduce to his own ambition.

The festivities of Knaresdean gave occasion to Lord Raby
to unite at his house the more prominent of those who thought
and acted in concert with Lord Vargrave; and in this secret
senate the operations for the following session were to be seriously discussed and gravely determined.

On the day which was to be concluded with the ball at
Knaresdean, Lord Vargrave went before the rest of the Merton party, for he was engaged to dine with the marquess.

On arriving at Knaresdean, Lumley found Lord Saxingham
and some other politicians, who had arrived the preceding day,
closeted with Lord Raby; and Vargrave, who shone to yet
greater advantage in the diplomacy of party management than
in the arena of parliament, brought penetration, energy, and
decision to timid and fluctuating counsels.   Lord Vargrave
lingered in the room after the first bell had summoned the
other guests to depart.

"My dear lord," said he then, "though no one would be
more glad than myself to secure Maltravers to our side, I very
much doubt whether you will succeed in doing so.   On the
one hand, he appears altogether disgusted with politics and
parliament; and on the other hand, I fancy that reports of his
change of opinions are, if not wholly unfounded, very unduly

coloured. Moreover, to do him justice, I think that he is not one to be blinded and flattered into the pale of a party; and your bird will fly away after you have wasted a bucketful of salt on his tail."

"Very possibly," said Lord Raby, laughing, — "you know him better than I do. But there are many purposes to serve in this matter, -— purposes too provincial to interest you. In the first place, we shall humble the Nelthorpe interest, merely by showing that we *do* think of a new member; secondly, we shall get up a manifestation of feeling that would be impossible, unless we were provided with a centre of attraction, thirdly, we shall rouse a certain emulation among other county gentlemen, and if Maltravers decline, we shall have many applicants; and fourthly, suppose Maltravers has not changed his opinions, we shall make him suspected by the party he really does belong to, and which would be somewhat formidable if he were to head them. In fact, these are mere county tactics that you can't be expected to understand."

"I see you are quite right. meanwhile you will at least have an opportunity (though I say it, who should not say it) to present to the county one of the prettiest young ladies that ever graced the halls of Knaresdean."

"Ah, Miss Cameron! I have heard much of her beauty: you are a lucky fellow, Vargrave! By the by, are we to say anything of the engagement?"

"Why, indeed, my dear lord, it is now so publicly known, that it would be false delicacy to affect concealment."

"Very well; I understand."

"How long I have detained you — a thousand pardons! — I have but just time to dress. In four or five months I must remember to leave you a longer time for your toilet."

"Me — how?"

"Oh, the Duke of —— can't live long; and I always observe that when a handsome man has the Garter, he takes a long time pulling up his stockings."

"Ha, ha! you are so droll, Vargrave."

"Ha, ha! I must be off."

"The more publicity is given to this arrangement, the more

difficult for Evelyn to shy at the leap," muttered Vargrave to himself as he closed the door. "Thus do I make all things useful to myself!"

The dinner party were assembled in the great drawing-room, when Maltravers and Cleveland, also invited guests to the banquet, were announced. Lord Raby received the former with marked *empressement ;* and the stately marchioness honoured him with her most gracious smile. Formal presentations to the rest of the guests were interchanged; and it was not till the circle was fully gone through that Maltravers perceived, seated by himself in a corner, to which he had shrunk on the entrance of Maltravers, a gray-haired solitary man, — it was Lord Saxingham! The last time they had met was in the death-chamber of Florence; and the old man forgot for the moment the anticipated dukedom, and the dreamed-of premiership, and his heart flew back to the grave of his only child! They saluted each other, and shook hands in silence. And Vargrave — whose eye was on them — Vargrave, whose arts had made that old man childless, felt not a pang of remorse! Living ever in the future, Vargrave almost seemed to have lost his memory. He knew not what regret was. It is a condition of life with men thoroughly worldly that they never look behind!

The signal was given: in due order the party were marshalled into the great hall, — a spacious and lofty chamber, which had received its last alteration from the hand of Inigo Jones; though the massive ceiling, with its antique and grotesque masques, betrayed a much earlier date, and contrasted with the Corinthian pilasters that adorned the walls, and supported the music-gallery, from which waved the flags of modern warfare and its mimicries, — the eagle of Napoleon, a token of the services of Lord Raby's brother (a distinguished cavalry officer in command at Waterloo), in juxtaposition with a much gayer and more glittering banner, emblematic of the martial fame of Lord Raby himself, as Colonel of the B——shire volunteers!

The music pealed from the gallery, the plate glittered on the board; the ladies wore diamonds, and the gentlemen who had them wore stars. It was a very fine sight, that banquet! — such as became the festive day of a lord-lieutenant whose ancestors had now defied, and now intermarried, with roy- alty. But there was very little talk, and no merriment. People at the top of the table drank wine with those at the bottom; and gentlemen and ladies seated next to each other whispered languidly in monosyllabic commune. On one side, Maltravers was flanked by a Lady Somebody Some- thing, who was rather deaf, and very much frightened for fear he should talk Greek; on the other side he was relieved by Sir John Merton, — very civil, very pompous, and talking, at strictured intervals, about county matters, in a measured intonation, savouring of the House-of-Commons jerk at the end of the sentence.

As the dinner advanced to its close, Sir John became a little more diffuse, though his voice sank into a whisper.

"I fear there will be a split in the Cabinet before parlia- ment meets."

"Indeed!"

"Yes; Vargrave and the premier cannot pull together very long. Clever man, Vargrave! but he has not enough stake in the country for a leader!"

"All men have public character to stake; and if that be good, I suppose no stake can be better?"

"Humph! — yes — very true; but still, when a man has land and money, his opinions, in a country like this, very properly carry more weight with them. If Vargrave, for instance, had Lord Raby's property, no man could be more fit for a leader, — a prime minister. We might then be sure that he would have no selfish interest to further: he would not play tricks with his party — you understand?"

"Perfectly."

"I am not a party man, as you may remember; indeed, you and I have voted alike on the same questions. Measures, not men, — that is my maxim; but still I don't like to see men placed above their proper stations."

"Maltravers, a glass of wine," said Lord Vargrave across the table. "Will you join us, Sir John?"

Sir John bowed.

"Certainly," he resumed, "Vargrave is a pleasant man and a good speaker; but still they say he is far from rich, — embarrassed, indeed. However, when he marries Miss Cameron it may make a great difference, — give him more respectability; do you know what her fortune is — something immense?"

"Yes, I believe so; I don't know."

"My brother says that Vargrave is most amiable. The young lady is very handsome, almost too handsome for a wife — don't you think so? Beauties are all very well in a ball-room; but they are not calculated for domestic life. I am sure you agree with me. I have heard, indeed, that Miss Cameron is rather learned; but there is so much scandal in a country neighbourhood, — people are so ill-natured. I dare say she is not more learned than other young ladies, poor girl! What do you think?"

"Miss Cameron is — is very accomplished, I believe. And so you think the Government cannot stand?"

"I don't say that, — very far from it; but I fear there must be a change. However, if the country gentlemen hold together, I do not doubt but what we shall weather the storm. The landed interest, Mr. Maltravers, is the great stay of this country, — the sheet-anchor, I may say. I suppose Lord Vargrave, who seems, I must say, to have right notions on this head, will invest Miss Cameron's fortune in land. But though one may buy an estate, one can't buy an old family, Mr. Maltravers! — you and I may be thankful for that. By the way, who was Miss Cameron's mother, Lady Vargrave? — something low, I fear; nobody knows."

"I am not acquainted with Lady Vargrave; your sister-in-law speaks of her most highly. And the daughter in herself is a sufficient guarantee for the virtues of the mother."

"Yes; and Vargrave on one side, at least, has himself nothing in the way of family to boast of."

The ladies left the hall, the gentlemen re-seated themselves. Lord Raby made some remark on politics to Sir John Merton, and the whole round of talkers immediately followed their leader.

"It is a thousand pities, Sir John," said Lord Raby, "that you have not a colleague more worthy of you; Nelthorpe never attends a committee, does he?"

"I cannot say that he is a very active member; but he is young, and we must make allowances for him," said Sir John, discreetly; for he had no desire to oust his colleague, — it was agreeable enough to be *the* efficient member.

"In these times," said Lord Raby, loftily, "allowances are not to be made for systematic neglect of duty; we shall have a stormy session; the Opposition is no longer to be despised; perhaps a dissolution may be nearer at hand than we think for. As for Nelthorpe, he cannot come in again."

"That I am quite sure of," said a fat country gentleman of great weight in the county; "he not only was absent on the great Malt question, but he never answered my letter respecting the Canal Company."

"Not answered your letter!" said Lord Raby, lifting up his hands and eyes in amaze and horror. "What conduct! Ah, Mr. Maltravers, you are the man for us!"

"Hear! hear!" cried the fat squire.

"Hear!" echoed Vargrave; and the approving sound went round the table.

Lord Raby rose. "Gentlemen, fill your glasses; a health to our distinguished neighbour!"

The company applauded; each in his turn smiled, nodded, and drank to Maltravers, who, though taken by surprise, saw at once the course to pursue. He returned thanks simply and shortly; and without pointedly noticing the allusion in which Lord Raby had indulged, remarked, incidentally, that he had retired, certainly for some years — perhaps forever — from political life.

Vargrave smiled significantly at Lord Raby, and hastened to lead the conversation into party discussion. Wrapped in his proud disdain of what he considered the contests of factions for toys and shadows, Maltravers remained silent; and the party soon broke up, and adjourned to the ballroom.

CHAPTER III.

Le plus grand défaut de la pénétration n'est pas de n'aller point jus-
qu'au but, — c'est de la passer.[1] — La Rochefoucauld.

Evelyn had looked forward to the ball at Knaresdean with
feelings deeper than those which usually inflame the fancy of
a girl proud of her dress and confident of her beauty.   Whether
or not she *loved* Maltravers, in the true acceptation of the word
"love," it is certain that he had acquired a most powerful command over her mind and imagination.   She felt the warmest
interest in his welfare, the most anxious desire for his esteem,
the deepest regret at the thought of their estrangement.   At
Knaresdean she should meet Maltravers, — in crowds, it is
true; but still she should meet him; she should see him towering superior above the herd; she should hear him praised;
she should mark him, the observed of all.   But there was another and a deeper source of joy within her.   A letter had
been that morning received from Aubrey, in which he had
announced his arrival for the next day.   The letter, though
affectionate, was short.   Evelyn had been some months absent,
— Lady Vargrave was anxious to make arrangements for her
return; but it was to be at her option whether she would
accompany the curate home.   Now, besides her delight at
seeing once more the dear old man, and hearing from his lips
that her mother was well and happy, Evelyn hailed in his
arrival the means of extricating herself from her position
with Lord Vargrave.   She would confide in him her increased
repugnance to that union, he would confer with Lord Vargrave; and then — and then — did there come once more the
thought of Maltravers?   No!   I fear it was not Maltravers

[1] "The greatest defect of penetration is not that of not going just up to
the point, — 't is the passing it."

who called forth that smile and that sigh! Strange girl, you know not your own mind!—but few of us, at your age, do.

In all the gayety of hope, in the pride of dress and half-conscious loveliness, Evelyn went with a light step into Caroline's room. Miss Merton had already dismissed her woman, and was seated by her writing-table, leaning her cheek thoughtfully on her hand.

"Is it time to go?" said she, looking up. "Well, we shall put Papa, and the coachman, and the horses, too, in excellent humour. How well you look! Really, Evelyn, you are indeed beautiful!" and Caroline gazed with honest but not unenvious admiration at the fairy form so rounded and yet so delicate, and the face that seemed to blush at its own charms.

"I am sure I can return the flattery," said Evelyn, laughing bashfully.

"Oh, as for me, I am well enough in my way: and hereafter, I dare say, we may be rival beauties. I hope we shall remain good friends, and rule the world with divided empire. Do you not long for the stir, and excitement, and ambition of London?—for ambition is open to us as to men!"

"No, indeed," replied Evelyn, smiling; "I could be ambitious, indeed; but it would not be for myself, but for—"

"A husband, perhaps; well, you will have ample scope for such sympathy. Lord Vargrave—"

"Lord Vargrave again?" and Evelyn's smile vanished, and she turned away.

"Ah," said Caroline, "I should have made Vargrave an excellent wife—pity he does not think so! As it is, I must set up for myself and become a *maîtresse femme*. So you think I look well to-night? I am glad of it—Lord Doltimore is one who will be guided by what other people say."

"You are not serious about Lord Doltimore?"

"Most sadly serious."

"Impossible! you could not speak so if you loved him."

"Loved him! no! but I intend to marry him."

Evelyn was revolted, but still incredulous.

"And you, too, will marry one whom you do not love—'t is our fate—"

"Never!"

"We shall see."

Evelyn's heart was damped, and her spirits fell.

"Tell me now," said Caroline, pressing on the wrung withers, "do you not think this excitement, partial and provincial though it be — the sense of beauty, the hope of conquest, the consciousness of power — better than the dull monotony of the Devonshire cottage? Be honest — "

"No, no, indeed!" answered Evelyn, tearfully and passion- ately; "one hour with my mother, one smile from her lips, were worth it all."

"And in your visions of marriage, you think then of nothing but roses and doves, — love in a cottage!"

"Love *in a home*, no matter whether a palace or a cottage," returned Evelyn.

"Home!" repeated Caroline, bitterly; "home, — home is the English synonym for the French *ennui*. But I hear Papa on the stairs."

A ballroom — what a scene of commonplace! how hack- neyed in novels! how trite in ordinary life! and yet ball- rooms have a character and a sentiment of their own, for all tempers and all ages. Something in the lights, the crowd, the music, conduces to stir up many of the thoughts that belong to fancy and romance. It is a melancholy scene to men after a certain age. It revives many of those lighter and more graceful images connected with the wandering de- sires of youth, — shadows that crossed us, and seemed love, but were not; having much of the grace and charm, but none of the passion and the tragedy, of love. So many of our earliest and gentlest recollections are connected with those chalked floors, and that music painfully gay, and those quiet nooks and corners, where the talk that hovers about the heart and does not touch it has been held. Apart and unsympathiz- ing in that austerer wisdom which comes to us after deep pas- sions have been excited, we see form after form chasing the butterflies that dazzle us no longer among the flowers that have evermore lost their fragrance.

Somehow or other, it is one of the scenes that remind us

most forcibly of the loss of youth! We are brought so closely
in contact with the young and with the short-lived pleasures
that once pleased us, and have forfeited all bloom. Happy
the man who turns from "the tinkling cymbal" and "the gallery of pictures," and can think of some watchful eye and
some kind heart *at home;* but those who have no home — and
they are a numerous tribe — never feel lonelier hermits or
sadder moralists than in such a crowd.

Maltravers leaned abstractedly against the wall, and some
such reflections, perhaps, passed within, as the plumes waved
and the diamonds glittered around him. Ever too proud to
be vain, the *monstrari digito* had not flattered even in the
commencement of his career. And now he heeded not the
eyes that sought his look, nor the admiring murmur of lips
anxious to be overheard. Affluent, well-born, unmarried,
and still in the prime of life, — in the small circles of a
province, Ernest Maltravers would in himself have been an
object of interest to the diplomacy of mothers and daughters;
and the false glare of reputation necessarily deepened curiosity, and widened the range of speculators and observers.

Suddenly, however, a new object of attention excited new
interest; new whispers ran through the crowd, and these
awakened Maltravers from his revery. He looked up, and
beheld all eyes fixed upon one form! His own eyes encountered those of Evelyn Cameron!

It was the first time he had seen this beautiful young
person in all the *éclat,* pomp, and circumstance of her station,
as the heiress of the opulent Templeton, — the first time he
had seen her the cynosure of crowds, who, had her features
been homely, would have admired the charms of her fortune
in her face. And now, as radiant with youth, and the flush
of excitement on her soft cheek, she met his eye, he said to
himself: "And could I have wished one so new to the world
to have united her lot with a man for whom all that to her is
delight has grown wearisome and stale? Could I have been
justified in stealing her from the admiration that, at her age
and to her sex, has so sweet a flattery? Or, on the other
hand, could I have gone back to her years, and sympathized

with feelings that time has taught me to despise? Better as it is."

Influenced by these thoughts, the greeting of Maltravers disappointed and saddened Evelyn, she knew not why; it was constrained and grave.

"Does not Miss Cameron look well?" whispered Mrs. Merton, on whose arm the heiress leaned. "You observe what a sensation she creates?"

Evelyn overheard, and blushed as she stole a glance at Maltravers. There was something mournful in the admiration which spoke in his deep earnest eyes.

"Everywhere," said he, calmly, and in the same tone, "everywhere Miss Cameron appears, she must outshine all others." He turned to Evelyn, and said with a smile, "You must learn to inure yourself to admiration; a year or two hence, and you will not blush at your own gifts!"

"And you, too, contribute to spoil me! — fie!"

"Are you so easily spoiled? If I meet you hereafter, you will think. my compliments cold to the common language of others."

"You do not know me, — perhaps you never will."

"I am contented with the fair pages I have already read."

"Where is Lady Raby?" asked Mrs. Merton. "Oh, I see; Evelyn, my love, we must present ourselves to our hostess."

The ladies moved on; and when Maltravers next caught a glance of Evelyn, she was with Lady Raby, and Lord Vargrave also was by her side.

The whispers round him had grown louder.

"Very lovely indeed! so young, too! and she is really going to be married to Lord Vargrave; so much older than she is, — quite a sacrifice!"

"Scarcely so. He is so agreeable, and still handsome. But are you sure that the thing is settled?"

"Oh, yes. Lord Raby himself told me so. It will take place very soon."

"But do you know who her mother was? I cannot make out."

"Nothing particular. You know the late Lord Vargrave

was a man of low birth. I believe she was a widow of his
own rank; she lives quite in seclusion."

"How d' ye do, Mr. Maltravers? So glad to see you," said
the quick, shrill voice of Mrs. Hare. "Beautiful ball! Nobody does things like Lord Raby; don't you dance?"

"No, madam."

"Oh, you young gentlemen are so *fine* nowadays!" (Mrs.
Hare, laying stress on the word *young*, thought she had paid
a very elegant compliment, and ran on with increased
complacency.)

"You are going to let Burleigh, I hear, to Lord Doltimore,
— is it true? No! really now, what stories people do tell.
Elegant man, Lord Doltimore! Is it true, that Miss Caroline is going to marry his lordship? Great match! No scandal, I hope; you 'll excuse *me!* Two weddings on the *tapis*,
— quite stirring for our stupid county. Lady Vargrave and
Lady Doltimore, two new peeresses. Which do you think is
the handsomer? Miss Merton is the taller, but there is something fierce in her eyes. Don't you think so? By the by, I
wish you joy, — you 'll excuse *me*."

"Wish me joy, madam?"

"Oh, you are so close. Mr. Hare says he shall support you.
You will have all the ladies with you. Well, I declare, Lord
Vargrave is going to dance. How old is he, do you think?"

Maltravers uttered an audible *pshaw*, and moved away;
but his penance was not over. Lord Vargrave, much as he
disliked dancing, still thought it wise to ask the fair hand of
Evelyn; and Evelyn, also, could not refuse.

And now, as the crowd gathered round the red ropes,
Maltravers had to undergo new exclamations at Evelyn's
beauty and Vargrave's luck. Impatiently he turned from the
spot, with that gnawing sickness of the heart which none but
the jealous know. He longed to depart, yet dreaded to do so.
It was the last time he should see Evelyn, perhaps for years;
the last time he should see her as Miss Cameron!

He passed into another room, deserted by all save four old
gentlemen — Cleveland one of them — immersed in whist; and
threw himself upon an ottoman, placed in a recess by the oriel

window. There, half concealed by the draperies, he communed and reasoned with himself. His heart was sad within
him; he never felt before *how* deeply and *how* passionately he
loved Evelyn; how firmly that love had fastened upon the
very core of his heart! Strange, indeed, it was in a girl so
young, of whom he had seen but little, — and that little in
positions of such quiet and ordinary interest, — to excite a
passion so intense in a man who had gone through strong
emotions and stern trials! But all love is unaccountable.
The solitude in which Maltravers had lived, the absence of
all other excitement, perhaps had contributed largely to fan
the flame. And his affections had so long slept, and after
long sleep the passions wake with such giant strength! He
felt now too well that the last rose of life had bloomed for
him; it was blighted in its birth, but it could never be replaced. Henceforth, indeed, he should be alone, the hopes
of home were gone forever; and the other occupations of mind
and soul — literature, pleasure, ambition — were already for-
sworn at the very age in which by most men they are most
indulged!

O Youth! begin not thy career too soon, and let one passion
succeed in its due order to another; so that every season of
life may have its appropriate pursuit and charm!

The hours waned; still Maltravers stirred not; nor were his
meditations disturbed, except by occasional ejaculations from
the four old gentlemen, as between each deal they moralized
over the caprices of the cards.

At length, close beside him he heard that voice, the lightest
sound of which could send the blood rushing through his
veins; and from his retreat he saw Caroline and Evelyn,
seated close by.

"I beg pardon," said the former, in a low voice, — "I beg
pardon, Evelyn, for calling you away; but I longed to tell
you. The die is cast. Lord Doltimore has proposed, and I
have accepted him! Alas, alas! I half wish I could retract!"

"Dearest Caroline!" said the silver voice of Evelyn, "for
Heaven's sake, do not thus wantonly resolve on your own
unhappiness! You wrong yourself, Caroline! you do, indeed!

You are not the vain ambitious character you affect to be!
Ah, what is it you require? Wealth? Are you not my
friend; am I not rich enough for both? Rank? What can
it give you to compensate for the misery of a union without
love? Pray, forgive me for speaking thus. Do not think me
presumptuous, or romantic; but, indeed, indeed, I know from
my own heart what yours must undergo! "

Caroline pressed her friend's hand with emotion.

" You are a bad comforter, Evelyn. My mother, my father,
will preach a very different doctrine. I am foolish, indeed,
to be so sad in obtaining the very object I have sought! Poor
Doltimore! he little knows the nature, the feelings of her
whom he thinks he has made the happiest of her sex; he little
knows — " Caroline paused, turned pale as death, and then
went rapidly on, " but you, Evelyn, *you* will meet the same
fate; we shall bear it together."

" No! no! do not think so! Where I give my hand, there
shall I give my heart."

At this time Maltravers half rose, and sighed audibly.

" Hush! " said Caroline, in alarm. At the same moment,
the whist-table broke up, and Cleveland approached
Maltravers.

" I am at your service," said he ; " I know you will not stay
the supper. You will find me in the next room; I am just
going to speak to Lord Saxingham." The gallant old gentleman then paid a compliment to the young ladies, and walked
away.

" So you too are a deserter from the ballroom! " said Miss
Merton to Maltravers as she rose.

" I am not very well; but do not let me frighten you away."

" Oh, no! I hear the music; it is the last quadrille before
supper : and here is my fortunate partner looking for me."

" I have been everywhere in search of you," said Lord
Doltimore, in an accent of tender reproach : " come, we are
almost too late now."

Caroline put her arm into Lord Doltimore's, who hurried
her into the ballroom.

Miss Cameron looked irresolute whether or not to follow,

when Maltravers seated himself beside her; and the paleness
of his brow, and something that bespoke pain in the compressed lip, went at once to her heart. In her childlike tenderness, she would have given worlds for the sister's privilege
of sympathy and soothing. The room was now deserted; they
were alone.

The words that he had overheard from Evelyn's lips,
"Where I shall give my hand, there shall I give my heart,"
Maltravers interpreted but in one sense, — "she loved her betrothed;" and strange as it may seem, at that thought, which
put the last seal upon his fate, selfish anguish was less felt
than deep compassion. So young, so courted, so tempted as
she must be — and with such a protector! — the cold, the
unsympathizing, the heartless Vargrave! She, too, whose
feelings, so warm, ever trembled on her lip and eye. Oh!
when she awoke from her dream, and knew whom she had
loved, what might be her destiny, what her danger!

"Miss Cameron," said Maltravers, "let me for one moment
detain you; I will not trespass long. May I once, and for the
last time, assume the austere rights of friendship? I have
seen much of life, Miss Cameron, and my experience has been
purchased dearly; and harsh and hermit-like as I may have
grown, I have not outlived such feelings as you are well
formed to excite. Nay," — and Maltravers smiled sadly — "I
am not about to compliment or flatter, I speak not to you as
the young to the young; the difference of our years, that takes
away sweetness from flattery, leaves still sincerity to friendship. You have inspired me with a deep interest, — deeper
than I thought that living beauty could ever rouse in me
again! It may be that something in the tone of your voice,
your manner, a nameless grace that I cannot define, reminds
me of one whom I knew in youth, — one who had not your
advantages of education, wealth, birth; but to whom Nature
was more kind than Fortune."

He paused a moment; and without looking towards Evelyn,
thus renewed, —

"You are entering life under brilliant auspices. Ah, let
me hope that the noonday will keep the promise of the dawn!

You are susceptible, imaginative; do not demand too much, or dream too fondly. When you are wedded, do not imagine that wedded life is exempt from its trials and its cares; if you know yourself beloved — and beloved you must be — do not ask from the busy and anxious spirit of man all which Romance promises and Life but rarely yields. And oh! " continued Maltravers, with an absorbing and earnest passion, that poured forth its language with almost breathless rapidity, — " if ever your heart rebels, if ever it be dissatisfied, fly the false sentiment as a sin! Thrown, as from your rank you must be, on a world of a thousand perils, with no guide so constant and so safe as your own innocence, make not that world too dear a friend. Were it possible that your own home ever could be lonely or unhappy, reflect that to woman the unhappiest home is happier than all excitement abroad. You will have a thousand suitors hereafter: believe that the asp lurks under the flatterer's tongue, and resolve, come what may, to be contented with your lot. How many have I known, lovely and pure as you, who have suffered the very affections — the very beauty of their nature — to destroy them! Listen to me as a warner, as a brother, as a pilot who has passed the seas on which your vessel is about to launch. And ever, ever let me know, in whatever lands your name may reach me, that one who has brought back to me all my faith in human excellence, while the idol of our sex, is the glory of her own. Forgive me this strange impertinence; my heart is full, and has overflowed. And now, Miss Cameron — Evelyn Cameron — this is my last offence, and my last farewell! "

He held out his hand, and involuntarily, unknowingly, she clasped it, as if to detain him till she could summon words to reply. Suddenly he heard Lord Vargrave's voice behind. The spell was broken; the next moment Evelyn was alone, and the throng swept into the room towards the banquet, and laughter and gay voices were heard, and Lord Vargrave was again by Evelyn's side!

14

CHAPTER IV.

To you
This journey is devoted.
Lover's Progress, Act iv. sc. 1.

As Cleveland and Maltravers returned homeward, the latter abruptly checked the cheerful garrulity of his friend. "I have a favour, a great favour to ask of you."

"And what is that?"

"Let us leave Burleigh to-morrow; I care not at what hour; we need go but two or three stages if you are fatigued."

"Most hospitable host! and why?"

"It is torture, it is agony to me, to breathe the air of Burleigh," cried Maltravers, wildly. "Can you not guess my secret? Have I then concealed it so well? I love, I adore Evelyn Cameron, and she is betrothed to — she loves — another!"

Mr. Cleveland was breathless with amaze; Maltravers had indeed so well concealed his secret, and now his emotion was so impetuous, that it startled and alarmed the old man, who had never himself experienced a passion, though he had indulged a sentiment. He sought to console and soothe; but after the first burst of agony, Maltravers recovered himself, and said gently, —

"Let us never return to this subject again: it is right that I should conquer this madness, and conquer it I will! Now you know my weakness, you will indulge it. My cure cannot commence until I can no longer see from my casements the very roof that shelters the affianced bride of another."

"Certainly, then, we will set off to-morrow: my poor friend! is it indeed — "

"Ah, cease," interrupted the proud man; "no compassion, I implore: give me but time and silence, — they are the only remedies."

Before noon the next day, Burleigh was once more deserted by its lord. As the carriage drove through the village, Mrs. Elton saw it from her open window; but her patron, too absorbed at that hour even for benevolence, forgot her existence: and yet so complicated are the webs of fate, that in the breast of that lowly stranger was locked a secret of the most vital moment to Maltravers.

"Where is he going; where is the squire going?" asked Mrs. Elton, anxiously.

"Dear heart!" said the cottager, "they do say he be going for a short time to foren parts. But he will be back at Christmas."

"And at Christmas I may be gone hence forever," muttered the invalid; "but what will that matter to him — to any one?"

At the first stage Maltravers and his friend were detained a short time for the want of horses. Lord Raby's house had been filled with guests on the preceding night, and the stables of this little inn, dignified with the sign of the Raby Arms, and about two miles distant from the great man's place, had been exhausted by numerous claimants returning homeward from Knaresdean. It was a quiet, solitary post-house, and patience, till some jaded horses should return, was the only remedy; the host, assuring the travellers that he expected four horses every moment, invited them within. The morning was cold, and the fire not unacceptable to Mr. Cleveland; so they went into the little parlour. Here they found an elderly gentleman of very prepossessing appearance, who was waiting for the same object. He moved courteously from the fireplace as the travellers entered, and pushed the "B——shire Chronicle" towards Cleveland: Cleveland bowed urbanely. "A cold day, sir; the autumn begins to show itself."

"It is true, sir," answered the old gentleman; "and I feel the cold the more, having just quitted the genial atmosphere of the South."

"Of Italy?"

"No, of England only. I see by this paper (I am not much of a politician) that there is a chance of a dissolution of par-

liament, and that Mr. Maltravers is likely to come forward
for this county; are you acquainted with him, sir?"

"A little," said Cleveland, smiling.

"He is a man I am much interested in," said the old
gentleman; "and I hope soon to be honoured with his
acquaintance."

"Indeed! and you are going into his neighbourhood?" asked
Cleveland, looking more attentively at the stranger, and much
pleased with a certain simple candour in his countenance and
manner.

"Yes, to Merton Rectory."

Maltravers, who had been hitherto stationed by the window,
turned round.

"To Merton Rectory?" repeated Cleveland. "You are
acquainted with Mr. Merton, then?"

"Not yet; but I know some of his family. However, my
visit is rather to a young lady who is staying at the rectory,
— Miss Cameron."

Maltravers sighed heavily; and the old gentleman looked
at him curiously. "Perhaps, sir, if you know that neighbourhood, you may have seen — "

"Miss Cameron! Certainly; it is an honour not easily
forgotten."

The old gentleman looked pleased.

"The dear child!" said he, with a burst of honest affection,
and he passed his hand over his eyes. Maltravers drew near
to him.

"You know Miss Cameron; you are to be envied, sir,"
said he.

"I have known her since she was a child; Lady Vargrave
is my dearest friend."

"Lady Vargrave must be worthy of such a daughter. Only
under the light of a sweet disposition and pure heart could
that beautiful nature have been trained and reared."

Maltravers spoke with enthusiasm; and, as if fearful to
trust himself more, left the room.

"That gentleman speaks not more warmly than justly," said
the old man, with some surprise. "He has a countenance

which, if physiognomy be a true science, declares his praise
to be no common compliment; may I inquire his name?"

"Maltravers," replied Cleveland, a little vain of the effect
his ex-pupil's name was to produce.

The curate — for it was he — started and changed countenance.

"Maltravers! but he is not about to leave the county?"

"Yes, for a few months."

Here the host entered. Four horses, that had been only
fourteen miles, had just re-entered the yard. If Mr. Maltravers could spare two to that gentleman, who had, indeed,
pre-engaged them?

"Certainly," said Cleveland; "but be quick."

"And is Lord Vargrave still at Mr. Merton's?" asked the
curate, musingly.

"Oh, yes, I believe so. Miss Cameron is to be married to
him very shortly, — is it not so?"

"I cannot say," returned Aubrey, rather bewildered. "You
know Lord Vargrave, sir?"

"Extremely well!"

"And you think him worthy of Miss Cameron?"

"That is a question for her to answer. But I see the
horses are put to. Good-day, sir! Will you tell your fair
young friend that you have met an old gentleman who
wishes her all happiness; and if she ask you his name, say
Cleveland?"

So saying, Mr. Cleveland bowed, and re-entered the carriage. But Maltravers was yet missing. In fact, he returned
to the house by the back way, and went once more into the
little parlour. It was something to see again one who would
so soon see Evelyn!

"If I mistake not," said Maltravers, "you are that Mr.
Aubrey on whose virtues I have often heard Miss Cameron
delight to linger? Will you believe my regret that our
acquaintance is now so brief?"

As Maltravers spoke thus simply, there was in his countenance, his voice, a melancholy sweetness, which greatly con-
ciliated the good curate; and as Aubrey gazed upon his noble

features and lofty mien, he no longer wondered at the fascination he had appeared to exercise over the young Evelyn.

"And may I not hope, Mr. Maltravers," said he, "that
before long our acquaintance may be renewed? Could not
Miss Cameron," he added, with a smile and a penetrating
look, "tempt you into Devonshire?"

Maltravers shook his head, and, muttering something not
very audible, quitted the room. The curate heard the whirl
of the wheels, and the host entered to inform him that his
own carriage was now ready.

"There is something in this," thought Aubrey, "which I
do not comprehend. His manner, his trembling voice, bespoke emotions he struggled to conceal. Can Lord Vargrave
have gained his point? Is Evelyn, indeed, no longer free?"

CHAPTER V.

CERTES, c'est un grand cas, Icas,
Que toujours tracas ou fracas
Vous faites d'une ou d'autre sort ;
C'est le diable qui vous emporte ! [1] — VOITURE.

LORD VARGRAVE had passed the night of the ball and the
following morning at Knaresdean. It was necessary to bring
the counsels of the scheming conclave to a full and definite
conclusion; and this was at last effected. Their strength
numbered, friends and foes alike canvassed and considered,
and due account taken of the waverers to be won over, it
really did seem, even to the least sanguine, that the Saxingham or Vargrave party was one that might well aspire either
to dictate to, or to break up, a government. Nothing now
was left to consider but the favourable hour for action. In
high spirits, Lord Vargrave returned about the middle of the
day to the rectory.

[1] "Certes, it is the fact, Icas, that you are always engaged in tricks or
scrapes of some sort or other ; it must be the devil that bewitches you."

"So," thought he, as he reclined in his carriage, — "so, in politics, the prospect clears as the sun breaks out. The party I have espoused is one that must be the most durable, for it possesses the greatest property and the most stubborn prejudice — what elements for Party! All that I now require is a sufficient fortune to back my ambition. Nothing can clog my way but these cursed debts, this disreputable want of gold. And yet Evelyn alarms me! Were I younger, or had I not made my position too soon, I would marry her by fraud or by force, — run off with her to Gretna, and make Vulcan minister to Plutus. But this would never do at my years, and with my reputation. A pretty story for the newspapers, d—n them! Well, nothing venture, nothing have; I will brave the hazard! Meanwhile, Doltimore is mine; Caroline will rule him, and I rule her. His vote and his boroughs are something, — his money will be more immediately useful: I must do him the honour to borrow a few thousands, — Caroline must manage that for me. The fool is miserly, though a spendthrift; and looked black when I delicately hinted the other day that I wanted a friend — *id est*, a loan! money and friendship same thing, — distinction without a difference!" Thus cogitating, Vargrave whiled away the minutes till his carriage stopped at Mr. Merton's door.

As he entered the hall he met Caroline, who had just quitted her own room.

"How lucky I am that you have on your bonnet! I long for a walk with you round the lawn."

"And I, too, am glad to see you, Lord Vargrave," said Caroline, putting her arm in his.

"Accept my best congratulations, my own sweet friend," said Vargrave, when they were in the grounds. "You have no idea how happy Doltimore is. He came to Knaresdean yesterday to communicate the news, and his neckcloth was primmer than ever. C'est un bon enfant."

"Ah, how can you talk thus? Do you feel no pain at the thought that — that I am another's?"

"Your heart will be ever mine, — and that is the true fidelity. What else, too, could be done? As for Lord Dolti-

more, we will go shares in him. Come, cheer thee, *m'amie;*
I rattle on thus to keep up your spirits. Do not fancy I
am happy!"

Caroline let fall a few tears; but beneath the influence of
Vargrave's sophistries and flatteries, she gradually recovered
her usual hard and worldly tone of mind.

"And where is Evelyn?" asked Vargrave. "Do you know,
the little witch seemed to be half mad the night of the ball.
Her head was turned; and when she sat next me at supper, she not only answered every question I put to her *à
tort et à travers,* but I fancied every moment she was going
to burst out crying. Can you tell what was the matter with
her?"

"She was grieved to hear that I was to be married to the
man I do not love. Ah, Vargrave, she has more heart than
you have!"

"But she never fancies that you love me?" asked Lumley,
in alarm. "You women are so confoundedly confidential!"

"No, she does not suspect our secret."

"Then I scarcely think your approaching marriage was a
sufficient cause for so much distraction."

"Perhaps she may have overheard some of the impertinent
whispers about her mother, — 'Who was Lady Vargrave?'
and 'What Cameron was Lady Vargrave's first husband?' *I*
overheard a hundred such vulgar questions; and provincial
people whisper so loud."

"Ah, that is a very probable solution of the mystery; and
for my part, I am almost as much puzzled as any one else can
be to know who Lady Vargrave was!"

"Did not your uncle tell you?"

"He told me that she was of no very elevated birth and
station, — nothing more; and she herself, with her quiet,
say-nothing manner, slips through all my careless question-
ings like an eel. She is still a beautiful creature, more regularly handsome than even Evelyn; and old Templeton had a
very sweet tooth at the back of his head, though he never
opened his mouth wide enough to show it."

"She must ever at least have been blameless, to judge by

an air which, even now, is more like that of a child than a matron."

"Yes; she has not much of the widow about her, poor soul! But her education, except in music, has not been very carefully attended to; and she knows about as much of the world as the Bishop of Autun (better known as Prince Talleyrand) knows of the Bible. If she were not so simple, she would be silly; but silliness is never simple, — always cunning; however, there is some cunning in her keeping her past Cameronian Chronicles so close. Perhaps I may know more about her in a short time, for I intend going to C——, where my uncle once lived, in order to see if I can revive under the rose — since peers are only contraband electioneerers — his old parliamentary influence in that city: and they may tell me more there than I now know."

"Did the late lord marry at C——?"

"No; in Devonshire. I do not even know if Mrs. Cameron ever was at C——."

"You must be curious to know who the father of your intended wife was?"

"Her father! No; I have no curiosity in that quarter. And, to tell you the truth, I am much too busy about the Present to be raking into that heap of rubbish we call the Past. I fancy that both your good grandmother and that comely old curate of Brook-Green know everything about Lady Vargrave; and, as they esteem her so much, I take it for granted she is *sans tache*."

"How could I be so stupid! *À propos* of the curate, I forgot to tell you that he is here. He arrived about two hours ago, and has been closeted with Evelyn ever since!"

"The deuce! What brought the old man hither?"

"That I know not. Papa received a letter from him yesterday morning, to say that he would be here to-day. Perhaps Lady Vargrave thinks it time for Evelyn to return home."

"What am I to do?" said Vargrave, anxiously. "Dare I yet venture to propose?"

"I am sure it will be in vain, Vargrave. You must prepare for disappointment."

"And ruin," muttered Vargrave, gloomily. "Hark you, Caroline, she may refuse me if she pleases. But I am not a man to be baffled. Have her I will, by one means or another; revenge urges me to it almost as much as ambition. That girl's thread of life has been the dark line in my woof; she has robbed me of fortune, she now thwarts me in my career, she humbles me in my vanity. But, like a hound that has tasted blood, I will run her down, whatever winding she takes."

"Vargrave, you terrify me! Reflect; we do not live in an age when violence — "

"Tush!" interrupted Lumley, with one of those dark looks which at times, though very rarely, swept away all its customary character from that smooth, shrewd countenance. "Tush! We live in an age as favourable to intellect and to energy as ever was painted in romance. I have that faith in fortune and myself that I tell you, with a prophet's voice, that Evelyn shall fulfil the wish of my dying uncle. But the bell summons us back."

On returning to the house, Lord Vargrave's valet gave him a letter which had arrived that morning. It was from Mr. Gustavus Douce, and ran thus: —

FLEET STREET, —— 20, 18—.

MY LORD, — It is with the greatest regret that I apprise you, for Self & Co., that we shall not be able in the present state of the Money Market to renew your Lordship's bill for £10,000, due the 28th instant. Respectfully calling your Lordship's attention to the same, I have the honour to be, for Self & Co., my Lord,

Your Lordship's most obedient and most obliged humble servant,

GUSTAVUS DOUCE.

To the Right Hon. LORD VARGRAVE, etc.

This letter sharpened Lord Vargrave's anxiety and resolve; nay, it seemed almost to sharpen his sharp features as he muttered sundry denunciations on Messrs. Douce and Co., while arranging his neckcloth at the glass.

CHAPTER VI.

Sol. Why, please your honourable lordship, we were talking here and there, — this and that. — *The Stranger.*

AUBREY had been closeted with Evelyn the whole morning; and, simultaneous with his arrival, came to her the news of the departure of Maltravers. It was an intelligence that greatly agitated and unnerved her; and, coupling that event with his solemn words on the previous night, Evelyn asked herself, in wonder, what sentiments she could have inspired in Maltravers. Could he love her, — her, so young, so inferior, so uninformed? Impossible! Alas! alas! for Maltravers! His genius, his gifts, his towering qualities, — all that won the admiration, almost the awe, of Evelyn, — placed him at a distance from her heart! When she asked herself if he loved her, she did not ask, even in that hour, if she loved him. But even the question she did ask, her judgment answered erringly in the negative. Why should he love, and yet fly her? She understood not his high-wrought scruples, his self-deluding belief. Aubrey was more puzzled than enlightened by his conversation with his pupil; only one thing seemed certain, — her delight to return to the cottage and her mother.

Evelyn could not sufficiently recover her composure to mix with the party below; and Aubrey, at the sound of the second dinner-bell, left her to her solitude, and bore her excuses to Mrs. Merton.

"Dear me!" said that worthy lady; "I am so sorry. I thought Miss Cameron looked fatigued at breakfast, and there was something hysterical in her spirits; and I suppose the surprise of your arrival has upset her. Caroline, my dear, you had better go and see what she would like to have taken up to her room, — a little soup and the wing of a chicken."

"My dear," said Mr. Merton, rather pompously, "I think it would be but a proper respect to Miss Cameron, if you yourself accompanied Caroline."

"I assure you," said the curate, alarmed at the avalanche of politeness that threatened poor Evelyn, — "I assure you that Miss Cameron would prefer being left alone at present; as you say, Mrs. Merton, her spirits are rather agitated."

But Mrs. Merton, with a sliding bow, had already quitted the room, and Caroline with her.

"Come back, Sophy! Cecilia, come back!" said Mr. Merton, settling his *jabot*.

"Oh, dear Evy! poor dear Evy! — Evy is ill!" said Sophy; "I may go to Evy? I must go, Papa!"

"No, my dear, you are too noisy; these children are quite spoiled, Mr. Aubrey."

The old man looked at them benevolently, and drew them to his knee; and, while Cissy stroked his long white hair, and Sophy ran on about dear Evy's prettiness and goodness, Lord Vargrave sauntered into the room.

On seeing the curate, his frank face lighted up with surprise and pleasure; he hastened to him, seized him by both hands, expressed the most heartfelt delight at seeing him, inquired tenderly after Lady Vargrave, and, not till he was out of breath, and Mrs. Merton and Caroline returning apprised him of Miss Cameron's indisposition, did his rapture vanish; and, as a moment before he was all joy, so now he was all sorrow.

The dinner passed off dully enough; the children, readmitted to dessert, made a little relief to all parties; and when they and the two ladies went, Aubrey himself quickly rose to join Evelyn.

"Are you going to Miss Cameron?" said Lord Vargrave; "pray say how unhappy I feel at her illness. I think these grapes — they are very fine — could not hurt her. May I ask you to present them with my best — best and most anxious regards? I shall be so uneasy till you return. Now, Merton (as the door closed on the curate), let's have another bottle of this famous claret! Droll old fellow that, — quite a character!"

"He is a great favourite with Lady Vargrave and Miss Cameron, I believe," said Mr. Merton. "A mere village priest, I suppose; no talent, no energy — or he could not be a curate at that age."

"Very true, — a shrewd remark. The Church is as good a profession as any other for getting on, if a man has anything in him. I shall live to see *you* a bishop!"

Mr. Merton shook his head.

"Yes, I shall; though you have hitherto disdained to exhibit any one of the three orthodox qualifications for a mitre."

"And what are they, my lord?"

"Editing a Greek play, writing a political pamphlet, and apostatizing at the proper moment."

"Ha, ha ! your lordship is severe on us."

"Not I; I often wish I had been brought up to the Church, — famous profession, properly understood. By Jupiter, I should have been a capital bishop!"

In his capacity of parson, Mr. Merton tried to look grave; in his capacity of a gentlemanlike, liberal fellow, he gave up the attempt, and laughed pleasantly at the joke of the rising man.

CHAPTER VII.

WILL nothing please you?
What do you think of the Court ? — *The Plain Dealer.*

ON one subject Aubrey found no difficulty in ascertaining Evelyn's wishes and condition of mind. The experiment of her visit, so far as Vargrave's hopes were concerned, had utterly failed; she could not contemplate the prospect of his alliance, and she poured out to the curate, frankly and fully, all her desire to effect a release from her engagement. As it was now settled that she should return with Aubrey to Brook-Green, it was indeed necessary to come to the long-delayed

understanding with her betrothed. Yet this was difficult, for
he had so little pressed, so distantly alluded to, their engagement, that it was like a forwardness, an indelicacy in Evelyn to
forestall the longed-for yet dreaded explanation. This, however, Aubrey took upon himself; and at this promise Evelyn
felt as the slave may feel when the chain is stricken off.

At breakfast, Mr. Aubrey communicated to the Mertons
Evelyn's intention to return with him to Brook-Green on the
following day. Lord Vargrave started, bit his lip, but said
nothing.

Not so silent was Mr. Merton.

"Return with you! my dear Mr. Aubrey, just consider; it is
impossible! You see Miss Cameron's rank of life, her position, — so very strange; no servants of her own here but her
woman, — no carriage even! You would not have her travel
in a post-chaise such a long journey! Lord Vargrave, you
can never consent to that, I am sure?"

"Were it only as Miss Cameron's *guardian*," said Lord
Vargrave, pointedly, "I should certainly object to such a
mode of performing such a journey. Perhaps Mr. Aubrey
means to perfect the project by taking two outside places on
the top of the coach?"

"Pardon me," said the curate, mildly, "but I am not so
ignorant of what is due to Miss Cameron as you suppose.
Lady Vargrave's carriage, which brought me hither, will be
no unsuitable vehicle for Lady Vargrave's daughter; and Miss
Cameron is not, I trust, quite so spoiled by all your friendly
attentions as to be unable to perform a journey of two days
with no other protector than myself."

"I forgot Lady Vargrave's carriage, — or rather I was not
aware that you had used it, my dear sir," said Mr. Merton.
"But you must not blame us, if we are sorry to lose Miss
Cameron so suddenly; I was in hopes that *you* too would stay
at least a week with us."

The curate bowed at the rector's condescending politeness;
and just as he was about to answer, Mrs. Merton put in, —

"And you see I had set my heart on her being Caroline's
bridesmaid."

Caroline turned pale, and glanced at Vargrave, who appeared solely absorbed in breaking toast into his tea, — a delicacy he had never before been known to favour.

There was an awkward pause. The servant opportunely entered with a small parcel of books, a note to Mr. Merton, and that most blessed of all blessed things in the country, — the letter-bag.

"What is this?" said the rector, opening his note, while Mrs. Merton unlocked the bag and dispensed the contents: "Left Burleigh for some months, a day or two sooner than he had expected; excuse French leave-taking; return Miss Merton's books, much obliged; gamekeeper has orders to place the Burleigh preserves at my disposal. So we have lost our neighbour!"

"Did you not know Mr. Maltravers was gone?" said Caroline. "I heard so from Jenkins last night; he accompanies Mr. Cleveland to Paris."

"Indeed!" said Mrs. Merton, opening her eyes. "What could take him to Paris?"

"Pleasure, I suppose," answered Caroline. "I'm sure I should rather have wondered what could detain him at Burleigh."

Vargrave was all this while breaking open seals and running his eyes over sundry scrawls with the practised rapidity of the man of business; he came to the last letter. His countenance brightened.

"Royal invitation, or rather command, to Windsor," he cried. "I am afraid I, too, must leave you, this very day."

"Bless me!" exclaimed Mrs. Merton; "is that from the king? Do let me see!"

"Not exactly from the king; the same thing though:" and Lord Vargrave, carelessly pushing the gracious communication towards the impatient hand and loyal gaze of Mrs. Merton, carefully put the other letters in his pocket, and walked musingly to the window.

Aubrey seized the opportunity to approach him. "My lord, can I speak with you a few moments?"

"Me! certainly; will you come to my dressing-room?"

CHAPTER VIII.

. . . THERE was never
Poor gentleman had such a sudden fortune.
BEAUMONT AND FLETCHER : *The Captain*, Act v. sc. 5

"MY LORD," said the curate, as Vargrave, leaning back in
his chair, appeared to examine the shape of his boots, while
in reality "his sidelong looks," not "of love," were fixed
upon his companion, — "I need scarcely refer to the wish of
the late lord, your uncle, relative to Miss Cameron and yourself; nor need I, to one of a generous spirit, add that an
engagement could be only so far binding as both the parties
whose happiness is concerned should be willing in proper time
and season to fulfil it."

"Sir!" said Vargrave, impatiently waving his hand; and,
in his irritable surmise of what was to come, losing his habitual self-control, "I know not what all this has to do with
you; surely you trespass upon ground sacred to Miss Cameron
and myself? Whatever you have to say, let me beg you to
come at once to the point."

"My lord, I will obey you. Miss Cameron — and, I may
add, with Lady Vargrave's consent — deputes me to say
that, although she feels compelled to decline the honour of
your lordship's alliance, yet if in any arrangement of the fortune bequeathed to her she could testify to you, my lord, her
respect and friendship, it would afford her the most sincere
gratification."

Lord Vargrave started.

"Sir," said he, "I know not if I am to thank you for this
information, the announcement of which so strangely coin-
cides with your arrival. But allow me to say that there needs
no ambassador between Miss Cameron and myself. It is due,
sir, to my station, to my relationship, to my character of
guardian, to my long and faithful affection, to all considera-

tions which men of the world understand, which men of feeling sympathize with, to receive from Miss Cameron alone the
rejection of my suit."

"Unquestionably Miss Cameron will grant your lordship
the interview you have a right to seek; but pardon me, I
thought it might save you both much pain, if the meeting
were prepared by a third person; and on any matter of business, any atonement to your lordship — "

"Atonement! what can atone to me?" exclaimed Vargrave,
as he walked to and fro the room in great disorder and excitement.   "Can you give me back years of hope and expectancy,
— the manhood wasted in a vain dream?   Had I not been
taught to look to this reward, should I have rejected all occasion — while my youth was not yet all gone, while my heart
was not yet all occupied — to form a suitable alliance?   Nay,
should I have indulged in a high and stirring career, for
which **my** own fortune is by no means qualified?   Atonement! atonement!   Talk of atonement to boys!   Sir, I stand
before you a man whose private happiness is blighted, whose
public prospects are darkened, life wasted, fortunes ruined, the
schemes of an existence built upon one hope, which was law-
fully indulged, overthrown; and you talk to me of *atonement!*"

Selfish as the nature of this complaint might be, Aubrey
was struck with its justice.

"My lord," said he, a little embarrassed, "I cannot deny
that there is truth in much of what you say.   Alas! it proves
how vain it is for man to calculate on the future; how unhappily your uncle erred in imposing conditions, which the
chances of life and the caprices of affection could at any
time dissolve!   But this is blame that attaches only to the
dead: can you blame the living?"

"Sir, I considered myself bound by my uncle's prayer to
keep my hand and heart disengaged, that this title — miserable and barren distinction though it be! — might, as he so
ardently desired, descend to Evelyn.   I had a right to expect
similar honour upon her side!"

"Surely, my lord, you, to whom the late lord on his death-
bed confided all the motives of his conduct and the secret of

his life, cannot but be aware that, while desirous of promoting your worldly welfare, and uniting in one line his rank and
his fortune, your uncle still had Evelyn's happiness at heart
as his warmest wish; you must know that, if that happiness
were forfeited by a marriage with you, the marriage became
but a secondary consideration.   Lord Vargrave's will in itself
was a proof of this.   He did not impose as an absolute condition upon Evelyn her union with yourself; he did not make
the forfeiture of her whole wealth the penalty of her rejection
of that alliance.   By the definite limit of the forfeit, he intimated a distinction between a command and à desire.   And
surely, when you consider all circumstances, your lordship
must think that, what with that forfeit and the estate settled
upon the title, your uncle did all that in a worldly point of
view equity and even affection could exact from him."

Vargrave smiled bitterly, but said nothing.

"And if this be doubted, I have clearer proof of his intentions.   Such was his confidence in Lady Vargrave, that in the
letter he addressed to her before his death, and which I now
submit to your lordship, you will observe that he not only
expressly leaves it to Lady Vargrave's discretion to communicate to Evelyn that history of which she is at present ignorant, but that he also clearly defines the line of conduct he
wished to be adopted with respect to Evelyn and yourself.
Permit me to point out the passage."

Impatiently Lord Vargrave ran his eye over the letter
placed in his hand, till he came to these lines: —

" And if, when she has arrived at the proper age to form a judgment,
Evelyn should decide against Lumley's claims, you know that on no account would I sacrifice her happiness; that all I require is, that fair
play be given to his pretensions, due indulgence to the scheme I have
long had at heart.   Let her be brought up to consider him her future
husband ; let her not be prejudiced against him ; let her fairly judge for
herself, when the time arrives."

"You see, my lord," said Mr. Aubrey, as he took back the
letter, "that this letter bears the same date as your uncle's
will.   What he desired has been done.   Be just, my lord, be

just, and exonerate us all from blame: who can dictate to the affections?"

"And I am to understand that I have no chance, now or hereafter, of obtaining the affections of Evelyn? Surely, at your age, Mr. Aubrey, you cannot encourage the heated romance common to all girls of Evelyn's age. Persons of our rank do not marry like the Corydon and Phyllis of a pastoral. At my years, I never was fool enough to expect that I should inspire a girl of seventeen with what is called a passionate attachment. But happy marriages are based upon suitable circumstances, mutual knowledge and indulgence, respect, esteem. Come, sir, let me hope yet, — let me hope that, on the same day, I may congratulate you on your preferment and you may congratulate me upon my marriage."

Vargrave said this with a cheerful and easy smile; and the tone of his voice was that of a man who wished to convey serious meaning in a jesting accent.

Mr. Aubrey, meek as he was, felt the insult of the hinted bribe, and coloured with a resentment no sooner excited than checked. "Excuse me, my lord, I have now said all; the rest had better be left to your ward herself."

"Be it so, sir. I will ask you, then, to convey my request to Evelyn to honour me with a last and parting interview."

Vargrave flung himself on his chair, and Aubrey left him.

CHAPTER IX.

THUS airy Strephon tuned his lyre. — SHENSTONE.

IN his meeting with Evelyn, Vargrave certainly exerted to the utmost all his ability and all his art. He felt that violence, that sarcasm, that selfish complaint would not avail in a man who was not loved, — though they are often admirable cards in the hands of a man who is. As his own heart was

perfectly untouched in the matter, except by rage and disappointment, — feelings which with him never lasted very long,
— he could play coolly his losing game. His keen and ready
intellect taught him that all he could now expect was to be-
queath sentiments of generous compassion and friendly interest; to create a favourable impression, which he might
hereafter improve; to reserve, in short, some spot of vantage-
ground in the country from which he was to affect to withdraw all his forces. He had known, in his experience of
women, which, whether as an actor or a spectator, was large
and various — though not among very delicate and refined
natures — that a lady often takes a fancy to a suitor *after* she
has rejected him; that precisely *because* she has once rejected
she ultimately accepts him. And even this chance was, in
circumstances so desperate, not to be neglected. He assumed,
therefore, the countenance, the postures, and the voice of
heart-broken but submissive despair; he affected a nobleness
and magnanimity in his grief, which touched Evelyn to the
quick, and took her by surprise.

"It is enough," said he, in sad and faltering accents; "quite
enough for me to know that you cannot love me, — that I
should fail in rendering you happy. Say no more, Evelyn,
say no more! Let me spare you, at least, the pain your generous nature must feel in my anguish. I resign all pretensions to your hand; you are free! — may you be happy!"

"Oh, Lord Vargrave! oh, Lumley!" said Evelyn, weeping,
and moved by a thousand recollections of early years. "If I
could but prove in any other way my grateful sense of your
merits, your too partial appreciation of me, my regard for my
lost benefactor, then, indeed, nor till then, could I be happy.
Oh that this wealth, so little desired by me, had been more at
my disposal! but as it is, the day that sees me in possession
of it, shall see it placed under your disposition, your control.
This is but justice, — common justice to you; you were the
nearest relation of the departed. I had no claim on him, —
none but affection. Affection! and yet I disobey him!"

There was much in all this that secretly pleased Vargrave;
but it only seemed to redouble his grief.

"Talk not thus, my ward, my friend — ah, still my friend,"
said he, putting his handkerchief to his eyes.   "I repine not;
I am more than satisfied.   Still let me preserve my privilege
of guardian, of adviser, — a privilege dearer to me than all
the wealth of the Indies! "

Lord Vargrave had some faint suspicion that Legard had
created an undue interest in Evelyn's heart; and on this point
he delicately and indirectly sought to sound her.   Her replies
convinced him that if Evelyn had conceived any prepossession
for Legard, there had not been time or opportunity to ripen it
into deep attachment.   Of Maltravers he had no fear.   The
habitual self-control of that reserved personage deceived him
partly; and his low opinion of mankind deceived him still
more.   For if there had been any love between Maltravers
and Evelyn, why should the former not have stood his ground,
and declared his suit?   Lumley would have "bah'd" and
"pish'd" at the thought of any punctilious regard for engagements so easily broken having power either to check passion
for beauty, or to restrain self-interest in the chase of an
heiress.   He had known Maltravers ambitious; and with
him, ambition and self-interest meant the same.   Thus, by
the very *finesse* of his character — while Vargrave ever with
the worldly was a keen and almost infallible observer — with
natures of a more refined, or a higher order, he always missed
the mark by overshooting.   Besides, had a suspicion of Maltravers ever crossed him, Caroline's communications would
have dispelled it.   It was more strange that Caroline should
have been blind; nor would she have been so had she been
less absorbed in her own schemes and destinies.   All her usual
penetration had of late settled in self; and an uneasy feeling
— half arising from conscientious reluctance to aid Vargrave's
objects, half from jealous irritation at the thought of Vargrave's marrying another — had prevented her from seeking
any very intimate or confidential communication with Evelyn
herself.

The dreaded conference was over; Evelyn parted from Vargrave with the very feelings he had calculated on exciting, —
the moment he ceased to be her lover, her old childish regard

for him recommenced. She pitied his dejection, she respected his generosity, she was deeply grateful for his forbearance. But still — still she was free; and her heart bounded within her at the thought.

Meanwhile, Vargrave, after his solemn farewell to Evelyn, retreated again to his own room, where he remained till his post-horses arrived. Then, descending into the drawing-room, he was pleased to find neither Aubrey nor Evelyn there. He knew that much affectation would be thrown away upon Mr. and Mrs. Merton; he thanked them for their hospitality, with grave and brief cordiality, and then turned to Caroline, who stood apart by the window.

"All is up with me at present," he whispered. "I leave you, Caroline, in anticipation of fortune, rank, and prosperity; that is some comfort. For myself, I see only difficulties, embarrassment, and poverty in the future; but I despond of nothing. Hereafter you may serve me, as I have served you. Adieu! — I have been advising Caroline not to spoil Doltimore, Mrs. Merton; he is conceited enough already. Good-by! God bless you all! love to your little girls. Let me know if I can serve you in any way, Merton, — good-by again!" And thus, sentence by sentence, Vargrave talked himself into his carriage. As it drove by the drawing-room windows, he saw Caroline standing motionless where he had left her; he kissed his hand, — her eyes were fixed mournfully on his. Hard, wayward, and worldly as Caroline Merton was, Vargrave was yet not worthy of the affection he had inspired; for she could *feel*, and he could not, — the distinction, perhaps, between the sexes. And there still stood Caroline Merton, recalling the last tones of that indifferent voice, till she felt her hand seized, and turned round to see Lord Doltimore, and smile upon the happy lover, persuaded that he was adored!

BOOK VI.

Πῦρ σοὶ προσοίσω, κοὐ τὸ σὸν προσκέψομαι. — EURIPIDES : *Andromache,* 214.

"I will bring fire to thee — I reck not of the place."

CHAPTER I.

. . . THIS ancient city,
How wanton sits she amidst Nature's smiles!

. . . Various nations meet,
As in the sea, yet not confined in space,
But streaming freely through the spacious streets. — YOUNG.

. . . His teeth he still did grind,
And grimly gnash, threatening revenge in vain. — SPENSER.

"PARIS is a delightful place, — that is allowed by all. It
is delightful to the young, to the gay, to the idle; to the literary lion, who likes to be petted; to the wiser epicure, who
indulges a more justifiable appetite. It is delightful to ladies,
who wish to live at their ease, and buy beautiful caps; delightful to philanthropists, who wish for listeners to schemes
of colonizing the moon; delightful to the haunters of balls
and ballets, and little theatres and superb *cafés*, where men
with beards of all sizes and shapes scowl at the English, and
involve their intellects in the fascinating game of dominos.
For these, and for many others, Paris is delightful. I say
nothing against it. But, for my own part, I would rather
live in a garret in London than in a palace in the Chaussée
d'Antin. — 'Chacun à son mauvais goût.'

"I don't like the streets, in which I cannot walk but in the
kennel; I don't like the shops, that contain nothing except

what's at the window; I don't like the houses, like prisons which look upon a courtyard; I don't like the *beaux jardins*, which grow no plants save a Cupid in plaster; I don't like the wood fires, which demand as many *petits soins* as the women, and which warm no part of one but one's eyelids, I don't like the language, with its strong phrases about nothing, and vibrating like a pendulum between ' rapture ' and ' desolation; ' I don't like the accent, which one cannot get, without speaking through one's nose; I don't like the eternal fuss and jabber about books without nature, and revolutions without fruit; I have no sympathy with tales that turn on a dead jackass, nor with constitutions that give the ballot to the representatives, and withhold the suffrage from the people; neither have I much faith in that enthusiasm for the *beaux arts*, which shows its produce in execrable music, detestable pictures, abominable sculpture, and a droll something that I believe the *French* call POETRY. Dancing and cookery, — these are the arts the French excel in, I grant it; and excellent things they are; but oh, England! oh, Germany! you need not be jealous of your rival! "

These are not the author's remarks, — he disowns them; they were Mr. Cleveland's. He was a prejudiced man; Maltravers was more liberal, but then Maltravers did not pretend to be a wit.

Maltravers had been several weeks in the city of cities, and now he had his apartments in the gloomy but interesting Faubourg St. Germain, all to himself. For Cleveland, having attended eight days at a sale, and having moreover ransacked all the curiosity shops, and shipped off bronzes and cabinets, and Genoese silks and *objets de vertu*, enough to have half furnished Fonthill, had fulfilled his mission, and returned to his villa. Before the old gentleman went, he flattered himself that change of air and scene had already been serviceable to his friend; and that time would work a complete cure upon that commonest of all maladies, — an unrequited passion, or an ill-placed caprice.

Maltravers, indeed, in the habit of conquering, as well as of concealing emotion, vigorously and earnestly strove to dethrone the image that had usurped his heart. Still vain of his self-command, and still worshipping his favourite virtue of Fortitude and his delusive philosophy of the calm Golden Mean, he would not weakly indulge the passion, while he so sternly fled from its object.

But yet the image of Evelyn pursued, — it haunted him; it came on him unawares, in solitude, in crowds. That smile so cheering, yet so soft, that ever had power to chase away the shadow from his soul; that youthful and luxurious bloom of pure and eloquent thoughts, which was as the blossom of genius before its fruit, bitter as well as sweet, is born; that rare union of quick feeling and serene temper, which forms the very ideal of what we dream of in the mistress, and exact from the wife, — all, even more, far more, than the exquisite form and the delicate graces of the less durable beauty, returned to him, after every struggle with himself; and time only seemed to grave, in deeper if more latent folds of his heart, the ineradicable impression.

Maltravers renewed his acquaintance with some persons not unfamiliar to the reader.

Valerie de Ventadour — how many recollections of the fairer days of life were connected with that name! Precisely as she had never reached to his love, but only excited his fancy (the fancy of twenty-two), had her image always retained a pleasant and grateful hue; it was blended with no deep sorrow, no stern regret, no dark remorse, no haunting shame.

They met again. Madame de Ventadour was still beautiful, and still admired, — perhaps more admired than ever; for to the great, fashion and celebrity bring a second and yet more popular youth. But Maltravers, if rejoiced to see how gently Time had dealt with the fair Frenchwoman, was yet more pleased to read in her fine features a more serene and contented expression than they had formerly worn. Valerie de Ventadour had preceded her younger admirer through the " MYSTERIES OF LIFE; " she had learned the real objects of being; she distinguished between the Actual and the Visionary, the Shadow and the Substance; she had acquired content for the present, and looked with quiet hope towards the future.

Her character was still spotless; or rather, every year of temptation and trial had given it a fairer lustre.   Love, that might
have ruined, being once subdued, preserved her from all after
danger.   The first meeting between Maltravers and Valerie
was, it is true, one of some embarrassment and reserve: not
so the second.   They did but once, and that slightly, recur to
the past, and from that moment, as by a tacit understanding,
true friendship between them dated.   Neither felt mortified
to see that an illusion had passed away, — they were no longer
the same in each other's eyes.   Both might be improved, and
were so; but the Valerie and the Ernest of Naples were as
things dead and gone!   Perhaps Valerie's heart was even more
reconciled to the cure of its soft and luxurious malady by the
renewal of their acquaintance.   The mature and experienced
reasoner, in whom enthusiasm had undergone its usual change,
with the calm brow and commanding aspect of sober manhood,
was a being so different from the romantic boy, new to the
actual world of civilized toils and pleasures, fresh from the
adventures of Eastern wanderings, and full of golden dreams
of poetry before it settles into authorship or action!   She
missed the brilliant errors, the daring aspirations, — even the
animated gestures and eager eloquence, — that had interested
and enamoured her in the loiterer by the shores of Baiæ, or
amidst the tomb-like chambers of Pompeii.   For the Maltravers now before her — wiser, better, nobler, even handsomer
than of yore (for he was one whom manhood became better
than youth) — the Frenchwoman could at any period have felt
friendship without danger.   It seemed to her, not as it really
was, the natural *development*, but the very *contrast*, of the
ardent, variable, imaginative boy, by whose side she had
gazed at night on the moonlit waters and rosy skies of the
soft Parthenope!   How does time, after long absence, bring
to us such contrasts between the one we remember and the
one we see!   And what a melancholy mockery does it seem of
our own vain hearts, dreaming of impressions never to be
changed, and affections that never can grow cool!

And now, as they conversed with all the ease of cordial and
guileless friendship, how did Valerie rejoice in secret that

upon that friendship there rested no blot of shame! and that she had not forfeited those consolations for a home without love, which had at last settled into cheerful nor unhallowed resignation, — consolations only to be found in the conscience and the pride!

M. de Ventadour had not altered, except that his nose was longer, and that he now wore a peruque in full curl instead of his own straight hair. But somehow or other — perhaps by the mere charm of custom — he had grown more pleasing in Valerie's eyes; habit had reconciled her to his foibles, deficiencies, and faults; and, by comparison with others, she could better appreciate his good qualities, such as they were, — generosity, good-temper, good-nature, and unbounded indulgence to herself. Husband and wife have so many interests in common, that when they have jogged on through the ups and downs of life a sufficient time, the leash which at first galled often grows easy and familiar; and unless the *temper*, or rather the disposition and the heart, of either be insufferable, what was once a grievous yoke becomes but a companionable tie. And for the rest, Valerie, now that sentiment and fancy were sobered down, could take pleasure in a thousand things which her pining affections once, as it were, overlooked and overshot. She could feel grateful for all the advantages her station and wealth procured her; she could cull the roses in her reach, without sighing for the amaranths of Elysium.

If the great have more temptations than those of middle life, and if their senses of enjoyment become more easily pampered into a sickly apathy, so at least (if they can once outlive satiety) they have many more resources at their command. There is a great deal of justice in the old line, displeasing though it be to those who think of love in a cottage, "'T is best repenting in a coach and six!" If among the Eupatrids, the Well Born, there is less love in wedlock, less quiet happiness at home, still they are less chained each to each, — they have more independence, both the woman and the man, and occupations and the solace without can be so easily obtained! Madame de Ventadour, in retiring from the mere frivolities of society — from crowded rooms, and the

inane talk and hollow smiles of mere acquaintanceship — became more sensible of the pleasures that her refined and elegant intellect could derive from art and talent, and the
communion of friendship. She drew around her the most
cultivated minds of her time and country. Her abilities, her
wit, and her conversational graces enabled her not only to
mix on equal terms with the most eminent, but to amalgamate
and blend the varieties of talent into harmony. The same
persons, when met elsewhere, seemed to have lost their charm;
under Valerie's roof every one breathed a congenial atmosphere. And music and letters, and all that can refine and
embellish civilized life, contributed their resources to this
gifted and beautiful woman. And thus she found that the
mind has excitement and occupation, as well as the heart;
and, unlike the latter, the culture we bestow upon the first
ever yields us its return. We talk of education for the poor,
but we forget how much it is needed by the rich. Valerie was
a living instance of the advantages to women of knowledge
and intellectual resources. By them she had purified her
fancy, by them she had conquered discontent, by them she
had grown reconciled to life and to her lot! When the heavy
heart weighed down the one scale, it was the mind that restored the balance.

The spells of Madame de Ventadour drew Maltravers into
this charmed circle of all that was highest, purest, and most
gifted in the society of Paris. There he did not meet, as
were met in the times of the old *régime,* sparkling abbés
intent upon intrigues; or amorous old dowagers, eloquent on
Rousseau; or powdered courtiers, uttering epigrams against
kings and religions, — straws that foretold the whirlwind.
Paul Courier was right! Frenchmen are Frenchmen still;
they are full of fine phrases, and their thoughts smell of the
theatre; they mistake foil for diamonds, the Grotesque for
the Natural, the Exaggerated for the Sublime: but still I
say, Paul Courier was right, — there is more honesty now in
a single *salon* in Paris than there was in all France in the
days of Voltaire. Vast interests and solemn causes are no
longer tossed about like shuttlecocks on the battledores of

empty tongues. In the *bouleversement* of Revolutions the French have fallen on their feet!

Meeting men of all parties and all classes, Maltravers was struck with the heightened tone of public morals, the earnest sincerity of feeling which generally pervaded all, as compared with his first recollections of the Parisians. He saw that true elements for national wisdom were at work, though he saw also that there was no country in which their operations would be more liable to disorder, more slow and irregular in their results. The French are like the Israelites in the Wilderness, when, according to a Hebrew tradition, every morning they seemed on the verge of Pisgah, and every evening they were as far from it as ever. But still time rolls on, the pilgrimage draws to its close, and the Canaan must come at last!

At Valerie's house, Maltravers once more met the De Montaignes. It was a painful meeting, for they thought of Cesarini when they met.

It is now time to return to that unhappy man. Cesarini had been removed from England when Maltravers quitted it after Lady Florence's death; and Maltravers had thought it best to acquaint De Montaigne with all the circumstances that had led to his affliction. The pride and the honour of the high-spirited Frenchman were deeply shocked by the tale of fraud and guilt, softened as it was; but the sight of the criminal, his awful punishment, merged every other feeling in compassion. Placed under the care of the most skilful practitioners in Paris, great hopes of Cesarini's recovery had been at first entertained. Nor was it long, indeed, before he appeared entirely restored, so far as the external and superficial tokens of sanity could indicate a cure. He testified complete consciousness of the kindness of his relations, and clear remembrance of the past: but to the incoherent ravings of delirium, an intense melancholy, still more deplorable, succeeded. In this state, however, he became once more the inmate of his brother-in-law's house; and though avoiding all society, except that of Teresa, whose affectionate nature never wearied of its cares, he resumed many of his old occupations. Again he appeared to take delight in desultory and unprofit-

able studies, and in the cultivation of that luxury of solitary
men, "the thankless muse." By shunning all topics connected with the gloomy cause of his affliction, and talking
rather of the sweet recollections of Italy and childhood than
of more recent events, his sister was enabled to soothe the
dark hour, and preserve some kind of influence over the ill-
fated man. One day, however, there fell into his hands an
English newspaper, which was full of the praises of Lord
Vargrave; and the article in lauding the peer referred to his
services as the commoner Lumley Ferrers.

This incident, slight as it appeared, and perfectly untrace-
able by his relations, produced a visible effect on Cesarini;
and three days afterwards he attempted his own life. The
failure of the attempt was followed by the fiercest paroxysms.
His disease returned in all its dread force: and it became
necessary to place him under yet stricter confinement than he
had endured before. Again, about a year from the date now
entered upon, he had appeared to recover; and again he was
removed to De Montaigne's house. His relations were not
aware of the influence which Lord Vargrave's name exercised
over Cesarini; in the melancholy tale communicated to them
by Maltravers, that name had not been mentioned. If Maltravers had at one time entertained some vague suspicions that
Lumley had acted a treacherous part with regard to Florence,
those suspicions had long since died away for want of confirmation; nor did he (nor did therefore the De Montaignes)
connect Lord Vargrave with the affliction of Cesarini. De
Montaigne himself, therefore, one day at dinner, alluding to
a question of foreign politics which had been debated that
morning in the Chamber, and in which he himself had taken
an active part, happened to refer to a speech of Vargrave upon
the subject, which had made some sensation abroad, as well as
at home. Teresa asked innocently who Lord Vargrave was;
and De Montaigne, well acquainted with the biography of
the principal English statesmen, replied that he had commenced his career as Mr. Ferrers, and reminded Teresa that
they had once been introduced to him in Paris. Cesarini suddenly rose and left the room; his absence was not noted, for

his comings and goings were ever strange and fitful. Teresa soon afterwards quitted the apartment with her children, and De Montaigne, who was rather fatigued by the exertions and excitement of the morning, stretched himself in his chair to enjoy a short *siesta*. He was suddenly awakened by a feeling of pain and suffocation, — awakened in time to struggle against a strong gripe that had fastened itself at his throat. The room was darkened in the growing shades of the evening; and, but for the glittering and savage eyes that were fixed on him, he could scarcely discern his assailant. He at length succeeded, however, in freeing himself, and casting the intended assassin on the ground. He shouted for assistance; and the lights borne by the servants who rushed into the room revealed to him the face of his brother-in-law. Cesarini, though in strong convulsions, still uttered cries and imprecations of revenge; he denounced De Montaigne as a traitor and a murderer! In the dark confusion of his mind, he had mistaken the guardian for the distant foe, whose name sufficed to conjure up the phantoms of the dead, and plunge reason into fury.

It was now clear that there was danger and death in Cesarini's disease. His madness was pronounced to be capable of no certain and permanent cure; he was placed at a new asylum (the superintendents of which were celebrated for humanity as well as skill), a little distance from Versailles, and there he still remained. Recently his lucid intervals had become more frequent and prolonged; but trifles that sprang from his own mind, and which no care could prevent or detect, sufficed to renew his calamity in all its fierceness. At such times he required the most unrelaxing vigilance, for his madness ever took an alarming and ferocious character; and had he been left unshackled, the boldest and stoutest of the keepers would have dreaded to enter his cell unarmed, or alone.

What made the disease of the mind appear more melancholy and confirmed was, that all this time the frame seemed to increase in health and strength. This is not an uncommon case in instances of mania — and it is generally the worst

symptom. In earlier youth, Cesarini had been delicate even
to effeminacy; but now his proportions were enlarged, his
form, though still lean and spare, muscular and vigorous, —
as if in the torpor which usually succeeded to his bursts of
frenzy, the animal portion gained by the repose or disorgani-
zation of the intellectual. When in his better and calmer
mood — in which indeed none but the experienced could have
detected his malady — books made his chief delight. But
then he complained bitterly, if briefly, of the confinement he
endured, of the injustice he suffered; and as, shunning all
companions, he walked gloomily amidst the grounds that surrounded that House of Woe, his unseen guardians beheld him
clenching his hands, as at some visionary enemy, or overheard
him accuse some phantom of his brain of the torments he
endured.

Though the reader can detect in Lumley Ferrers the cause
of the frenzy, and the object of the imprecation, it was not so
with the De Montaignes, nor with the patient's keepers and
physicians; for in his delirium he seldom or never gave name
to the shadows that he invoked, — not even to that of Florence. It is, indeed, no unusual characteristic of madness to
shun, as by a kind of cunning, all mention of the names of
those by whom the madness has been caused. It is as if the
unfortunates imagined that the madness might be undiscov-
ered if the images connected with it were unbetrayed.

Such, at this time, was the wretched state of the man,
whose talents had promised a fair and honourable career,
had it not been the wretched tendency of his mind, from boy-
hood upward, to pamper every unwholesome and unhallowed
feeling as a token of the exuberance of genius. De Montaigne, though he touched as lightly as possible upon this
dark domestic calamity in his first communications with Maltravers, whose conduct in that melancholy tale of crime and
woe had, he conceived, been stamped with generosity and
feeling, still betrayed emotions that told how much his peace
had been embittered.

"I seek to console Teresa," said he, turning away his manly
head, "and to point out all the blessings yet left to her; but

that brother so beloved, from whom so much was so vainly expected, — still ever and ever, though she strives to conceal it from me, this affliction comes back to her, and poisons every thought! Oh, better a thousand times that he had died! When reason, sense, almost the soul, are dead, how dark and fiend-like is the life that remains behind! And if it should be in the blood — if Teresa's children — dreadful thought!"

De Montaigne ceased, thoroughly overcome.

"Do not, my dear friend, so fearfully exaggerate your misfortune, great as it is; Cesarini's disease evidently arose from no physical conformation, — it was but the crisis, the development, of a long-contracted malady of mind, passions morbidly indulged, the reasoning faculty obstinately neglected; and yet too he may recover. The further memory recedes from the shock he has sustained, the better the chance that his mind will regain its tone."

De Montaigne wrung his friend's hand.

"It is strange that from you should come sympathy and comfort! — you whom he so injured; you whom his folly or his crime drove from your proud career, and your native soil! But Providence will yet, I trust, redeem the evil of its erring creature, and I shall yet live to see you restored to hope and home, a happy husband, an honoured citizen. Till then, I feel as if the curse lingered upon my race."

"Speak not thus. Whatever my destiny, I have recovered from that wound; and still, De Montaigne, I find in life that suffering succeeds to suffering, and disappointment to disappointment, as wave to wave. To endure is the only philosophy; to believe that we shall live again in a brighter planet, is the only hope that our reason should accept from our desires."

16

CHAPTER II.

Monstra evenerunt mihi :
Introit in ædes ater alienus canis,
Anguis per impluvium decidit de tegulis,
Gallina cecinit ! [1] — TERENCE.

WITH his constitutional strength of mind, and conformably
with his acquired theories, Maltravers continued to struggle
against the latest and strongest passion of his life.   It might
be seen in the paleness of his brow, and that nameless expression of suffering which betrays itself in the lines about the
mouth, that his health was affected by the conflict within
him; and many a sudden fit of absence and abstraction, many
an impatient sigh, followed by a forced and unnatural gayety,
told the observant Valerie that he was the prey of a sorrow
he was too proud to disclose.   He compelled himself, however, to take, or to affect, an interest in the singular phenomena of the social state around him, — phenomena that, in
a happier or serener mood, would indeed have suggested no
ordinary food for conjecture and meditation.

The state of *visible transition* is the state of nearly all the
enlightened communities in Europe.   But nowhere is it so
pronounced as in that country which may be called the Heart
of European Civilization.   There, all to which the spirit of
society attaches itself appears broken, vague, and half developed, — the Antique in ruins, and the New not formed.   It
is, perhaps, the only country in which the Constructive principle has not kept pace with the Destructive.   The Has Been
is blotted out; the To Be is as the shadow of a far land in a
mighty and perturbed sea.[2]

---

[1] " Prodigies have occurred   a strange black dog came into the house ; a
snake glided from the tiles, through the court; the hen crowed."

[2] The reader will remember that these remarks were written long before
the last French Revolution, and when the dynasty of Louis Philippe was generally considered most secure.

Maltravers, who for several years had not examined the progress of modern literature, looked with mingled feelings of surprise, distaste, and occasional and most reluctant admiration, on the various works which the successors of Voltaire and Rousseau have produced, and are pleased to call the offspring of Truth united to Romance.

Profoundly versed in the mechanism and elements of those masterpieces of Germany and England, from which the French have borrowed so largely while pretending to be original, Maltravers was shocked to see the monsters which these Frankensteins had created from the relics and the offal of the holiest sepulchres. The head of a giant on the limbs of a dwarf, incongruous members jumbled together, parts fair and beautiful, — the whole a hideous distortion!

"It may be possible," said he to De Montaigne, "that these works are admired and extolled; but how they can be vindicated by the examples of Shakspeare and Goethe, or even of Byron, who redeemed poor and melodramatic conceptions with a manly vigour of execution, an energy and completeness of purpose, that Dryden himself never surpassed, is to me utterly inconceivable."

"I allow that there is a strange mixture of fustian and maudlin in all these things," answered De Montaigne; "but they are but the windfalls of trees that may bear rich fruit in due season; meanwhile, any new school is better than eternal imitations of the old. As for critical vindications of the works themselves, the age that produces the phenomena is never the age to classify and analyze them. We have had a deluge, and now new creatures spring from the new soil."

"An excellent simile: they come forth from slime and mud, — fetid and crawling, unformed and monstrous. I grant exceptions; and even in the New School, as it is called, I can admire the real genius, the vital and creative power of Victor Hugo. But oh, that a nation which has known a Corneille should ever spawn forth a ——! And with these rickety and drivelling abortions — all having followers and adulators — your Public can still bear to be told that they have improved wonderfully on the day when they gave laws and models to

the literature of Europe; they can bear to hear —— proclaimed a sublime genius in the same circles which sneer
down Voltaire! "

Voltaire is out of fashion in France, but Rousseau still
maintains his influence, and boasts his imitators. Rousseau
was the worse man of the two; perhaps he was also the more
dangerous writer. But his reputation is more durable, and
sinks deeper into the heart of his nation; and the danger of
his unstable and capricious doctrines has passed away. In
Voltaire we behold the fate of all writers purely destructive;
their uses cease with the evils they denounce. But Rousseau
sought to construct as well as to destroy; and though nothing
could well be more absurd than his constructions, still man
loves to look back and see even delusive images — castles in
the air — reared above the waste where cities have been.
Rather than leave even a burial-ground to solitude, we popu-
late it with ghosts.

By degrees, however, as he mastered all the features of the
French literature, Maltravers become more tolerant of the
present defects, and more hopeful of the future results. He
saw in one respect that that literature carried with it its own
ultimate redemption.

Its general characteristic — contradistinguished from the
literature of the old French classic school — is to take the
heart for its study; to bring the passions and feelings into
action, and let the Within have its record and history as well
as the Without. In all this our contemplative analyst began
to allow that the French were not far wrong when they contended that Shakspeare made the fountain of their inspira-
tion, — a fountain which the majority of our later English
Fictionists have neglected. It is not by a story woven of
interesting incidents, relieved by delineations of the exter-
nals and surface of character, humorous phraseology, and
every-day ethics, that Fiction achieves its grandest ends.

In the French literature, thus characterized, there is much
false morality, much depraved sentiment, and much hollow
rant; but still it carries within it the germ of an excellence,
which, sooner or later, must in the progress of national genius

arrive at its full development.   Meanwhile, it is a consola-
tion to know that nothing really immoral is ever permanently
popular, or ever, therefore, long deleterious; what is dangerous in a work of genius cures itself in a few years.   We can
now read "Werther," and instruct our hearts by its exposition
of weakness and passion, our taste by its exquisite and unrivalled simplicity of construction and detail,' without any fear
that we shall shoot ourselves in top-boots!   We can feel ourselves elevated by the noble sentiments of "The Robbers," and
our penetration sharpened as to the wholesale immorality of
conventional cant and hypocrisy, without any danger of turning banditti and becoming cutthroats from the love of virtue.
Providence, that has made the genius of the few in all times
and countries the guide and prophet of the many, and appointed
Literature as the sublime agent of Civilization, of Opinion, and
of Law, has endowed the elements it employs with a divine
power of self-purification.   The stream settles of itself by
rest and time; the impure particles fly off, or are neutralized
by the healthful.   It is only fools that call the works of a
master-spirit immoral.   There does not exist in the literature
of the world one *popular* book that is immoral two centuries
after it is produced.   For, in the heart of nations, the False
does not live so long; and the True is the Ethical to the end
of time.

From the literary Maltravers turned to the political state
of France his curious and thoughtful eye.   He was struck by
the resemblance which this nation — so civilized, so thoroughly European — bears in one respect to the despotisms of
the East: the convulsions of the capital decide the fate of the
country; Paris is the tyrant of France.   He saw in this inflammable concentration of power, which must ever be preg-
nant with great evils, one of the causes why the revolutions of
that powerful and polished people are so incomplete and unsatisfactory, why, like Cardinal Fleury, system after system,
and Government after Government —

> . . . "floruit sine fructu,
> Defloruit sine luctu." [1]

---

[1] "Flourished without fruit, and was destroyed without regret."

Maltravers regarded it as a singular instance of perverse ratiocination, that, unwarned by experience, the French should still persist in perpetuating this political vice; that all their policy should still be the policy of Centralization, — a principle which secures the momentary strength, but ever ends in the abrupt destruction of States. It is, in fact, the perilous tonic, which seems to brace the system, but drives the blood to the head, — thus come apoplexy and madness. By centralization the provinces are weakened, it is true, — but weak to assist as well as to oppose a government, weak to withstand a mob. Nowhere, nowadays, is a mob so powerful as in Paris: the political history of Paris is the history of mobs. Centralization is an excellent quackery for a despot who desires power to last only his own life, and who has but a life-interest in the State; but to true liberty and permanent order centralization is a deadly poison. The more the provinces govern their own affairs, the more we find everything, even to roads and post-horses, are left to the people; the more the Municipal Spirit pervades every vein of the vast body, the more certain may we be that reform and change must come from universal opinion, which is slow, and constructs ere it destroys, — not from public clamour, which is sudden, and not only pulls down the edifice but sells the bricks!

Another peculiarity in the French Constitution struck and perplexed Maltravers. This people so pervaded by the republican sentiment; this people, who had sacrificed so much for Freedom; this people, who, in the name of Freedom, had perpetrated so much crime with Robespierre, and achieved so much glory with Napoleon, — this people were, *as* a people, contented to be utterly excluded from all power and voice in the State! Out of thirty-three millions of subjects, less than two hundred thousand electors! Where was there ever an oligarchy equal to this? What a strange infatuation, to demolish an aristocracy and yet to exclude a people! What an anomaly in political architecture, to build an inverted pyramid! Where was the safety-valve of governments, where the natural vents of excitement in a population so inflammable ? The people itself were left a mob, — no stake in the State, no action in its affairs, no legislative interest in its security.[1]

On the other hand, it was singular to see how — the aristocracy of birth broken down — the aristocracy of letters had arisen. A Peerage, half composed of journalists, philosophers, and authors! This was the beau-ideal of Algernon Sidney's Aristocratic Republic, of the Helvetian vision of what ought to be the dispensation of public distinctions; yet was it, after all, a desirable aristocracy ? Did society gain; did literature lose ? Was the priesthood of Genius made more sacred and more pure by these worldly decorations and hollow titles ; or was aristocracy itself thus rendered a more disinterested, a more powerful, or a more sagacious element in the administration of law, or the elevation of opinion ? These questions, not lightly to be answered, could not fail to arouse the speculation and curiosity of a man who had been familiar with the closet and the forum ; and in proportion as he found his interest excited in these problems to be solved by a foreign nation, did the thoughtful Englishman feel the old instinct — which binds the citizen to the fatherland — begin to stir once more earnestly and vividly within him.

"You, yourself individually, are passing like us," said De Montaigne one day to Maltravers, "through a state of transition. You have forever left the Ideal, and you are carrying your cargo of experience over to the Practical. When you reach that haven, you will have completed the development of your forces."

"You mistake me, — I am but a spectator."

"Yes; but you desire to go behind the scenes ; and he who once grows familiar with the green-room, longs to be an actor."

With Madame de Ventadour and the De Montaignes Maltravers passed the chief part of his time. They knew how to appreciate his nobler and to love his gentler attributes and qualities ; they united in a warm interest for his future fate ; they combated his Philosophy of Inaction ; and they felt that

[1] Has not all this proved prophetic ?

it was because he was not happy that he was not wise. Experience was to him what ignorance had been to Alice. His
faculties were chilled and dormant. As affection to those who
are unskilled in all things, so is affection to those who despair
of all things. The mind of Maltravers was a world without
a sun!

CHAPTER III.

CŒLEBS, quid agam? [1] — HORACE.

IN a room at Fenton's Hotel sat Lord Vargrave and Caroline
Lady Doltimore, — two months after the marriage of the
latter.

"Doltimore has positively fixed, then, to go abroad on your
return from Cornwall?"

"Positively, — to Paris. You can join us at Christmas, I
trust?"

"I have no doubt of it; and before then I hope that I shall
have arranged certain public matters, which at present harass
and absorb me even more than my private affairs."

"You have managed to obtain terms with Mr. Douce, and
to delay the repayment of your debt to him?"

"Yes, I hope so, till I touch Miss Cameron's income; which
will be mine, I trust, by the time she is eighteen."

"You mean the forfeit money of thirty thousand pounds?"

"Not I; I mean what I said!"

"Can you really imagine she will still accept your hand?"

"With your aid, I do imagine it! Hear me. You must
take Evelyn with you to Paris. I have no doubt but that she
will be delighted to accompany you; nay, I have paved the
way so far. For, of course, as a friend of the family, and
guardian to Evelyn, I have maintained a correspondence with
Lady Vargrave. She informs me that Evelyn has been unwell

---

[1] "What shall I do, a bachelor ? "

and low-spirited; that she fears Brook-Green is dull for her, etc. I wrote, in reply, to say that the more my ward saw of the world, prior to her accession, when of age, to the position she would occupy in it, the more she would fulfil my late uncle's wishes with respect to her education and so forth. I added that as you were going to Paris, and as you loved her so much, there could not be a better opportunity for her entrance into life under the most favourable auspices. Lady Vargrave's answer to this letter arrived this morning: she will consent to such an arrangement should you propose it."

"But what good will result to yourself in this project? At Paris you will be sure of rivals, and — "

"Caroline," interrupted Lord Vargrave, "I know very well what you would say: I also know all the danger I must incur. But it is a choice of evils, and I choose the least. You see that while she is at Brook-Green, and under the eye of that sly old curate, I can effect nothing with her. There, she is entirely removed from my influence: not so abroad; not so under your roof. Listen to me still further. In this country, and especially in the seclusion and shelter of Brook-Green, I have no scope for any of those means which I shall be compelled to resort to, in failure of all else."

"What can you intend?" said Caroline, with a slight shudder.

"I don't know what I intend yet. But this, at least, I can tell you, — that Miss Cameron's fortune I must and will have. I am a desperate man; and I can play a desperate game, if need be."

"And do you think that *I* will aid, will abet?"

"Hush, not so loud! Yes, Caroline, you will, and you must aid and abet me in any project I may form."

"Must! Lord Vargrave?"

"Ay," said Lumley, with a smile, and sinking his voice into a whisper, — "ay! *you are in my power!*"

"Traitor! — you cannot dare! you cannot mean — "

"I mean nothing more than to remind you of the ties that exist between us, — ties which ought to render us the firmest and most confidential of friends. Come, Caroline, recollect all the benefit must not lie on one side. I have obtained for you rank and wealth; I have procured you a husband, — you must help me to a wife!"

Caroline sank back, and covered her face with her hands.

"I allow," continued Vargrave, coldly, — "I allow that your beauty and talent were sufficient of themselves to charm a wiser man than Doltimore; but had I not suppressed jealousy, sacrificed love, had I dropped a hint to your liege lord, — nay, had I not fed his lap-dog vanity by all the cream and sugar of flattering falsehoods, — you would be Caroline Merton still!"

"Oh, would that I were! Oh that I were anything but your tool, your victim! Fool that I was! wretch that I am! I am rightly punished!"

"Forgive me, forgive me, dearest," said Vargrave, soothingly; "I was to blame, forgive me: but you irritated, you maddened me, by your seeming indifference to my prosperity, my fate. I tell you again and again, pride of my soul, I tell you, that you are the only being I love! and if you will allow me, if you will rise superior, as I once fondly hoped, to all the cant and prejudice of convention and education, the only woman I could ever respect, as well as love. Oh, hereafter, when you see me at that height to which I feel that I am born to climb, let me think that to your generosity, your affection, your zeal, I owed the ascent. At present I am on the precipice; without your hand I fall forever. My own fortune is gone; the miserable forfeit due to me, if Evelyn continues to reject my suit, when she has arrived at the age of eighteen, is deeply mortgaged. I am engaged in vast and daring schemes, in which I may either rise to the highest station or lose that which I now hold. In either case, how necessary to me is wealth: in the one instance, to maintain my advancement; in the other, to redeem my fall."

"But did you not tell me," said Caroline, "that Evelyn proposed and promised to place her fortune at your disposal, even while rejecting your hand?"

"Absurd mockery!" exclaimed Vargrave; "the foolish boast of a girl, — an impulse liable to every caprice. Can

you suppose that when she launches into the extravagance
natural to her age and necessary to her position, she will not
find a thousand demands upon her rent-roll not dreamed of
now; a thousand vanities and baubles that will soon erase my
poor and hollow claim from her recollection? Can you suppose that, if she marry another, her husband will ever consent to a child's romance? And even were all this possible,
were it possible that girls were not extravagant, and that
husbands had no common-sense, is it for me, Lord Vargrave,
to be a mendicant upon reluctant bounty, — a poor cousin, a
pensioned led-captain? Heaven knows I have as little false
pride as any man, but still this is a degradation I cannot
stoop to. Besides, Caroline, I am no miser, no Harpagon: I
do not want wealth for wealth's sake, but for the advantages
it bestows, — respect, honour, position; and these I get as the
husband of the great heiress. Should I get them as her
dependant? No: for more than six years I have built my
schemes and shaped my conduct according to one assured and
definite object; and that object I shall not now, at the
eleventh hour, let slip from my hands. Enough of this:
you will pass Brook-Green in returning from Cornwall; you
will take Evelyn with you to Paris, — leave the rest to me.
Fear no folly, no violence, from my plans, whatever they may
be: I work in the dark. Nor do I despair that Evelyn will
love, that Evelyn will voluntarily accept me yet: my disposition is sanguine; I look to the bright side of things; do the
same!"

Here their conference was interrupted by Lord Doltimore,
who lounged carelessly into the room, with his hat on one
side. "Ah, Vargrave, how are you? You will not forget the
letters of introduction? Where are you going, Caroline?"

"Only to my own room, to put on my bonnet; the carriage
will be here in a few minutes." And Caroline escaped.

"So you go to Cornwall to-morrow, Doltimore?"

"Yes; cursed bore! but Lady Elizabeth insists on seeing
us, and I don't object to a week's good shooting. The old
lady, too, has something to leave, and Caroline had no dowry,
— not that I care for it; but still marriage is expensive."

"By the by, you will want the five thousand pounds you lent me?"

"Why, whenever it is convenient."

"Say no more, — it shall be seen to. Doltimore, I am very anxious that Lady Doltimore's *début* at Paris should be brilliant: everything depends on falling into the right set. For myself, I don't care about fashion, and never did; but if I were married, and an idle man like you, it might be different."

"Oh, you will be very useful to us when we return to London. Meanwhile, you know, you have my proxy in the Lords. I dare say there will be some sharp work the first week or two after the recess."

"Very likely; and depend on one thing, my dear Doltimore, that when I am in the Cabinet, a certain friend of mine shall be an earl. Adieu."

"Good-by, my dear Vargrave, good-by; and, I say, — I say, don't distress yourself about that trifle; a few months hence it will suit me just as well."

"Thanks. I will just look into my accounts, and use you without ceremony. Well, I dare say we shall meet at Paris. Oh, I forgot, — I observe that you have renewed your intimacy with Legard. Now, he is a very good fellow, and I gave him that place to oblige you; still, as you are no longer a *garçon* — but perhaps I shall offend you?"

"Not at all. What is there against Legard?"

"Nothing in the world, — but he is a bit of a boaster. I dare say his ancestor was a Gascon, poor fellow! — and he affects to say that you can't choose a coat, or buy a horse, without his approval and advice, — that he can turn you round his finger. Now this hurts your consequence in the world, — you don't get credit for your own excellent sense and taste. Take my advice, avoid these young hangers-on of fashion, these club-room lions. Having no importance of their own, they steal the importance of their friends. *Verbum sap.*"

"You are very right, — Legard *is* a coxcomb; and now I see why he talked of joining us at Paris."

"Don't let him do any such thing! He will be telling

" 'FORGIVE ME,' SAID VARGRAVE, SOOTHINGLY."

the Frenchmen that her ladyship is in love with him, ha, ha!"

"Ha, ha! — a very good joke — poor Caroline! — very good joke!"

"Well, good-by, once more." And Vargrave closed the door.

"Legard go to Paris — not if Evelyn goes there!" muttered Lumley. "Besides, I want no partner in the little that one can screw out of this blockhead."

CHAPTER IV.

Mr. BUMBLECASE, a word with you — I have a little business.
Farewell, the goodly Manor of Blackacre, with all its woods, underwoods, and appurtenances whatever. — WYCHERLEY : *Plain Dealer*.

IN quitting Fenton's Hotel, Lord Vargrave entered into one of the clubs in St. James's Street: this was rather unusual with him, for he was not a club man. It was not his system to spend his time for nothing. But it was a wet December day; the House was not yet assembled, and he had done his official business. Here, as he was munching a biscuit and reading an article in one of the ministerial papers — the heads of which he himself had supplied — Lord Saxingham joined and drew him to the window.

"I have reason to think," said the earl, "that your visit to Windsor did good."

"Ah, indeed; so I fancied."

"I do not think that a certain personage will ever consent to the —— question; and the premier, whom I saw to-day, seems chafed and irritated."

"Nothing can be better; I know that we are in the right boat."

"I hope it is not true, Lumley, that your marriage with Miss Cameron is broken off; such was the *on dit* in the club, just before you entered."

"Contradict it, my dear lord, — contradict it. I hope by the spring to introduce Lady Vargrave to you. But who broached the absurd report?"

"Why, your *protégé*, Legard, says he heard so from his uncle, who heard it from Sir John Merton."

"Legard is a puppy, and Sir John Merton a jackass. Legard had better attend to his office, if he wants to get on; and I wish you 'd tell him so. I have heard somewhere that he talks of going to Paris, — you can just hint to him that he must give up such idle habits. Public functionaries are not now what they were, — people are expected to work for the money they pocket; otherwise Legard is a cleverish fellow, and deserves promotion. A word or two of caution from you will do him a vast deal of good."

"Be sure I will lecture him. Will you dine with me to-day, Lumley?"

"No. I expect my co-trustee, Mr. Douce, on matters of business, — a *tête-à-tête* dinner."

Lord Vargrave had, as he conceived, very cleverly talked over Mr. Douce into letting his debt to that gentleman run on for the present; and in the meanwhile, he had overwhelmed Mr. Douce with his condescensions. That gentleman had twice dined with Lord Vargrave, and Lord Vargrave had twice dined with him. The occasion of the present more familiar entertainment was in a letter from Mr. Douce, begging to see Lord Vargrave on particular business; and Vargrave, who by no means liked the word *business* from a gentleman to whom he owed money, thought that it would go off more smoothly if sprinkled with champagne.

Accordingly, he begged "My dear Mr. Douce" to excuse ceremony, and dine with him on Thursday at seven o'clock, — he was really so busy all the mornings.

At seven o'clock, Mr. Douce came. The moment he entered Vargrave called out, at the top of his voice, "Dinner immediately!" And as the little man bowed and shuffled,

and fidgeted and wriggled (while Vargrave shook him by the
hand), as if he thought he was going himself to be spitted,
his host said, "With your leave, we'll postpone the budget
till after dinner. It is the fashion nowadays to postpone
budgets as long as we can, — eh? Well, and how are all at
home? Devilish cold; is it not? So you go to your villa
every day? That's what keeps you in such capital health.
You know I had a villa too, — though I never had time to go
there."

"Ah, yes; I think, I remember, at Ful-Ful-Fulham!"
gasped out Mr. Douce. "Your poor uncle's — now Lady
Var-Vargrave's jointure-house. So — so — "

"She don't live there!" burst in Vargrave (far too impatient
to be polite). "Too cockneyfied for her, — gave it up to me;
very pretty place, but d—d expensive. I could not afford it,
never went there, and so I have let it to my wine-merchant;
the rent just pays his bill. You will taste some of the sofas
and tables to-day in his champagne. I don't know how it is,
I always fancy my sherry smells like my poor uncle's old
leather chair: very odd smell it had, — a kind of respectable
smell! I hope you're hungry, — dinner's ready."

Vargrave thus rattled away in order to give the good banker
to understand that his affairs were in the most flourishing
condition: and he continued to keep up the ball all dinner-
time, stopping Mr. Douce's little, miserable, gasping, dacelike
mouth, with "a glass of wine, Douce?" or "by the by, Douce,"
whenever he saw that worthy gentleman about to make the
Æschylean improvement of a second person in the dialogue.

At length, dinner being fairly over, and the servants withdrawn, Lord Vargrave, knowing that sooner or later Douce
would have his say, drew his chair to the fire, put his feet on
the fender, and cried, as he tossed off his claret, "Now,
Douce, what can i do for you?"

Mr. Douce opened his eyes to their full extent, and then as
rapidly closed them; and this operation he continued till,
having snuffed them so much that they could by no possibility burn any brighter, he was convinced that he had not mis-
understood his lordship.

"Indeed, then," he began, in his most frightened manner, "indeed — I — really, your lordship is very good — I — I wanted to speak to you on business."

"Well, what can I do for you, — some little favour, eh? Snug sinecure for a favourite clerk, or a place in the Stamp-Office for your fat footman — John, I think you call him? You know, my dear Douce, you may command me."

"Oh, indeed, you are all good-good-goodness — but — but — "

Vargrave threw himself back, and shutting his eyes and pursing up his mouth, resolutely suffered Mr. Douce to unbosom himself without interruption. He was considerably relieved to find that the business referred to related only to Miss Cameron.

Mr. Douce having reminded Lord Vargrave, as he had often done before, of the wishes of his uncle, that the greater portion of the money bequeathed to Evelyn should be invested in land, proceeded to say that a most excellent opportunity presented itself for just such a purchase as would have rejoiced the heart of the late lord, — a superb place, in the style of Blickling, — deer-park six miles round, ten thousand acres of land, bringing in a clear eight thousand pounds a year, purchase money only two hundred and forty thousand pounds. The whole estate was, indeed, much larger, — eighteen thousand acres; but then the more distant farms could be sold in different lots, in order to meet the exact sum Miss Cameron's trustees were enabled to invest.

"Well," said Vargrave, "and where is it? My poor uncle was after De Clifford's estate, but the title was not good."

"Oh! this — is much — much — much fi-fi-finer; famous investment — but rather far off — in — in the north, Li-Li-Lisle Court."

"Lisle Court! Why, does not that belong to Colonel Maltravers?"

"Yes. It is, indeed, quite, I may say, a secret — yes — really — a se-se-secret — not in the market yet — not at all — soon snapped up."

"Humph! Has Colonel Maltravers been extravagant?"

"No; but he does not — I hear — or rather Lady — Julia —
so I 'm told, yes, indeed — does not li-like — going so far, and
so they spend the winter in Italy instead.   Yes — very odd —
very fine place."

Lumley was slightly acquainted with the elder brother of
his old friend, — a man who possessed some of Ernest's faults,
— very proud, and very exacting, and very fastidious; but all
these faults were developed in the ordinary commonplace
world, and were not the refined abstractions of his younger
brother.

Colonel Maltravers had continued, since he entered the
Guards, to be thoroughly the man of fashion, and nothing
more.   But rich and well-born, and highly connected, and
thoroughly *à la mode* as he was, his pride made him uncom-
fortable in London, while his fastidiousness made him un-
comfortable in the country.   He was *rather* a great person,
but he wanted to be a *very* great person.   This he was at
Lisle Court; but that did not satisfy him.   He wanted not
only to be a very great person, but a very great person among
very great persons — and squires and parsons bored him.
Lady Julia, his wife, was a fine lady, inane and pretty, who
saw everything through her husband's eyes.   He was quite
master *chez lui*, was Colonel Maltravers!   He lived a great
deal abroad; for on the Continent his large income seemed
princely, while his high character, thorough breeding, and
personal advantages, which were remarkable, secured him a
greater position in foreign courts than at his own.   Two
things had greatly disgusted him with Lisle Court, — trifles
they might be with others, but they were not trifles to Cuth-
bert Maltravers; in the first place, a man who had been his
father's attorney, and who was the very incarnation of coarse
unrepellable familiarity, had bought an estate close by the
said Lisle Court, and had, *horresco referens*, been made a baronet!   Sir Gregory Gubbins took precedence of Colonel Maltravers!   He could not ride out but he met Sir Gregory; he
could not dine out but he had the pleasure of walking behind
Sir Gregory's bright blue coat with its bright brass buttons.
In his last visit to Lisle Court, which he had then crowded

with all manner of fine people, he had seen — the very first morning after his arrival — seen from the large window of his state saloon, a great staring white, red, blue, and gilt thing, at the end of the stately avenue planted by Sir Guy Maltravers in honour of the victory over the Spanish armada. He looked in mute surprise, and everybody else looked; and a polite German count, gazing through his eye-glass, said, "Ah! dat is vat you call a vim in your *pays*, — the vim of Colonel Maltravers!"

This "vim" was the pagoda summer-house of Sir Gregory Gubbins, erected in imitation of the Pavilion at Brighton. Colonel Maltravers was miserable: the *vim* haunted him; it seemed ubiquitous; he could not escape it, — it was built on the highest spot in the county. Ride, walk, sit where he would, the *vim* stared at him; and he thought he saw little mandarins shake their round little heads at him. This was one of the great curses of Lisle Court; the other was yet more galling. The owners of Lisle Court had for several generations possessed the dominant interest in the county town. The colonel himself meddled little in politics, and was too fine a gentleman for the drudgery of parliament. He had offered the seat to Ernest, when the latter had commenced his public career; but the result of a communication proved that their political views were dissimilar, and the negotiation dropped without ill-feeling on either side. Subsequently a vacancy occurred; and Lady Julia's brother (just made a Lord of the Treasury) wished to come into parliament, so the county town was offered to him. Now, the proud commoner had married into the family of a peer as proud as himself, and Colonel Maltravers was always glad whenever he could impress his consequence on his connections by doing them a favour. He wrote to his steward to see that the thing was properly settled, and came down on the nomination-day "to share the triumph and partake the gale." Guess his indigna-tion, when he found the nephew of Sir Gregory Gubbins was already in the field! The result of the election was that Mr. Augustus Gubbins came in, and that Colonel Maltravers was pelted with cabbage-stalks, and accused of attempting to *sell*

the worthy and independent electors to a government nomi-
nee! In shame and disgust, Colonel Maltravers broke up his
establishment at Lisle Court, and once more retired to the
Continent.

About a week from the date now touched upon, Lady Julia
and himself had arrived in London from Vienna; and a new
mortification awaited the unfortunate owner of Lisle Court.
A railroad company had been established, of which Sir Gregory Gubbins was a principal shareholder; and the speculator,
Mr. Augustus Gubbins, one of the "most useful men in the
House," had undertaken to carry the bill through parliament.
Colonel Maltravers received a letter of portentous size, inclos-
ing the map of the places which this blessed railway was to
bisect; and lo! just at the bottom of his park ran a portentous
line, which informed him of the sacrifice he was expected to
make for the public good, — especially for the good of that
very county town, the inhabitants of which had pelted him
with cabbage-stalks!

Colonel Maltravers lost all patience. Unacquainted with
our wise legislative proceedings, he was not aware that a railway planned is a very different thing from a railway made;
and that parliamentary committees are not by any means
favourable to schemes for carrying the public through a gentleman's park.

"This country is not to be lived in," said he to Lady Julia;
"it gets worse and worse every year. I am sure I never had
any comfort in Lisle Court. I 've a great mind to sell it."

"Why, indeed, as we have no sons, only daughters, and
Ernest is so well provided for," said Lady Julia, "and the
place is so far from London, and the neighbourhood is so disagreeable, I think we could do very well without it."

Colonel Maltravers made no answer, but he revolved the
pros and *cons ;* and then he began to think how much it cost
him in gamekeepers and carpenters and bailiffs and gardeners
and Heaven knows whom besides; and then the pagoda flashed
across him; and then the cabbage-stalks, and at last he went
to his solicitor.

"You may sell Lisle Court," said he, quietly.

The solicitor dipped his pen in the ink. "The particulars, Colonel?"

"Particulars of Lisle Court! everybody, that is, every gen-tleman, knows Lisle Court!"

"Price, sir?"

"You know the rents; calculate accordingly. It will be too large a purchase for one individual; sell the outlying woods and farms separately from the rest."

"We must draw up an advertisement, Colonel."

"Advertise Lisle Court! out of the question, sir. I can have no publicity given to my intention: mention it quietly to any capitalist; but keep it out of the papers till it is all settled. In a week or two you will find a purchaser, — the sooner the better."

Besides his horror of newspaper comments and newspaper puffs, Colonel Maltravers dreaded that his brother — then in Paris — should learn his intention, and attempt to thwart it; and, somehow or other, the colonel was a little in awe of Ernest, and a little ashamed of his resolution. He did not know that, by a singular coincidence, Ernest himself had thought of selling Burleigh.

The solicitor was by no means pleased with this way of settling the matter. However, he whispered it about that Lisle Court was in the market; and as it really was one of the most celebrated places of its kind in England, the whis-per spread among bankers and brewers and soap-boilers and other rich people — the Medici of the New Noblesse rising up amongst us — till at last it reached the ears of Mr. Douce.

Lord Vargrave, however bad a man he might be, had not many of those vices of character which belong to what I may call the *personal class of vices*, — that is, he had no ill-will to individuals. He was not, ordinarily, a jealous man, nor a spiteful, nor a malignant, nor a vindictive man: his vices arose from utter indifference to all men, and all things — ex-cept as conducive to his own ends. He would not have in-jured a worm if it did him no good; but he would have set any house on fire if he had no other means of roasting his own eggs. Yet still, if any feeling of personal rancour could harbour in his breast, it was, first, towards Evelyn Cameron, and, secondly, towards Ernest Maltravers. For the first time in his life, he did long for revenge, — revenge against the one for stealing his patrimony, and refusing his hand; and that revenge he hoped to gratify.

As to the other, it was not so much dislike he felt, as an uneasy sentiment of inferiority. However well he himself had got on in the world, he yet grudged the reputation of a man whom he had remembered a wayward, inexperienced boy: he did not love to hear any one praise Maltravers. He fancied, too, that this feeling was reciprocal, and that Maltravers was pained at hearing of any new step in his own career. In fact, it was that sort of jealousy which men often feel for the companions of their youth, whose characters are higher than their own, and whose talents are of an order they do not quite comprehend. Now, it certainly did seem at that moment to Lord Vargrave that it would be a most splendid triumph over Mr. Maltravers of Burleigh to be lord of Lisle Court, the hereditary seat of the elder branch of the family: to be, as it were, in the very shoes of Mr. Ernest Maltravers's elder brother. He knew, too, that it was a property of great consequence. Lord Vargrave of Lisle Court would hold a very different post in the peerage from Lord Vargrave of ——, Fulham! Nobody would call the owner of Lisle Court an adventurer; nobody would suspect such a man of caring three straws about place and salary. And if he married Evelyn, and if Evelyn bought Lisle Court, would not Lisle Court be his? He vaulted over the *ifs*, stiff monosyllables though they were, with a single jump. Besides, even should the thing come to nothing, there was the very excuse he sought for joining Evelyn at Paris, for conversing with her, consulting her. It was true that the will of the late lord left it solely at the discretion of the trustees to select such landed invest-ment as seemed best to them; but still it was, if not legally necessary, at least but a proper courtesy to consult Evelyn. And plans, and drawings, and explanations, and rent-rolls, would justify him in spending morning after morning alone with her.

Thus cogitating, Lord Vargrave suffered Mr. Douce to stammer out sentence upon sentence, till at length, as he rang for coffee, his lordship stretched himself with the air of a man stretching himself into self-complacency or a good thing, and said, —

"Mr. Douce, I will go down to Lisle Court as soon as I can; I will see it; I will ascertain all about it; I will consider favourably of it. I agree with you, I think it will do famously."

"But," said Mr. Douce, who seemed singularly anxious about the matter, "we must make haste, my lord; for really — yes, indeed — if — if — if Baron Roths — Rothschild should — that is to say — "

"Oh, yes, I understand; keep the thing close, my dear Douce; make friends with the colonel's lawyer; play with him a little, till I can run down."

"Besides, you see, you are such a good man of business, my lord — that you see, that — yes, really — there must be time to draw out the purchase-money — sell out at a prop — prop — "

"To be sure, to be sure! Bless me, how late it is! I am afraid my carriage is ready. I must go to Madame de L——'s."

Mr. Douce, who seemed to have much more to say, was forced to keep it for another time, and to take his leave.

Lord Vargrave went to Madame de L——'s. His position in what is called Exclusive Society was rather peculiar. By those who affected to be the best judges, the frankness of his manner and the easy oddity of his conversation were pronounced at variance with the tranquil serenity of thorough breeding. But still he was a great favourite both with fine ladies and dandies. His handsome keen countenance, his talents, his politics, his intrigues, and an animated boldness in his bearing, compensated for his constant violation of all the minutiæ of orthodox conventionalism.

At this house he met Colonel Maltravers, and took an opportunity to renew his acquaintance with that gentleman. He then referred, in a confidential whisper, to the communication he had received touching Lisle Court.

"Yes," said the colonel, "I suppose I must sell the place, if I can do so quietly. To be sure, when I first spoke to my lawyer it was in a moment of vexation, on hearing that the —— railroad was to go through the park, but I find that I overrated that danger. Still, if you will do me the honour to go and look over the place, you will find very good shoot-ing; and when you come back, you can see if it will suit you. Don't say anything about it when you are there; it is better not to publish my intention all over the county. I shall have Sir Gregory Gubbins offering to buy it if you do!"

"You may depend on my discretion. Have you heard any-thing of your brother lately?"

"Yes; I fancy he is going to Switzerland. He would soon be in England, if he heard I was going to part with Lisle Court!"

"What, it would vex him so?"

"I fear it would; but he has a nice old place of his own, not half so large, and therefore not half so troublesome as Lisle Court."

"Ay! and he *did* talk of selling that nice old place."

"Selling Burleigh! you surprise me. But really country places in England *are* a bore. I suppose he has his Gubbins as well as myself!"

Here the chief minister of the government adorned by Lord Vargrave's virtues passed by, and Lumley turned to greet him.

The two ministers talked together most affectionately in a close whisper, — so affectionately, that one might have seen, with half an eye, that they hated each other like poison!

CHAPTER V.

Inspicere tanquam in speculum, in vitas omnium
Jubeo.[1] — Terence.

Ernest Maltravers still lingered at Paris: he gave up all
notion of proceeding farther. He was, in fact, tired of travel.
But there was another reason that chained him to that "Navel
of the Earth," — there is not anywhere a better sounding-board
to London rumours than the English *quartier* between the
Boulevard des Italiennes and the Tuileries; here, at all
events, he should soonest learn the worst: and every day,
as he took up the English newspapers, a sick feeling of apprehension and fear came over him. No! till the seal was set
upon the bond, till the Rubicon was passed, till Miss Cameron was the wife of Lord Vargrave, he could neither return to
the home that was so eloquent with the recollections of Evelyn, nor, by removing farther from England, delay the receipt
of an intelligence which he vainly told himself he was prepared to meet.

He continued to seek such distractions from thought as
were within his reach; and as his heart was too occupied for
pleasures which had, indeed, long since palled, those distractions were of the grave and noble character which it is a pre-
rogative of the intellect to afford to the passions.

De Montaigne was neither a Doctrinaire nor a Republican,
— and yet, perhaps, he was a little of both. He was one who
thought that the tendency of all European States is towards
Democracy; but he by no means looked upon Democracy as a
panacea for all legislative evils. He thought that, while
a writer should be in advance of his time, a statesman should
content himself with marching by its side; that a nation
could not be ripened, like an exotic, by artificial means; that
it must be developed only by natural influences. He believed

---

[1] "I bid you look into the lives of all men, as it were into a mirror."

that forms of government are never universal in their effects. Thus, De Montaigne conceived that we were wrong in attaching more importance to legislative than to social reforms. He considered, for instance, that the surest sign of our progressive civilization is in our growing distaste to capital punishments. He believed, not in the ultimate *perfection* of mankind, but in their progressive *perfectibility*. He thought that improvement was indefinite; but he did not place its advance more under Republican than under Monarchical forms. "Provided," he was wont to say, "all our checks to power are of the right kind, it matters little to what hands the power itself is confided."

"Ægina and Athens," said he, "were republics — commercial and maritime — placed under the same sky, surrounded by the same neighbours, and rent by the same struggles between Oligarchy and Democracy. Yet, while one left the world an immortal heirloom of genius, where are the poets, the philosophers, the statesmen of the other? Arrian tells us of republics in India, still supposed to exist by modern investigators; but they are not more productive of liberty of thought, or ferment of intellect, than the principalities. In Italy there were commonwealths as liberal as the Republic of Florence; but they did not produce a Machiavelli or a Dante. What daring thought, what gigantic speculation, what democracy of wisdom and genius, have sprung up amongst the despotisms of Germany! You cannot educate two individuals so as to produce the same results from both; you cannot, by similar constitutions (which are the education of nations) produce the same results from different communities. The proper object of statesmen should be to give every facility to the people to develop themselves, and every facility to philosophy to dispute and discuss as to the ultimate objects to be obtained. But you cannot, as a practical legislator, place your country under a melon-frame: it must grow of its own accord."

I do not say whether or not De Montaigne was wrong! but Maltravers saw at least that he was faithful to his theories; that all his motives were sincere, all his practice pure. He could not but allow, too, that in his occupations and labours, De Montaigne appeared to feel a sublime enjoyment; that, in linking all the powers of his mind to active and useful objects, De Montaigne was infinitely happier than the Philosophy of Indifference, the scorn of ambition, had made Maltravers. The influence exercised by the large-souled and practical Frenchman over the fate and the history of Maltravers was very peculiar.

De Montaigne had not, apparently and directly, operated upon his friend's outward destinies; but he had done so indirectly, by operating on his mind. Perhaps it was he who had consolidated the first wavering and uncertain impulses of Maltravers towards literary exertion; it was he who had consoled him for the mortifications at the earlier part of his career; and now, perhaps he might serve, in the full vigour of his intellect, permanently to reconcile the Englishman to the claims of life.

There were, indeed, certain conversations which Maltravers held with De Montaigne, the germ and pith of which it is necessary that I should place before the reader, — for I write the inner as well as the outer history of a man; and the great incidents of life are not brought about only by the dramatic agencies of others, but also by our own reasonings and habits of thought. What I am now about to set down may be wearisome, but it is not episodical; and I promise that it shall be the last didactic conversation in the work.

One day Maltravers was relating to De Montaigne all that he had been planning at Burleigh for the improvement of his peasantry, and all his theories respecting Labour-Schools and Poor-rates, when De Montaigne abruptly turned round, and said, —

"You have, then, really found that in your own little village your exertions — exertions not very arduous, not demanding a tenth part of your time — have done practical good?"

"Certainly I think so," replied Maltravers, in some surprise.

"And yet it was but yesterday that you declared that all the labours of Philosophy and Legislation were labours vain; their benefits equivocal and uncertain; that as the sea, where it loses in one place, gains in another, so civilization only partially profits us, stealing away one virtue while it yields another, and leaving the large proportions of good and evil eternally the same."

"True; but I never said that man might not relieve individuals by individual exertion: though he cannot by abstract theories — nay, even by practical action in the wide circle — benefit the mass."

"Do you not employ on behalf of individuals the same moral agencies that wise legislation or sound philosophy would adopt towards the multitude? For example, you find that the children of your village are happier, more orderly, more obedient, promise to be wiser and better men in their own station of life, from the new, and, I grant, excellent system of school discipline and teaching that you have established. What you have done in one village, why should not legislation do throughout a kingdom? Again, you find that, by simply holding out hope and emulation to industry, by making stern distinctions between the energetic and the idle, the independent exertion and the pauper-mendicancy, you have found a lever by which you have literally moved and shifted the little world around you. But what is the difference here between the rules of a village lord and the laws of a wise legislature? The moral feelings you have appealed to exist universally, the moral remedies you have practised are as open to legislation as to the individual proprietor."

"Yes; but when you apply to a nation the same principles which regenerate a village, new counterbalancing principles arise. If I give education to my peasants, I send them into the world with advantages *superior* to their fellows, — advantages which, not being common to their class, enable them to *outstrip* their fellows. But if this education were universal to the whole tribe, no man would have an advantage superior to the others; the knowledge they would have acquired being shared by all, would leave all as they now are, hewers of wood and drawers of water: the principle of individual hope, which springs from knowledge, would soon be baffled by the vast competition that *universal* knowledge would produce. Thus by the universal improvement would be engendered a universal discontent.

"Take a broader view of the subject. Advantages given to the *few* around me — superior wages, lighter toils, a greater sense of the dignity of man — are not productive of any change in society. Give these advantages to the *whole mass* of the labouring classes, and what in the small orbit is the desire of the *individual* to rise becomes in the large circumference the desire of the *class* to rise; hence social restlessness, social change, revolution, and its hazards. For revolutions are produced but by the aspirations of one order, and the resistance of the other. Consequently, legislative improvement differs widely from individual amelioration; the same principle, the same agency, that purifies the small body, becomes destructive when applied to the large one. Apply the flame to the log on the hearth, or apply it to the forest, is there no distinction in the result? The breeze that freshens the fountain passes to the ocean, current impels current, wave urges wave, and the breeze becomes the storm."

"Were there truth in this train of argument," replied De Montaigne, "had we ever abstained from communicating to the Multitude the enjoyments and advantages of the Few, had we shrunk from the good, because the good is a parent of the change and its partial ills, what now would be society? Is there no difference in collective happiness and virtue between the painted Picts and the Druid worship, and the glorious harmony, light, and order of the great English nation?"

"The question is popular," said Maltravers, with a smile; "and were you my opponent in an election, would be cheered on any hustings in the kingdom. But I have lived among savage tribes, — savage, perhaps, as the race that resisted Cæsar; and their happiness seems to me, not perhaps the same as that of the few whose sources of enjoyment are numerous, refined, and, save by their own passions, unalloyed; but equal to that of the mass of men in States the most civilized and advanced. The artisans, crowded together in the fetid air of factories, with physical ills gnawing at the core of the constitution, from the cradle to the grave; drudging on from dawn to sunset and flying for recreation to the dread excitement of the dram-shop, or the wild and vain hopes of political fanaticism, — are not in my eyes happier than the wild Indians with hardy frames and calm tempers, seasoned to the privations for which you pity them, and uncursed with desires of that better state never to be theirs. The Arab in his desert has seen all the luxuries of the pasha in his harem; but he envies them not. He is contented with his barb, his tent, his desolate sands, and his spring of refreshing water.

"Are we not daily told, do not our priests preach it from their pulpits, that the cottage shelters happiness equal to that within the palace? Yet what the distinction between the peasant and the prince, differing from that between the peasant and the savage? There are more enjoyments and more privations in the one than in the other; but if, in the latter case, the enjoyments, though fewer, be more keenly felt, — if the privations, though apparently sharper, fall upon duller sensibilities and hardier frames, — your gauge of proportion loses all its value. Nay, in civilization there is for the multitude an evil that exists not in the savage state. The poor man sees daily and hourly all the vast disparities produced by civilized society; and reversing the divine parable, it is Lazarus who from afar, and from the despondent pit, looks upon Dives in the lap of Paradise: therefore, his privations, his sufferings, are made more keen by comparison with the luxuries of others. Not so in the desert and the forest. There but small distinctions, and those softened by immemorial and hereditary usage — that has in it the sanctity of religion — separate the savage from his chief. The fact is, that in civilization we behold a splendid aggregate, — literature and science, wealth and luxury, commerce and glory; but we see not the million victims crushed beneath the wheels of the machine, — the health sacrificed, the board breadless, the jails filled, the hospitals reeking, the human life poisoned in every spring, and poured forth like water! Neither do we remember all the steps, marked by desolation, crime, and bloodshed, by which this barren summit has been reached. Take the his-

tory of any civilized state, — England, France, Spain before
she rotted back into second childhood, the Italian Republics,
the Greek Commonwealths, the Empress of the Seven Hills —
what struggles, what persecutions, what crimes, what mas-
sacres! Where, in the page of history, shall we look back
and say, ' Here improvement has diminished the sum of
evil '? Extend, too, your scope beyond the State itself: each
State has won its acquisitions by the woes of others. Spain
springs above the Old World on the blood-stained ruins of
the New; and the groans and the gold of Mexico produce the
splendours of the Fifth Charles!

"Behold England, the wise, the liberal, the free England
— through what struggles she has passed; and is she yet contented? The sullen oligarchy of the Normans; our own criminal invasions of Scotland and France; the plundered people,
the butchered kings; the persecutions of the Lollards; the
wars of Lancaster and York; the new dynasty of the Tudors,
that at once put back Liberty, and put forward Civilization!
the Reformation, cradled in the lap of a hideous despot, and
nursed by violence and rapine; the stakes and fires of Mary,
and the craftier cruelties of Elizabeth, — England, strengthened by the desolation of Ireland, the Civil Wars, the reign
of hypocrisy, followed by the reign of naked vice; the nation
that beheaded the graceful Charles gaping idly on the scaffold
of the lofty Sidney; the vain Revolution of 1688, which, if a
jubilee in England, was a massacre in Ireland; the bootless
glories of Marlborough; the organized corruption of Walpole,
the frantic war with our own American sons, the exhausting
struggles with Napoleon!

"Well, we close the page; we say, Lo! a thousand years
of incessant struggles and afflictions! millions have perished,
but Art has survived; our boors wear stockings, our women
drink tea, our poets read Shakspeare, and our astronomers
improve on Newton! Are we now contented? No! more
restless than ever. New classes are called into power; new
forms of government insisted on. Still the same catch-
words, — Liberty here, Religion there; Order with one faction, Amelioration with the other. Where is the goal, and

what have we gained?   Books are written, silks are woven, palaces are built, — mighty acquisitions for the few — but the peasant is a peasant still!   The crowd are yet at the bottom of the wheel; better off, you say.   No, for they are not more contented!   The artisan is as anxious for change as ever the serf was; and the steam-engine has its victims as well as the sword.

"Talk of legislation: all isolated laws pave the way to wholesale changes in the form of government!   Emancipate Catholics, and you open the door to democratic principle, that Opinion should be free.   If free with the sectarian, it should be free with the elector.   The Ballot is a corollary from the Catholic Relief-bill.   Grant the Ballot, and the new corollary of enlarged suffrage.   Suffrage enlarged is divided but by a yielding surface (a circle widening in the waters, from universal suffrage.   Universal suffrage is Democracy.   Is Democracy better than the aristocratic commonwealth?   Look at the Greeks, who knew both forms; are they agreed which is the best?   Plato, Thucydides, Xenophon, Aristophanes — the Dreamer, the Historian, the Philosophic Man of Action, the penetrating Wit — have no ideals in Democracy.   Algernon Sidney, the martyr of liberty, allows no government to the multitude.   Brutus died for a republic, but a republic of Patricians!   What form of government is then the best?   All dispute, the wisest cannot agree.   The many still say ' a Republic; ' yet, as you yourself will allow, Prussia, the Despotism, does all that Republics do.   Yes, but a good despot is a lucky accident; true, but a just and benevolent Republic is as yet a monster equally short-lived.   When the People have no other tyrant, their own public opinion becomes one.   No secret espionage is more intolerable to a free spirit than the broad glare of the American eye.

"A rural republic is but a patriarchal tribe — no emulation, no glory; peace and stagnation.   What Englishman, what Frenchman, would wish to be a Swiss?   A commercial republic is but an admirable machine for making money.   Is man created for nothing nobler than freighting ships and speculating on silk and sugar?   In fact, there is no certain goal in legislation; we go on colonizing Utopia, and fighting phan-

toms in the clouds. Let us content ourselves with injuring
no man, and doing good only in our own little sphere. Let
us leave States and senates to fill the sieve of the Danaides,
and roll up the stone of Sisyphus."

"My dear friend," said De Montaigne, "you have certainly
made the most of an argument, which, if granted, would con-
sign government to fools and knaves, and plunge the communities of mankind into the Slough of Despond. But a very
commonplace view of the question might suffice to shake your
system. Is life, mere animal life, on the whole, a curse or a
blessing?"

"The generality of men in all countries," answered Maltravers, "enjoy existence, and apprehend death; were it
otherwise, the world had been made by a Fiend, and not a
God!"

"Well, then, observe how the progress of society cheats
the grave! In great cities, where the effect of civilization
must be the most visible, the diminution of mortality in a
corresponding ratio with the increase of civilization is most
remarkable. In Berlin, from the year 1747 to 1755, the
annual mortality was as one to twenty-eight; but from 1816
to 1822, it was as one to thirty-four! You ask what England
has gained by her progress in the arts? I will answer you by
her bills of mortality. In London, Birmingham, and Liverpool, deaths have decreased in less than a century from one
to twenty, to one to forty (precisely one-half!). Again, whenever a community — nay, a single city, decreases in civilization, and in its concomitants, activity and commerce, its
mortality instantly increases. But if civilization be favourable to the prolongation of life, must it not be favourable to
all that blesses life, — to bodily health, to mental cheerfulness, to the capacities for enjoyment? And how much more
grand, how much more sublime, becomes the prospect of gain,
if we reflect that, to each life thus called forth, there is a
soul, a destiny beyond the grave, multiplied immortalities!
What an apology for the continued progress of States! But
you say that, however we advance, we continue impatient and
dissatisfied: can you really suppose that, because man in every
state is discontented with his lot, there is no difference in the

degree and *quality* of his discontent, no distinction between
pining for bread and longing for the moon? Desire is implanted within us, as the very principle of existence; the
physical desire fills the world, and the moral desire improves
it. Where there is desire, there must be discontent: if we
are satisfied with all things, desire is extinct. But a certain
degree of discontent is not incompatible with happiness, nay,
it has happiness of its own; what happiness like hope, —
what is hope but desire? The European serf, whose seigneur
could command his life, or insist as a right on the chastity of
his daughter, desires to better his condition. God has compassion on his state; Providence calls into action the ambition of leaders, the contests of faction, the movement of men's
aims and passions: a change passes through society and legislation, and the serf becomes free! He desires still, but what?
No longer personal security, no longer the privileges of life
and health; but higher wages, greater comforts, easier justice
for diminished wrongs. Is there no difference in the quality
of that desire? Was one a greater torment than the other
is? Rise a scale higher: a new class is created — the Middle
Class, — the express creature of Civilization. Behold the
burgher and the citizen, and still struggling, still contending,
still desiring, and therefore still discontented. But the discontent does not prey upon the springs of life: it is the discontent of *hope*, not *despair;* it calls forth faculties, energies, and
passions, in which there is more joy than sorrow. It is this
desire which makes the citizen in private life an anxious
father, a careful master, an *active*, and therefore not an unhappy, man. You allow that individuals can effect individual
good: this very restlessness, this very discontent with the exact place that he occupies, makes the citizen a benefactor in
his narrow circle. Commerce, better than Charity, feeds the
hungry and clothes the naked. Ambition, better than brute
affection, gives education to our children, and teaches them
the love of industry, the pride of independence, the respect
for others and themselves!

"In other words, a deference to such qualities as can best
fit them to get on in the world, and make the most money!"

"Take that view if you will; but the wiser, the more civilized the State, the worse chances for the rogue to get on!
There may be some art, some hypocrisy, some avarice, — nay,
some hardness of heart, — in paternal example and professional tuition.   But what are such sober infirmities to the
vices that arise from defiance and despair?   Your savage has
his virtues, but they are mostly physical, — fortitude, absti-
nence, patience: mental and moral virtues must be numerous
or few, in proportion to the range of ideas and the exigencies
of social life.   With the savage, therefore, they must be fewer
than with civilized men; and they are consequently limited
to those simple and rude elements which the safety of his
state renders necessary to him.   He is usually hospitable;
sometimes honest.   But vices are necessary to his existence
as well as virtues: he is at war with a tribe that may destroy
his own; and treachery without scruple, cruelty without remorse, are essential to him; he feels their necessity, and calls
them *virtues!*   Even the half-civilized man, the Arab whom
you praise, imagines he has a necessity for your money; and
his robberies become virtues to him.   But in civilized States,
vices are at least not necessary to the existence of the majority; they are not, therefore, worshipped as virtues.   Society
unites against them; treachery, robbery, massacre, are not
essential to the strength or safety of the community: they
exist, it is true, but they are not cultivated, but punished.
The thief in St. Giles's has the virtues of your savage: he is
true to his companions, he is brave in danger, he is patient in
privation; he practises the virtues necessary to the bonds of
his calling and the tacit laws of his vocation.   He might have
made an admirable savage: but surely the mass of civilized
men are better than the thief? "

Maltravers was struck, and paused a little before he replied;
and then he shifted his ground.   "But at least all our laws,
all our efforts, must leave the multitude in every State condemned to a labour that deadens intellect, and a poverty that
embitters life."

"Supposing this were true, still there are multitudes besides
the multitude.   In each State Civilization produces a middle

class, more numerous to-day than the whole peasantry of a thousand years ago. Would Movement and Progress be without their divine uses, even if they limited their effect to the production of such a class? Look also to the effect of art, and refinement, and just laws, in the wealthier and higher classes. See how their very habits of life tend to increase the sum of enjoyment; see the mighty activity that their very luxury, the very frivolity of their pursuits, create! Without an aristocracy, would there have been a middle class? Without a middle class, would there ever have been an interposition between lord and slave? Before commerce produces a middle class, Religion creates one. The Priesthood, whatever its errors, was the curb to Power. But, to return to the multitude, — you say that in all times they are left the same. Is it so? I come to statistics again: I find that not only civilization, but liberty, has a prodigious effect upon human life. It is, as it were, by the instinct of self-preservation that liberty is so passionately desired by the multitude. A negro slave, for instance, dies annually as one to five or six, but a free African in the English service only as one to thirty-five! Freedom is not, therefore, a mere abstract dream, a beautiful name, a Platonic aspiration: it is interwoven with the most practical of all blessings, — life itself! And can you say fairly that by laws labour cannot be lightened and poverty diminished? We have granted already that since *there are degrees in discontent, there is a difference between the peasant and the serf: how know you what the peasant a thousand years hence may be? Discontented, you will say, — still discontented. Yes; but if he had not been discontented, he would have been a serf still! Far from quelling this desire to better himself, we ought to hail it as the source of his perpetual progress. That desire to him is often like imagination to the poet, it transports him into the Future —

   "'Crura sonant ferro, sed canit inter opus.'

It is, indeed, the gradual transformation from the desire of Despair to the desire of Hope, that makes the difference between man and man, between misery and bliss."

"And then comes the crisis. Hope ripens into deeds; the stormy revolution, perhaps the armed despotism; the relapse into the second infancy of States!"

"Can we, with new agencies at our command, new morality, new wisdom, predicate of the Future by the Past? In ancient States, the mass were slaves; civilization and freedom rested with oligarchies; in Athens twenty thousand citizens, four hundred thousand slaves! How easy decline, degeneracy, overthrow in such States, — a handful of soldiers and philosophers without a People! Now we have no longer barriers to the circulation of the blood of States. The absence of slavery, the existence of the Press; the healthful proportions of kingdoms, neither too confined nor too vast, have created new hopes, which history cannot destroy. As a proof, look to all late revolutions: in England the Civil Wars, the Reformation, — in France her awful Saturnalia, her military despotism! Has either nation fallen back? The deluge passes, and, behold, the face of things more glorious than before! Compare the French of to-day with the French of the old *régime*. You are silent; well, and if in all States there is ever some danger of evil in their activity, is that a reason why you are to lie down inactive; why you are to leave the crew to battle for the helm? How much may individuals by the diffusion of their own thoughts in letters or in action regulate the order of vast events, — now prevent, now soften, now animate, now guide! And is a man to whom Providence and Fortune have imparted such prerogatives to stand aloof, because he can neither foresee the Future nor create Perfection? And you talk of no certain and definite goal! How know we that there is a certain and definite goal, even in heaven? How know we that excellence may not be illimitable? Enough that we improve, that we proceed. Seeing in the great design of earth that benevolence is an attribute of the Designer, let us leave the rest to Posterity and to God."

"You have disturbed many of my theories," said Maltravers, candidly; "and I will reflect on our conversation; but, after all, is every man to aspire to influence others; to throw his opinion into the great scales in which human destinies are weighed?

Private life is not criminal.   It is no virtue to write a book, or to make a speech.   Perhaps, I should be as well engaged in returning to my country village, looking at my schools, and wrangling with the parish overseers — ”

"Ah," interrupted the Frenchman, laughing; "if I have driven you to this point, I will go no further.   Every state of life has its duties; every man must be himself the judge of what he is most fit for.   It is quite enough that he desires to be active, and labours to be useful; that he acknowledges the precept, ' Never to be weary in well-doing.'   The divine appetite once fostered, let it select its own food.   But the man who, after fair trial of his capacities, and with all opportunity for their full development before him, is convinced that he has faculties which private life cannot wholly absorb, must not repine that Human Nature is not perfect, when he refuses even to exercise the gifts he himself possesses. ”

Now these arguments have been very tedious; in some places they have been old and trite; in others they may appear too much to appertain to the abstract theory of first principles.   Yet from such arguments, *pro* and *con*, unless I greatly mistake, are to be derived corollaries equally practical and sublime, — the virtue of Action, the obligations of Genius, and the philosophy that teaches us to confide in the destinies, and labour in the service, of mankind.

CHAPTER VI.

I 'LL tell you presently her very picture ;
Stay — yes, it is so — Lelia.
                              The Captain, Act v. sc. 1.

MALTRAVERS had not shrunk into a system of false philosophy from wayward and sickly dreams, from resolute self-delusion; on the contrary, his errors rested on his convictions: the convictions disturbed, the errors were rudely shaken.

But when his mind began restlessly to turn once more towards the duties of active life; when he recalled all the former drudgeries and toils of political conflict, or the wearing fatigues of literature, with its small enmities, its false friendships, and its meagre and capricious rewards, — ah, then, indeed, he shrank in dismay from the thoughts of the solitude at home! No lips to console in dejection, no heart to sympathize in triumph, no love within to counterbalance the hate without, — and the best of man, his household affections, left to wither away, or to waste themselves on ideal images, or melancholy remembrance.

It may, indeed, be generally remarked (contrary to a common notion), that the men who are most happy at home are the most active abroad. The animal spirits are necessary to healthful action; and dejection and the sense of solitude will turn the stoutest into dreamers. The hermit is the antipodes of the citizen; and no gods animate and inspire us like the Lares.

One evening, after an absence from Paris of nearly a fortnight, at De Montaigne's villa, in the neighbourhood of St. Cloud, Maltravers, who, though he no longer practised the art, was not less fond than heretofore of music, was seated in Madame de Ventadour's box at the Italian Opera; and Valerie, who was above all the woman's jealousy of beauty, was expatiating with great warmth of eulogium upon the charms of a young English lady whom she had met at Lady G——'s the preceding evening.

"She is just my beau-ideal of the true English beauty," said Valerie: "it is not only the exquisite fairness of the complexion, nor the eyes so purely blue, — which the dark lashes relieve from the coldness common to the light eyes of the Scotch and German, — that are so beautifully national, but the simplicity of manner, the unconsciousness of admiration, the mingled modesty and sense of the expression. No, I have seen women more beautiful, but I never saw one more lovely: you are silent; I expected some burst of patriotism in return for my compliment to your countrywoman!"

"But I am so absorbed in that wonderful Pasta—"

"You are no such thing; your thoughts are far away. But can you tell me anything about my fair stranger and her friends? In the first place, there is a Lord Doltimore, whom I knew before — you need say nothing about him; in the next there is his new married bride, handsome, dark — but you are not well!"

"It was the draught from the door; go on, I beseech you, the young lady, the friend, her name?"

"Her name I do not remember; but she was engaged to be married to one of your statesmen, Lord Vargrave; the marriage is broken off — I know not if that be the cause of a certain melancholy in her countenance, — a melancholy I am sure not natural to its Hebe-like expression. But who have just entered the opposite box? Ah, Mr. Maltravers, do look, there is the beautiful English girl!"

And Maltravers raised his eyes, and once more beheld the countenance of Evelyn Cameron!

BOOK VII.

Λύκησις ἀγνῶς λόγων
ἦλθε. — SOPHOCLES : *Œd. Tyr.* 681.

Words of dark import gave suspicion birth. — POTTER.

CHAPTER I.

Luce. Is the wind there ?
That makes for me.
Isab. Come, I forget a business.
Wit without Money.

LORD VARGRAVE's travelling-carriage was at his door, and he himself was putting on his greatcoat in his library, when Lord Saxingham entered.

"What! you are going into the country?"

"Yes; I wrote you word, — to see Lisle Court."

"Ay, true; I had forgot. Somehow or other my memory is not so good as it was. But, let me see, Lisle Court is in ——shire. Why, you will pass within ten miles of C——."

"C——! Shall I? I am not much versed in the geography of England, — never learned it at school. As for Poland, Kamschatka, Mexico, Madagascar, or any other place as to which knowledge would be *useful*, I have every inch of the way at my finger's end. But *à propos* of C——, it is the town in which my late uncle made his fortune."

"Ah, so it is. I recollect you were to have stood for C——, but gave it up to Staunch; very handsome in you. Have you any interest there still?"

"I think my ward has some tenants, — a street or two, — one called Richard Street, and the other Templeton Place. I had intended some weeks ago to have gone down there, and seen what interest was still left to our family; but Staunch himself told me that C—— was a sure card."

"So he thought; but he has been with me this morning in great alarm: he now thinks he shall be thrown out. A Mr. Winsley, who has a great deal of interest there, and was a supporter of his, hangs back on account of the —— question. This is unlucky, as Staunch is quite with *us ;* and if he were to rat now it would be most unfortunate."

"Winsley! Winsley! — my poor uncle's right-hand man. A great brewer, — always chairman of the Templeton Committee. I know the name, though I never saw the man."

"If you could take C—— in your way?"

"To be sure. Staunch must not be lost. We cannot throw away a single vote, much more one of such weight, — eighteen stone at the least! I'll stop at C—— on pretence of seeing after my ward's houses, and have a quiet conference with Mr. Winsley. Hem! Peers must not interfere in elections, eh? Well, good-by: take care of yourself. I shall be back in a week, I hope, — perhaps less."

In a minute more Lord Vargrave and Mr. George Frederick Augustus Howard, a slim young gentleman of high birth and connections, but who, having, as a portionless cadet, his own way to make in the world, condescended to be his lordship's private secretary, were rattling over the streets the first stage to C——.

It was late at night when Lord Vargrave arrived at the head inn of that grave and respectable cathedral city, in which once Richard Templeton, Esq., — saint, banker, and politician, — had exercised his dictatorial sway. "Sic transit gloria mundi!" As he warmed his hands by the fire in the large wainscoted apartment into which he was shown, his eye met a full length engraving of his uncle, with a roll of papers in his hand, — meant for a parliamentary bill for the turnpike trusts in the neighbourhood of C——. The sight brought back his recollections of that pious and saturnine relation, and insensibly the minister's thoughts flew to his death-bed, and to the strange secret which in that last hour he had

revealed to Lumley, — a secret which had done much in deepening Lord Vargrave's contempt for the forms and conven-
tionalities of decorous life.   And here it may be mentioned
— though in the course of this volume a penetrating reader
may have guessed as much — that, whatever that secret, it
did not refer expressly or exclusively to the late lord's singular and ill-assorted marriage.   Upon that point much was
still left obscure to arouse Lumley's curiosity, had he been a
man whose curiosity was very vivacious.   But on this he felt
but little interest.   He knew enough to believe that no further
information could benefit himself personally; why should he
trouble his head with what never would fill his pockets?

An audible yawn from the slim secretary roused Lord Vargrave from his revery.

"I envy you, my young friend," said he, good-humouredly.
"It is a pleasure we lose as we grow older, — that of being
sleepy.   However, ' to bed,' as Lady Macbeth says.   Faith, I
don't wonder the poor devil of a thane was slow in going to
bed with such a tigress.   Good-night to you."

CHAPTER II.

MA fortune va prendre une face nouvelle.[1]
RACINE Androm., Act i. sc. 1.

THE next morning Vargrave inquired the way to Mr.
Winsley's, and walked alone to the house of the brewer.
The slim secretary went to inspect the cathedral.

Mr. Winsley was a little, thickset man, with a civil but
blunt electioneering manner.   He started when he heard Lord
Vargrave's name, and bowed with great stiffness.   Vargrave
saw at a glance that there was some cause of grudge in the

---

[1] "My fortune is about to take a turn."

mind of the worthy man; nor did Mr. Winsley long hesitate before he cleansed his bosom of its perilous stuff.

"This is an unexpected honour, my lord: I don't know how to account for it."

"Why, Mr. Winsley, your friendship with my late uncle can, perhaps, sufficiently explain and apologize for a visit from a nephew sincerely attached to his memory."

"Humph! I certainly did do all in my power to promote Mr. Templeton's interests. No man, I may say, did more; and yet I don't think it was much thought of the moment he turned his back upon the electors of C——. Not that I bear any malice; I am well to do, and value no man's favour, — no man's, my lord!"

"You amaze me! I always heard my poor uncle speak of you in the highest terms."

"Oh, well, it don't signify; pray say no more of it. Can I offer your lordship a glass of wine?"

"No, I am much obliged to you; but we really must set this little matter right. You know that after his marriage my uncle never revisited C——; and that shortly before his death he sold the greater part of his interest in this city. His young wife, I suppose, liked the neighbourhood of London; and when elderly gentlemen *do* marry, you know they are no longer their own masters; but if you had ever come to Fulham — ah! then, indeed, my uncle would have rejoiced to see his old friend."

"Your lordship thinks so," said Mr. Winsley with a sardonic smile. "You are mistaken; I did call at Fulham; and though I sent in my card, Lord Vargrave's servant (he was then My Lord) brought back word that his lordship was not at home."

"But that must have been true; he was out, you may depend on it."

"I saw him at the window, my lord," said Mr. Winsley, taking a pinch of snuff.

"Oh, the deuce! I'm in for it," thought Lumley. — "Very strange, indeed! but how can you account for it? Ah, perhaps the health of Lady Vargrave — she was so very delicate then, and my poor uncle lived for her — you know that he left all his fortune to Miss Cameron? "

"Miss Cameron!   Who is she, my lord? "

"Why, his daughter-in-law; Lady Vargrave was a widow, — a Mrs. Cameron."

"Mrs. Cam —   I remember now, — they put Cameron in the newspapers; but I thought it was a mistake.   But, perhaps " (added Winsley, with a sneer of peculiar malignity), — "perhaps, when your worthy uncle thought of being a peer, he did not like to have it known that he married so much beneath him."

"You quite mistake, my dear sir; my uncle never denied that Mrs. Cameron was a lady of no fortune or connections, — widow to some poor Scotch gentleman, who died I think in India."

"He left her very ill off, poor thing; but she had a great deal of merit, and worked hard; she taught my girls to play — "

"Your girls! did Mrs. Cameron ever reside in C——? "

"To be sure; but she was then called Mrs. Butler — just as pretty a name to my fancy."

"You must make a mistake: my uncle married this lady in Devonshire."

"Very possibly," quoth the brewer, doggedly.   "Mrs. Butler left the town with her little girl some time before Mr. Templeton married."

"Well, you are wiser than I am," said Lumley, forcing a smile.   "But how can you be sure that Mrs. Butler and Mrs. Cameron are one and the same person?   You did not go into the house, you could not have seen Lady Vargrave " (and here Lumley shrewdly guessed — if the tale were true — at the cause of his uncle's exclusion of his old acquaintance).

"No! but I saw her ladyship on the lawn," said Mr. Winsley, with another sardonic smile; "and I asked the porter at the lodge as I went out if that was Lady Vargrave, and he said, ' yes.'   However, my lord, bygones are bygones, — I bear no malice; your uncle was a good man: and if he had but said to me, ' Winsley, don't say a word about Mrs.

Butler,' he might have reckoned on me just as much as when in his elections he used to put five thousand pounds in my hands, and say, ' Winsley, no bribery, — it is wicked; let this be given in charity.' Did any one ever know how that money went? Was your uncle ever accused of corruption? But, my lord, surely you will take some refreshment? "

"No, indeed; but if you will let me dine with you to-morrow, you 'll oblige me much; and, whatever my uncle's faults (and latterly, poor man, he was hardly in his senses; what a will he made!) let not the nephew suffer for them. Come, Mr. Winsley," and Lumley held out his hand with enchanting frankness, "you know my motives are disinterested; I have no parliamentary interest to serve, we have no constituents for our Hospital of Incurables; and — oh! that 's right, — we 're friends, I see! Now I must go and look after my ward's houses. Let me see, the agent's name is — is — "

"Perkins, I think, my lord," said Mr. Winsley, thoroughly softened by the charm of Vargrave's words and manner. "Let me put on my hat, and show you his house."

"Will you? That 's very kind; give me all the election news by the way — you know I was once within an ace of being your member."

Vargrave learned from his new friend some further particulars relative to Mrs. Butler's humble habits and homely mode of life at C——, which served completely to explain to him why his proud and worldly uncle had so carefully abstained from all intercourse with that city, and had prevented the nephew from standing for its vacant representation. It seemed, however, that Winsley — whose resentment was not of a very active or violent kind — had not communicated the discovery he had made to his fellow townspeople; but had contented himself with hints and aphorisms, whenever he had heard the subject of Mr. Templeton's marriage discussed, which had led the gossips of the place to imagine that he had made a much worse selection than he really had. As to the accuracy of Winsley's assertion, Vargrave, though surprised at first, had but little doubt on consideration, especially when he heard that Mrs. Butler's principal patroness had been the Mrs.

Leslie, now the intimate friend of Lady Vargrave. But what had been the career, what the earlier condition and struggles of this simple and interesting creature? With her appearance at C——, commenced all that surmise could invent. Not greater was the mystery that wrapped the apparition of Manco Capac by the lake Titiaca, than that which shrouded the places and the trials whence the lowly teacher of music had emerged amidst the streets of C——.

Weary, and somewhat careless, of conjecture, Lord Vargrave, in dining with Mr. Winsley, turned the conversation upon the business on which he had principally undertaken his journey, — namely, the meditated purchase of Lisle Court.

"I myself am not a very good judge of landed property," said Vargrave; "I wish I knew of an experienced surveyor to look over the farms and timber: can you help me to such a one?"

Mr. Winsley smiled, and glanced at a rosy-cheeked young lady, who simpered and turned away. "I think my daughter could recommend one to your lordship, if she dared."

"Oh, Pa!"

"I see. Well, Miss Winsley, I will take no recommendation but yours."

Miss Winsley made an effort.

"Indeed, my lord, I have always heard Mr. Robert Hobbs considered very clever in his profession."

"Mr. Robert Hobbs is my man! His good health — and a fair wife to him."

Miss Winsley glanced at Mamma, and then at a younger sister; and then there was a titter, and then a fluttering, and then a rising, and Mr. Winsley, Lord Vargrave, and the slim secretary were left alone.

"Really, my lord," said the host, resettling himself, and pushing the wine, "though you have guessed our little family arrangement, and I have some interest in the recommendation, since Margaret will be Mrs. Robert Hobbs in a few weeks, yet I do not know a more acute, intelligent young man anywhere. Highly respectable, with an independent fortune; his father is lately dead, and made at least thirty thousand pounds in trade. His brother Edward is also dead; so he has the bulk of the property, and he follows his profession merely for amusement. He would consider it a great honour."

"And where does he live?"

"Oh, not in this county, — a long way off; close to ——; but it is all in your lordship's road. A very nice house he has, too. I have known his family since I was a boy; it is astonishing how his father improved the place, — it was a poor little lath-and-plaster cottage when the late Mr. Hobbs bought it, and it is now a very excellent family house."

"Well, you shall give me the address and a letter of introduction, and so much for that matter. But to return to politics;" and here Lord Vargrave ran eloquently on, till Mr. Winsley thought him the only man in the world who could save the country from that utter annihilation, the possibility of which he had never even suspected before.

It may be as well to add, that, on wishing Lord Vargrave good-night, Mr. Winsley whispered in his ear, "Your lordship's friend, Lord Staunch, need be under no apprehension, — we are all right!"

———◆———

CHAPTER III.

THIS is the house, sir. — *Love's Pilgrimage*, Act iv sc. 2.

Redeunt Saturnia regna.[1] — VIRGIL.

THE next morning, Lumley and his slender companion were rolling rapidly over the same road on which, sixteen years ago, way-worn and weary, Alice Darvil had first met with Mrs. Leslie; they were talking about a new opera-dancer as they whirled by the very spot.

[1] "A former state of things returns."

It was about five o'clock in the afternoon, the next day, when the carriage stopped at a cast-iron gate, on which was inscribed this epigraph, "Hobbs' lodge — Ring the Bell."

"A snug place enough," said Lord Vargrave, as they were waiting the arrival of the footman to unbar the gate.

"Yes," said Mr. Howard. "If a retired Cit could be trans-formed into a house, such is the house he would be."

Poor Dale Cottage, — the home of Poetry and Passion! But change visits the Commonplace as well as the Romantic. Since Alice had pressed to that cold grating her wistful eyes, time had wrought his allotted revolutions; the old had died, the young grown up. Of the children playing on the lawn, death had claimed some, and marriage others, — and the holiday of youth was gone for all.

The servant opened the gate. Mr. Robert Hobbs *was* at home; he had friends with him, — he was engaged; Lord Vargrave sent in his card, and the introductory letter from Mr. Winsley. In two seconds, these missives brought to the gate Mr. Robert Hobbs himself, a smart young man, with a black stock, red whiskers, and an eye-glass pendant to a hair-chain which was possibly a *gage d'amour* from Miss Margaret Winsley.

A profusion of bows, compliments, apologies, etc., the carriage drove up the sweep, and Lord Vargrave descended, and was immediately ushered into Mr. Hobbs's private room. The slim secretary followed, and sat silent, melancholy, and upright, while the peer affably explained his wants and wishes to the surveyor.

Mr. Hobbs was well acquainted with the locality of Lisle Court, which was little more than thirty miles distant; he should be proud to accompany Lord Vargrave thither the next morning. But, might he venture, might he dare, might he presume — a gentleman who lived at the town of —— was to dine with him that day; a gentleman of the most profound knowledge of agricultural affairs; a gentleman who knew every farm, almost every acre, belonging to Colonel Mal-travers; if his lordship could be induced to waive ceremony, and dine with Mr. Hobbs, it might be really useful to meet this gentleman. The slim secretary, who was very hungry, and who thought he sniffed an uncommonly savoury smell, looked up from his boots. Lord Vargrave smiled.

"My young friend here is too great an admirer of Mrs. Hobbs — who is to be — not to feel anxious to make the acquaintance of any member of the family she is to enter."

Mr. George Frederick Augustus Howard blushed indignant refutation of the calumnious charge. Vargrave continued, —

"As for me, I shall be delighted to meet any friends of yours, and am greatly obliged for your consideration. We may dismiss the postboys, Howard; and what time shall we summon them, — ten o'clock?"

"If your lordship would condescend to accept a bed, we can accommodate your lordship and this gentleman, and start at any hour in the morning that — "

"So be it," interrupted Vargrave. "You speak like a man of business. Howard, be so kind as to order the horses for six o'clock to-morrow. We'll breakfast at Lisle Court."

This matter settled, Lord Vargrave and Mr. Howard were shown into their respective apartments. Travelling dresses were changed, the dinner put back, and the fish over-boiled; but what mattered common fish, when Mr. Hobbs had just caught such a big one? Of what consequence he should be henceforth and ever! A peer, a minister, a stranger to the county, — to come all this way to consult *him!* to be *his* guest! to be shown off, and patted, and trotted out before all the rest of the company! Mr. Hobbs was a made man! Careless of all this, ever at home with any one, and delighted, perhaps, to escape a *tête-à-tête* with Mr. Howard in a strange inn, Vargrave lounged into the drawing-room, and was formally presented to the expectant family and the famishing guests.

During the expiring bachelorship of Mr. Robert Hobbs, his sister, Mrs. Tiddy (to whom the reader was first introduced as a bride gathering the wisdom of economy and large joints from the frugal lips of her mamma), officiated as lady of the house, — a comely matron, and well-preserved, — except that she had lost a front tooth, — in a jaundiced satinet gown, with

a fall of British blonde, and a tucker of the same, Mr. Tiddy
being a starch man, and not willing that the luxuriant charms
of Mrs. T. should be too temptingly exposed! There was
also Mr. Tiddy, whom his wife had married for love, and who
was now well to do, — a fine-looking man, with large whiskers,
and a Roman nose, a little awry. Moreover, there was a Miss
Biddy or Bridget Hobbs, a young lady of four or five and
twenty, who was considering whether she might ask Lord
Vargrave to write something in her album, and who cast a
bashful look of admiration at the slim secretary, as he now
sauntered into the room, in a black coat, black waistcoat,
black trousers, and a black neckcloth, with a black pin, —
looking much like an ebony cane split half-way up. Miss
Biddy was a fair young lady, a *leetle* faded, with uncommonly
thin arms and white satin shoes, on which the slim secretary
cast his eyes and — shuddered!

In addition to the family group were the Rector of ——,
an agreeable man, who published sermons and poetry; also
Sir William Jekyll, who was employing Mr. Hobbs to make
a map of an estate he had just purchased; also two country
squires and their two wives; moreover, the physician of the
neighbouring town, — a remarkably tall man, who wore spectacles and told anecdotes; and, lastly, Mr. Onslow, the gentleman to whom Mr. Hobbs had referred, — an elderly man of
prepossessing exterior, of high repute as the most efficient
magistrate, the best farmer, and the most sensible person in
the neighbourhood. This made the party, to each individual
of which the great man bowed and smiled; and the great
man's secretary bent, condescendingly, three joints of his
backbone.

The bell was now rung, dinner announced. Sir William
Jekyll led the way with one of the she-squires, and Lord Vargrave offered his arm to the portly Mrs. Tiddy.

Vargrave, as usual, was the life of the feast. Mr. Howard,
who sat next to Miss Bridget, conversed with her between
the courses, "in dumb show." Mr. Onslow and the physician played second and third to Lord Vargrave. When the
dinner was over, and the ladies had retired, Vargrave found

himself seated next to Mr. Onslow, and discovered in his neighbour a most agreeable companion. They talked principally about Lisle Court, and from Colonel Maltravers the conversation turned naturally upon Ernest. Vargrave proclaimed his early intimacy with the latter gentleman, complained, feelingly, that politics had divided them of late, and told two or three anecdotes of their youthful adventures in the East. Mr. Onslow listened to him with much attention.

"I made the acquaintance of Mr. Maltravers many years ago," said he, "and upon a very delicate occasion. I was greatly interested in him; I never saw one so young (for he was then but a boy) manifest feelings so deep. By the dates you have referred to, your acquaintance with him must have commenced very shortly after mine. Was he at that time cheerful, in good spirits?"

"No, indeed; hypochondriacal to the greatest degree."

"Your lordship's intimacy with him, and the confidence that generally exists between young men, induce me to suppose that he may have told you a little romance connected with his early years."

Lumley paused to consider; and this conversation, which had been carried on apart, was suddenly broken into by the tall doctor, who wanted to know whether his lordship had ever heard the anecdote about Lord Thurlow and the late king. The anecdote was as long as the doctor himself; and when it was over, the gentlemen adjourned to the drawing-room, and all conversation was immediately drowned by "Row, brothers, row," which had only been suspended till the arrival of Mr. Tiddy, who had a fine bass voice.

Alas! eighteen years ago, in that spot of earth, Alice Darvil had first caught the soul of music from the lips of Genius and of Love! But better as it is, — less romantic, but more proper, — as Hobbs' Lodge was less pretty, but more safe from the winds and rains, than Dale Cottage.

Miss Bridget ventured to ask the good-humoured Lord Vargrave if he sang. "Not I, Miss Hobbs; but Howard, there! — ah, if you heard *him!*" The consequence of this hint was, that the unhappy secretary, who, alone, in a distant corner, was unconsciously refreshing his fancy with some cool weak coffee, was instantly beset with applications from Miss Bridget, Mrs. Tiddy, Mr. Tiddy, and the tall doctor, to favour the company with a specimen of his talents. Mr. Howard could sing, — he could even play the guitar. But to sing at Hobbs' Lodge, to sing to the accompaniment of Mrs. Tiddy, to have his gentle tenor crushed to death in a glee by the heavy splayfoot of Mr. Tiddy's manly bass — the thought was insufferable! He faltered forth assurances of his ignorance, and hastened to bury his resentment in the retirement of a remote sofa. Vargrave, who had forgotten the significant question of Mr. Onslow, renewed in a whisper his conversation with that gentleman relative to the meditated investment, while Mr. and Mrs. Tiddy sang "Come dwell with me;" and Onslow was so pleased with his new acquaintance, that he volunteered to make a fourth in Lumley's carriage the next morning, and accompany him to Lisle Court. This settled, the party soon afterwards broke up. At midnight Lord Vargrave was fast asleep; and Mr. Howard, tossing restlessly to and fro on his melancholy couch, was revolving all the hardships that await a native of St. James's, who ventures forth among —

> "The Anthropophagi, and men whose heads
> Do grow beneath their shoulders!"

CHAPTER IV.

BUT how were these doubts to be changed into absolute certainty?
                                        EDGAR HUNTLEY.

THE next morning, while it was yet dark, Lord Vargrave's carriage picked up Mr. Onslow at the door of a large old-fashioned house, at the entrance of the manufacturing town of ——. The party were silent and sleepy till they arrived at Lisle Court. The sun had then appeared, the morning was clear, the air frosty and bracing; and as, after traversing a noble park, a superb quadrangular pile of brick flanked by huge square turrets coped with stone broke upon the gaze of Lord Vargrave, his worldly heart swelled within him, and the image of Evelyn became inexpressibly lovely and seductive.

Though the housekeeper was not prepared for Vargrave's arrival at so early an hour, yet he had been daily expected: the logs soon burned bright in the ample hearth of the breakfast-room; the urn hissed, the cutlets smoked; and while the rest of the party gathered round the fire, and unmuffled themselves of cloaks and shawl-handkerchiefs, Vargrave seized upon the housekeeper, traversed with delighted steps the magnificent suite of rooms, gazed on the pictures, admired the state bed-chambers, peeped into the offices, and recognized in all a mansion worthy of a Peer of England, — but which a more prudent man would have thought, with a sigh, required careful management of the rent-roll raised from the property adequately to equip and maintain. Such an idea did not cross the mind of Vargrave; he only thought how much he should be honoured and envied, when, as Secretary of State, he should yearly fill those feudal chambers with the pride and rank of England! It was characteristic of the extraordinary sanguineness and self-confidence of Vargrave, that he entirely overlooked one slight obstacle to this prospect, in the determined refusal of Evelyn to accept that passionate homage which he offered to — her fortune!

When breakfast was over the steward was called in, and the party, mounted upon ponies, set out to reconnoitre. After spending the short day most agreeably in looking over the gardens, pleasure-grounds, park, and home-farm, and settling to visit the more distant parts of the property the next day, the party were returning home to dine, when Vargrave's eye caught the glittering *whim* of Sir Gregory Gubbins.

He pointed it out to Mr. Onslow, and laughed much at hearing of the annoyance it occasioned to Colonel Maltravers. "Thus," said Lumley, "do we all crumple the rose-leaf under us, and quarrel with couches the most luxuriant! As for me,

I will wager, that were this property mine, or my ward's, in three weeks we should have won the heart of Sir Gregory, made him pull down his *whim*, and coaxed him out of his interest in the city of ——. A good seat for you, Howard, some day or other."

"Sir Gregory has prodigiously bad taste," said Mr. Hobbs. "For my part, I think that there ought to be a certain modest simplicity in the display of wealth got in business, — that was my poor father's maxim."

"Ah!" said Vargrave, "Hobbs' Lodge is a specimen. Who was your predecessor in that charming retreat?"

"Why, the place — then called Dale Cottage — belonged to a Mr. Berners, a rich bachelor in business, who was rich enough not to mind what people said of him, and kept a lady there. She ran off from him, and he then let it to some young man — a stranger, very eccentric, I hear — a Mr. — Mr. Butler — and he, too, gave the cottage an unlawful attraction, — a most beautiful girl, I have heard."

"Butler!" echoed Vargrave, — "Butler! Butler!" Lumley recollected that such had been the real name of Mrs. Cameron. Onslow looked hard at Vargrave.

"You recognize the name, my lord," said he in a whisper, as Hobbs had turned to address himself to Mr. Howard. "I thought you very discreet when I asked you, last night, if you remembered the early follies of your friend." A suspicion at once flashed upon the quick mind of Vargrave: Butler was a name on the mother's side in the family of Maltravers; the gloom of Ernest when he first knew him, the boy's hints that the gloom was connected with the affections, the extraordinary and single accomplishment of Lady Vargrave in that art of which Maltravers was so consummate a master, the similarity of name, — all taken in conjunction with the meaning question of Mr. Onslow, were enough to suggest to Vargrave that he might be on the verge of a family secret, the knowledge of which could be turned to advantage. He took care not to confess his ignorance, but artfully proceeded to draw out Mr. Onslow's communications.

"Why, it is true," said he, "that Maltravers and I had no

secrets. Ah, we were wild fellows then! The name of Butler is in his family, eh?"

"It is. I see you know all."

"Yes; he told me the story, but it is eighteen years ago. Do refresh my memory. Howard, my good fellow, just ride on and expedite dinner: Mr. Hobbs, will you go with Mr. What's-his-name, the steward, and look over the maps, out-goings, etc.? Now, Mr. Onslow — so Maltravers took the cottage, and a lady with it? — ay, I remember."

Mr. Onslow (who was in fact that magistrate to whom Ernest had confided his name and committed the search after Alice, and who was really anxious to know if any tidings of the poor girl had ever been ascertained) here related that history with which the reader is acquainted, — the robbery of the cottage, the disappearance of Alice, the suspicions that connected that disappearance with her ruffian father, the despair and search of Maltravers. He added that Ernest, both before his departure from England, and on his return, had written to him to learn if Alice had ever been heard of; the replies of the magistrate were unsatisfactory. "And do you think, my lord, that Mr. Maltravers has never to this day ascertained what became of the poor young woman?"

"Why, let me see, — what was her name?"

The magistrate thought a moment, and replied, "Alice Darvil."

"Alice!" exclaimed Vargrave. "Alice!" — aware that such was the Christian name of his uncle's wife, and now almost convinced of the truth of his first vague suspicion.

"You seem to know the name?"

"Of Alice; yes — but not Darvil. No, no; I believe he has never heard of the girl to this hour. Nor you either?"

"I have not. One little circumstance related to me by Mr. Hobbs, your surveyor's father, gave me some uneasiness. About two years after the young woman disappeared, a girl, of very humble dress and appearance, stopped at the gate of Hobbs' Lodge, and asked earnestly for Mr. Butler. On hearing he was gone, she turned away, and was seen no more. It seems that this girl had an infant in her arms — which rather

shocked the propriety of Mr. and Mrs. Hobbs. The old gentleman told me the circumstance a few days after it happened, and I caused inquiry to be made for the stranger; but
she could not be discovered. I thought at first this possibly
might be the lost Alice; but I learned that, during his stay
at the cottage, your friend — despite his error, which we will
not stop to excuse — had exercised so generous and wide a
charity amongst the poor in the town and neighbourhood, that
it was a more probable supposition of the two that the girl
belonged to some family he had formerly relieved, and her
visit was that of a mendicant, not a mistress. Accordingly,
after much consideration, I resolved not to mention the circumstances to Mr. Maltravers, when he wrote to me on his
return from the Continent. A considerable time had then
elapsed since the girl had applied to Mr. Hobbs; all trace of
her was lost; the incident might open wounds that time must
have nearly healed, might give false hopes — or, what was
worse, occasion a fresh and unfounded remorse at the idea of
Alice's destitution; it would, in fact, do no good, and might
occasion unnecessary pain. I therefore suppressed all mention of it."

"You did right: and so the poor girl had an infant in her
arms? — humph! What sort of looking person was this Alice
Darvil, — pretty, of course?"

"I never saw her; and none but the persons employed in
the premises knew her by sight; they described her as remarkably lovely."

"Fair and slight, with blue eyes, I suppose? — those are
the orthodox requisites of a heroine."

"Upon my word I forget; indeed I should never have
remembered as much as I do, if the celebrity of Mr. Maltravers, and the consequence of his family in these parts,
together with the sight of his own agony — the most painful
I ever witnessed — had not served to impress the whole affair
very deeply on my mind."

"Was the girl who appeared at the gate of Hobbs' Lodge
described to you?"

"No; they scarcely observed her countenance, except that

her complexion was too fair for a gypsy's; yet, now I think of it, Mrs. Tiddy, who was with her father when he told me the adventure, dwelt particularly on her having (as you so pleasantly conjecture) fair hair and blue eyes. Mrs. Tiddy, being just married, was romantic at that day."

"Well, it is an odd tale; but life is full of odd tales. Here we are at the house; it really is a splendid old place!"

CHAPTER V.

PENDENT opera intérrupta.[1] — VIRGIL.

THE history Vargrave had heard he revolved much when he retired to rest. He could not but allow that there was still little ground for more than conjecture that Alice Darvil and Alice Lady Vargrave were one and the same person. It might, however, be of great importance to him to trace this conjecture to certainty. The knowledge of a secret of early sin and degradation in one so pure, so spotless, as Lady Vargrave, might be of immense service in giving him a power over her, which he could turn to account with Evelyn. How could he best prosecute further inquiry, — by repairing at once to Brook-Green, or — the thought struck him — by visiting and "pumping" Mrs. Leslie, the patroness of Mrs. Butler, of C——, the friend of Lady Vargrave? It was worth trying the latter, — it was little out of his way back to London. His success in picking the brains of Mr. Onslow of a secret encouraged him in the hope of equal success with Mrs. Leslie. He decided accordingly, and fell asleep to dream of Christmas *battues*, royal visitors, the Cabinet, the premiership! Well, no possession equals the dream of it! Sleep on, my lord! you would be restless enough if you were to get all you want.

1 "The things begun are interrupted and suspended."

For the next three days, Lord Vargrave was employed in examining the general outlines of the estate; and the result of this survey satisfied him as to the expediency of the purchase. On the third day, he was several miles from the house when a heavy rain came on. Lord Vargrave was constitutionally hardy, and not having been much exposed to visitations of the weather of late years, was not practically aware that when a man is past forty, he cannot endure with impunity all that falls innocuously on the elasticity of twenty-six. He did not, therefore, heed the rain that drenched him to the skin, and neglected to change his dress till he had finished reading some letters and newspapers which awaited his return at Lisle Court. The consequence of this imprudence was, that the next morning when he woke, Lord Vargrave found himself, for almost the first time in his life, seriously ill. His head ached violently, cold shiverings shook his frame like an ague; the very strength of the constitution on which the fever had begun to fasten itself augmented its danger. Lumley — the last man in the world to think of the possibility of dying — fought up against his own sensations, ordered his post-horses, as his visit of survey was now over, and scarcely even alluded to his indisposition. About an hour before he set off, his letters arrived; one of these informed him that Caroline, accompanied by Evelyn, had already arrived in Paris; the other was from Colonel Legard, respectfully resigning his office, on the ground of an accession of fortune by the sudden death of the admiral, and his intention to spend the ensuing year in a Continental excursion. This last letter occasioned Vargrave considerable alarm; he had always felt a deep jealousy of the handsome ex-guardsman, and he at once suspected that Legard was about to repair to Paris as his rival. He sighed, and looked round the spacious apartment, and gazed on the wide prospects of grove and turf that extended from the window, and said to himself, "Is another to snatch these from my grasp?" His impatience to visit Mrs. Leslie, to gain ascendency over Lady Vargrave, to repair to Paris, to scheme, to manœuvre, to triumph, accelerated the progress of the disease that was now burning in his veins; and the hand that he held out to Mr. Hobbs, as he stepped into his carriage, almost scorched the cold, plump, moist fingers of the surveyor. Before six o'clock in the evening Lord Vargrave confessed reluctantly to himself that he was too ill to proceed much farther. "Howard," said he then, breaking a silence that had lasted some hours, "don't be alarmed; I feel that I am about to have a severe attack; I shall stop at M—— (naming a large town they were approaching); I shall send for the best physician the place affords; if I am delirious to-morrow, or unable to give my own orders, have the kindness to send express for Dr. Holland, — but don't leave me yourself, my good fellow. At my age, it is a hard thing to have no one in the world to care for me in illness; d—n affection when I am well!"

After this strange burst, which very much frightened Mr. Howard, Lumley relapsed into silence, not broken till he reached M——. The best physician was sent for; and the next morning, as he had half foreseen and foretold, Lord Vargrave *was* delirious!

CHAPTER VI.

NOUGHT under Heaven so strongly doth allure
The sense of man, and all his mind possess,
As Beauty's love-bait. — SPENSER.

LEGARD was, as I have before intimated, a young man of generous and excellent dispositions, though somewhat spoiled by the tenor of his education, and the gay and reckless society which had administered tonics to his vanity and opiates to his intellect. The effect which the beauty, the grace, the innocence of Evelyn had produced upon him had been most deep and most salutary. It had rendered dissipation tasteless and insipid; it had made him look more deeply into his own heart, and into the rules of life. Though, partly from the

irksomeness of dependence upon an uncle at once generous
and ungracious, partly from a diffident and feeling sense of
his own inadequate pretensions to the hand of Miss Cameron,
and partly from the prior and acknowledged claims of Lord
Vargrave, he had accepted, half in despair, the appointment
offered to him, he still found it impossible to banish that
image which had been the first to engrave upon ardent and
fresh affections an indelible impression. He secretly chafed
at the thought that it was to a fortunate rival that he owed
the independence and the station he had acquired, and resolved to seize an early opportunity to free himself from obligations that he deeply regretted he had incurred. At length
he learned that Lord Vargrave had been refused, — that Evelyn was free; and within a few days from that intelligence,
the admiral was seized with apoplexy; and Legard suddenly
found himself possessed, if not of wealth, at least of a competence sufficient to redeem his character as a suitor from the
suspicion attached to a fortune-hunter and adventurer. Despite the new prospects opened to him by the death of his
uncle, and despite the surly caprice which had mingled with
and alloyed the old admiral's kindness, Legard was greatly
shocked by his death; and his grateful and gentle nature was
at first only sensible to grief for the loss he had sustained.
But when, at last, recovering from his sorrow, he saw Evelyn
disengaged and free, and himself in a position honourably to
contest her hand, he could not resist the sweet and passionate
hopes that broke upon him. He resigned, as we have seen,
his official appointment, and set out for Paris. He reached
that city a day or two after the arrival of Lord and Lady
Doltimore. He found the former, who had not forgotten the
cautions of Vargrave, at first cold and distant; but partly
from the indolent habit of submitting to Legard's dictates on
matters of taste, partly from a liking to his society, and principally from the popular suffrages of fashion, which had
always been accorded to Legard, and which were nowadays
diminished by the news of his accession of fortune, Lord
Doltimore, weak and vain, speedily yielded to the influences
of his old associate, and Legard became quietly installed as

the *enfant de la maison*. Caroline was not in this instance a very faithful ally to Vargrave's views and policy. In his singular *liaison* with Lady Doltimore, the crafty manœuvrer had committed the vulgar fault of intriguers: he had over-refined and had overreached himself. At the commencement of their strange and unprincipled intimacy, Vargrave had had, perhaps, no other thought than that of piquing Evelyn, con-soling his vanity, amusing his *ennui*, and indulging rather his propensities as a gallant than promoting his more serious objects as a man of the world. By degrees, and especially at Knaresdean, Vargrave himself became deeply entangled by an affair that he had never before contemplated as more impor-tant than a passing diversion; instead of securing a friend to assist him in his designs on Evelyn, he suddenly found that he had obtained a mistress anxious for his love and jealous of his homage. With his usual promptitude and self-confidence, he was led at once to deliver himself of all the ill-consequences of his rashness, — to get rid of Caroline as a mistress, and to retain her as a tool, by marrying her to Lord Doltimore. By the great ascendency which his character acquired over her, and by her own worldly ambition, he succeeded in inducing her to sacrifice all romance to a union that gave her rank and fortune; and Vargrave then rested satisfied that the clever wife would not only secure him a permanent power over the political influence and private fortune of the weak husband, but also abet his designs in securing an alliance equally desir-able for himself. Here it was that Vargrave's incapacity to understand the refinements and scruples of a woman's affec-tion and nature, however guilty the one, and however worldly the other, foiled and deceived him. Caroline, though the wife of another, could not contemplate without anguish a similar bondage for her lover; and having something of the better qualities of her sex still left to her, she recoiled from being an accomplice in arts that were to drive the young, inexperi-enced, and guileless creature who called her "friend " into the arms of a man who openly avowed the most mercenary mo-tives, and who took gods and men to witness that his heart was sacred to another. Only in Vargrave's presence were these scruples overmastered; but the moment he was gone they returned in full force. She had yielded, from positive fear, to his commands that she should convey Evelyn to Paris; but she trembled to think of the vague hints and dark menaces that Vargrave had let fall as to ulterior proceedings, and was distracted at the thought of being implicated in some villanous or rash design. When, therefore, the man whose rivalry Vargrave most feared was almost established at her house, she made but a feeble resistance; she thought that, if Legard should become a welcome and accepted suitor before Lumley arrived, the latter would be forced to forego whatever hopes he yet cherished, and that she should be delivered from a dilemma, the prospect of which daunted and appalled her. Added to this, Caroline was now, alas! sensible that a fool is not so easily governed; her resistance to an intimacy with Legard would have been of little avail: Doltimore, in these matters, had an obstinate will of his own; and, whatever might once have been Caroline's influence over her liege, certain it is that such influence had been greatly impaired of late by the indulgence of a temper, always irritable, and now daily more soured by regret, remorse, contempt for her husband, — and the melancholy discovery that fortune, youth, beauty, and station are no talismans against misery.

It was the gayest season of Paris; and to escape from herself, Caroline plunged eagerly into the vortex of its dissipations. If Doltimore's heart was disappointed, his vanity was pleased at the admiration Caroline excited; and he himself was of an age and temper to share in the pursuits and amusements of his wife. Into these gayeties, new to their fascination, dazzled by their splendour, the young Evelyn entered with her hostess; and ever by her side was the unequalled form of Legard. Each of them in the bloom of youth, each of them at once formed to please, and to be pleased by that fair Armida which we call the World, there was, necessarily, a certain congeniality in their views and sentiments, their occupations and their objects; nor was there, in all that brilliant city, one more calculated to captivate the eye and fancy than George Legard. But still, to a certain degree diffident and fearful, Legard never yet spoke of love; nor did their intimacy at this time ripen to that point in which Evelyn could have asked herself if there were danger in the society of Legard, or serious meaning in his obvious admiration. Whether that melancholy, to which Lady Vargrave had alluded in her correspondence with Lumley, were occasioned by thoughts connected with Maltravers, or unacknowledged recollections of Legard, it remains for the acute reader himself to ascertain.

The Doltimores had been about three weeks in Paris; and for a fortnight of that time Legard had been their constant guest, and half the inmate of their hotel, when, on that night which has been commemorated in our last book, Maltravers suddenly once more beheld the face of Evelyn, and in the same hour learned that she was free. He quitted Valerie's box; with a burning pulse and a beating heart, joy and surprise and hope sparkling in his eyes and brightening his whole aspect, he hastened to Evelyn's side.

It was at this time Legard, who sat behind Miss Cameron, unconscious of the approach of a rival, happened by one of those chances which occur in conversation to mention the name of Maltravers. He asked Evelyn if she had yet met him.

"What! is he, then, in Paris?" asked Evelyn, quickly. "I heard, indeed," she continued, "that he left Burleigh for Paris, but imagined he had gone on to Italy."

"No, he is still here; but he goes, I believe, little into the society Lady Doltimore chiefly visits. Is he one of your favourites, Miss Cameron?"

There was a slight increase of colour in Evelyn's beautiful cheek, as she answered, —

"Is it possible not to admire and be interested in one so gifted?"

"He has certainly noble and fine qualities," returned Legard; "but I cannot feel at ease with him: a coldness, a *hauteur*, a measured distance of manner, seem to forbid even esteem. Yet *I* ought not to say so," he added, with a pang of self-reproach.

"No, indeed, you ought not to say so," said Evelyn, shaking her head with a pretty affectation of anger; "for I know that you pretend to like what I like, and admire what I admire; and I am an enthusiast in all that relates to Mr. Maltravers!"

"I know that I would wish to see all things in life through Miss Cameron's eyes," whispered Legard, softly; and this was the most meaning speech he had ever yet made.

Evelyn turned away, and seemed absorbed in the opera; and at that instant the door of the box opened, and Maltravers entered.

In her open, undisguised, youthful delight at seeing him again, Maltravers felt, indeed, "as if Paradise were opened in her face." In his own agitated emotions, he scarcely noticed that Legard had risen and resigned his seat to him; he availed himself of the civility, greeted his old acquaintance with a smile and a bow, and in a few minutes he was in deep converse with Evelyn.

Never had he so successfully exerted the singular, the master-fascination that he could command at will, — the more powerful from its contrast to his ordinary coldness. In the very expression of his eyes, the very tone of his voice, there was that in Maltravers, seen at his happier moments, which irres'stibly interested and absorbed your attention: he could make you forget everything but himself, and the rich, easy, yet earnest eloquence, which gave colour to his language and melody to his voice. In that hour of renewed intercourse with one who had at first awakened, if not her heart, at least her imagination and her deeper thoughts, certain it is that even Legard was not missed. As she smiled and listened, Evelyn dreamed not of the anguish she inflicted. Leaning against the box, Legard surveyed the absorbed attention of Evelyn, the adoring eyes of Maltravers, with that utter and crushing wretchedness which no passion but jealousy, and that only while it is yet a virgin agony, can bestow! He had never before even dreamed of rivalry in such a quarter; but there was that ineffable instinct, which lovers have, and which so seldom errs, that told him at once that in Maltravers

was the greatest obstacle his passion could encounter. He
waited in hopes that Evelyn would take the occasion to turn
to him at least — when the fourth act closed. She did not;
and, unable to constrain his emotions, and reply to the small-
talk of Lord Doltimore, he abruptly quitted the box.

When the opera was over, Maltravers offered his arm to
Evelyn; she accepted it, and then she looked round for
Legard. He was gone.

BOOK VIII.

’Ω Ζεῦ, τί μου δρᾶσαι βεβούλευσαι πέρι;

O Fate! O Heaven! — what have ye then decreed?

SOPHOCLES: Œd. Tyr. 738.

῞Υβρις, . . .

. . . . . .

ἀκροτάταν εἰσαναβᾶσ’ ἀπότομον
ὤρουσέν νιν εἰς ἀνάγκαν. — Ibid, 874.

“ Insolent pride . . .

. . . . . .

The topmost crag of the great precipice
Surmounts — to rush to ruin.”

CHAPTER I.

. . . SHE is young, wise, fair,
In these to Nature she’s immediate heir.

. . . Honours best thrive
When rather from our acts we them derive
Than our foregoers! — All’s Well that Ends Well.

LETTER FROM ERNEST MALTRAVERS TO THE HON. FREDERICK CLEVELAND.

EVELYN is free; she is in Paris; I have seen her, — I see her daily!

How true it is that we cannot make a philosophy of indifference! The affections are stronger than all our reasonings. We must take them into our alliance, or they will destroy all our theories of self-government. Such fools of fate are we, passing from system to system, from scheme to scheme, vainly

seeking to shut out passion and sorrow — forgetting that they
are born within us — and return to the soul as the seasons to
the earth!   Yet, — years, many years ago, when I first looked
gravely into my own nature and being here, when I first awakened to the dignity and solemn responsibilities of human life,
I had resolved to tame and curb myself into a thing of rule
and measure.   Bearing within me the wound scarred over but
never healed, the consciousness of wrong to the heart that had
leaned upon me, haunted by the memory of my lost Alice, I
shuddered at new affections bequeathing new griefs.   Wrapped
in a haughty egotism, I wished not to extend my empire over
a wider circuit than my own intellect and passions.   I turned
from the trader-covetousness of bliss, that would freight the
wealth of life upon barks exposed to every wind upon the seas
of Fate; I was contented with the hope to pass life alone,
honoured, though unloved.   Slowly and reluctantly I yielded
to the fascinations of Florence. Lascelles.   The hour that
sealed the compact between us was one of regret and alarm.
In vain I sought to deceive myself, — I felt that I did not
love.   And then I imagined that Love was no longer in my
nature, — that I had exhausted its treasures before my time,
and left my heart a bankrupt.   Not till the last — not till
that glorious soul broke out in all its brightness the nearer it
approached the source to which it has returned — did I feel
of what tenderness she was worthy and I was capable.   She
died, and the world was darkened!   Energy, ambition, my
former aims and objects, were all sacrificed at her tomb.   But
amidst ruins and through the darkness, my soul yet supported
me; I could no longer hope, but I could endure.   I was resolved that I would not be subdued, and that the world should
not hear me groan.   Amidst strange and far-distant scenes,
amidst hordes to whom my very language was unknown, in
wastes and forests, which the step of civilized man, with his
sorrows and his dreams, had never trodden, I wrestled with
my soul, as the patriarch of old wrestled with the angel, —
and the angel was at last the victor!   You do not mistake me:
you know that it was not the death of Florence alone that
worked in me that awful revolution; but with that death the

last glory fled from the face of things that had seemed to me beautiful of old. Hers was a love that accompanied and dignified the schemes and aspirations of manhood, — a love that was an incarnation of ambition itself; and all the evils and disappointments that belong to ambition seemed to crowd around my heart like vultures to a feast allured and invited by the dead. But this at length was over; the barbarous state restored me to the civilized. I returned to my equals, prepared no more to be an actor in the strife, but a calm spectator of the turbulent arena. I once more laid my head beneath the roof of my fathers; and if without any clear and definite object, I at least hoped to find amidst " my old hereditary trees" the charm of contemplation and repose. And scarce — in the first hours of my arrival — had I indulged that dream, when a fair face, a sweet voice, that had once before left deep and unobliterated impressions on my heart, scattered all my philosophy to the winds. I saw Evelyn! and if ever there was love at first sight, it was that which I felt for her: I lived in her presence, and forgot the Future! Or, rather, I was with the Past, — in the bowers of my springtide of life and hope! It was an after-birth of youth — my love for that young heart!

It is, indeed, only in maturity that we know how lovely were our earliest years! What depth of wisdom in the old Greek myth, that allotted Hebe as the prize to the god who had been the arch-labourer of life! and whom the satiety of all that results from experience had made enamoured of all that belongs to the Hopeful and the New!

This enchanting child, this delightful Evelyn, this ray of undreamed of sunshine, smiled away all my palaces of ice. I loved, Cleveland, — I loved more ardently, more passionately, more wildly than ever I did of old! But suddenly I learned that she was affianced to another, and felt that it was not for me to question, to seek the annulment of the bond. I had been unworthy to love Evelyn if I had not loved honour more! I fled from her presence, honestly and resolutely; I sought to conquer a forbidden passion; I believed that I had not won affection in return; I believed, from certain expressions that

I overheard Evelyn utter to another, that her heart as well as
her hand was given to Vargrave. I came hither; you know
how sternly and resolutely I strove to eradicate a weakness
that seemed without even the justification of hope! If I suffered, I betrayed it not. Suddenly Evelyn appeared again
before me! — and suddenly I learned that she was free! Oh,
the rapture of that moment! Could you have seen her bright
face, her enchanting smile, when we met again! Her ingenuous innocence did not conceal her gladness at seeing me!
What hopes broke upon me! Despite the difference of our
years, I think she loves me! that in that love I am about at
last to learn what blessings there are in life.

Evelyn has the simplicity, the tenderness, of Alice, with
the refinement and culture of Florence herself; not the
genius, not the daring spirit, not the almost fearful brilliancy of that ill-fated being, — but with a taste as true to the
Beautiful, with a soul as sensitive to the Sublime! In Evelyn's presence I feel a sense of peace, of security, of home!
Happy! thrice happy! he who will take her to his breast!
Of late she has assumed a new charm in my eyes, — a certain
pensiveness and abstraction have succeeded to her wonted
gayety. Ah, Love is pensive, — is it not, Cleveland? How
often I ask myself that question! And yet, amidst all my
hopes, there are hours when I tremble and despond! How
can that innocent and joyous spirit sympathize with all that
mine has endured and known? How, even though her imagination be dazzled by some prestige around my name, how can
I believe that I have awakened her heart to that deep and real
love of which it is capable, and which youth excites in youth?
When we meet at her home, or amidst the quiet yet brilliant
society which is gathered round Madame de Ventadour or the
Montaignes, with whom she is an especial favourite; when we
converse; when I sit by her, and her soft eyes meet mine, — I
feel not the disparity of years; my heart speaks to her, and
that is youthful still! But in the more gay and crowded
haunts to which her presence allures me, when I see that
fairy form surrounded by those who have not outlived the

pleasures that so naturally dazzle and captivate her, then, indeed, I feel that my tastes, my habits, my pursuits, belong to another season of life, and ask myself anxiously if my nature and my years are those that can make *her* happy? Then, indeed, I recognize the wide interval that time and trial place between one whom the world has wearied, and one for whom the world is new. If she should discover hereafter that youth should love only youth, my bitterest anguish would be that of remorse! I know how deeply I love by knowing how immeasurably dearer her happiness is than my own! I will wait, then, yet a while, I will examine, I will watch well that I do not deceive myself. As yet I think that I have no rivals whom I need fear: surrounded as she is by the young-est and the gayest, she still turns with evident pleasure to me, whom she calls her friend. She will forego the amuse-ments she most loves for society in which we can converse more at ease. You remember, for instance, young Legard? He is here; and, before I met Evelyn, was much at Lady Doltimore's house. I cannot be blind to his superior advan-tages of youth and person; and there is something striking and prepossessing in the gentle yet manly frankness of his manner, — and yet no fear of his rivalship ever haunts me. True, that of late he has been little in Evelyn's society; nor do I think, in the frivolity of his pursuits, he can have edu-cated his mind to appreciate Evelyn, or be possessed of those qualities which would render him worthy of her. But there is something good in the young man, despite his foibles, — something that wins upon me; and you will smile to learn, that he has even surprised from *me* — usually so reserved on such matters — the confession of my attachment and hopes! Evelyn often talks to me of her mother, and describes her in colours so glowing that I feel the greatest interest in one who has helped to form so beautiful and pure a mind. Can you learn who Lady Vargrave was? There is evidently some mys-tery thrown over her birth and connections; and, from what I can hear, this arises from their lowliness. You know that, though I have been accused of family pride, it is a pride of a peculiar sort. I am proud, not of the length of a mouldering pedigree, but of some historical quarterings in my escutcheon, — of some blood of scholars and of heroes that rolls in my veins; it is the same kind of pride that an Englishman may feel in belonging to a country that has produced Shakspeare and Bacon. I have never, I hope, felt the vulgar pride that disdains want of birth in others; and I care not three straws whether my friend or my wife be descended from a king or a peasant. It is myself, and not my connections, who alone can disgrace my lineage; therefore, however humble Lady Vargrave's parentage, do not scruple to inform me, should you learn any intelligence that bears upon it.

I had a conversation last night with Evelyn that delighted me. By some accident we spoke of Lord Vargrave; and she told me, with an enchanting candour, of the position in which she stood with him, and the conscientious and noble scruples she felt as to the enjoyment of a fortune, which her bene-factor and stepfather had evidently intended to be shared with his nearest relative. In these scruples I cordially con-curred; and if I marry Evelyn, my first care will be to carry them into effect, — by securing to Vargrave, as far as the law may permit, the larger part of the income; I should like to say all, — at least till Evelyn's children would have the right to claim it: a right not to be enforced during her own, and, therefore, probably not during Vargrave's life. I own that this would be no sacrifice, for I am proud enough to recoil from the thought of being indebted for fortune to the woman I love. It was that kind of pride which gave coldness and constraint to my regard for Florence; and for the rest, my own property (much increased by the simplicity of my habits of life for the last few years) will suffice for all Evelyn or myself could re-quire. Ah, madman that I am! I calculate already on mar-riage, even while I have so much cause for anxiety as to love. But my heart beats, — my heart has grown a dial that keeps the account of time; by its movements I calculate the mo-ments — in an hour I shall see her!

Oh, never, never, in my wildest and earliest visions, could I have fancied that I should love as I love now! Adieu, my

oldest and kindest friend! If I am happy at last, it will be
something to feel that at last I shall have satisfied your ex
pectations of my youth:

Affectionately yours,

E. MALTRAVERS.

Rue de ———. Paris,
January —, 18—.

◆

CHAPTER II.

In her youth
There is a prone and speechless dialect —
Such as moves men. — *Measure for Measure.*

Abbess.   Haply in private —
Adriana.   And in assemblies too. — *Comedy of Errors.*

It was true, as Maltravers had stated, that Legard had of
late been little at Lady Doltimore's, or in the same society as
Evelyn. With the vehemence of an ardent and passionate
nature, he yielded to the jealous rage and grief that devoured
him. He saw too clearly, and from the first, that Maltravers
adored Evelyn; and in her familiar kindness of manner
towards him, in the unlimited veneration in which she appeared to hold his gifts and qualities, he thought that that
love might become reciprocal. He became gloomy and almost
morose; he shunned Evelyn, he forbore to enter into the lists
against his rival. Perhaps the intellectual superiority of
Maltravers, the extraordinary conversational brilliancy that
he could display when he pleased, the commanding dignity of
his manners, even the matured authority of his reputation and
years, might have served to awe the hopes, as well as to wound
the vanity, of a man accustomed himself to be the oracle of a
circle. These might have strongly influenced Legard in with-
drawing himself from Evelyn's society; but there was one circumstance, connected with motives much more generous, that
mainly determined his conduct. It happened that Maltravers,

shortly after his first interview with Evelyn, was riding alone one day in the more sequestered part of the Bois de Boulogne, when he encountered Legard, also alone, and on horseback. The latter, on succeeding to his uncle's fortune, had taken care to repay his debt to Maltravers; he had done so in a short but feeling and grateful letter, which had been forwarded to Maltravers at Paris, and which pleased and touched him. Since that time he had taken a liking to the young man, and now, meeting him at Paris, he sought, to a certain extent, Legard's more intimate acquaintance. Maltravers was in that happy mood when we are inclined to be friends with all men. It is true, however, that, though unknown to himself, that pride of bearing, which often gave to the very virtues of Maltravers an unamiable aspect, occasionally irritated one who felt he had incurred to him an obligation of honour and of life never to be effaced; it made the sense of this obligation more intolerable to Legard; it made him more desirous to acquit himself of the charge. But on this day there was so much cordiality in the greeting of Maltravers, and he pressed Legard in so friendly a manner to join him in his ride, that the young man's heart was softened, and they rode together, conversing familiarly on such topics as were in common between them. At last the conversation fell on Lord and Lady Doltimore; and thence Maltravers, whose soul was full of one thought, turned it indirectly towards Evelyn.

"Did you ever see Lady Vargrave?"

"Never," replied Legard, looking another way; "but Lady Doltimore says she is as beautiful as Evelyn herself, if that be possible; and still so young in form and countenance, that she looks rather like her sister than her mother!"

"How I should like to know her!" said Maltravers, with a sudden energy.

Legard changed the subject. He spoke of the Carnival, of balls, of masquerades, of operas, of reigning beauties!

"Ah," said Maltravers, with a half sigh, "yours is the age for those dazzling pleasures; to me they are 'the twice-told tale.'"

Maltravers meant it not, but this remark chafed Legard.

He thought it conveyed a sarcasm on the childishness of his own mind or the levity of his pursuits; his colour mounted, as he replied, —

"It is not, I fear, the slight difference of years between us, — it is the difference of intellect you would insinuate; but you should remember all men have not your resources; all men cannot pretend to genius!"

"My dear Legard," said Maltravers, kindly, "do not fancy that I could have designed any insinuation half so presumptuous and impertinent. Believe me, I envy you, sincerely and sadly, all those faculties of enjoyment which I have worn away. Oh, how I envy you! for, were they still mine, then — then, indeed, I might hope to mould myself into greater congeniality with the beautiful and the young!"

Maltravers paused a moment, and resumed, with a grave smile: "I trust, Legard, that you will be wiser than I have been; that you will gather your roses while it is yet May: and that you will not live to thirty-six, pining for happiness and home, a disappointed and desolate man; till, when your ideal is at last found, you shrink back appalled, to discover that you have lost none of the tendencies to love, but many of the graces by which love is to be allured!"

There was so much serious and earnest feeling in these words that they went home at once to Legard's sympathies. He felt irresistibly impelled to learn the worst.

"Maltravers," said he, in a hurried tone, "it would be an idle compliment to say that you are not likely to love in vain; perhaps it is indelicate in me to apply a general remark; and yet — yet I cannot but fancy that I have discovered your secret, and that you are not insensible to the charms of Miss Cameron!"

"Legard!" said Maltravers, — and so strong was his fervent attachment to Evelyn, that it swept away all his natural coldness and reserve, — "I tell you plainly and frankly that in my love for Evelyn Cameron lie the last hopes I have in life. I have no thought, no ambition, no sentiment that is not vowed to her. If my love should be unreturned, I may strive to endure the blow, I may mix with the world, I may seem to occupy myself in the aims of others; but my heart will be broken! Let us talk of this no more; you have surprised my secret, though it must have betrayed itself. Learn from me how preternaturally strong, how generally fatal is love deferred to that day when — in the stern growth of all the feelings — love writes itself on granite! "

Maltravers, as if impatient of his own weakness, put spurs to his horse, and they rode on rapidly for some time without speaking.

That silence was employed by Legard in meditating over all he had heard and witnessed, in recalling all that he owed to Maltravers; and before that silence was broken the young man nobly resolved not even to attempt, not even to hope, a rivalry with Maltravers; to forego all the expectations he had so fondly nursed, to absent himself from the company of Evelyn, to requite faithfully and firmly that act of generosity to which he owed the preservation of his life, — the redemption of his honour.

Agreeably to this determination, he abstained from visiting those haunts in which Evelyn shone; and if accident brought them together, his manner was embarrassed and abrupt. She wondered, — at last, perhaps she resented, — it may be that she grieved; for certain it is that Maltravers was right in thinking that her manner had lost the gayety that distinguished it at Merton Rectory. But still it may be doubted whether Evelyn had seen enough of Legard, and whether her fancy and romance were still sufficiently free from the magical influences of the genius that called them forth in the eloquent homage of Maltravers, to trace, herself, to any causes connected with her younger lover the listless melancholy that crept over her. In very young women — new alike to the world and the knowledge of themselves — many vague and undefined feelings herald the dawn of Love; shade after shade and light upon light succeeds before the sun breaks forth, and the earth awakens to his presence.

It was one evening that Legard had suffered himself to be led into a party at the —— ambassador's; and there, as he stood by the door, he saw at a little distance Maltravers con-

versing with Evelyn.   Again he writhed beneath the tortures
of his jealous anguish; and there, as he gazed and suffered,
he resolved (as Maltravers had done before him) to fly from
the place that had a little while ago seemed to him Elysium!
He would quit Paris, he would travel, he would not see Evelyn again till the irrevocable barrier was passed, and she was
the wife of Maltravers!   In the first heat of this determination, he turned towards some young men standing near him,
one of whom was about to visit Vienna.   He gayly proposed
to join him, — a proposal readily accepted, and began conversing on the journey, the city, its splendid and proud society,
with all that cruel exhilaration which the forced spirits of a
stricken heart can alone display, when Evelyn (whose conference with Maltravers was ended) passed close by him.   She
was leaning on Lady Doltimore's arm, and the admiring murmur of his companions caused Legard to turn suddenly round.

"You are not dancing to-night, Colonel Legard," said Caroline, glancing towards Evelyn.   "The more the season for
balls advances, the more indolent you become."

Legard muttered a confused reply, one half of which
seemed petulant, while the other half was inaudible.

"Not so indolent as you suppose," said his friend.   "Legard
meditates an excursion sufficient, I hope, to redeem his character in your eyes.   It is a long journey, and, what is worse,
a very cold journey, to Vienna."

"Vienna! do you think of going to Vienna?" cried Caroline.

"Yes," said Legard.   "I hate Paris; any place better than
this odious city!" and he moved away.

Evelyn's eyes followed him sadly and gravely.   She remained by Lady Doltimore's side, abstracted and silent for
several minutes.

Meanwhile Caroline, turning to Lord Devonport (the friend
who had proposed the Viennese excursion), said, "It is cruel
in you to go to Vienna, — it is doubly cruel to rob Lord
Doltimore of his best friend and Paris of its best waltzer."

"Oh, it is a voluntary offer of Legard's, Lady Doltimore,
— believe me, I have used no persuasive arts.   But the fact
is, that we have been talking of a fair widow, the beauty of

Austria, and as proud and as unassailable as Ehrenbreitstein itself. Legard's vanity is piqued; and so — as a professed lady-killer — he intends to see what can be effected by the handsomest Englishman of his time."

Caroline laughed, and new claimants on her notice succeeded to Lord Devonport. It was not till the ladies were waiting their carriage in the shawl-room that Lady Doltimore noticed the paleness and thoughtful brow of Evelyn.

"Are you fatigued or unwell, dear?" she said.

"No," answered Evelyn, forcing a smile; and at that moment they were joined by Maltravers, with the intelligence that it would be some minutes before the carriage could draw up. Caroline amused herself in the interval by shrewd criticisms on the dresses and characters of her various friends. Caroline had grown an amazing prude in her judgment of others!

"What a turban! — prudent for Mrs. A—— to wear, — bright red; it puts out her face, as the sun puts out the fire. Mr. Maltravers, do observe Lady B—— with that *very* young gentleman. After all her experience in angling, it is odd that she should still only throw in for small fish. Pray, why is the marriage between Lady C—— D—— and Mr. F—— broken off? Is it true that he is so much in debt, and is so very — very profligate? They say she is heartbroken."

"Really, Lady Doltimore," said Maltravers, smiling, "I am but a bad scandal-monger. But poor F—— is not, I believe, much worse than others. How do we know whose fault it is when a marriage is broken off? Lady C—— D—— heartbroken! what an idea! Nowadays there is never any affection in compacts of that sort; and the chain that binds the frivolous nature is but a gossamer thread! Fine gentlemen and fine ladies, their loves and their marriages —

"'May flourish and may fade ;
A breath can make them, as a breath has made.'

Never believe that a heart long accustomed to beat only in good society can be broken, — it is rarely ever touched!"

Evelyn listened attentively, and seemed struck. She sighed,

and said in a very low voice, as to herself, "It is true — how could I think otherwise?"

For the next few days Evelyn was unwell, and did not quit her room.   Maltravers was in despair.   The flowers, the books, the music he sent; his anxious inquiries, his earnest and respectful notes, touched with that ineffable charm which Heart and Intellect breathe into the most trifling coinage from their mint, — all affected Evelyn sensibly.   Perhaps she contrasted them with Legard's indifference and apparent caprice; perhaps in that contrast Maltravers gained more than by all his brilliant qualities.   Meanwhile, without visit, without message, without farewell, — unconscious, it is true, of Evelyn's illness, — Legard departed for Vienna.

CHAPTER III.

A PLEASING land   .   .   .
Of dreams that wave before the half-shut eye,
   And of gay castles in the clouds that pass,
Forever flashing round a summer sky. — THOMSON.

DAILY, hourly, increased the influence of Evelyn over Maltravers.   Oh, what a dupe is a man's pride! what a fool his wisdom!   That a girl, a mere child, one who scarce knew her own heart, beautiful as it was, — whose deeper feelings still lay coiled up in their sweet buds, — that she should thus master this proud, wise man!   But as thou — our universal teacher — as thou, O Shakspeare! haply speaking from the hints of thine own experience, hast declared —

" None are so truly caught, when they are catched,
   As wit turned fool; folly in wisdom hatched,
      Hath wisdom's warrant."

Still, methinks that, in that surpassing and dangerously indulged affection which levelled thee, Maltravers, with the weakest, which overturned all thy fine philosophy of Stoicism, and made thee the veriest slave of the "Rose Garden,"

—still, Maltravers, thou mightest at least have seen that thou hast lost forever all right to pride, all privilege to disdain the herd! But thou wert proud of thine own infirmity! And far sharper must be that lesson which can teach thee that Pride —thine angel — is ever pre-doomed to fall.

What a mistake to suppose that the passions are strongest in youth! The passions are not stronger, but the control over them is weaker. They are more easily excited, they are more violent and more apparent; but they have less energy, less durability, less intense and concentrated power, than in maturer life. In youth, passion succeeds to passion, and one breaks upon the other, as waves upon a rock, till the heart frets itself to repose. In manhood, the great deep flows on, more calm, but more profound; its serenity is the proof of the might and terror of its course, were the wind to blow and the storm to rise.

A young man's ambition is but vanity, — it has no definite aim, it plays with a thousand toys. As with one passion, so with the rest. In youth, Love is ever on the wing, but, like the birds in April, it hath not yet built its nest. With so long a career of summer and hope before it, the disappointment of to-day is succeeded by the novelty of to-morrow, and the sun that advances to the noon but dries up its fervent tears. But when we have arrived at that epoch of life, — when, if the light fail us, if the last rose wither, we feel that the loss cannot be retrieved, and that the frost and the darkness are at hand, Love becomes to us a treasure that we watch over and hoard with a miser's care. Our youngest-born affection is our darling and our idol, the fondest pledge of the Past, the most cherished of our hopes for the Future. A certain melancholy that mingles with our joy at the possession only enhances its charm. We feel ourselves so dependent on it for all that is yet to come. Our other barks — our gay galleys of pleasure, our stately argosies of pride — have been swallowed up by the remorseless wave. On this last vessel we freight our all, to its frail tenement we commit ourselves. The star that guides it is our guide, and in the tempest that menaces we behold our own doom!

Still Maltravers shrank from the confession that trembled on his lips; still he adhered to the course he had prescribed to himself. If ever (as he had implied in his letter to Cleveland) — if ever Evelyn should discover they were not suited to each other! The possibility of such an affliction impressed his judgment, the dread of it chilled his heart. With all his pride, there was a certain humility in Maltravers that was perhaps one cause of his reserve. He knew what a beautiful possession is youth, — its sanguine hopes, its elastic spirit, its inexhaustible resources! What to the eyes of woman were the acquisitions which manhood had brought him, — the vast but the sad experience, the arid wisdom, the philosophy based on disappointment? He might be loved but for the vain glitter of name and reputation, — and love might vanish as custom dimmed the illusion. Men of strong affections are jealous of their own genius. They know how separate a thing from the household character genius often is, — they fear lest they should be loved for a quality, not for themselves.

Thus communed he with himself; thus, as the path had become clear to his hopes, did new fears arise; and thus did love bring, as it ever does, in its burning wake, —

> " The pang, the agony, the doubt ! "

Maltravers then confirmed himself in the resolution he had formed: he would cautiously examine Evelyn and himself; he would weigh in the balance every straw that the wind should turn up; he would not aspire to the treasure, unless he could feel secure that the coffer could preserve the gem. This was not only a prudent, it was a just and a generous determination. It was one which we all ought to form if the fervour of our passions will permit us. We have no right to sacrifice years to moments, and to melt the pearl that has no price in a single draught! But can Maltravers adhere to his wise precautions? The truth must be spoken, — it was, perhaps, the first time in his life that Maltravers had been really *in* love.

As the reader will remember, he had not been in love with the haughty Florence; admiration, gratitude, — the affection of the head, not that of the feelings, — had been the links that

bound him to the enthusiastic correspondent revealed in the
gifted beauty; and the gloomy circumstances connected with
her early fate had left deep furrows in his memory. Time
and vicissitude had effaced the wounds, and the Light of the
Beautiful dawned once more in the face of Evelyn. Valerie
de Ventadour had been but the fancy of a roving breast.
Alice, the sweet Alice! — her, indeed, in the first flower of
youth, he had loved with a boy's romance. He had loved
her deeply, fondly, — but perhaps he had never been *in* love
with her; he had mourned her loss for years, — insensibly to
himself her loss had altered his character and cast a melancholy gloom over all the colours of his life. But she whose
range of ideas was so confined, she who had but broke into
knowledge, as the chrysalis into the butterfly — how much in
that prodigal and gifted nature, bounding onwards into the
broad plains of life, must the peasant girl have failed to fill!
They had had nothing in common but their youth and their
love. It was a dream that had hovered over the poet-boy in
the morning twilight, — a dream he had often wished to recall,
a dream that had haunted him in the noon-day, — but had, as
all boyish visions ever have done, left the heart unexhausted,
and the passions unconsumed! Years, long years, since then
had rolled away, and yet, perhaps, one unconscious attraction
that drew Maltravers so suddenly towards Evelyn was a something indistinct and undefinable that reminded him of Alice.
There was no similarity in their features; but at times a tone
in Evelyn's voice, a "trick of the manner," an air, a gesture,
recalled him, over the gulfs of Time, to Poetry, and Hope,
and Alice.

In the youth of each — the absent and the present one —
there was resemblance, — resemblance in their simplicity,
their grace. Perhaps Alice, of the two, had in her nature
more real depth, more ardour of feeling, more sublimity of
sentiment, than Evelyn. But in her primitive ignorance half
her noblest qualities were embedded and unknown. And
Evelyn — his equal in rank; Evelyn, well cultivated; Evelyn, so long courted, so deeply studied — had such advantages
over the poor peasant girl! Still the poor peasant girl often

seemed to smile on him from that fair face; and in Evelyn he
half loved Alice again!

So these two persons now met daily; their intercourse was
even more familiar than before, their several minds grew
hourly more developed and transparent to each other. But
of love Maltravers still forbore to speak; they were friends,
— no more; such friends as the disparity of their years and
their experience might warrant them to be. And in that
young and innocent nature — with its rectitude, its enthusiasm, and its pious and cheerful tendencies — Maltravers found
freshness in the desert, as the camel-driver lingering at the
well. Insensibly his heart warmed again to his kind; and
as the harp of David to the ear of Saul, was the soft voice
that lulled remembrance and awakened hope in the lonely
man.

Meanwhile, what was the effect that the presence, the attentions, of Maltravers produced on Evelyn? Perhaps it
was of that kind which most flatters us and most deceives.
She never dreamed of comparing him with others. To her
thoughts he stood aloof and alone from all his kind. It may
seem a paradox, but it might be that she admired and ven-
erated him almost too much for love. Still her pleasure in
his society was so evident and unequivocal, her deference to
his opinion so marked, she sympathized in so many of his
objects, she had so much blindness or forbearance for his
faults (and he never sought to mask them), that the most
diffident of men might have drawn from so many symptoms
hopes the most auspicious. Since the departure of Legard,
the gayeties of Paris lost their charm for Evelyn, and more
than ever she could appreciate the society of her friend. He
thus gradually lost his earlier fears of her forming too keen
an attachment to the great world; and as nothing could be
more apparent than Evelyn's indifference to the crowd of
flatterers and suitors that hovered round her, Maltravers no
longer dreaded a rival. He began to feel assured that they
had both gone through the ordeal; and that he might ask for
love without a doubt of its immutability and faith. At this
period they were both invited, with the Doltimores, to spend

a few days at the villa of De Montaigne, near St. Cloud. And there it was that Maltravers determined to know his fate!

———◆———

CHAPTER IV.

CHAOS of Thought and Passion all confused. — POPE.

IT is to the contemplation of a very different scene that the course of our story now conducts us.

Between St. Cloud and Versailles there was at that time — perhaps there still is — a lone and melancholy house, appro- priated to the insane, — melancholy, not from its site, but the purpose to which it is devoted. Placed on an eminence, the windows of the mansion command — beyond the gloomy walls that gird the garden ground — one of those enchanting prospects which win for France her title to *La Belle*. There the glori- ous Seine is seen in the distance, broad and winding through the varied plains, and beside the gleaming villages and villas. There, too, beneath the clear blue sky of France, the forest- lands of Versailles and St. Germains stretch in dark luxuri- ance around and afar. There you may see sleeping on the verge of the landscape the mighty city, — crowned with the thousand spires from which, proud above the rest, rises the eyry of Napoleon's eagle, the pinnacle of Notre Dame.

Remote, sequestered, the place still commands the survey of the turbulent world below; and Madness gazes upon pros- pects that might well charm the thoughtful eyes of Imagina- tion or of Wisdom! In one of the rooms of this house sat Castruccio Cesarini. The apartment was furnished even with elegance; a variety of books strewed the table; nothing for comfort or for solace that the care and providence of affection could dictate was omitted. Cesarini was alone: leaning his cheek upon his hand, he gazed on the beautiful and tranquil view we have described. "And am I never to set a free foot on that soil again?" he muttered indignantly, as he broke from his revery.

The door opened, and the keeper of the sad abode (a surgeon of humanity and eminence) entered, followed by De Montaigne. Cesarini turned round and scowled upon the latter; the surgeon, after a few words of salutation, withdrew to a corner of the room, and appeared absorbed in a book. De Montaigne approached his brother-in-law, — "I have brought you some poems just published at Milan, my dear Castruccio, — they will please you."

"Give me my liberty!" cried Cesarini, clenching his hands. "Why am I to be detained here? Why are my nights to be broken by the groans of maniacs, and my days devoured in a solitude that loathes the aspect of things around me? Am I mad? You know I am not! It is an old trick to say that poets are mad, — you mistake our agonies for insanity. See, I am calm; I can reason: give me any test of sound mind — no matter how rigid — I will pass it; I am not mad, — I swear I am not!"

"No, my dear Castruccio," said De Montaigne, soothingly; "but you are still unwell, — you still have fever; when next I see you perhaps you may be recovered sufficiently to dismiss the doctor and change the air. Meanwhile is there anything you would have added or altered?"

Cesarini had listened to this speech with a mocking sarcasm on his lip, but an expression of such hopeless wretchedness in his eyes, as they alone can comprehend who have witnessed madness in its lucid intervals. He sank down, and his head drooped gloomily on his breast. "No," said he; "I want nothing but free air or death, — no matter which."

De Montaigne stayed some time with the unhappy man, and sought to soothe him; but it was in vain. Yet when he rose to depart, Cesarini started up, and fixing on him his large wistful eyes, exclaimed, "Ah! do not leave me yet. It is so dreadful to be alone with the dead and the worse than dead!"

The Frenchman turned aside to wipe his eyes, and stifle the rising at his heart; and again he sat, and again he sought to soothe. At length Cesarini, seemingly more calm, gave him leave to depart. "Go," said he, "go; tell Teresa I am better, that I love her tenderly, that I shall live to tell her children not to be poets. Stay, you asked if there was aught I wished changed: yes, this room; it is too still: I hear my own pulse beat so loudly in the silence, it is horrible! There is a room below, by the window of which there is a tree, and the winds rock its boughs to and fro, and it sighs and groans like a living thing; it will be pleasant to look at that tree, and see the birds come home to it, — yet that tree is wintry and blasted too! It will be pleasant to hear it fret and chafe in the stormy nights; it will be a friend to me, that old tree! let me have that room. Nay, look not at each other, — it is not so high as this; but the window is barred, — I cannot escape!" And Cesarini smiled.

"Certainly," said the surgeon, "if you prefer that room; but it has not so fine a view."

"I hate the view of the world that has cast me off. When may I change?"

"This very evening."

"Thank you; it will be a great revolution in my life."

And Cesarini's eyes brightened, and he looked happy. De Montaigne, thoroughly unmanned, tore himself away.

The promise was kept, and Cesarini was transferred that night to the chamber he had selected.

As soon as it was deep night, the last visit of the keeper paid, and, save now and then, by some sharp cry in the more distant quarter of the house, all was still, Cesarini rose from his bed; a partial light came from the stars that streamed through the frosty and keen air, and cast a sickly gleam through the heavy bars of the casement. It was then that Cesarini drew from under his pillow a long-cherished and carefully-concealed treasure. Oh, with what rapture had he first possessed himself of it! with what anxiety had it been watched and guarded! how many cunning stratagems and profound inventions had gone towards the baffling the jealous search of the keeper and his myrmidons! The abandoned and wandering mother never clasped her child more fondly to her bosom, nor gazed upon his features with more passionate visions for the future. And what had so enchanted the poor prisoner, so deluded the poor maniac? A large nail! He had found it accidentally in the garden; he had hoarded it for weeks, — it had inspired him with the hope of liberty. Often, in the days far gone, he had read of the wonders that had been effected, of the stones removed, and the bars filed, by the self-same kind of implement. He remembered that the most celebrated of those bold unfortunates who live a life against the law, had said, "Choose my prison, and give me but a rusty nail, and I laugh at your jailers and your walls!" He crept to the window; he examined his relic by the dim starlight; he kissed it passionately, and the tears stood in his eyes.

Ah, who shall determine the worth of things? No king that night so prized his crown as the madman prized that rusty inch of wire, — the proper prey of the rubbish-cart and dunghill. Little didst thou think, old blacksmith, when thou drewest the dull metal from the fire, of what precious price it was to become!

Cesarini, with the astuteness of his malady, had long marked out this chamber for the scene of his operations; he had observed that the framework in which the bars were set seemed old and worm-eaten; that the window was but a few feet from the ground; that the noise made in the winter nights by the sighing branches of the old tree without would deaden the sound of the lone workman. Now, then, his hopes were to be crowned. Poor fool! and even *thou* hast hope still! All that night he toiled and toiled, and sought to work his iron into a file; now he tried the bars, and now the framework. Alas! he had not learned the skill in such tools, possessed by his renowned model and inspirer; the flesh was worn from his fingers, the cold drops stood on his brow; and morning surprised him, advanced not a hair-breadth in his labour.

He crept back to bed, and again hid the useless implement, and at last he slept.

And, night after night, the same task, the same results! But at length, one day, when Cesarini returned from his moody walk in the gardens (*pleasure*-grounds they were called by the owner), he found better workmen than he at the window; they were repairing the framework, they were strengthening the bars, — all hope was now gone! The unfortunate said nothing; too cunning to show his despair he eyed them silently, and cursed them; but the old tree was left still, and that was something, — company and music.

A day or two after this barbarous counterplot, Cesarini was walking in the gardens towards the latter part of the afternoon (just when in the short days the darkness begins to steal apace over the chill and western sun), when he was accosted by a fellow-captive, who had often before sought his acquaintance; for they try to have friends, — those poor people! Even *we* do the same; though *we* say we are *not* mad! This man had been a warrior, had served with Napoleon, had received honours and ribbons, — might, for aught we know, have dreamed of being a marshal! But the demon smote him in the hour of his pride. It was his disease to fancy himself a monarch. He believed, for he forgot chronology, that he was at once the Iron Mask, and the true sovereign of France and Navarre, confined in state by the usurpers of his crown. On other points he was generally sane; a tall, strong man, with fierce features, and stern lines, wherein could be read many a bloody tale of violence and wrong, of lawless passions, of terrible excesses, to which madness might be at once the consummation and the curse. This man had taken a fancy to Cesarini; and, in some hours Cesarini had shunned him less than others, — for they could alike rail against all living things. The lunatic approached Cesarini with an air of dignity and condescension.

" It is a cold night, sir, — and there will be no moon. Has it never occurred to you that the winter is the season for escape? "

Cesarini started; the ex-officer continued, —

" Ay, I see by your manner that you, too, chafe at our ignominious confinement. I think that together we might brave the worst. You probably are confined on some state offence. I give you full pardon, if you assist me. For my-

self I have but to appear in my capital; old Louis le Grand
must be near his last hour."

"This madman my best companion!" thought Cesarini,
revolting at his own infirmity, as Gulliver started from the
Yahoo. "No matter, he talks of escape.

"And how think you," said the Italian, aloud, — "how
think you, that we have any chance of deliverance?"

"Hush, speak lower," said the soldier. "In the inner
garden, I have observed for the last two days that a gardener
is employed in nailing some fig-trees and vines to the wall.
Between that garden and these grounds there is but a paling,
which we can easily scale. He works till dusk; at the latest
hour we can, let us climb noiselessly over the paling, and
creep along the vegetable beds till we reach the man. He
uses a ladder for his purpose; the rest is clear, — we must
fell and gag him, — twist his neck if necessary, — I have
twisted a neck before," quoth the maniac, with a horrid smile.
"The ladder will help us over the wall, and the night soon
grows dark at this season."

Cesarini listened, and his heart beat quick. "Will it be
too late to try to-night?" said he in a whisper.

"Perhaps not," said the soldier, who retained all his military acuteness. "But are you prepared, — don't you require
time to man yourself?"

"No — no, — I have had time enough! — I am ready."

"Well, then, — hist! — we are watched — one of the jailers!
Talk easily, smile, laugh. This way."

They passed by one of the watch of the place, and just as
they were in his hearing, the soldier turned to Cesarini, "Sir,
will you favour me with your snuff-box?"

"I have none."

"None? what a pity! My good friend," and he turned to
the scout, "may I request you to look in my room for my
snuff-box? It is on the chimney-piece, — it will not take you
a minute."

The soldier was one of those whose insanity was deemed
most harmless, and his relations, who were rich and well-
born, had requested every indulgence to be shown to him.

The watch suspected nothing, and repaired to the house.   As soon as the trees hid him, — "Now," said the soldier, "stoop almost on all fours, and run quick."

So saying the maniac crouched low, and glided along with a rapidity which did not distance Cesarini.   They reached the paling that separated the vegetable garden from the pleasure-ground; the soldier vaulted over it with ease, Cesarini with more difficulty followed.   They crept along; the herbs and vegetable beds, with their long bare stalks, concealed their movements; the man was still on the ladder.   "*La bonne Espérance!*" said the soldier through his ground teeth, muttering some old watchword of the wars, and (while Cesarini, below, held the ladder steadfast) he rushed up the steps, and with a sudden effort of his muscular arm, hurled the gardener to the ground.   The man, surprised, half stunned, and wholly terrified, did not attempt to wrestle with the two madmen,— he uttered loud cries for help!   But help came too late; these strange and fearful comrades had already scaled the wall, had dropped on the other side, and were fast making across the dusky fields to the neighbouring forest.

CHAPTER V.

HOPES and Fears
Start up alarmed, and o'er life's narrow verge
Look down : on what ?— a fathomless abyss ! — YOUNG.

MIDNIGHT — and intense frost!   There they were — houseless and breadless — the two fugitives, in the heart of that beautiful forest which has rung to the horns of many a royal chase.   The soldier, whose youth had been inured to hardships, and to the conquests which our mother-wit wrings from the stepdame Nature, had made a fire by the friction of two pieces of dry wood; such wood was hard to be found, for the snow whitened the level ground, and lay deep in the hollows;

and when it was discovered, the fuel was slow to burn; however, the fire blazed red at last. On a little mound, shaded by a semicircle of huge trees, sat the Outlaws of Human Reason. They cowered over the blaze opposite to each other, and the glare crimsoned their features. And each in his heart longed to rid himself of his mad neighbour; and each felt the awe of solitude, — the dread of sleep beside a comrade whose soul had lost God's light!

"Ho!" said the warrior, breaking a silence that had been long kept, "this is cold work at the best, and hunger pinches me; I almost regret the prison."

"I do not feel the cold," said Cesarini, "and I do not care for hunger: I am revelling only in the sense of liberty!"

"Try and sleep," quoth the soldier, with a coaxing and sinister softness of voice; "we will take it by turns to watch."

"I cannot sleep, — take you the first turn."

"Hark ye, sir!" said the soldier sullenly; "I must not have my commands disputed; now we are free, we are no longer equal: I am heir to the crowns of France and Navarre. Sleep, I say!"

"And what Prince or Potentate, King or Kaiser," cried Cesarini, catching the quick contagion of the fit that had seized his comrade, "can dictate to the monarch of Earth and Air, the Elements and the music-breathing Stars? I am Cesarini the Bard! and the huntsman Orion halts in his chase above to listen to my lyre! Be stilled, rude man! — thou scarest away the angels, whose breath even now was rushing through my hair!"

"It is too horrible!" cried the grim man of blood, shivering; "my enemies are relentless, and give me a madman for a jailer!"

"Ha! a madman!" exclaimed Cesarini, springing to his feet, and glaring at the soldier with eyes that caught and rivalled the blaze of the fire. "And who are you? — what devil from the deep hell, that art leagued with my persecutors against me?"

With the instinct of his old calling and valour, the soldier also rose when he saw the movement of his companion; and his fierce features worked with rage and fear.

"Avaunt!" said he, waving his arm; "we banish thee from our presence! This is our palace! — and our guards are at hand!" pointing to the still and skeleton trees that grouped round in ghastly bareness. "Begone!"

At that moment they heard at a distance the deep barking of a dog, and each cried simultaneously, "They are after me! — betrayed!" The soldier sprang at the throat of Cesarini; but the Italian, at the same instant, caught a half-burned brand from the fire, and dashed the blazing end in the face of his assailant. The soldier uttered a cry of pain, and recoiled back, blinded and dismayed. Cesarini, whose madness, when fairly roused, was of the most deadly nature, again raised his weapon, and probably nothing but death could have separated the foes; but again the bay of the dog was heard, and Cesarini, answering the sound by a wild yell, threw down the brand, and fled away through the forest with inconceivable swiftness. He hurried on through bush and dell, — and the boughs tore his garments and mangled his flesh, — but stopped not his progress till he fell at last on the ground, breathless and exhausted, and heard from some far-off clock the second hour of morning. He had left the forest; a farmhouse stood before him, and the whitened roofs of scattered cottages sloped to the tranquil sky. The witness of man — the social tranquil sky and the reasoning man — operated like a charm upon the senses which recent excitement had more than usually disturbed. The unhappy wretch gazed at the peaceful abodes, and sighed heavily; then, rising from the earth, he crept into one of the sheds that adjoined the farmhouse, and throwing himself on some straw, slept sound and quietly till daylight, and the voices of peasants in the shed awakened him.

He rose refreshed, calm, and, for ordinary purposes, sufficiently sane to prevent suspicion of his disease. He approached the startled peasants, and representing himself as a traveller who had lost his way in the night and amidst the forest, begged for food and water. Though his garments

were torn, they were new and of good fashion; his voice was
mild; his whole appearance and address those of one of some
station — and the French peasant is a hospitable fellow.
Cesarini refreshed and rested himself an hour or two at the
farm, and then resumed his wanderings; he offered no money,
for the rules of the asylum forbade money to its inmates, —
he had none with him; but none was expected from him, and
they bade him farewell as kindly as if he had bought their
blessings. He then began to consider where he was to take
refuge, and how provide for himself; the feeling of liberty
braced, and for a time restored, his intellect.

Fortunately, he had on his person, besides some rings of
trifling cost, a watch of no inconsiderable value, the sale of
which might support him, in such obscure and humble quarter as he could alone venture to inhabit, for several weeks,
perhaps months. This thought made him cheerful and elated;
he walked lustily on, shunning the high road. The day was
clear, the sun bright, the air full of racy health. Oh, what
soft raptures swelled the heart of the wanderer, as he gazed
around him! The Poet and the Freeman alike stirred within
his shattered heart! He paused to contemplate the berries of
the icy trees, to listen to the sharp glee of the blackbird; and
once — when he found beneath a hedge a cold, scentless group
of hardy violets — he laughed aloud in his joy. In that laughter there was no madness, no danger; but when as he jour-
neyed on, he passed through a little hamlet, and saw the
children at play upon the ground, and heard from the open
door of a cabin the sound of rustic music, then indeed he
paused abruptly; the past gathered over him: *he knew that
which he had been, that which he was now!* — an awful memory! a dread revelation! And, covering his face with his
hands, he wept aloud. In those tears were the peril and
method of madness. He woke from them to think of his
youth, his hopes, of Florence, of revenge! Lumley Lord
Vargrave! better, from that hour, to encounter the tiger in
his lair than find thyself alone with that miserable man!

CHAPTER VI.

It seemed the laurel chaste and stubborn oak,
And all the gentle trees on earth that grew,
It seemed the land, the sea, and heaven above,
All breathed out fancy sweet, and sighed out love.
FAIRFAX's *Tasso.*

AT De Montaigne's villa, Evelyn, for the first time, gathered from the looks, the manners, of Maltravers that she was beloved. It was no longer possible to mistake the evidences of affection. Formerly, Maltravers had availed himself of his advantage of years and experience, and would warn, admonish, dispute, even reprove; formerly, there had been so much of seeming caprice, of cold distance, of sudden and wayward haughtiness, in his bearing; but now the whole man was changed, — the Mentor had vanished in the Lover; he held his being on her breath. Her lightest pleasure seemed to have grown his law, no coldness ever alternated the deep devotion of his manner; an anxious, a timid, a watchful softness replaced all his stately self-possession. Evelyn saw that she was loved; and she then looked into her own heart.

I have said before that Evelyn was gentle, even to *yieldingness ;* that her susceptibility made her shrink from the thought of pain to another: and so thoroughly did she revere Maltravers, so grateful did she feel for a love that could not but flatter pride, and raise her in her self-esteem, that she felt it impossible that she could reject his suit. "Then, do I love him as I dreamed I could love?" she asked herself; and her heart gave no intelligible reply. "Yes, it must be so; in his presence I feel a tranquil and eloquent charm; his praise delights me; his esteem is my most high ambition; — and yet — and yet — " she sighed and thought of Legard; "but *he* loved me not!" and she turned restlessly from that image. "He thinks but of the world, of pleasure; Maltravers is right, — the spoiled children of society cannot love: why should I think of him?"

There were no guests at the villa, except Maltravers, Evelyn, and Lord and Lady Doltimore. Evelyn was much captivated by the graceful vivacity of Teresa, though that vivacity was not what it had been before her brother's affliction; their children, some of whom had grown up, constituted an amiable and intelligent family; and De Montaigne himself was agreeable and winning, despite his sober manners and his love of philosophical dispute. Evelyn often listened thoughtfully to Teresa's praises of her husband, — to her account of the happiness she had known in a marriage where there had been so great a disparity of years; Evelyn began to question the truth of her early visions of romance.

Caroline saw the unequivocal attachment of Maltravers with the same indifference with which she had anticipated the suit of Legard. It was the same to her what hand delivered Evelyn and herself from the designs of Vargrave; but Vargrave occupied nearly all her thoughts. The newspapers had reported him as seriously ill, — at one time in great danger. He was now recovering, but still unable to quit his room. He had written to her once, lamenting his ill-fortune, trusting soon to be at Paris; and touching, with evident pleasure, upon Legard's departure for Vienna, which he had seen in the "Morning Post." But he was afar — alone, ill, untended; and though Caroline's guilty love had been much abated by Vargrave's icy selfishness, by absence and remorse, still she had the heart of a woman, — and Vargrave was the only one that had ever touched it. She felt for him, and grieved in silence; she did not dare to utter sympathy aloud, for Doltimore had already given evidence of a suspicious and jealous temper.

Evelyn was also deeply affected by the account of her guardian's illness. As I before said, the moment he ceased to be her lover, her childish affection for him returned. She even permitted herself to write to him; and a tone of melancholy depression which artfully pervaded his reply struck her with something like remorse. He told her in the letter that he had much to say to her relative to an investment, in conformity with her stepfather's wishes, and he should hasten to Paris, even before the doctor would sanction his removal. Vargrave forbore to mention what the meditated investment was. The last public accounts of the minister had, however, been so favourable, that his arrival might be almost daily expected; and both Caroline and Evelyn felt relieved.

To De Montaigne, Maltravers confided his attachment, and both the Frenchman and Teresa sanctioned and encouraged it. Evelyn enchanted them; and they had passed that age when they could have imagined it possible that the man they had known almost as a boy was separated by years from the lively feelings and extreme youth of Evelyn. They could not believe that the sentiments he had inspired were colder than those that animated himself.

One day, Maltravers had been absent for some hours on his solitary rambles, and De Montaigne had not yet returned from Paris, which he visited almost daily. It was so late in the noon as almost to border on evening, when Maltravers, on his return, entered the grounds by a gate that separated them from an extensive wood. He saw Evelyn, Teresa, and two of her children walking on a terrace immediately before him. He joined them; and, somehow or other, it soon chanced that Teresa and himself loitered behind the rest, a little out of hearing. "Ah, Mr. Maltravers," said the former, "we miss the soft skies of Italy and the beautiful hues of Como."

"And, for my part, I miss the youth that gave 'glory to the grass and splendour to the flower.'"

"Nay; we are happier now, believe me, — or at least I should be, if — But I must not think of my poor brother. Ah, if his guilt deprived you of one who was worthy of you, it would be some comfort to his sister to think at last that the loss was repaired. And you still have scruples?"

"Who that loves truly has not? How young, how lovely, how worthy of lighter hearts and fairer forms than mine! Give me back the years that have passed since we last met at Como, and I might hope!"

"And this to me who have enjoyed such happiness with one older, when we married, by ten years than you are now!"

"But you, Teresa, were born to see life through the Claude glass."

"Ah, you provoke me with these refinements; you turn from a happiness you have but to demand."

"Do not — do not raise my hopes too high," cried Maltravers, with great emotion; "I have been schooling myself all day. But if I *am* deceived!"

"Trust me, you are not. See, even now she turns round to look for you; she loves you, — loves you as you deserve. This difference of years that you so lament does but deepen and elevate her attachment!"

Teresa turned to Maltravers, surprised at his silence. How joyous sat his heart upon his looks, — no gloom on his brow, no doubt in his sparkling eyes! He was mortal, and he yielded to the delight of believing himself beloved. He pressed Teresa's hand in silence, and, quitting her abruptly, gained the side of Evelyn. Madame de Montaigne comprehended all that passed within him; and as she followed, she soon contrived to detach her children, and returned with them to the house on a whispered pretence of seeing if their father had yet arrived. Evelyn and Maltravers continued to walk on, — not aware, at first, that the rest of the party were not close behind.

The sun had set; and they were in a part of the grounds which, by way of contrast to the rest, was laid out in the English fashion; the walk wound, serpent-like, among a profusion of evergreens irregularly planted; the scene was shut in and bounded, except where at a distance, through an opening of the trees, you caught the spire of a distant church, over which glimmered, faint and fair, the smile of the evening star.

"This reminds me of home," said Evelyn, gently.

"And hereafter it will remind me of you," said Maltravers, in whispered accents. He fixed his eyes on her as he spoke. Never had his look been so true to his heart; never had his voice so undisguisedly expressed the profound and passionate sentiment which had sprung up within him, — to constitute, as he then believed, the latest bliss, or the crowning misery,

of his life! At that moment, it was a sort of instinct that
told him they were *alone ;* for who has not felt — in those few
and memorable hours of life when love long suppressed over-
flows the fountain, and seems to pervade the whole frame and
the whole spirit — that there is a magic around and within us
that hath a keener intelligence than intellect itself? Alone
at such an hour with the one we love, the whole world besides
seems to vanish, and our feet to have entered the soil, and our
lips to have caught the air, of Fairyland.

They were alone. And why did Evelyn tremble? Why
did she feel that a crisis of existence was at hand?

"Miss Cameron — Evelyn," said Maltravers, after they had
walked some moments in silence, "hear me — and let your
reason as well as your heart reply. From the first moment
we met, you became dear to me. Yes, even when a child,
your sweetness and your fortitude foretold so well what you
would be in womanhood; even then you left upon my memory a delightful and mysterious shadow, — too prophetic of
the light that now hallows and wraps your image! We met
again, — and the attraction that had drawn me towards you
years before was suddenly renewed. I love you, Evelyn! I
love you better than all words can tell! Your future fate,
your welfare, your happiness, contain and embody all the
hopes left to me in life! But our years are different, Evelyn;
I have known sorrows, — and the disappointments and the
experience that have severed me from the common world have
robbed me of more than time itself hath done. They have
robbed me of that zest for the ordinary pleasures of our race,
— which may it be yours, sweet Evelyn, ever to retain! To
me, the time foretold by the Preacher as the lot of age has
already arrived, when the sun and the moon are darkened,
and when, save in you and through you, I have no pleasure
in anything. Judge, if such a being you can love! Judge,
if my very confession does not revolt and chill, if it does not
present to you a gloomy and cheerless future, were it possible
that you could unite your lot to mine! Answer not from
friendship or from pity; the love I feel for you can have a
reply from love alone, and from that reasoning which love, in

its enduring power, in its healthful confidence, in its prophetic foresight, alone supplies! I can resign you without a
murmur; but I could not live with you and even fancy that
you had one care I could not soothe, though you might have
happiness I could not share. And fate does not present to
me any vision so dark and terrible — no, not your loss itself;
no, not your indifference; no, not your aversion — as your
discovery, after time should make regret in vain, that you
had mistaken fancy or friendship for affection, a sentiment for
love. Evelyn, I have confided to you all, — all this wild
heart, now and evermore your own. My destiny is with
you."

Evelyn was silent; he took her hand, and her tears fell
warm and fast upon it. Alarmed and anxious, he drew her
towards him and gazed upon her face.

"You fear to wound me," he said, with pale lips and trembling voice. "Speak on, — I can bear all."

"No, no," said Evelyn, falteringly; "I have no fear but
not to deserve you."

"You love me, then, — you love me!" cried Maltravers
wildly, and clasping her to his heart.

The moon rose at that instant, and the wintry sward and
the dark trees were bathed in the sudden light. The time —
the light — so exquisite to all, even in loneliness and in sorrow — how divine in such companionship! in such overflow-
ing and ineffable sense of bliss! There and then for the first
time did Maltravers press upon that modest and blushing
cheek the kiss of Love, of Hope, — the seal of a union he
fondly hoped the grave itself could not dissolve!

Maltravers and Evelyn.

CHAPTER VII.

Queen. Whereon do you look ?
Hamlet. On him, on him, — look you how pale he glares ! — *Hamlet.*

PERHAPS to Maltravers those few minutes which ensued, as
they walked slowly on, compensated for all the troubles and
cares of years; for natures like his feel joy even yet more intensely than sorrow. It might be that the transport, the delirium of passionate and grateful thoughts that he poured forth,
when at last he could summon words, expressed feelings the
young Evelyn could not comprehend, and which less delighted
than terrified her with the new responsibility she had incurred.
But love so honest, so generous, so intense, dazzled and bewildered and carried her whole soul away.   Certainly at that
hour she felt no regret — no thought but that one in whom
she had so long recognized something nobler than is found in
the common world was thus happy and thus made happy by a
word, a look from her! Such a thought is woman's dearest
triumph; and one so thoroughly unselfish, so yielding, and so
soft, could not be insensible to the rapture she had caused.
"And oh!" said Maltravers, as he clasped again and again
the hand that he believed he had won forever, "now, at length,
have I learned how beautiful is life! For this — for this I
have been reserved! Heaven is merciful to me, and the waking world is brighter than all my dreams!"
He ceased abruptly.   At that instant they were once more
on the terrace where he had first joined Teresa, facing the
wood, which was divided by a slight and low palisade from
the spot where they stood. He ceased abruptly, for his eyes
encountered a terrible and ominous apparition, — a form connected with dreary associations of fate and woe. The figure
had raised itself upon a pile of firewood on the other side of
the fence, and hence it seemed almost gigantic in its stature.
It gazed upon the pair with eyes that burned with a preter-

natural blaze, and a voice which Maltravers too well remembered shrieked out "Love! love! What! *thou* love again? Where is the Dead! Ha, ha! Where is the Dead?"

Evelyn, startled by the words, looked up, and clung in speechless terror to Maltravers. He remained rooted to the spot.

"Unhappy man," said he, at length, and soothingly, "how came you hither? Fly not, you are with friends."

"Friends!" said the maniac, with a scornful laugh. "I know thee, Ernest Maltravers, — I know thee: but it is not thou who hast locked me up in darkness and in hell, side by side with the mocking fiend! Friends! ah, but no Friends shall catch me now! I am free! I am free! Air and wave are not more free!" And the madman laughed with horrible glee. "She is fair — fair," he said, abruptly checking himself, and with a changed voice, "but not so fair as the Dead. Faithless that thou art — and yet she loved *thee!* Woe to thee! woe! Maltravers, the perfidious! Woe to thee — and remorse — and shame!"

"Fear not, Evelyn, — fear not," whispered Maltravers, gently, and placing her behind him; "support your courage, — nothing shall harm you."

Evelyn, though very pale, and trembling from head to foot, retained her senses. Maltravers advanced towards the madman. But no sooner did the quick eye of the last perceive the movement, than, with the fear which belongs to that dread disease, — the fear of losing liberty, — he turned, and with a loud cry fled into the wood. Maltravers leaped over the fence, and pursued him some way in vain. The thick copses of the wood snatched every trace of the fugitive from his eye.

Breathless and exhausted, Maltravers returned to the spot where he had left Evelyn. As he reached it, he saw Teresa and her husband approaching towards him, and Teresa's merry laugh sounded clear and musical in the racy air. The sound appalled him; he hastened his steps to Evelyn.

"Say nothing of what we have seen to Madame de Montaigne, I beseech you," said he; "I will explain why hereafter."

Evelyn, too overcome to speak, nodded her acquiescence. They joined the De Montaignes, and Maltravers took the Frenchman aside.

But before he could address him, De Montaigne said, —

"Hush! do not alarm my wife — she knows nothing; but I have just heard at Paris, that — that he has escaped — you know whom I mean?"

"I do; he is at hand; send in search of him! I have seen him. Once more I have seen Castruccio Cesarini!"

BOOK IX.

Αἲ αἲ· τάδ' ἤδη διαφανῆ. — SOPHOCLES : *Œd. Tyr.* 754.

"Woe, woe : all things are clear."

CHAPTER I.

THE privilege that statesmen ever claim,
Who private interest never yet pursued,
But still pretended 't was for others' good.

.   .   .   .   .   .

From hence on every humorous wind that veered
With shifted sails a several course you steered.
Absalom and Achitophel, **Part ii.**

LORD VARGRAVE had for more than a fortnight remained at the inn at M——, too ill to be removed with safety in a season so severe. Even when at last, by easy stages, he reached London, he was subjected to a relapse; and his recovery was slow and gradual. Hitherto unused to sickness, he bore his confinement with extreme impatience; and against the commands of his physician insisted on continuing to transact his official business, and consult with his political friends in his sick-room; for Lumley knew well, that it is most pernicious to public men to be considered failing in health, — turkeys are not more unfeeling to a sick brother than politicians to an ailing statesman; they give out that his head is touched, and see paralysis and epilepsy in every speech and every despatch. The time, too, nearly ripe for his great schemes, made it doubly necessary that he should exert himself, and prevent being shelved with a plausible excuse of tender compassion for his infirmities. As soon therefore as he learned that Legard had left Paris, he thought himself safe for a while in that quarter, and surrendered his thoughts wholly to his ambitious projects. Perhaps, too, with the susceptible vanity of a middle-aged man, who has had his *bonnes fortunes*, Lumley deemed, with Rousseau, that a lover, pale and haggard — just raised from the bed of suffering — is more interesting to friendship than attractive to love. He and Rousseau were, I believe, both mistaken; but that is a matter of opinion: they both thought very coarsely of women, — one from having no sentiment, and the other from having a sentiment that was but a disease. At length, just as Lumley was sufficiently recovered to quit his house, to appear at his office, and declare that his illness had wonderfully improved his constitution, intelligence from Paris, the more startling from being wholly unexpected, reached him. From Caroline he learned that Maltravers had proposed to Evelyn, and been accepted. From Maltravers himself he heard the confirmation of the news. The last letter was short, but kind and manly. He addressed Lord Vargrave as Evelyn's guardian; slightly alluded to the scruples he had entertained till Lord Vargrave's suit was broken off; and feeling the subject too delicate for a letter, expressed a desire to confer with Lumley respecting Evelyn's wishes as to certain arrangements in her property.

And for this was it that Lumley had toiled! for this had he visited Lisle Court! and for this had he been stricken down to the bed of pain! Was it only to make his old rival the purchaser, if he so pleased it, of the possessions of his own family? Lumley thought at that moment less of Evelyn than of Lisle Court. As he woke from the stupor and the first fit of rage into which these epistles cast him, the recollection of the story he had heard from Mr. Onslow flashed across him. Were his suspicions true, what a secret he would possess! How fate might yet befriend him! Not a moment was to be lost. Weak, suffering as he still was, he ordered his carriage, and hastened down to Mrs. Leslie.

In the interview that took place, he was careful not to

alarm her into discretion. He managed the conference with his usual consummate dexterity. He did not appear to believe that there had been any actual connection between Alice and the supposed Butler. He began by simply asking whether Alice had ever, in early life, been acquainted with a person of that name, and when residing in the neighbourhood of ——. The change of countenance, the surprised start of Mrs. Leslie, convinced him that his suspicions were true.

"And why do you ask, my lord?" said the old lady. "Is it to ascertain this point that you have done me the honour to visit me?"

"Not exactly, my dear madam," said Lumley, smiling. "But I am going to C—— on business; and besides that I wished to give an account of your health to Evelyn, whom I shall shortly see at Paris, I certainly did desire to know whether it would be any gratification to Lady Vargrave, for whom I have the deepest regard, to renew her acquaintance with the said Mr. Butler."

"What does your lordship know of him? What is he; who is he?"

"Ah, my dear lady, you turn the tables on me, I see, — for my one question you would give me fifty. But, seriously, before I answer you, you must tell me whether Lady Vargrave does know a gentleman of that name; yet, indeed, to save trouble, I may as well inform you, that I know it was under that name that she resided at C——, when my poor uncle first made her acquaintance. What I ought to ask is this, — sup- posing Mr. Butler be still alive, and a gentleman of character and fortune, would it please Lady Vargrave to meet with him once more?"

"I cannot tell you," said Mrs. Leslie, sinking back in her chair, much embarrassed.

"Enough, I shall not stir further in the matter. Glad to see you looking so well. Fine place, beautiful trees. Any commands at C——, or any message for Evelyn?"

Lumley rose to depart.

"Stay," said Mrs. Leslie, recalling all the pining, restless, untiring love that Lady Vargrave had manifested towards the

lost, and feeling that she ought not to sacrifice to slight scruples the chance of happiness for her friend's future years, —
"stay; I think this question you should address to Lady Vargrave, — or shall I?"

"As you will, — perhaps I had better write. Good-day,"
and Vargrave hurried away.

He had satisfied himself, but he had another yet to satisfy,
— and that, from certain reasons known but to himself, without bringing the third person in contact with Lady Vargrave.
On arriving at C—— he wrote, therefore, to Lady Vargrave
as follows: —

> My dear Friend, — Do not think me impertinent or intrusive —
> but you know me too well for that. A gentleman of the name of Butler
> is exceedingly anxious to ascertain if you once lived near ——, in a
> pretty little cottage, — Dove, or Dale, or Dell cottage (some such appel-
> lation), — and if you remember a person of his name. Should you
> care to give a reply to these queries, send me a line addressed to Lon-
> don, which I shall get on my way to Paris.
>
> Yours most truly,
>
> VARGRAVE.

As soon as he had concluded, and despatched this letter,
Vargrave wrote to Mr. Winsley as follows: —

> My dear Sir, — I am so unwell as to be unable to call on you, or
> even to see any one, however agreeable (nay, the more agreeable the
> more exciting!). I hope, however, to renew our personal acquaintance
> before quitting C——. Meanwhile, oblige me with a line to say if I did
> not understand you to signify that you could, if necessary, prove that
> Lady Vargrave once resided in this town as Mrs. Butler, a very short
> time before she married my uncle, under the name of Cameron, in Dev-
> onshire; and had she not also at that time a little girl, — an infant, or
> nearly so, — who must necessarily be the young lady who is my uncle's
> heiress, Miss Evelyn Cameron. My reason for thus troubling you is
> obvious. As Miss Cameron's guardian, I have very shortly to wind up
> certain affairs connected with my uncle's will; and, what is more, there
> is some property bequeathed by the late Mr. Butler, which *may* make it
> necessary to prove identity.
>
> Truly yours,
>
> VARGRAVE.

The answer to the latter communication ran thus: —

"My Lord, — I am very sorry to hear your lordship is so unwell, and will pay my respects to-morrow.   I certainly can swear that the present Lady Vargrave was the Mrs. Butler who resided at C——, and taught music.   And as the child with her was of the same sex, and about the same age as Miss Cameron, there can, I should think, be no difficulty in establishing the identity between that young lady and the child Lady Vargrave had by her first husband, Mr. Butler; but of this, of course, I cannot speak.

"I have the honour, etc."

The next morning Vargrave despatched a note to Mr. Winsley, saying that his health required him to return to town immediately, — and to town, in fact, he hastened.   The day after his arrival, he received, in a hurried hand — strangely blurred and blotted, perhaps by tears — this short letter: —

For Heaven's sake, tell me what you mean!   Yes, yes, I did once reside at Dale Cottage, I did know one of the name of Butler!   Has *he* discovered the name *I* bear?   Where is he?   I implore you to write, or let me see you before you leave England!

ALICE VARGRAVE.

Lumley smiled triumphantly when he read and carefully put up this letter.

"I must now amuse and put her off — at all events for the present."

In answer to Lady Vargrave's letter, he wrote a few lines to say that he had only heard through a third person (a lawyer) of a Mr. Butler residing somewhere abroad, who had wished these inquiries to be made; that he believed it only related to some disposition of property; that, *perhaps*, the Mr. Butler who made the inquiry was heir to the Mr. Butler she had known; that he could learn nothing else at present, as the purport of her reply must be sent abroad, — the lawyer would or could say nothing more; that directly he received a further communication it should be despatched to her, that he was most affectionately and most truly hers.

The rest of that morning Vargrave devoted to Lord Saxingham and his allies; and declaring, and believing, that he should not be long absent at Paris, he took an early dinner, and was about once more to commit himself to the risks of travel, when, as he crossed the hall, Mr. Douce came hastily upon him.

"My lord — my lord — I must have a word with your l-l-lordship; — you are going to — that is — " (and the little man looked frightened) "you intend to — to go to — that is — ab-ab-ab — "

"Not abscond, Mr. Douce; come into the library: I am in a great hurry, but I have always time for *you*. What's the matter?"

"Why, then, my lord, — I — I have heard nothing m-m-more from your lordship about the pur-pur — "

"Purchase? — I am going to Paris, to settle all particulars with Miss Cameron; tell the lawyers so."

"May — may — we draw out the money to — to — show — that — that we are in earnest? Otherwise I fear — that is, I suspect — I mean I know, that Colonel Maltravers will be off the bargain."

"Why, Mr. Douce, really I must just see my ward first; but you shall hear from me in a day or two; — and the ten thousand pounds I owe you!"

"Yes, indeed, the ten — ten — ten! — my partner is very — "

"Anxious for it, no doubt! My compliments to him. God bless you! — take care of yourself, — must be off to save the packet;" and Vargrave hurried away, muttering, "Heaven sends money, and the devil sends duns!"

Douce gasped like a fish for breath, as his eyes followed the rapid steps of Vargrave; and there was an angry scowl of disappointment on his small features. Lumley, by this time, seated in his carriage, and wrapped up in his cloak, had forgotten the creditor's existence, and whispered to his aristocratic secretary, as he bent his head out of the carriage window, "I have told Lord Saxingham to despatch you to me, if there is any — the least — necessity for me in London. I leave you behind, Howard, because your sister being at court, and your cousin with our notable premier, you will find out every change in the wind — you understand. And, I say, Howard, don't think I forget your kindness! — you know that no man ever served me in vain! Oh, there's that horrid little Douce behind you, — tell them to drive on!"

------◆------

CHAPTER II.

HEARD you that ?
What prodigy of horror is disclosing ? — LILLO : *Fatal Curiosity.*

THE unhappy companion of Cesarini's flight was soon discovered and recaptured; but all search for Cesarini himself proved ineffectual, not only in the neighbourhood of St. Cloud, but in the surrounding country and in Paris. The only comfort was in thinking that his watch would at least preserve him for some time from the horrors of want; and that by the sale of the trinket, he might be traced. The police, too, were set at work, — the vigilant police of Paris! Still day rolled on day, and no tidings. The secret of the escape was carefully concealed from Teresa; and public cares were a sufficient excuse for the gloom on De Montaigne's brow.

Evelyn heard from Maltravers with mingled emotions of compassion, grief, and awe the gloomy tale connected with the history of the maniac. She wept for the fate of Florence; she shuddered at the curse that had fallen on Cesarini; and perhaps Maltravers grew dearer to her from the thought that there was so much in the memories of the past that needed a comforter and a soother.

They returned to Paris, affianced and plighted lovers; and then it was that Evelyn sought carefully and resolutely to banish from her mind all recollection, all regret, of the absent Legard: she felt the solemnity of the trust confided in her, and she resolved that no thought of hers should ever be of a nature to gall the generous and tender spirit that had confided its life of life to her care. The influence of Maltravers over her increased in their new and more familiar position, and yet still it partook too much of veneration, too little of passion; but that might be her innocence and youth. He, at least, was sensible of no want, — she had chosen him from the world; and fastidious as he deemed himself, he reposed, without a doubt, on the security of her faith. None of those presentiments which had haunted him when first betrothed to Florence disturbed him now. The affection of one so young and so guileless seemed to bring back to him all his own youth — we are ever young while the young can love us! Suddenly, too, the world took to his eyes a brighter and fairer aspect. Hope, born again, reconciled him to his career and to his race! The more he listened to Evelyn, the more he watched every evidence of her docile but generous nature, the more he felt assured that he had found at last a heart suited to his own. Her beautiful serenity of temper, cheerful, yet never fitful or unquiet, gladdened him with its insensible contagion. To be with Evelyn was like basking in the sunshine of some happy sky! It was an inexpressible charm to one wearied with "the hack sights and sounds" of this jaded world, — to watch the ever-fresh and sparkling thoughts and fancies which came from a soul so new to life! It enchanted one, painfully fastidious in what relates to the true nobility of character, that, however various the themes discussed, no low or mean thought ever sullied those beautiful lips. It was not the mere innocence of inexperience, but the moral incapability of guile, that charmed him in the companion he had chosen on his path to Eternity! He was also delighted to notice Evelyn's readiness of resources: she had that faculty, without which woman has no independence from the world, no pledge that domestic retirement will not soon languish into wearisome monotony, — the faculty of making trifles contribute to occupation or amusement; she was easily pleased, and yet she so soon reconciled herself to disappointment. He felt, and chid his own dulness for not feeling it

before, that, young and surpassingly lovely as she was, she
required no stimulant from the heated pursuits and the hollow admiration of the crowd.

"Such," thought he, "are the natures that alone can preserve through years the poetry of the first passionate illusion,
that can alone render wedlock the seal that confirms affection,
and not the mocking ceremonial that vainly consecrates its
grave!"

Maltravers, as we have seen, formally wrote to Lumley
some days after their return to Paris. He would have written also to Lady Vargrave, but Evelyn thought it best to prepare her mother by a letter from herself.

Miss Cameron now wanted but a few weeks to the age of
eighteen, at which she was to be the sole mistress of her own
destiny. On arriving at that age the marriage was to take
place. Valerie heard with sincere delight of the new engagement her friend had formed. She eagerly sought every opportunity to increase her intimacy with Evelyn, who was
completely won by her graceful kindness; the result of
Valerie's examination was, that she did not wonder at the
passionate love of Maltravers, but that her deep knowledge of
the human heart (that knowledge so remarkable in the women
of her country!) made her doubt how far it was adequately
returned, how far Evelyn deceived herself. Her first satisfaction became mingled with anxiety, and she relied more for
the future felicity of her friend on Evelyn's purity of thought
and general tenderness of heart than on the exclusiveness and
ardour of her love. Alas! few at eighteen are not too young
for the irrevocable step, — and Evelyn was younger than her
years! One evening at Madame de Ventadour's Maltravers
asked Evelyn if she had yet heard from Lady Vargrave.
Evelyn expressed her surprise that she had not, and the conversation fell, as was natural, upon Lady Vargrave herself.
"Is she as fond of music as you are?" asked Maltravers.

"Yes, indeed, I think so — and of the songs of a certain
person in particular; they always had for her an indescriba-
ble charm. Often have I heard her say that to read your
writings was like talking to an early friend. Your name and

genius seemed to make her solitary connection with the great
world. Nay — but you will not be angry — I half think it
was her enthusiasm, so strange and rare, that first taught me
interest in yourself."

"I have a double reason, then, for loving your mother,"
said Maltravers, much pleased and flattered. "And does she
not like Italian music?"

"Not much; she prefers some rather old-fashioned German
airs, very simple, but very touching."

"My own early passion," said Maltravers, more and more
interested.

"But there are also one or two English songs which I have
occasionally, but very seldom, heard her sing. One in especial affects her so deeply, even when she plays the air, that I
have always attached to it a certain mysterious sanctity. I
should not like to sing it before a crowd, but to-morrow, when
you call on me, and we are alone — "

"Ah, to-morrow I will not fail to remind you."

Their conversation ceased; yet, somehow or other, that
night when he retired to rest the recollection of it haunted
Maltravers. He felt a vague, unaccountable curiosity respecting this secluded and solitary mother; all concerning her early
fate seemed so wrapped in mystery. Cleveland, in reply to
his letter, had informed him that all inquiries respecting the
birth and first marriage of Lady Vargrave had failed. Evelyn
evidently knew but little of either, and he felt a certain delicacy in pressing questions which might be ascribed to the
inquisitiveness of a vulgar family pride. Moreover, lovers
have so much to say to each other, that he had not time to
talk at length to Evelyn about third persons. He slept ill
that night, — dark and boding dreams disturbed his slumber.
He rose late and dejected by presentiments he could not master: his morning meal was scarcely over, and he had already
taken his hat to go to Evelyn's for comfort and sunshine,
when the door opened, and he was surprised by the entrance
of Lord Vargrave.

Lumley seated himself with a formal gravity very unusual
to him, and as if anxious to waive unnecessary explanations,

began as follows, with a serious and impressive voice and
aspect: —

"Maltravers, of late years we have been estranged from
each other. I do not presume to dictate to you your friendships or your dislikes. Why this estrangement has happened
you alone can determine. For my part I am conscious of no
offence; that which I was I am still. It is you who have
changed. Whether it be the difference of our political opinions, or any other and more secret cause, I know not. I
lament, but it is now too late to attempt to remove it. If you
suspect me of ever seeking, or even wishing, to sow dissen-
sion between yourself and my ill-fated cousin, now no more,
you are mistaken. I ever sought the happiness and union of
you both. And yet, Maltravers, you then came between me
and an early and cherished dream. But I suffered in silence;
my course was at least disinterested, perhaps generous: let it
pass. A second time you cross my path, — you win from me
a heart I had long learned to consider mine. You have no
scruple of early friendship, you have no forbearance towards
acknowledged and affianced ties. You are my rival with
Evelyn Cameron, and your suit has prospered."

"Vargrave," said Maltravers, "you have spoken frankly;
and I will reply with an equal candour. A difference of
tastes, tempers, and opinions led us long since into opposite
paths. I am one who cannot disunite public morality from
private virtue. From motives best known to you, but which
I say openly I hold to have been those of interest or ambition, you did not change your opinions (there is no sin in
that), but retaining them in private, professed others in public, and played with the destinies of mankind as if they were
but counters to mark a mercenary game. This led me to
examine your character with more searching eyes; and I
found it one I could no longer trust. With respect to the
Dead, let the pall drop over that early grave, — I acquit you
of all blame. He who sinned has suffered more than would
atone the crime! You charge me with my love to Evelyn.
Pardon me, but I seduced no affection, I have broken no tie.
Not till she was free in heart and in hand to choose between

us, did I hint at love. Let me think that a way may be found to soften one portion at least of the disappointment you cannot but feel acutely."

"Stay!" said Lord Vargrave (who, plunged in a gloomy revery, had scarcely seemed to hear the last few sentences of his rival): "stay, Maltravers. Speak not of love to Evelyn! A horrible foreboding tells me that, a few hours hence, you would rather pluck out your tongue by the roots than couple the words of love with the thought of that unfortunate girl! Oh, if I were vindictive, what awful triumph would await me now! What retaliation on your harsh judgment, your cold contempt, your momentary and wretched victory over me! Heaven is my witness, that my only sentiment is that of terror and woe! Maltravers, in your earliest youth, did you form connection with one whom they called Alice Darvil?"

"Alice! merciful Heaven! what of her?"

"Did you never know that the Christian name of Evelyn's mother is Alice?"

"I never asked, I never knew; but it is a common name," faltered Maltravers.

"Listen to me," resumed Vargrave: "with Alice Darvil you lived in the neighbourhood of ——, did you not?"

"Go on, go on!"

"You took the name of Butler; by that name Alice Darvil was afterwards known in the town in which my uncle resided — there are gaps in the history that I cannot of my own knowledge fill up, — she taught music; my uncle became enamoured of her, but he was vain and worldly. She removed into Devonshire, and he married her there, under the name of Cameron, by which name he hoped to conceal from the world the lowness of her origin, and the humble calling she had followed. Hold! do not interrupt me. Alice had one daughter, as was supposed, by a former marriage; that daughter was the offspring of him whose name she bore — yes, of the false Butler! — that daughter is Evelyn Cameron!"

"Liar! devil!" cried Maltravers, springing to his feet, as if a shot had pierced his heart. "Proofs! proofs!"

23

"Will these suffice?" said Vargrave, as he drew forth the letters of Winsley and Lady Vargrave. Maltravers took them, but it was some moments before he could dare to read. He supported himself with difficulty from falling to the ground; there was a gurgle in his throat like the sound of the death-rattle; at last he read, and dropped the letters from his hand.

"Wait me here," he said very faintly, and moved mechanically to the door.

"Hold!" said Lord Vargrave, laying his hand upon Ernest's arm. "Listen to me for Evelyn's sake, for her mother's. You are about to seek Evelyn, — be it so! I know that you possess the god-like gift of self-control. You will not suffer her to learn that her mother has done that which dishonours alike mother and child? You will not consummate your wrong to Alice Darvil by robbing her of the fruit of a life of penitence and remorse? You will not unveil her shame to her own daughter? Convince yourself, and master yourself while you do so!"

"Fear me not," said Maltravers, with a terrible smile; "I will not afflict my conscience with a double curse. As I have sowed, so must I reap. Wait me here!"

---◆---

CHAPTER III.

. . . MISERY
That gathers force each moment as it rolls,
And must, at last, o'erwhelm me. — LILLO : *Fatal Curiosity.*

MALTRAVERS found Evelyn alone; she turned towards him with her usual sweet smile   welcome; but the smile vanished at once, as her eyes met his changed and working countenance; cold drops stood upon the rigid and marble brow, the lips writhed as if in bodily torture, the muscles of the face had fallen, and there was a wildness which appalled her in the fixed and feverish brightness of the eyes.

"You are ill, Ernest, — dear Ernest, you are ill, — your look freezes me!"

"Nay, Evelyn," said Maltravers, recovering himself by one of those efforts of which men who have *suffered without sympathy* are alone capable, — "nay, I am better now; I have been ill — very ill — but I am better!"

"Ill! and I not know of it?" She attempted to take his hand as she spoke. Maltravers recoiled.

"It is fire! it burns! Avaunt!" he cried, frantically. "O Heaven! spare me, spare me!"

Evelyn was not seriously alarmed; she gazed on him with the tenderest compassion. Was this one of those moody and overwhelming paroxysms to which it had been whispered abroad that he was subject? Strange as it may seem, despite her terror, he was dearer to her in that hour — as she believed, of gloom and darkness — than in all the glory of his majestic intellect, or all the blandishments of his soft address.

"What has happened to you?" she said, approaching him again; "have you seen Lord Vargrave? I know that he has arrived, for his servant has been here to say so; has he uttered anything to distress you? or has — " (she added falteringly and timidly) — "has poor Evelyn offended you? Speak to me, — only speak!"

Maltravers turned, and his face was now calm and serene: save by its extreme and almost ghastly paleness, no trace of the hell within him could be discovered.

"Pardon me," said he, gently, "I know not this morning what I say or do; think not of it, think not of me, — it will pass away when I hear your voice."

"Shall I sing to you the words I spoke of last night? See, I have them ready; I know them by heart, but I thought you might like to read them, they are so full of simple but deep feeling."

Maltravers took the song from her hands, and bent over the paper; at first, the letters seemed dim and indistinct, for there was a mist before his eyes; but at last a chord of mem-

ory was struck, — he recalled the words: they were some of
those he had composed for Alice in the first days of their delicious intercourse, — links of the golden chain, in which he had
sought to bind the spirit of knowledge to that of love.

"And from whom," said he, in a faint voice, as he calmly
put down the verses, — "from whom did your mother learn
these words?"

"I know not; some dear friend, years ago, composed and
gave them to her. It must have been one very dear to her,
to judge by the effect they still produce."

"Think you," said Maltravers, in a hollow voice, "think
you IT WAS YOUR FATHER?"

"My father! She never speaks of him! I have been early
taught to shun all allusion to his memory. My father! — it
is probable; yes, it may have been my father; whom else
could she have loved so fondly?"

There was a long silence; Evelyn was the first to break it.

"I have heard from my mother to-day, Ernest; her letter
alarms me, — I scarce know why!"

"Ah! and how — "

"It is hurried and incoherent, — almost wild: she says she
has learned some intelligence that has unsettled and unstrung
her mind; she has requested me to inquire if any one I am
acquainted with has heard of, or met abroad, some person of
the name of Butler. You start! — have you known one of
that name?"

"I! — did your mother never allude to that name before?"

"Never! — and yet, once I remember — "

"What?"

"That I was reading an account in the papers of the sudden
death of some Mr. Butler; and her agitation made a powerful
and strange impression upon me, — in fact, she fainted, and
seemed almost delirious when she recovered; she would not
rest till I had completed the account, and when I came to
the particulars of his age, etc. (he was old, I think) she
clasped her hands, and wept; but they seemed tears of joy.
The name is so common — whom of that name have you
known?"

"It is no matter. Is that your mother's letter; is that her handwriting?"

"Yes;" and Evelyn gave the letter to Maltravers. He glanced over the characters; he had once or twice seen Lady Vargrave's handwriting before, and had recognized no likeness between that handwriting and such early specimens of Alice's art as he had witnessed so many years ago; but now, "trifles light as air" had grown "confirmation strong as proof of Holy Writ," — he thought he detected Alice in every line of the hurried and blotted scroll; and when his eye rested on the words, "Your affectionate MOTHER, *Alice!*" his blood curdled in his veins.

"It is strange!" said he, still struggling for self-composure; "strange that I never thought of asking her name before! Alice! her name is Alice?"

"A sweet name, is it not? It accords so well with her simple character — how you would love her!"

As she said this, Evelyn turned to Maltravers with enthusiasm, and again she was startled by his aspect; for again it was haggard, distorted, and convulsed.

"Oh, if you love me," she cried, "do send immediately for advice! And yet, is it illness, Ernest, or is it some grief that you hide from me?"

"It is illness, Evelyn," said Maltravers, rising: and his knees knocked together. "I am not fit even for your companionship, — I will go home."

"And send instantly for advice?"

"Ay; it waits me there already."

"Thank Heaven! and you will write to me one little word — to relieve me? I am so uneasy!"

"I will write to you."

"This evening?"

"Ay!"

"Now go, — I will not detain you."

He walked slowly to the door, but when he reached it he turned, and catching her anxious gaze, he opened his arms; overpowered with strange fear and affectionate sympathy, she burst into passionate tears; and surprised out of the timidity and reserve which had hitherto characterized her pure and meek attachment to him, she fell on his breast, and sobbed aloud. Maltravers raised his hands, and, placing them solemnly on her young head, his lips muttered as if in prayer. He paused, and strained her to his heart; but he shunned that parting kiss, which, hitherto, he had so fondly sought. That embrace was one of agony, and not of rapture; and yet Evelyn dreamed not that he designed it for the last!

Maltravers re-entered the room in which he had left Lord Vargrave, who still awaited his return.

He walked up to Lumley, and held out his hand. "You have saved me from a dreadful crime, — from an everlasting remorse. I thank you!"

Hardened and frigid as his nature was, Lumley was touched; the movement of Maltravers took him by surprise. "It has been a dreadful duty, Ernest," said he, pressing the hand he held; "but to come, too, from *me*, — your rival!"

"Proceed, proceed, I pray you; explain all this — yet explanation! what do I want to know? Evelyn is my daughter, — Alice's child ! For Heaven's sake, give me hope; say it is not so; say that she is Alice's child, but not *mine!* Father! father! — and they call it a holy name — it is a horrible one!"

"Compose yourself, my dear friend: recollect what you have escaped! You will recover this shock. Time, travel — "

"Peace, man, — peace! Now then I am calm! When Alice left me she had no child. I knew not that she bore within her the pledge of our ill-omened and erring love. Verily, the sins of my youth have arisen against me; and the curse has come home to roost!"

"I cannot explain to you all details."

"But why not have told me of this? Why not have warned me; why not have said to me, when my heart could have been satisfied by so sweet a tie, ' Thou hast a daughter: thou art not desolate '? Why reserve the knowledge of the blessing until it has turned to poison? Fiend that you are! you have waited this hour to gloat over the agony from which a word from you a year, nay, a month ago — a little month ago — might have saved me and her!"

Maltravers, as he spoke, approached Vargrave, with eyes sparkling with fierce passion, his hand clenched, his form dilated, the veins on his forehead swelled like cords. Lumley, brave as he was, recoiled.

"I knew not of this secret," said he, deprecatingly, "till a few days before I came hither; and I came hither at once to disclose it to you. Will you listen to me? I knew that my uncle had married a person much beneath him in rank; but he was guarded and cautious, and I knew no more, except that by a first husband that lady had one daughter, — Evelyn. A chain of accidents suddenly acquainted me with the rest."

Here Vargrave pretty faithfully repeated what he had learned from the brewer at C——, and from Mr. Onslow; but when he came to the tacit confirmation of all his suspicions received from Mrs. Leslie, he greatly exaggerated and greatly distorted the account. "Judge, then," concluded Lumley, "of the horror with which I heard that you had declared an attachment to Evelyn, and that it was returned. Ill as I was, I hastened hither: you know the rest. Are you satisfied?"

"I will go to Alice! I will learn from her own lips — yet, how can I meet her again? How say to her, ' I have taken from thee thy last hope, — I have broken thy child's heart'?"

"Forgive me, but I should confess to you, that, from all I can learn from Mrs. Leslie, Lady Vargrave has but one prayer, one hope in life, — that she may never again meet with her betrayer. You may, indeed, in her own letter perceive how much she is terrified by the thought of your discovering her. She has, at length, recovered peace of mind and tranquillity of conscience. She shrinks with dread from the prospect of ever again encountering one once so dear, now associated in her mind with recollections of guilt and sorrow. More than this, she is sensitively alive to the fear of shame, to the dread of detection. If ever her daughter were to know her sin, it would be to her as a death-blow. Yet in her nervous state of health, her ever-quick and uncontrollable feelings, if you were to meet her, she would disguise nothing, conceal nothing. The veil would be torn aside: the menials in her own house would tell the tale, and curiosity circulate, and scandal blacken the story of her early errors. No, Maltravers, at least wait awhile before you see her; wait till her mind can be prepared for such an interview, till precautions can be taken, till you yourself are in a calmer state of mind."

Maltravers fixed his piercing eyes on Lumley while he thus spoke, and listened in deep attention.

"It matters not," said he, after a long pause, "whether these be your real reasons for wishing to defer or prevent a meeting between Alice and myself. The affliction that has come upon me bursts with too clear and scorching a blaze of light for me to see any chance of escape or mitigation. Even if Evelyn were the daughter of Alice by another, she would be forever separated from me. The mother and the child! there is a kind of incest even in that thought! But such an alleviation of my anguish is forbidden to my reason. No, poor Alice, I will not disturb the repose thou hast won at last! Thou shalt never have the grief to know that our error has brought upon thy lover so black a doom! All is over! the world never shall find me again. Nothing is left for me but the desert and the grave!"

"Speak not so, Ernest," said Lord Vargrave, soothingly; "a little while, and you will recover this blow: your control over passion has, even in youth, inspired me with admiration and surprise; and now, in calmer years, and with such incentives to self-mastery, your triumph will come sooner than you think. Evelyn, too, is so young; she has not known you long; perhaps her love, after all, is that caused by some mystic, but innocent working of nature, and she would rejoice to call you 'father.' Happy years are yet in store for you."

Maltravers did not listen to these vain and hollow consolations. With his head drooping on his bosom, his whole form unnerved, the large tears rolling unheeded down his cheeks, he seemed the very picture of a broken-hearted man, whom fate never again could raise from despair. He, who had, for

years, so cased himself in pride, on whose very front was
engraved the victory over passion and misfortune, whose step
had trod the earth in the royalty of the conqueror; the veriest
slave that crawls bore not a spirit more humbled, fallen, or
subdued! He who had looked with haughty eyes on the infirmities of others, who had disdained to serve his race because
of their human follies and partial frailties, — *he*, even *he*, the
Pharisee of Genius, — had but escaped by a chance, and by
the hand of the man he suspected and despised, from a crime
at which nature herself recoils, — which all law, social and
divine, stigmatizes as inexpiable, which the sternest imagination of the very heathen had invented as the gloomiest catas-
trophe that can befall the wisdom and the pride of mortals!
But one step farther, and the fabulous Œdipus had not been
more accursed!

Such thoughts as these, unformed, confused, but strong
enough to bow him to the dust, passed through the mind of
this wretched man. He had been familiar with grief, he had
been dull to enjoyment; sad and bitter memories had consumed his manhood: but pride had been left him still; and
he had dared in his secret heart to say, "I can defy Fate!"
Now the bolt had fallen; Pride was shattered into fragments,
Self-abasement was his companion, Shame sat upon his pros-
trate soul. The Future had no hope left in store. Nothing
was left for him but to die!

Lord Vargrave gazed at him in real pain, in sincere compassion; for his nature, wily, deceitful, perfidious though it
was, had cruelty only so far as was necessary to the unrelent-
ing execution of his schemes. No pity could swerve him
from a purpose; but he had enough of the *man* within him to
feel pity not the less, even for his own victim! At length
Maltravers lifted his head, and waved his hand gently to Lord
Vargrave.

"All is now explained," said he, in a feeble voice; "our
interview is over. I must be alone; I have yet to collect my
reason, to commune calmly and deliberately with myself; I
have to write to her — to invent, to lie, — I, who believed
I could never, never utter, even to an enemy, what was false!

And I must not soften the blow to her. I must not utter a word of love, — love, it is incest! I must endeavour brutally to crush out the very affection I created! She must hate me! — oh, *teach* her to hate me! Blacken my name, traduce my motives, — let her believe them levity or perfidy, what you will. So will she forget me the sooner; so will she the easier bear the sorrow which the father brings upon the child. And *she* has not sinned! O Heaven, the sin was mine! Let my punishment be a sacrifice that Thou wilt accept for her!"

Lord Vargrave attempted again to console; but this time the words died upon his lips. His arts failed him. Maltravers turned impatiently away and pointed to the door.

"I will see you again," said he, "before I quit Paris; leave your address below."

Vargrave was not, perhaps, unwilling to terminate a scene so painful: he muttered a few incoherent words, and abruptly withdrew. He heard the door locked behind him as he departed. Ernest Maltravers was alone! — what a solitude!

CHAPTER IV.

PITY me not, but lend thy serious hearing
To what I shall unfold. — *Hamlet.*

LETTER FROM ERNEST MALTRAVERS TO EVELYN
CAMERON.

EVELYN!

All that you have read of faithlessness and perfidy will seem tame to you when compared with that conduct which you are doomed to meet from me. We must part, and forever. We have seen each other for the last time. It is bootless even to ask the cause. Believe that I am fickle, false, heartless, — that a whim has changed me, if you will. My resolve is unalterable. We meet no more even as friends. I do not ask you either to forgive or to remember me. Look on

me as one wholly unworthy even of resentment! Do not think
that I write this in madness or in fever or excitement. Judge
me not by my seeming illness this morning. I invent no
excuse, no extenuation, for my broken faith and perjured vows.
Calmly, coldly, and deliberately I write; and thus writing, I
renounce your love.

This language is wanton cruelty, — it is fiendish insult, —
is it not, Evelyn? Am I not a villain? Are you not grateful
for your escape? Do you not look on the past with a shudder
at the precipice on which you stood?

I have done with this subject, — I turn to another. We are
parted, Evelyn, and forever. Do not fancy, — I repeat, do
not fancy that there is any error, any strange infatuation on
my mind, that there is any possibility that the sentence can
be annulled. It were almost easier to call the dead from the
grave than bring us again together, as we were and as we
hoped to be. Now that you are convinced of that truth,
learn, as soon as you have recovered the first shock of knowing how much wickedness there is on earth, — learn to turn
to the future for happier and more suitable ties than those
you could have formed with me. You are very young; in
youth our first impressions are lively but evanescent, — you
will wonder hereafter at having fancied you loved me. Another and a fairer image will replace mine. This is what I
desire and pray for. *As soon as I learn that you love another,
that you are wedded to another, I will re-appear in the world ;
till then, I am a wanderer and an exile. Your hand alone can
efface from my brow the brand of Cain!* When I am gone,
Lord Vargrave will probably renew his suit. I would rather
you married one of your own years, — one whom you could
love fondly, one who would chase away every remembrance of
the wretch who now forsakes you. But perhaps I have mistaken Lord Vargrave's character; perhaps he may be worthier
of you than I deemed (*I* who set up for the censor of other
men!); perhaps he may both win and deserve your affection.

Evelyn, farewell! God, who tempers the wind to the shorn
lamb, will watch over you!

ERNEST MALTRAVERS.

CHAPTER V.

Our acts our angels are, or good or ill,
The fatal shadows that walk by us still. — John Fletcher.

The next morning came; the carriage was at the door of
Maltravers, to bear him away he cared not whither. Where
could he fly from memory? He had just despatched the letter
to Evelyn, — a letter studiously written for the object of de-
stroying all the affection to which he had so fondly looked as
the last charm of life. He was now only waiting for Vargrave, to whom he had sent, and who hastened to obey the
summons.

When Lumley arrived, he was shocked at the alteration
which a single night had effected in the appearance of Maltravers; but he was surprised and relieved to find him calm
and self-possessed.

"Vargrave," said Maltravers, "whatever our past coldness,
henceforth I owe to you an eternal gratitude; and henceforth
this awful secret makes between us an indissoluble bond. If
I have understood you rightly, neither Alice nor other living
being than yourself know that in me, Ernest Maltravers,
stands the guilty object of Alice's first love. Let that secret
still be kept; relieve Alice's mind from the apprehension of
learning that the man who betrayed her yet lives: he will not
live long! I leave time and method of explanation to your
own judgment and acuteness. Now for Evelyn." Here Maltravers stated generally the tone of the letter he had written.
Vargrave listened thoughtfully.

"Maltravers," said he, "it is right to try first the effect of
your letter. But if it fail, if it only serve to inflame the
imagination and excite the interest, if Evelyn still continue
to love you, if that love preys upon her, if it should under-
mine health and spirit, if it should destroy her?"

Maltravers groaned. Lumley proceeded: "I say this not to wound you, but to provide against all circumstances. I too have spent the night in revolving what is best to be done in such a case; and this is the plan I have formed. Let us, if need be, tell the truth to Evelyn, robbing the truth only of its shame. Nay, nay, listen. Why not say that under a borrowed name and in the romance of early youth you knew and loved Alice (though in innocence and honour)? Your tender age, the difference of rank, forbade your union. Her father, discovering your clandestine correspondence, suddenly removed her from the country, and destroyed all clew for your inquiries. You lost sight of each other, — each was taught to believe the other dead. Alice was compelled by her father to marry Mr. Cameron; and after his death, her poverty and her love for her only child induced her to accept my uncle. You have now learned all, — have learned that Evelyn is the daughter of your first love, the daughter of one who adores you still, and whose life your remembrance has for so many years embittered. Evelyn herself will at once comprehend all the scruples of a delicate mind; Evelyn herself will recoil from the thought of making the child the rival to the mother. She will understand why you have flown from her; she will sympathize with your struggles; she will recall the constant melancholy of Alice; she will hope that the ancient love may be renewed, and efface all grief; Generosity and Duty alike will urge her to conquer her own affection! And hereafter, when time has restored you both, father and child may meet with such sentiments as father and child may own!"

Maltravers was silent for some minutes; at length he said abruptly, "And you really loved her, Vargrave, — you love her still? Your dearest care must be her welfare."

"It is! indeed, it is!"

"Then I must trust to your discretion; I can have no other confidant; I myself am not fit to judge. My mind is darkened — you may be right — I think so."

"One word more, — she may discredit my tale, if unsupported. Will you write one line to me to say that I am authorized to reveal the secret, and that it is known only to me? I will not use it unless I should think it absolutely required."

Hastily and mechanically Maltravers wrote a few words to the effect of what Lumley had suggested. "I will inform you," he said to Vargrave as he gave him the paper, "of whatever spot may become my asylum; and you can communicate to me all that I dread and long to hear; but let no man know the refuge of despair!"

There was positively a tear in Vargrave's cold eye, — the only tear that had glistened there for many years; he paused irresolute, then advanced, again halted, muttered to himself, and turned aside.

"As for the world," Lumley resumed, after a pause, "your engagement has been public, — some public account of its breach must be invented. You have always been considered a proud man; we will say that it was low birth on the side of both mother and father (the last only just discovered) that broke off the alliance!"

Vargrave was talking to the deaf; what cared Maltravers for the world? He hastened from the room, threw himself into his carriage, and Vargrave was left to plot, to hope, and to aspire.

BOOK X.

Οὖλον Ὄνειρον. — HOMER, I, 3.

"A dream!"

CHAPTER I.

QUALIS ubi in lucem coluber
. . . Mala gramina pastus.[1] — VIRGIL.

Pars minima est ipsa puella sui.[2] — OVID.

IT would be superfluous, and, perhaps, a sickening task, to detail at length the mode and manner in which Vargrave coiled his snares round the unfortunate girl whom his destiny had marked out for his prey. He was right in foreseeing that, after the first amazement caused by the letter of Maltravers, Evelyn would feel resentment crushed beneath her certainty of his affection her incredulity at his self-accusations, and her secret conviction that some reverse, some misfortune he was unwilling she should share, was the occasion of his farewell and flight. Vargrave therefore very soon communicated to Evelyn the tale he had suggested to Maltravers. He reminded her of the habitual sorrow, the evidence of which was so visible in Lady Vargrave; of her indifference to the pleasures of the world; of her sensitive shrinking from all recurrence to her early fate. "The secret of this," said he, "is in a youthful and most fervent attachment; your mother loved a young stranger above her in rank,

---

[1] " As when a snake glides into light, having fed on pernicious pastures."
[2] " The girl is the least part of himself."

who (his head being full of German romance) was then roam
ing about the country on pedestrian and adventurous excursions, under the assumed name of Butler. By him she was
most ardently beloved in return. Her father, perhaps, suspected the rank of her lover, and was fearful of her honour
being compromised. He was a strange man, that father! and
I know not his real character and motives; but he suddenly
withdrew his daughter from the suit and search of her lover,
— they saw each other no more; her lover mourned her as one
dead. In process of time your mother was constrained by her
father to marry Mr. Cameron, and was left a widow with an
only child, — yourself: she was poor, — very poor! and her
love and anxiety for you at last induced her to listen to the
addresses of my late uncle; for your sake she married again;
again death dissolved the tie! But still, unceasingly and
faithfully, she recalled that first love, the memory of which
darkened and embittered all her life, and still she lived upon
the hope to meet with the lost again. At last, and most
recently, it was my fate to discover that the object of this
unconquerable affection lived, — was still free in hand if not
in heart: you behold the lover of your mother in Ernest Maltravers! It devolved on me (an invidious — a reluctant duty)
to inform Maltravers of the identity of Lady Vargrave with
the Alice of his boyish passion; to prove to him her suffering,
patient, unsubdued affection; to convince him that the sole
hope left to her in life was that of one day or other beholding
him once again. You know Maltravers, — his high-wrought,
sensitive, noble character; he recoiled in terror from the
thought of making his love to the daughter the last and bitterest affliction to the mother he had so loved; knowing too
how completely that mother had entwined herself round your
affections, he shuddered at the pain and self-reproach that
would be yours when you should discover to whom you had
been the rival, and whose the fond hopes and dreams that
your fatal beauty had destroyed. Tortured, despairing, and
half beside himself, he fled from this ill-omened passion,
and in solitude he now seeks to subdue that passion. Touched
by the woe, the grief, of the Alice of his youth, it is his inten-

tion, as soon as he can know you restored to happiness and content, to hasten to your mother, and offer his future devotion as the fulfilment of former vows. On you, and you alone, it depends to restore Maltravers to the world, — on you alone it depends to bless the remaining years of the mother who so dearly loves you! "

It may be easily conceived with what sensations of wonder, compassion, and dismay, Evelyn listened to this tale, the progress of which her exclamations, her sobs, often interrupted. She would write instantly to her mother, to Maltravers. Oh, how gladly she would relinquish his suit! How cheerfully promise to rejoice in that desertion which brought happiness to the mother she had so loved!

"Nay," said Vargrave, "your mother must not know, till the intelligence can be breathed by his lips, and softened by his protestations of returning affection, that the mysterious object of her early romance is that Maltravers whose vows have been so lately offered to her own child. Would not such intelligence shock all pride, and destroy all hope? How could she then consent to the sacrifice which Maltravers is prepared to make? No! not till you are another's — not (to use the words of Maltravers) till you are a happy and beloved wife — must your mother receive the returning homage of Maltravers; not till ,then can she know where that homage has been recently rendered; not till then can Maltravers feel justified in the atonement he meditates. He is willing to sacrifice himself; he trembles at the thought of sacrificing you! Say nothing to your mother, till from her own lips she tells you that she has learned all."

Could Evelyn hesitate; could Evelyn doubt? To allay the fears, to fulfil the prayers of the man whose conduct appeared so generous, to restore him to peace and the world; above all, to pluck from the heart of that beloved and gentle mother the rankling dart, to shed happiness over her fate, to reunite her with the loved and lost, — what sacrifice too great for this?

Ah, why was Legard absent? Why did she believe him capricious, light, and false? Why had she shut her softest thoughts from her soul? But he — the true lover — was afar,

and his true love unknown! and Vargrave, the watchful serpent, was at hand.

In a fatal hour, and in the transport of that enthusiasm
which inspires alike our more rash and our more sublime
deeds, which makes us alike dupes and martyrs, — the enthusiasm that tramples upon self, that forfeits all things to a
high-wrought zeal for others, Evelyn consented to become the
wife of Vargrave!   Nor was she at first sensible of the sacrifice, — sensible of anything but the glow of a noble spirit and
an approving conscience.   Yes, thus, and thus alone, did she
obey both duties, — that, which she had well-nigh abandoned,
to her dead benefactor, and that to the living mother.   Afterwards came a dread reaction; and then, at last, that passive
and sleep-like resignation, which is Despair under a milder
name.   Yes, — such a lot had been predestined from the first;
in vain had she sought to fly it: Fate had overtaken her, and
she must submit to the decree!

She was most anxious that the intelligence of the new bond
might be transmitted instantly to Maltravers.   Vargrave
promised, but took care not to perform.   He was too acute
not to know that in so sudden a step Evelyn's motives would
be apparent, and his own suit indelicate and ungenerous.
He was desirous that Maltravers should learn nothing till
the vows had been spoken, and the indissoluble chain forged.
Afraid to leave Evelyn, even for a day, afraid to trust her in
England to an interview with her mother, — he remained at
Paris, and hurried on all the requisite preparations.   He sent
to Douce, who came in person, with the deeds necessary for
the transfer of the money for the purchase of Lisle Court,
which was now to be immediately completed.   The money
was to be lodged in Mr. Douce's bank till the lawyers had
completed their operations; and in a few weeks, when Evelyn
had attained the allotted age, Vargrave trusted to see himself
lord alike of the betrothed bride, and the hereditary lands of
the crushed Maltravers.   He refrained from stating to Evelyn
who was the present proprietor of the estate to become hers;
he foresaw all the objections she would form; — and, indeed,
she was unable to think, to talk, of such matters.   One

favour she had asked, and it had been granted, — that she was to be left unmolested to her solitude till the fatal day. Shut up in her lonely room, condemned not to confide her thoughts, to seek for sympathy even in her mother, — the poor girl in vain endeavoured to keep up to the tenor of her first enthusiasm, and reconcile herself to a step, which, however, she was heroine enough not to retract or to repent, even while she recoiled from its contemplation.

Lady Doltimore, amazed at what had passed, — at the flight of Maltravers, the success of Lumley, — unable to account for it, to extort explanation from Vargrave or from Evelyn, was distracted by the fear of some villanous deceit which she could not fathom. To escape herself she plunged yet more eagerly into the gay vortex. Vargrave, suspicious, and fearful of trusting to what she might say in her nervous and excited temper if removed from his watchful eye, deemed himself compelled to hover round her. His manner, his conduct, were most guarded; but Caroline herself, jealous, irritated, unsettled, evinced at times a right both to familiarity and anger, which drew upon her and himself the sly vigilance of slander. Meanwhile Lord Doltimore, though too cold and proud openly to notice what passed around him, seemed disturbed and anxious. His manner to Vargrave was distant; he shunned all *tête-à-têtes* with his wife. Little, however, of this did Lumley heed. A few weeks more, and all would be well and safe. Vargrave did not publish his engagement with Evelyn: he sought carefully to conceal it till the very day was near at hand; but it was whispered abroad; some laughed, some believed. Evelyn herself was seen nowhere. De Montaigne had, at first, been indignantly incredulous at the report that Maltravers had broken off a connection he had so desired from a motive so weak and unworthy as that of mere family pride. A letter from Maltravers, who confided to him and Vargrave alone the secret of his retreat, reluctantly convinced him that the wise are but pompous fools; he was angry and disgusted; and still more so when Valerie and Teresa (for female friends stand by us right or wrong) hinted at excuses, or surmised that other causes lurked behind the one alleged. But his thoughts were much drawn from this subject by increasing anxiety for Cesarini, whose abode and fate still remained an alarming mystery.

It so happened that Lord Doltimore, who had always had a taste for the antique, and who was greatly displeased with his own family-seat because it was comfortable and modern, fell, from *ennui*, into a habit, fashionable enough in Paris, of buying curiosities and cabinets, — high-back chairs and oak-carvings; and with this habit returned the desire and the affection for Burleigh. Understanding from Lumley that Maltravers had probably left his native land forever, he imagined it extremely probable that the latter would now consent to the sale, and he begged Vargrave to forward a letter from him to that effect.

Vargrave made some excuse, for he felt that nothing could be more indelicate than such an application forwarded through his hands at such a time; and Doltimore, who had acciden-tally heard De Montaigne confess that he knew the address of Maltravers, quietly sent his letter to the Frenchman, and, without mentioning its contents, begged him to forward it. De Montaigne did so. Now it is very strange how slight men and slight incidents bear on the great events of life; but that simple letter was instrumental to a new revolution in the strange history of Maltravers.

CHAPTER II.

QUID frustra simulacra fugacia captas ? —
Quod petis est nusquam.[1] — OVID : *Met.* iii. 432.

To no clime dedicated to the indulgence of majestic griefs or to the soft melancholy of regret — not to thy glaciers, or thy dark-blue lakes, beautiful Switzerland, mother of many

[1] " Why, in vain, do you catch at fleeting shadows ? That which you seek is nowhere."

exiles; nor to thy fairer earth and gentler heaven, sweet Italy, — fled the agonized Maltravers. Once, in his wanderings, he had chanced to pass by a landscape so steeped in sullen and desolate gloom, that it had made a powerful and uneffaced impression upon his mind: it was amidst those swamps and morasses that formerly surrounded the castle of Gil de Retz, the ambitious Lord, the dreaded Necromancer, who perished at the stake, after a career of such power and splendour as seemed almost to justify the dark belief in his preternatural agencies.[1]

Here, in a lonely and wretched inn, remote from other habitations, Maltravers fixed himself. In gentler griefs there is a sort of luxury in bodily discomfort; in his inexorable and unmitigated anguish, bodily discomfort was not felt. There is a kind of magnetism in extreme woe, by which the body itself seems laid asleep, and knows no distinction between the bed of Damiens and the rose-couch of the Sybarite. He left his carriage and servants at a post-house some miles distant. He came to this dreary abode alone; and in that wintry season, and that most disconsolate scene, his gloomy soul found something congenial, something that did not mock him, in the frowns of the haggard and dismal Nature. Vain would it be to describe what he then felt, what he then endured. Suffice it that, through all, the diviner strength of man was not wholly crushed, and that daily, nightly, hourly, he prayed to the Great Comforter to assist him in wrestling against a guilty love. No man struggles so honestly, so ardently as he did, utterly in vain; for in us all, if we would but cherish it, there is a spirit that must rise at last — a crowned, if bleeding conqueror — over Fate and all the Demons!

One day after a prolonged silence from Vargrave, whose letters all breathed comfort and assurance in Evelyn's progressive recovery of spirit and hope, his messenger returned from the post-town with a letter in the hand of De Montaigne. It contained, in a blank envelope (De Montaigne's silence told

---

[1] See, for description of this scenery, and the fate of De Retz, the high-wrought and glowing romance by Mr. Ritchie called "The Magician."

him how much he had lost in the esteem of his friend), the
communication of Lord Doltimore.   It ran thus: —

MY DEAR SIR, — As I hear that your plans are likely to make you a
long resident on the Continent, may I again inquire if you would be induced to dispose of Burleigh ?   I am willing to give more than its real
value, and would raise a mortgage on my own property sufficient to pay
off, at once, the whole purchase-money.   Perhaps you may be the more
induced to the sale from the circumstance of having an example in the
head of your family, Colonel Maltravers, as I learn through Lord Vargrave, having resolved to dispose of Lisle Court.   Waiting your answer,
                  I am, dear Sir, truly yours,
                                               DOLTIMORE.

"Ay," said Maltravers, bitterly, crushing the letter in his
hand, "let our name be blotted out from the land, and our
hearths pass to the stranger.   How could I ever visit the
place where I first saw *her?* "

He resolved at once, — he would write to England, and
place the matter in the hands of agents.   This was but a
short-lived diversion to his thoughts, and their cloudy darkness soon gathered round him again.

What I am now about to relate may appear, to a hasty
criticism, to savour of the Supernatural; but it is easily
accounted for by ordinary agencies, and it is strictly to the
letter of the truth.

In his sleep that night a dream appeared to Maltravers.
He thought he was alone in the old library at Burleigh, and
gazing on the portrait of his mother; as he so gazed, he fancied
that a cold and awful tremor seized upon him, that he in vain
endeavoured to withdraw his eyes from the canvas — his sight
was chained there by an irresistible spell.   Then it seemed
to him that the portrait gradually changed, — the features the
same, but the bloom vanished into a white and ghastly hue;
the colours of the dress faded, their fashion grew more large
and flowing, but heavy and rigid as if cut in stone, — the
robes of the grave.   But on the face there was a soft and
melancholy smile, that took from its livid aspect the natural
horror; the lips moved, and, it seemed as if without a sound,
the released soul spoke to that which the earth yet owned.

"Return," it said, "to thy native land, and thine own home. Leave not the last relic of her who bore and yet watches over thee to stranger hands.' Thy good Angel shall meet thee at thy hearth!"

The voice ceased. With a violent effort Maltravers broke the spell that had forbidden his utterance. He called aloud, and the dream vanished: he was broad awake, his hair erect, the cold dews on his brow. The pallet, rather than bed on which he lay, was opposite to the window, and the wintry moonlight streamed wan and spectral into the cheerless room. But between himself and the light there seemed to stand a shape, a shadow, that into which the portrait had changed in his dream, — that which had accosted and chilled his soul. He sprang forward, "My mother! even in the grave canst thou bless thy wretched son! Oh, leave me not — say that thou — " The delusion vanished, and Maltravers fell back insensible.

It was long in vain, when, in the healthful light of day, he revolved this memorable dream, that Maltravers sought to convince himself that dreams need no ministers from heaven or hell to bring the gliding falsehoods along the paths of sleep; that the effect of that dream itself, on his shattered nerves, his excited fancy, was the real and sole raiser of the spectre he had thought to behold on waking. Long was it before his judgment could gain the victory, and reason disown the empire of a turbulent imagination; and even when at length reluctantly convinced, the dream still haunted him, and he could not shake it from his breast. He longed anxiously for the next night; it came, but it brought neither dreams nor sleep, and the rain beat, and the winds howled, against the casement. Another night, and the moon was again bright; and he fell into a deep sleep; no vision disturbed or hallowed it. He woke ashamed of his own expectation. But the event, such as it was, by giving a new turn to his thoughts, had roused and relieved his spirit, and misery sat upon him with a lighter load. Perhaps, too, to that still haunting recollection was mainly owing a change in his former purpose. He would still sell the old Hall; but he would first return, and remove that holy portrait, with pious hands; he would garner up and save all that had belonged to her whose death had been his birth. Ah, never had she known for what trials the infant had been reserved!

CHAPTER III.

THE weary hours steal on
And flaky darkness breaks. — *Richard III.*

ONCE more, suddenly and unlooked for, the lord of Burleigh appeared at the gates of his deserted hall! and again the old housekeeper and her satellites were thrown into dismay and consternation. Amidst blank and welcomeless faces, Maltravers passed into his study: and as soon as the logs burned and the bustle was over, and he was left alone, he took up the light and passed into the adjoining library. It was then about nine o'clock in the evening; the air of the room felt damp and chill, and the light but faintly struggled against the mournful gloom of the dark book-lined walls and sombre tapestry. He placed the candle on the table, and drawing aside the curtain that veiled the portrait, gazed with deep emotion, not unmixed with awe, upon the beautiful face whose eyes seemed fixed upon him with mournful sweetness. There is something mystical about those painted ghosts of ourselves, that survive our very dust! Who, gazing upon them long and wistfully, does not half fancy that they seem not insensible to his gaze, as if we looked our own life into them, and the eyes that followed us where we moved were animated by a stranger art than the mere trick of the limner's colours?

With folded arms, rapt and motionless, Maltravers contemplated the form that, by the upward rays of the flickering light, seemed to bend down towards the desolate son. How had he ever loved the memory of his mother! how often in his childish years had he stolen away, and shed wild tears for the loss of that dearest of earthly ties, never to be compensated, never to be replaced! How had he respected, how sympathized with the very repugnance which his father had at first testified towards him, as the innocent cause of her untimely death! He had never seen her, — never felt her passionate kiss; and yet it seemed to him, as he gazed, as if he had known her for years. That strange kind of inner and spiritual memory which often recalls to us places and persons we have never seen before, and which Platonists would resolve to the unquenched and struggling consciousness of a former life, stirred within him, and seemed to whisper, "You were united in the old time." "Yes!" he said, half aloud, "we will never part again. Blessed be the delusion of the dream that recalled to my heart the remembrance of thee, which, at least, I can cherish without a sin. ' My good angel shall meet me at my hearth!' so didst thou say in the solemn vision. Ah, does thy soul watch over me still? How long shall it be before the barrier is broken! how long before we meet, but not in dreams!"

The door opened, the housekeeper looked in. "I beg pardon, sir, but I thought your honour would excuse the liberty, though I know it is very bold to — "

"What is the matter? What do you want?"

"Why, sir, poor Mrs. Elton is dying, — they say she cannot get over the night; and as the carriage drove by the cottage window, the nurse told her that the squire was returned; and she has sent up the nurse to entreat to see your honour before she dies. I am sure I was most loth to disturb you, sir, with such a message; and says I, the squire has only just come off a journey — "

"Who is Mrs. Elton?"

"Don't your honour remember the poor woman that was run over, and you were so good to, and brought into the house the day Miss Cameron — "

"I remember, — say I will be with her in a few minutes. About to die!" muttered Maltravers; "she is to be envied, — the prisoner is let loose, the bark leaves the desert isle!"

He took his hat and walked across the park, dimly lighted
by the stars, to the cottage of the sufferer. He reached her
bedside, and took her hand kindly. She seemed to rally at the
sight of him; the nurse was dismissed, they were left alone.

Before morning, the spirit had left that humble clay; and
the mists of dawn were heavy on the grass as Maltravers
returned home. There were then on his countenance the
traces of recent and strong emotion, and his step was elastic,
and his cheek flushed. Hope once more broke within him,
but mingled with doubt, and faintly combated by reason. In
another hour Maltravers was on his way to Brook-Green.
Impatient, restless, fevered, he urged on the horses, he sowed
the road with gold; and at length the wheels stopped before
the door of the village inn. He descended, asked the way
to the curate's house; and crossing the burial-ground, and
passing under the shadow of the old yew-tree, entered
Aubrey's garden. The curate was at home, and the conference that ensued was of deep and breathless interest to the
visitor.

It is now time to place before the reader, in due order and
connection, the incidents of that story, the knowledge of
which, at that period, broke in detached and fragmentary
portions on Maltravers.

———◆———

CHAPTER IV.

I CANNA chuse, but ever will
Be luving to thy father still,
Whaireir he gae, whaireir he ryde,
My luve with him maun still abyde;
In weil or wae, whaireir he gae,
Mine heart can neir depart him frae.
Lady Anne Bothwell's Lament.

IT may be remembered that in the earlier part of this
continuation of the history of Maltravers it was stated that
Aubrey had in early life met with the common lot of a disap-

pointed affection. Eleanor Westbrook, a young woman of his own humble rank, had won, and seemed to return, his love; but of that love she was not worthy. Vain, volatile, and ambitious, she forsook the poor student for a more brilliant marriage. She accepted the hand of a merchant, who was caught by her beauty, and who had the reputation of great wealth. They settled in London, and Aubrey lost all traces of her. She gave birth to an only daughter: and when that child had attained her fourteenth year, her husband suddenly, and seemingly without cause, put an end to his existence. The cause, however, was apparent before he was laid in his grave. He was involved far beyond his fortune, — he had died to escape beggary and a jail. A small annuity, not exceeding one hundred pounds, had been secured on the widow. On this income she retired with her child into the country; and chance, the vicinity of some distant connections, and the cheapness of the place, concurred to fix her residence in the outskirts of the town of C——. Characters that in youth have been most volatile and most worldly, often when bowed down and dejected by the adversity which they are not fitted to encounter, become the most morbidly devout; they ever require an excitement, and when earth denies, they seek it impatiently from heaven.

This was the case with Mrs. Westbrook; and this new turn of mind brought her naturally into contact with the principal saint of the neighbourhood, Mr. Richard Templeton. We have seen that that gentleman was not happy in his first marriage; death had not then annulled the bond. He was of an ardent and sensual temperament, and quietly, under the broad cloak of his doctrines, he indulged his constitutional tendencies. Perhaps in this respect he was not worse than nine men out of ten. But then he professed to be better than nine hundred thousand nine hundred and ninety-nine men out of a million! To a fault of temperament was added the craft of hypocrisy, and the vulgar error became a dangerous vice. Upon Mary Westbrook, the widow's daughter, he gazed with eyes that were far from being the eyes of the spirit. Even at the age of fourteen she charmed him; but when, after watching her ripening beauty expand, three years were added to that age, Mr. Templeton was most deeply in love. Mary was indeed lovely, — her disposition naturally good and gentle, but her education worse than neglected. To the frivolities and meannesses of a second-rate fashion, inculcated into her till her father's death, had now succeeded the quackeries, the slavish subservience, the intolerant bigotries, of a transcendental superstition. In a change so abrupt and violent, the whole character of the poor girl was shaken; her principles unsettled, vague, and unformed, and naturally of mediocre and even feeble intellect, she clung to the first plank held out to her in "that wide sea of wax" in which "she halted." Early taught to place the most implicit faith in the dictates of Mr. Templeton, fastening her belief round him as the vine winds its tendrils round the oak, yielding to his ascendency, and pleased with his fostering and almost caressing manner, no confessor in Papal Italy ever was more dangerous to village virtue than Richard Templeton (who deemed himself the archetype of the only pure Protestantism) to the morals and heart of Mary Westbrook.

Mrs. Westbrook, whose constitution had been prematurely broken by long participation in the excesses of London dissipation and by the reverse of fortune which still preyed upon a spirit it had rather soured than humbled, died when Mary was eighteen. Templeton became the sole friend, comforter, and supporter of the daughter.

In an evil hour (let us trust not from premeditated villany), — an hour when the heart of one was softened by grief and gratitude, and the conscience of the other laid asleep by passion, the virtue of Mary Westbrook was betrayed. Her sorrow and remorse, his own fears of detection and awakened self-reproach, occasioned Templeton the most anxious and poignant regret. There had been a young woman in Mrs. Westbrook's service, who had left it a short time before the widow died, in consequence of her marriage. Her husband ill-used her; and glad to escape from him and prove her gratitude to her employer's daughter, of whom she had been extremely fond, she had returned to Miss Westbrook after the

funeral of her mother. The name of this woman was Sarah
Miles. Templeton saw that Sarah more than suspected his
connection with Mary; it was necessary to make a confidant,
— he selected her. Miss Westbrook was removed to a distant
part of the country, and Templeton visited her cautiously and
rarely. Four months afterwards, Mrs. Templeton died, and
the husband was free to repair his wrong. Oh, how he then
repented of what had passed! but four months' delay, and all
this sin and sorrow might have been saved! He was now
racked with perplexity and doubt: his unfortunate victim was
advanced in her pregnancy. It was necessary, if he wished
his child to be legitimate — still more if he wished to preserve
the honour of its mother — that he should not hesitate long in
the reparation to which duty and conscience urged him. But
on the other hand, he, the saint, the oracle, the immaculate
example for all forms, proprieties, and decorums, to scandal-
ize the world by so rapid and premature a hymen —

> " Ere yet the salt of most unrighteous tears
> Had left the flushing in his galled eyes,
> To marry."

No! he could not brave the sneer of the gossips, the triumph
of his foes, the dejection of his disciples, by so rank and rash
a folly. But still Mary pined so, he feared for her health —
for his own unborn offspring. There was a middle path, — a
compromise between duty and the world; he grasped at it as
most men similarly situated would have done, — they were
married, but privately, and under feigned names: the secret
was kept close. Sarah Miles was the only witness acquainted
with the real condition and names of the parties.

Reconciled to herself, the bride recovered health and spirits,
Templeton formed the most sanguine hopes. He resolved, as
soon as the confinement was over, to go abroad; Mary should
follow; in a foreign land they should be publicly married;
they would remain some years on the Continent; when he
returned, his child's age could be put back a year. Oh,
nothing could be more clear and easy!

Death shivered into atoms all the plans of Mr. Templeton.

Mary suffered most severely in childbirth, and died a few weeks afterwards. Templeton at first was inconsolable, but worldly thoughts were great comforters. He had done all that conscience could do to atone a sin, and he was freed from a most embarrassing dilemma, and from a temporary banishment utterly uncongenial and unpalatable to his habits and ideas. But now he had a child, — a legitimate child, successor to his name, his wealth; a first-born child, — the only one ever sprung from him, the prop and hope of advancing years! On this child he doted with all that paternal passion which the hardest and coldest men often feel the most for their own flesh and blood — for fatherly love is sometimes but a transfer of self-love from one fund to another.

Yet this child — this darling that he longed to show to the whole world — it was absolutely necessary, for the present, that he should conceal and disown. It had happened that Sarah's husband died of his own excesses a few weeks before the birth of Templeton's child, she having herself just recovered from her confinement; Sarah was therefore free forever from her husband's vigilance and control. To her care the destined heiress was committed, and her own child put out to nurse. And this was the woman and this the child who had excited so much benevolent curiosity in the breasts of the worthy clergyman and the three old maids of C——.[1] Alarmed at Sarah's account of the scrutiny of the parson, and at his own rencontre with that hawk-eyed pastor, Templeton lost no time in changing the abode of the nurse; and to her new residence had the banker bent his way, with rod and angle, on that evening which witnessed his adventure with Luke Darvil.[2] When Mr. Templeton first met Alice, his own child was only about thirteen or fourteen months old, — but little older than Alice's. If the beauty of Mrs. Leslie's *protégée* first excited his coarser nature, her maternal tenderness, her anxious care for her little one, struck a congenial chord in the father's heart. It connected him with her by a mute and unceasing sympathy. Templeton had felt so deeply

[1] See "Ernest Maltravers," book iv., p. 164.
[2] "Ernest Maltravers," book iv., p. 181.

the alarm and pain of illicit love, he had been (as he profanely believed) saved from the brink of public shame by so signal an interference of grace, that he resolved no more to hazard his good name and his peace of mind upon such perilous rocks. The dearest desire at his heart was to have his daughter under his roof, — to fondle, to play with her, to watch her growth, to win her affection. This, at present, seemed impossible. But if he were to marry, — marry a widow, to whom he might confide all, or a portion, of the truth; if that child could be passed off as hers — ah, that was the best plan! And Templeton wanted a wife! Years were creeping on him, and the day would come when a wife would be useful as a nurse. But Alice was supposed to be a widow; and Alice was so meek, so docile, so motherly. If she could be induced to remove from C——, either part with her own child or call it her niece, — and adopt his. Such, from time to time, were Templeton's thoughts, as he visited Alice, and found, with every visit, fresh evidence of her tender and beautiful disposition; such the objects which, in the First Part of this work, we intimated were different from those of mere admiration for her beauty.[1] But again, worldly doubts and fears — the dislike of so unsuitable an alliance, the worse than lowness of Alice's origin, the dread of discovery for her early error — held him back, wavering and irresolute. To say truth, too, her innocence and purity of thought kept him at a certain distance. He was acute enough to see that he — even he, the great Richard Templeton — might be refused by the faithful Alice.

At last Darvil was dead; he breathed more freely, he revolved more seriously his projects; and at this time, Sarah, wooed by her first lover, wished to marry again; his secret would pass from her breast to her second husband's, and thence how far would it travel? Added to this, Sarah's con-

---

[1] "Our banker always seemed more struck by Alice's moral feelings than even by her physical beauty. Her love for her child, for instance, impressed him powerfully," etc. "His feelings altogether for Alice, the designs he entertained towards her, were of a very complicated nature, and it will be long, perhaps, before the reader can thoroughly comprehend them." — See "Ernest Maltravers," book iv., p. 178.

science grew uneasy; the brand ought to be effaced from the memory of the dead mother, the legitimacy of the child proclaimed; she became importunate, she wearied and she alarmed the pious man. He therefore resolved to rid himself of the only witness to his marriage whose testimony he had cause to fear, — of the presence of the only one acquainted with his sin and the real name of the husband of Mary Westbrook. He consented to Sarah's marriage with William Elton, and offered a liberal dowry on the condition that she should yield to the wish of Elton himself, an adventurous young man, who desired to try his fortunes in the New World. His daughter he must remove elsewhere.

While this was going on, Alice's child, long delicate and drooping, became seriously ill. Symptoms of decline appeared; the physician recommended a milder air, and Devonshire was suggested. Nothing could equal the generous, the fatherly kindness which Templeton evinced on this most painful occasion. He insisted on providing Alice with the means to undertake the journey with ease and comfort; and poor Alice, with a heart heavy with gratitude and sorrow, consented for her child's sake to all he offered.

Now the banker began to perceive that all his hopes and wishes were in good train. He foresaw that the child of Alice was doomed! — that was one obstacle out of the way. Alice herself was to be removed from the sphere of her humble calling. In a distant county she might appear of better station, and under another name. Conformably to these views, he suggested to her that, in proportion to the seeming wealth and respectability of patients, did doctors attend to their complaints. He proposed that Alice should depart privately to a town many miles off; that there he would provide for her a carriage, and engage a servant; that he would do this for her as for a relation, and that she should take that relation's name. To this, Alice rapt in her child, and submissive to all that might be for the child's benefit, passively consented. It was arranged then as proposed, and under the name of Cameron, which, as at once a common yet a well-sounding name, occurred to his invention, Alice departed with her sick charge and a female attendant (who knew nothing of her previous calling or story), on the road to Devonshire. Templeton himself resolved to follow her thither in a few days; and it was fixed that they should meet at Exeter.

It was on this melancholy journey that occurred that memorable day when Alice once more beheld Maltravers; and, as she believed, uttering the vows of love to another.[1] The indisposition of her child had delayed her some hours at the inn: the poor sufferer had fallen asleep; and Alice had stolen from its couch for a little while, when her eyes rested on the father. Oh, how then she longed, she burned to tell him of the new sanctity, that, by a human life, had been added to their early love! And when, crushed and sick at heart, she turned away, and believed herself forgotten and replaced, it was the pride of the mother rather than of the mistress that supported her. She, meek creature, felt not the injury to herself; but *his* child, — the sufferer, perhaps the dying one, — *there, there* was the wrong! No! she would not hazard the chance of a cold — great Heaven! perchance an *incredulous* — look upon the hushed, pale face above. But little time was left for thought, for explanation, for discovery. She saw him — unconscious of the ties so near, and thus lost — depart as a stranger from the spot; and henceforth was gone the sweet hope of living for the future. Nothing was left her but the pledge of that which had been. Mournful, despondent, half broken-hearted, she resumed her journey. At Exeter she was joined, as agreed, by Mr. Templeton; and with him came a fair, a blooming, and healthful girl to contrast her own drooping charge. Though but a few weeks older, you would have supposed the little stranger by a year the senior of Alice's child: the one was so well grown, so advanced; the other so backward, so nipped in the sickly bud.

"You can repay me for all, for more than I have done; more than I ever can do for you and yours," said Templeton, "by taking this young stranger also under your care. It is the child of one dear, most dear to me; an orphan; I know

[1] See "Ernest Maltravers," book v., p. 221.

not with whom else to place it. Let it for the present be
supposed your own, — the elder child."

Alice could refuse nothing to her benefactor; but her heart
did not open at first to the beautiful girl, whose sparkling
eyes and rosy cheeks mocked the languid looks and faded
hues of her own darling. But the sufferer seemed to hail a
playmate; it smiled, it put forth its poor, thin hands; it
uttered its inarticulate cry of pleasure, and Alice burst into
tears, and clasped them *both* to her heart.

Mr. Templeton took care not to rest under the same roof
with her he now seriously intended to make his wife; but he
followed Alice to the seaside, and visited her daily. Her
infant rallied; it was tenacious of the upper air; it clung to
life so fondly; poor child, it could not foresee what a bitter
thing to some of us life is! And now it was that Templeton,
learning from Alice her adventure with her absent lover,
learning that all hope in that quarter was gone, seized the
occasion, and pressed his suit. Alice at the hour was over-
flowing with gratitude; in her child's reviving looks she
read all her obligations to her benefactor. But still, at the
word *love*, at the name of *marriage*, her heart recoiled; and
the lost, the faithless, came back to his fatal throne. In
choked and broken accents, she startled the banker with the
refusal — the faltering, tearful, but resolute refusal — of his
suit.

But Templeton brought new engines to work: he wooed her
through her child; he painted all the brilliant prospects that
would open to the infant by her marriage with him. He
would cherish, rear, provide for it as his own. This shook
her resolves; but this did not prevail. He had recourse to a
more generous appeal: he told her so much of his history
with Mary Westbrook as commenced with his hasty and inde-
corous marriage, — attributing the haste to love! made her
comprehend his scruples in owning the child of a union the
world would be certain to ridicule or condemn; he expatiated
on the inestimable blessings she could afford him, by deliver-
ing him from all embarrassment, and restoring his daughter,
though under a borrowed name, to her father's roof. At this

Alice mused; at this she seemed irresolute. She had long seen how inexpressibly dear to Templeton was the child confided to her care; how he grew pale if the slightest ailment reached her; how he chafed at the very wind if it visited her cheek too roughly; and she now said to him simply, —

"Is your child, in truth, your dearest object in life? Is it with her, and her alone, that your dearest hopes are connected?"

"It is, — it is indeed!" said the banker, honestly surprised out of his gallantry; "at least," he added, recovering his self-possession, "as much so as is compatible with my affection for you."

"And only if I marry you, and adopt her as my own, do you think that your secret may be safely kept, and all your wishes with respect to her be fulfilled?"

"Only so."

"And for that reason, chiefly, nay entirely, you condescend to forget what I have been, and seek my hand? Well, if that were all, I owe you too much; my poor babe tells me too loudly what I owe you to draw back from anything that can give you so blessed an enjoyment. Ah, one's child! one's own child, under one's own roof, it *is* such a blessing! But then, if I marry you, it can be only to secure to you that object; to be as a mother to your child; but wife only in name to you! I am not so lost as to despise myself. I know now, though I knew it not at first, that I have been guilty; nothing can excuse that guilt but fidelity to *him!* Oh, yes! I never, never can be unfaithful to my babe's father! As for all else, dispose of me as you will." And Alice, who from very innocence had uttered all this without a blush, now clasped her hands passionately, and left Templeton speechless with mortification and surprise.

When he recovered himself, he affected not to understand her; but Alice was not satisfied, and all further conversation ceased. He began slowly, and at last, and after repeated conferences and urgings, to comprehend how strange and stubborn in some points was the humble creature whom his proposals so highly honoured. Though his daughter was indeed his first object in life; though for her he was willing to make a *mésalliance*, the extent of which it would be incumbent on him studiously to conceal, — yet still, the beauty of Alice awoke an earthlier sentiment that he was not disposed to conquer. He was quite willing to make promises, and talk generously; but when it came to an oath, — a solemn, a binding oath — and this Alice rigidly exacted, — he was startled, and drew back. Though hypocritical, he was, as we have before said, a most sincere believer. He might creep through a promise with unbruised conscience; but he was not one who could have dared to violate an oath, and lay the load of perjury on his soul. Perhaps, after all, the union never would have taken place, but Templeton fell ill; that soft and relaxing air did not agree with him; a low but dangerous fever seized him, and the worldly man trembled at the aspect of Death. It was in this illness that Alice nursed him with a daughter's vigilance and care; and when at length he recovered, impressed with her zeal and kindness, softened by illness, afraid of the approach of solitary age, — and feeling more than ever his duties to his motherless child, he threw himself at Alice's feet, and solemnly vowed all that she required.

It was during this residence in Devonshire, and especially during his illness, that Templeton made and cultivated the acquaintance of Mr. Aubrey. The good clergyman prayed with him by his sick-bed; and when Templeton's danger was at its height, he sought to relieve his conscience by a confession of his wrongs to Mary Westbrook. The name startled Aubrey; and when he learned that the lovely child who had so often sat on his knee, and smiled in his face, was the granddaughter of his first and only love, he had a new interest in her welfare, a new reason to urge Templeton to reparation, a new motive to desire to procure for the infant years of Eleanor's grandchild the gentle care of the young mother, whose own bereavement he sorrowfully foretold. Perhaps the advice and exhortations of Aubrey went far towards assisting the conscience of Mr. Templeton, and reconciling him to the sacrifice he made to his affection for his daughter.

Be that as it may, he married Alice, and Aubrey solemnized and blessed the chill and barren union.

But now came a new and inexpressible affliction; the child of Alice had rallied but for a time. The dread disease had but dallied with its prey; it came on with rapid and sudden force; and within a month from the day that saw Alice the bride of Templeton, the last hope was gone, and the mother was bereft and childless!

The blow that stunned Alice was not, after the first natural shock of sympathy, an unwelcome event to the banker. Now *his* child would be Alice's sole care; now there could be no gossip, no suspicion why, in life and after death, he should prefer one child, supposed not his own, to the other.

He hastened to remove Alice from the scene of her affliction. He dismissed the solitary attendant who had accompanied her on her journey; he bore his wife to London, and finally settled, as we have seen, at a villa in its vicinity. And there, more and more, day by day, centred his love upon the supposed daughter of Mrs. Templeton, his darling and his heiress, the beautiful Evelyn Cameron.

For the first year or two, Templeton evinced some alarming disposition to escape from the oath he had imposed upon himself; but on the slightest hint there was a sternness in the wife, in all else so respectful, so submissive, that repressed and awed him. She even threatened — and at one time was with difficulty prevented carrying the threat into effect — to leave his roof forever, if there were the slightest question of the sanctity of his vow. Templeton trembled; such a separation would excite gossip, curiosity, scandal, a noise in the world, public talk, possible discovery. Besides, Alice was necessary to Evelyn, necessary to his own comfort; something to scold in health, something to rely upon in illness. Gradually then, but sullenly, he reconciled himself to his lot; and as years and infirmities grew upon him, he was contented at least to have secured a faithful friend and an anxious nurse. Still a marriage of this sort was not blessed: Templeton's vanity was wounded; his temper, always harsh, was soured; he avenged his affront by a thousand petty tyrannies; and, without a murmur, Alice perhaps in those years of rank and opulence suffered more than in all her wander ings, with love at her heart and her infant in her arms.

Evelyn was to be the heiress to the wealth of the banker. But the *title* of the new peer! — if he could unite wealth and title, and set the coronet on that young brow! This had led him to seek the alliance with Lumley. And on his death-bed, it was not the secret of Alice, but that of Mary West-brook and his daughter, which he had revealed to his dismayed and astonished nephew, in excuse for the apparently unjust alienation of his property, and as the cause of the alliance he had sought.

While her husband, if husband he might be called, lived, Alice had seemed to bury in her bosom her regret — deep, mighty, passionate, as it was — for her lost child, the child of the unforgotten lover, to whom, through such trials, and amid such new ties, she had been faithful from first to last. But when once more free, her heart flew back to the far and lowly grave. Hence her yearly visits to Brook-Green; hence her purchase of the cottage, hallowed by memories of the dead. There, on that lawn, had she borne forth the fragile form, to breathe the soft noontide air; there, in that chamber, had she watched and hoped, and prayed and despaired; there, in that quiet burial-ground, rested the beloved dust! But Alice, even in her holiest feelings, was not selfish: she for-bore to gratify the first wish of her heart till Evelyn's edu-cation was sufficiently advanced to enable her to quit the neighbourhood; and then, to the delight of Aubrey (who saw in Evelyn a fairer, and nobler, and purer Eleanor), she came to the solitary spot, which, in all the earth, was the *least* solitary to her!

And now the image of the lover of her youth — which during her marriage she had *sought*, at least, to banish — returned to her, and at times inspired her with the only hopes that the grave had not yet transferred to heaven! In relating her tale to Aubrey or in conversing with Mrs. Leslie, whose friendship she still maintained, she found that both concurred in thinking that this obscure and wandering Butler, so skilled

in an art in which eminence in man is generally professional, must be of mediocre or perhaps humble station.   Ah!
now that she was free and rich, if she were to meet him again,
and his love was not all gone, and he would believe in *her*
strange and constant truth; now, *his* infidelity could be forgiven, — forgotten in the benefits it might be hers to bestow!
And how, poor Alice, in that remote village, was chance to
throw him in your way?   She knew not: but something often
whispered to her, "Again you shall meet those eyes; again you
shall hear that voice; and you shall tell him, weeping on his
breast, how you loved his child!"   And would he not have
forgotten her; would he not have formed new ties? — could
he read the loveliness of unchangeable affection in that pale
and pensive face!   Alas, when we love intensely, it is difficult to make us fancy that there is no love in return!

The reader is acquainted with the adventures of Mrs.
Elton, the sole confidant of the secret union of Templeton
and Evelyn's mother.   By a singular fatality, it was the selfish and characteristic recklessness of Vargrave that had, in
fixing her home at Burleigh, ministered to the revelation of
his own villanous deceit.   On returning to England she had
inquired for Mr. Templeton; she had learned that he had
married again, had been raised to the peerage under the title
of Lord Vargrave, and was gathered to his fathers.   She had
no claim on his widow or his family.   But the unfortunate
child who should have inherited his property, she could only
suppose her dead.

When she first saw Evelyn, she was startled by her likeness to her unfortunate mother.   But the unfamiliar name
of Cameron, the intelligence received from Maltravers that
Evelyn's mother still lived, dispelled her suspicions; and
though at times the resemblance haunted her, she doubted
and inquired no more.   In fact, her own infirmities grew
upon her, and pain usurped her thoughts.

Now it so happened that the news of the engagement of
Maltravers to Miss Cameron became known to the county but
a little time before he arrived, — for news travels slow from
the Continent to our provinces, — and, of course, excited all

the comment of the villagers. Her nurse repeated the tale to Mrs. Elton, who instantly remembered the name, and recalled the resemblance of Miss Cameron to the unfortunate Mary Westbrook.

"And," said the gossiping nurse, "she was engaged, they say, to a great lord, and gave him up for the squire, — a great lord in the court, who had been staying at Parson Merton's, Lord Vargrave!"

"Lord Vargrave!" exclaimed Mrs. Elton, remembering the title to which Mr. Templeton had been raised.

"Yes; they do say as how the late lord left Miss Cameron all his money — such a heap of it — though she was not his child, over the head of his nevy, the present lord, on the understanding like that they were to be married when she came of age. But she would not take to him after she had seen the squire. And, to be sure, the squire is the finest-looking gentleman in the county."

"Stop! stop!" said Mrs. Elton, feebly; "the late lord left all his fortune to Miss Cameron, — not his child! I guess the riddle! I understand it all! my foster-child!" she murmured, turning away; "how could I have mistaken that likeness?"

The agitation of the discovery she supposed she had made, her joy at the thought that the child she had loved as her own was alive and possessed of its rights, expedited the progress of Mrs. Elton's disease; and Maltravers arrived just in time to learn her confession (which she naturally wished to make to one who was at once her benefactor, and supposed to be the destined husband of her foster-child), and to be agitated with hope, with joy, at her solemn conviction of the truth of her surmises. If Evelyn were not his daughter — even if not to be his bride — what a weight from his soul! He hastened to Brook-Green; and dreading to rush at once to the presence of Alice, he recalled Aubrey to his recollection. In the interview he sought, all, or at least much, was cleared up. He saw at once the premeditated and well-planned villany of Vargrave. And Alice, her tale — her sufferings — her indomitable love! — how should he meet *her?*

CHAPTER V.

Yet once more, O ye laurels! and once more,
Ye myrtles! — Lycidas.

While Maltravers was yet agitated and excited by the
disclosure of the curate, to whom, as a matter of course, he
had divulged his own identity with the mysterious Butler,
Aubrey, turning his eyes to the casement, saw the form of
Lady Vargrave slowly approaching towards the house.

"Will you withdraw to the inner room?" said he; "she is
coming; you are not yet prepared to meet her! — nay, would
it be well?"

"Yes, yes; I am prepared. We must be alone. I will
await her here."

"But — "

"Nay, I implore you!"

The curate, without another word, retired into the inner
apartment, and Maltravers sinking in a chair breathlessly
awaited the entrance of Lady Vargrave. He soon heard the
light step without; the door, which opened at once on the
old-fashioned parlour, was gently unclosed, and Lady Vargrave was in the room! In the position he had taken, only
the outline of Ernest's form was seen by Alice, and the daylight came dim through the cottage casement; and seeing
some one seated in the curate's accustomed chair, she could
but believe that it was Aubrey himself.

"Do not let me interrupt you," said that sweet, low voice,
whose music had been dumb for so many years to Maltravers,
"but I have a letter from France, from a stranger. It alarms
me so; it is about Evelyn;" and, as if to imply that she meditated a longer visit than ordinary, Lady Vargrave removed
her bonnet, and placed it on the table. Surprised that the
curate had not answered, had not come forward to welcome
her, she then approached; Maltravers rose, and they stood

before each other face to face. And how lovely still was
Alice! lovelier he thought even than of old! And those eyes,
so divinely blue, so dovelike and soft, yet with some spiritual
and unfathomable mystery in their clear depth, were once
more fixed upon him. Alice seemed turned to stone; she
moved not, she spoke not, she scarcely breathed; she gazed
spellbound, as if her senses — as if life itself — had deserted
her.

"Alice!" murmured Maltravers, — "Alice, we meet at
last!"

His voice restored memory, consciousness, youth, at once
to her! She uttered a loud cry of unspeakable joy, of rapture! She sprang forward — reserve, fear, time, change, all
forgotten; she threw herself into his arms, she clasped him
to her heart again and again! — the faithful dog that has
found its master expresses not his transport more uncontrolla-
bly, more wildly. It was something fearful — the excess of
her ecstasy! She kissed his hands, his clothes; she laughed,
she wept; and at last, as words came, she laid her head on
his breast, and said passionately, "I have been true to thee!
I have been true to thee! — or this hour would have killed
me!" Then, as if alarmed by his silence, she looked up into
his face, and as his burning tears fell upon her cheek, she
said again and with more hurried vehemence, "I *have* been
faithful, — do you not believe me?"

"I do, I do, noble, unequalled Alice! Why, why were you
so long lost to me? Why now does your love so shame my
own?"

At these words, Alice appeared to awaken from her first
oblivion of all that had chanced since they met; she blushed
deeply, and drew herself gently and bashfully from his embrace. "Ah," she said, in altered and humbled accents, "you
have loved another! Perhaps you have no love left for me!
Is it so; is it? No, no; those eyes — you love me — you love
me still!"

And again she clung to him, as if it were heaven to believe
all things, and death to doubt. Then, after a pause, she drew
him gently with both her hands towards the light, and gazed

upon him fondly, proudly, as if to trace, line by line, and feature by feature, the countenance which had been to her sweet thoughts as the sunlight to the flowers. "Changed, changed," she muttered; "but still the same, — still beautiful, still divine!" She stopped. A sudden thought struck her: his garments were worn and soiled by travel, and that princely crest, fallen and dejected, no longer towered in proud defiance above the sons of men. "You are not rich," she exclaimed eagerly, — "say you are not rich! I am rich enough for both; it is all yours, — all yours; I did not betray you for it; there is no shame in it. Oh, we shall be so happy! Thou art come back to thy poor Alice! thou knowest how she loved thee!"

There was in Alice's manner, her wild joy, something so different from her ordinary self, that none who could have seen her — quiet, pensive, subdued — would have fancied her the same being. All that Society and its woes had taught were gone; and Nature once more claimed her fairest child. The very years seemed to have fallen from her brow, and she looked scarcely older than when she had stood with him beneath the moonlight by the violet banks far away. Suddenly, her colour faded; the smile passed from the dimpled lips; a sad and solemn aspect succeeded to that expression of passionate joy. "Come," she said, in a whisper, "come, follow;" and still clasping his hand, she drew him to the door. Silent and wonderingly he followed her across the lawn, through the moss-grown gate, and into the lonely burial-ground. She moved on with a noiseless and gliding step, — so pale, so hushed, so breathless, that even in the noonday you might have half fancied the fair shape was not owned by earth. She paused where the yew-tree cast its gloomy shadow; and the small and tombless mound, separated from the rest, was before them. She pointed to it, and falling on her knees beside it, murmured, "Hush, it sleeps below, — thy child!" She covered her face with both her hands, and her form shook convulsively.

Beside that form and before that grave knelt Maltravers. There vanished the last remnant of his stoic pride; and there — Evelyn herself forgotten — there did he pray to Heaven for pardon to himself, and blessings on the heart he had betrayed. There solemnly did he vow, the remainder of his years, to guard from all future ill the faithful and childless mother.

———◆———

CHAPTER VI.

WILL Fortune never come with both hands full,
But write her fair words still in foulest letters ?

Henry IV. Part ii.

I PASS over those explanations, that record of Alice's eventful history, which Maltravers learned from her own lips, to confirm and add to the narrative of the curate, the purport of which is already known to the reader.

It was many hours before Alice was sufficiently composed to remember the object for which she had sought the curate. But she had laid the letter which she had brought, and which explained all, on the table at the vicarage; and when Maltravers, having at last induced Alice, who seemed afraid to lose sight of him for an instant, to retire to her room, and seek some short repose, returned towards the vicarage, he met Aubrey in the garden. The old man had taken the friend's acknowledged license to read the letter evidently meant for his eye; and, alarmed and anxious, he now eagerly sought a consultation with Maltravers. The letter, written in English, as familiar to the writer as her own tongue, was from Madame de Ventadour. It had been evidently dictated by the kindest feelings. After apologizing briefly for her interference, she stated that Lord Vargrave's marriage with Miss Cameron was now a matter of public notoriety; that it would take place in a few days; that it was observed with suspicion that Miss Cameron appeared nowhere; that she seemed almost a prisoner in her room; that certain expressions which had dropped from Lady Doltimore had alarmed her greatly. According to these expressions, it would seem that Lady Vargrave was not apprised of the approaching event; that, considering Miss Cameron's recent engagement to Mr. Maltravers suddenly (and, as Valerie thought, unaccountably) broken off on the arrival of Lord Vargrave; considering her extreme youth, her brilliant fortune; and, Madame de Ventadour delicately hinted, considering also Lord Vargrave's character for unscrupulous determination in the furtherance of any object on which he was bent, — considering all this, Madame de Ventadour had ventured to address Miss Cameron's mother, and to guard her against the possibility of design or deceit. Her best apology for her intrusion must be her deep interest in Miss Cameron, and her long friendship for one to whom Miss Cameron had been so lately betrothed. If Lady Vargrave were aware of the new engagement, and had sanctioned it, of course her intrusion was unseasonable and superfluous; but if ascribed to its real motive, would not be the less forgiven.

It was easy for Maltravers to see in this letter how generous and zealous had been that friendship for himself which could have induced the woman of the world to undertake so officious a task. But of this he thought not, as he hurried over the lines, and shuddered at Evelyn's urgent danger.

"This intelligence," said Aubrey, "must be, indeed, a surprise to Lady Vargrave. For we have not heard a word from Evelyn or Lord Vargrave to announce such a marriage; and she (and myself till this day) believed that the engagement between Evelyn and Mr. ——, I mean," said Aubrey with confusion, — "I mean yourself, was still in force. Lord Vargrave's villany is apparent; we must act immediately. What is to be done?"

"I will return to Paris to-morrow; I will defeat his machination, expose his falsehood!"

"You may need a proxy for Lady Vargrave, an authority . for Evelyn; one whom Lord Vargrave knows to possess the secret of her birth, her rights: I will go with you. We must speak to Lady Vargrave."

Maltravers turned sharply round. "And Alice knows not who I am; that I — I am, or was, a few weeks ago, the suitor of another; and that other the child she has reared as her own! Unhappy Alice! in the very hour of her joy at my return, is she to writhe beneath this new affliction?"

"Shall I break it to her?" said Aubrey, pityingly.

"No, no; these lips must inflict the last wrong!"

Maltravers walked away, and the curate saw him no more till night.

In the interval, and late in the evening, Maltravers rejoined Alice.

The fire burned clear on the hearth, the curtains were drawn, the pleasant but simple drawing-room of the cottage smiled its welcome as Maltravers entered, and Alice sprang up to greet him! It was as if the old days of the music-lesson and the meerschaum had come back.

"This is yours," said Alice, tenderly, as he looked round the apartment. "Now — now I know what a blessed thing riches are! Ah, you are looking on that picture; it is of her who supplied your daughter's place, — she is so beautiful, so good, you will love her as a daughter. Oh, that letter — that — that letter — I forgot it till now — it is at the vicarage — I must go there immediately, and you will come too, — you will advise us."

"Alice, I have read the letter, — I know all. Alice, sit down and hear me, — it is you who have to learn from me. In our young days I was accustomed to tell you stories in winter nights like these, — stories of love like our own, of sorrows which, at that time, we only knew by hearsay. I have one now for your ear, truer and sadder than they were. Two children, for they were then little more — children in ignorance of the world, children in freshness of heart, children almost in years — were thrown together by strange vicissitudes, more than eighteen years ago. They were of different sexes, — they loved and they erred. But the error was solely with the boy; for what was innocence in her was but passion in him. He loved her dearly; but at that age her qualities were half developed. He knew her beautiful, simple, tender; but he knew not all the virtue, the faith, and the nobleness that Heaven had planted in her soul. They parted, — they knew not each other's fate. He sought her anxiously, but in vain; and sorrow and remorse long consumed him, and her memory threw a shadow over his existence. But again — for his love had not the exalted holiness of hers (*she* was true!) — he sought to renew in others the charm he had lost with her. In vain, — long, long in vain. Alice, you know to whom the tale refers. Nay, listen yet. I have heard from the old man yonder that you were witness to a scene many years ago which deceived you into the belief that you beheld a rival. It was not so: that lady yet lives, — then, as now, a friend to me; nothing more. I grant that, at one time, my fancy allured me to her, but my heart was still true to thee."

"Bless you for those words!" murmured Alice; and she crept more closely to him.

He went on. "Circumstances, which at some calmer occasion you shall hear, again nearly connected my fate by marriage to another. I had then seen you at a distance, unseen by you, — seen you apparently surrounded by respectability and opulence; and I blessed Heaven that your lot, at least, was not that of penury and want." (Here Maltravers related, where he had caught that brief glimpse of Alice,[1] — how he had sought for her again and again in vain.) "From that hour," he continued, "seeing you in circumstances of which I could not have dared to dream, I felt more reconciled to the past; yet, when on the verge of marriage with another — beautiful, gifted, generous as she was — a thought, a memory half acknowledged, dimly traced, chained back my sentiments; and admiration, esteem, and gratitude were not love! Death — a death melancholy and tragic — forbade this union; and I went forth in the world, a pilgrim and a wanderer. Years rolled away, and I thought I had conquered the desire for love, — a desire that had haunted me since I lost thee. But, suddenly and recently, a being, beautiful as yourself — sweet, guileless, and young as you were when we met — woke in me a new and a strange sentiment. I will not conceal it from you: Alice, at last I loved another! Yet, singular as it may seem to you, it was a certain resemblance to yourself, not

[1] See "Ernest Maltravers," book v., p. 228.

in feature, but in the tones of the voice, the nameless grace of
gesture and manner, the very music of your once happy laugh,
— those traits of resemblance which I can now account for,
and which children catch not from their parents only, but
from those they most see, and, loving most, most imitate in
their tender years, — all these, I say, made perhaps a chief
attraction, that drew me towards — Alice, are you prepared
for it? — drew me towards Evelyn Cameron. Know me in my
real character, by my true name: I am that Maltravers to
whom the hand of Evelyn was a few weeks ago betrothed!"

He paused, and ventured to look up at Alice; she was
exceedingly pale, and her hands were tightly clasped together, but she neither wept nor spoke. The worst was over;
he continued more rapidly, and with less constrained an
effort: "By the art, the duplicity, the falsehood of Lord
Vargrave, I was taught in a sudden hour to believe that
Evelyn was our daughter, that you recoiled from the prospect
of beholding once more the author of so many miseries. I
need not tell you, Alice, of the horror that succeeded to love.
I pass over the tortures I endured. By a train of incidents
to be related to you hereafter, I was led to suspect the truth of
Vargrave's tale. I came hither; I have learned all from
Aubrey. I regret no more the falsehood that so racked me for
the time; I regret no more the rupture of my bond with
Evelyn; I regret nothing that brings me at last free and
unshackled to thy feet, and acquaints me with thy sublime
faith and ineffable love. Here then — here beneath your own
roof — here he, at once your earliest friend and foe, kneels to
you for pardon and for hope! He woos you as his wife, his
companion to the grave! Forget all his errors, and be to him,
under a holier name, all that you were to him of old!"

"And you are then Evelyn's suitor, — you are he whom she
loves? I see it all — all!" Alice rose, and, before he was
even aware of her purpose, or conscious of what she felt, she
had vanished from the room.

Long, and with the bitterest feelings, he awaited her
return; she came not. At last he wrote a hurried note,
imploring her to join him again, to relieve his suspense; to

believe his sincerity; to accept his vows. He sent it to her own room, to which she had hastened to bury her emotions. In a few minutes there came to him this answer, written in pencil, blotted with tears.

" I thank you, I understand your heart; but forgive me — I cannot see you yet. She is so beautiful and good, she is worthy of you. I shall soon be reconciled. God bless you, — bless you both ! "

The door of the vicarage was opened abruptly, and Maltravers entered with a hasty but heavy tread.

"Go to her, go to that angel; go, I beseech you! Tell her that she wrongs me, if she thinks I can ever wed another, ever have an object in life, but to atone to, to merit her. Go, plead for me."

Aubrey, who soon gathered from Maltravers what had passed, departed to the cottage. It was near midnight before he returned. Maltravers met him in the churchyard, beside the yew-tree. "Well, well, what message do you bring?"

"She wishes that we should both set off for Paris to-morrow. Not a day is to be lost, — we must save Evelyn from this snare."

"Evelyn! Yes, Evelyn shall be saved; but the rest — the rest — why do you turn away?"

" ' You are not the poor artist, the wandering adventurer; you are the high-born, the wealthy, the renowned Maltravers: Alice has nothing to confer on you. You have won the love of Evelyn, — Alice cannot doom the child confided to her care to hopeless affection; you love Evelyn, — Alice cannot compare herself to the young and educated and beautiful creature, whose love is a priceless treasure. Alice prays you not to grieve for her; she will soon be content and happy in your happiness.' This is the message."

"And what said you, — did you not tell her such words would break my heart? "

"No matter what I said; I mistrust myself when I advise her. Her feelings are truer than all our wisdom! "

Maltravers made no answer, and the curate saw him gliding rapidly away by the starlit graves towards the village.

CHAPTER VII.

Think you I can a resolution fetch
From flowery tenderness ? — *Measure for Measure.*

They were on the road to Dover. Maltravers leaned back in the corner of the carriage with his hat over his brows, though the morning was yet too dark for the curate to perceive more than the outline of his features. Milestone after milestone glided by the wheels, and neither of the travellers broke the silence. It was a cold, raw morning, and the mists rose sullenly from the dank hedges and comfortless fields.

Stern and self-accusing was the scrutiny of Maltravers into the recesses of his conscience, and the blotted pages of the Past. That pale and solitary mother, mourning over the grave of her — of his own — child, rose again before his eyes, and seemed silently to ask him for an account of the heart he had made barren, and of the youth to which his love had brought the joylessness of age. With the image of Alice, — afar, alone, whether in her wanderings, a beggar and an outcast, or in that hollow prosperity, in which the very ease of the frame allowed more leisure to the pinings of the heart, — with that image, pure, sorrowing, and faithful from first to last, he compared his own wild and wasted youth, his resort to fancy and to passion for excitement. He contrasted with her patient resignation his own arrogant rebellion against the trials, the bitterness of which his proud spirit had exaggerated; his contempt for the pursuits and aims of others; the imperious indolence of his later life, and his forgetfulness of the duties which Providence had fitted him to discharge. His mind, once so rudely hurled from that complacent pedestal, from which it had so long looked down on men, and said, "I am wiser and better than you," became even too acutely sensitive to its own infirmities; and that desire for Virtue, which he had ever deeply entertained, made itself more distinctly and loudly heard amidst the ruins and the silence of his pride.

From the contemplation of the Past, he roused himself to face the Future. Alice had refused his hand, Alice herself had ratified and blessed his union with another! Evelyn, so madly loved, — Evelyn might still be his! No law — from the violation of which, even in thought, Human Nature recoils appalled and horror-stricken — forbade him to reclaim her hand, to snatch her from the grasp of Vargrave, to woo again, and again to win her! But did Maltravers welcome, did he embrace that thought? Let us do him justice: he did not. He felt that Alice's resolution, in the first hour of mortified affection, was not to be considered final; and even if it were so, he felt yet more deeply that her love — the love that had withstood so many trials — never could be subdued. Was he to make her nobleness a curse? Was he to say, "Thou hast passed away in thy generation, and I leave thee again to thy solitude for her whom thou hast cherished as a child?" He started in dismay from the thought of this new and last blow upon the shattered spirit; and then fresh and equally sacred obstacles between Evelyn and himself broke slowly on his view. Could Templeton rise from his grave, with what resentment, with what just repugnance, would he have regarded in the betrayer of his wife (even though wife but in name) the suitor to his child!

These thoughts came in fast and fearful force upon Maltravers, and served to strengthen his honour and his conscience. He felt that though, in law, there was no shadow of connection between Evelyn and himself, yet his tie with Alice had been of a nature that ought to separate him from one who had regarded Alice as a mother. The load of horror, the agony of shame, were indeed gone; but still a voice whispered as before, "Evelyn is lost to thee forever!" But so shaken had already been her image in the late storms and convulsion of his soul, that this thought was preferable to the thought of sacrificing Alice. If *that* were all — but Evelyn might still love him; and justice to Alice might be misery to her! He started from his revery with a vehement gesture, and groaned audibly.

The curate turned to address to him some words of inquiry and surprise; but the words were unheard, and he perceived, by the advancing daylight, that the countenance of Maltravers was that of a man utterly rapt and absorbed by some mastering and irresistible thought. Wisely, therefore, he left his companion in peace, and returned to his own anxious and engrossing meditations.

The travellers did not rest till they arrived at Dover. The vessel started early the following morning, and Aubrey, who was much fatigued, retired to rest. Maltravers glanced at the clock upon the mantelpiece; it was the hour of nine. For him there was no hope of sleep; and the prospect of the slow night was that of dreary suspense and torturing self-commune.

As he turned restlessly in his seat, the waiter entered to say that there was a gentleman who had caught a glimpse of him below on his arrival, and who was anxious to speak with him. Before Maltravers could answer, the gentleman himself entered, and Maltravers recognized Legard.

"I beg your pardon," said the latter, in a tone of great agitation, "but I was most anxious to see you for a few moments. I have just returned to England — all places alike hateful to me! I read in the papers — an — an announcement — which — which occasions me the greatest — I know not what I would say, — but is it true? Read this paragraph;" and Legard placed "The Courier" before Maltravers.

The passage was as follows: —

"It is whispered that Lord Vargrave, who is now at Paris, is to be married in a few days to the beautiful and wealthy Miss Cameron, to whom he has been long engaged."

"Is it possible?" exclaimed Legard, following the eyes of Maltravers, as he glanced over the paragraph. "Were not *you* the lover, — the accepted, the happy lover of Miss Cameron? Speak, tell me, I implore you! — that it was for you, who saved my life and redeemed my honour, and not for that cold schemer, that I renounced all my hopes of earthly happiness, and surrendered the dream of winning the heart and hand of the only woman I ever loved!"

A deep shade fell over the features of Maltravers. He gazed earnestly and long upon the working countenance of Legard, and said, after a pause, —

"You, too, loved her, then? I never knew it, — never guessed it; or, if once I suspected, it was but for a moment; and — "

"Yes," interrupted Legard, passionately, "Heaven is my witness how fervently and truly I did love — I do still love Evelyn Cameron! But when you confessed to me your affection — your hopes — I felt all that I owed you; I felt that I never ought to become your rival. I left Paris abruptly. What I have suffered I will not say; but it was some comfort to think that I had acted as became one who owed you a debt never to be cancelled nor repaid. I travelled from place to place, each equally hateful and wearisome; at last, I scarce know why, I returned to England. I have arrived this day; and now — but tell me, is it true?"

"I believe it true," said Maltravers, in a hollow voice, "that Evelyn is at this moment engaged to Lord Vargrave. I believe it equally true that that engagement, founded upon false impressions, never will be fulfilled. With that hope and that belief, I am on my road to Paris."

"And she will be yours, still?" said Legard, turning away his face: "well, that I can bear. May you be happy, sir!"

"Stay, Legard," said Maltravers, in a voice of great feeling: "let us understand each other better; you have renounced your passion to your sense of honour." Maltravers paused thoughtfully. "It was noble in you, it was more than just to me; I thank you and respect you. But, Legard, was there aught in the manner, the bearing of Evelyn Cameron, that could lead you to suppose that she would have returned your affection? True, had we started on equal terms, I am not vain enough to be blind to your advantages of youth and person; but I believed that the affections of Evelyn were already mine, before we met at Paris."

"It might be so," said Legard, gloomily; "nor is it for me

to say that a heart so pure and generous as Evelyn's could deceive yourself or me. Yet I *had* fancied, I *had* hoped, while you stood aloof, that the partiality with which she regarded you was that of admiration more than love; that you had dazzled her imagination rather than won her heart. I had hoped that I should win, that I was winning, my way to her affection! But let this pass; I drop the subject forever — only, Maltravers, only do me justice. You are a proud man, and your pride has often irritated and stung me, in spite of my gratitude. Be more lenient to me than you have been; think that, though I have my errors and my follies, I am still capable of some conquests over myself. And most sincerely do I now wish that Evelyn's love may be to you that blessing it would have been to me!"

This was, indeed, a new triumph over the pride of Maltravers, — a new humiliation. He had looked with a cold contempt on this man, because he affected not to be above the herd; and this man had preceded him in the very sacrifice he himself meditated.

"Legard," said Maltravers, and a faint blush overspread his face, "you rebuke me justly. I acknowledge my fault, and I ask you to forgive it. From this night, whatever happens, I shall hold it an honour to be admitted to your friendship; from this night, George Legard never shall find in me the offences of arrogance and harshness."

Legard wrung the hand held out to him warmly, but made no answer; his heart was full, and he would not trust himself to speak.

"You think, then," resumed Maltravers, in a more thoughtful tone, — "you think that Evelyn could have loved you, had my pretensions not crossed your own? And you think, also — pardon me, dear Legard — that you could have acquired the steadiness of character, the firmness of purpose, which one so fair, so young, so inexperienced and susceptible, so surrounded by a thousand temptations, would need in a guardian and protector?"

"Oh, do not judge of me by what I have been. I feel that Evelyn could have reformed errors worse than mine; that her love would have elevated dispositions yet more light and commonplace. You do not know what miracles love works! But now, what is there left for me? What matters it how frivolous and poor the occupations which can distract my thoughts, and bring me forgetfulness? Forgive me; I have no right to obtrude all this egotism on you."

"Do not despond, Legard," said Maltravers, kindly; "there may be better fortunes in store for you than you yet anticipate. I cannot say more now; but will you remain at Dover a few days longer? Within a week you shall hear from me. I will not raise hopes that it may not be mine to realize. But if it be as you think it was, why little, indeed, would rest with me. Nay, look not on me so wistfully," added Maltravers, with a mournful smile; "and let the subject close for the present. You will stay at Dover?"

"I will; but —"

"No buts, Legard; it is so settled."

BOOK XI.

'Ο Ἄνθρωπος εὐεργετὸς πεφυκώς. — MARCUS ANTONINUS, lib. iii.

" Man is born to be a doer of good."

CHAPTER I.

His teeth he still did grind,
And grimly gnash, threatening revenge in vain. — SPENSER.

IT is now time to return to Lord Vargrave. His most
sanguine hopes were realized; all things seemed to prosper.
The hand of Evelyn Cameron was pledged to him, the wedding-day was fixed. In less than a week she was to confer
upon the ruined peer a splendid dowry, that would smooth
all obstacles in the ascent of his ambition. From Mr. Douce
he learned that the deeds, which were to transfer to himself
the baronial possessions of the head of the house of Maltravers, were nearly completed; and on his wedding-day he
hoped to be able to announce that the happy pair had set out
for their princely mansion of Lisle Court. In politics, though
nothing could be finally settled till his return, letters from
Lord Saxingham assured him that all was auspicious: the
court and the heads of the aristocracy daily growing more
alienated from the premier, and more prepared for a Cabinet
revolution. And Vargrave, perhaps, like most needy men,
overrated the advantages he should derive from, and the ser-
vile opinions he should conciliate in, his new character of
landed proprietor and wealthy peer. He was not insensible
to the silent anguish that Evelyn seemed to endure, nor to
the bitter gloom that hung on the brow of Lady Doltimore.

But these were clouds that foretold no storm, — light shadows that obscured not the serenity of the favouring sky. He continued to seem unconscious to either; to take the coming event as a matter of course, and to Evelyn he evinced so gentle, unfamiliar, respectful, and delicate an attachment, that he left no opening, either for confidence or complaint. Poor Evelyn! her gayety, her enchanting levity, her sweet and infantine playfulness of manner, were indeed vanished. Pale, wan, passive, and smileless, she was the ghost of her former self! But days rolled on, and the evil one drew near; she recoiled, but she never dreamed of resisting. How many equal victims of her age and sex does the altar witness!

One day, at early noon, Lord Vargrave took his way to Evelyn's. He had been to pay a political visit in the Faubourg St. Germain, and he was now slowly crossing the more quiet and solitary part of the gardens of the Tuileries, his hands clasped behind him, after his old, unaltered habit, and his eyes downcast, — when suddenly a man, who was seated alone beneath one of the trees, and who had for some moments watched his steps with an anxious and wild aspect, rose and approached him. Lord Vargrave was not conscious of the intrusion, till the man laid his hand on Vargrave's arm, and exclaimed, —

"It is he! it is! Lumley Ferrers, we meet again!"

Lord Vargrave started and changed colour, as he gazed on the intruder.

"Ferrers," continued Cesarini (for it was he), and he wound his arm firmly into Lord Vargrave's as he spoke, "you have not changed; your step is light, your cheek healthful; and yet I — you can scarcely recognize me. Oh, I have suffered so horribly since we parted! Why is this? Why have I been so heavily visited, and why have you gone free? Heaven is not just!"

Castruccio was in one of his lucid intervals; but there was that in his uncertain eye, and strange unnatural voice, which showed that a breath might dissolve the avalanche. Lord Vargrave looked anxiously round; none were near: but he knew that the more public parts of the garden were thronged, and through the trees he saw many forms moving in the distance. He felt that the sound of his voice could summon assistance in an instant, and his assurance returned to him.

"My poor friend," said he soothingly, as he quickened his pace, "it grieves me to the heart to see you look ill; do not think so much of what is past."

"There is no past!" replied Cesarini, gloomily. "The Past is my Present! And I have thought and thought, in darkness and in chains, over all that I have endured, and a light has broken on me in the hours when they told me I was mad! Lumley Ferrers, it was not for my sake that you led me, devil as you are, into the lowest hell! You had some object of your own to serve in separating *her* from Maltravers. You made me your instrument. What was I to you that you should have sinned for *my* sake? Answer me, and truly, if those lips can utter truth!"

"Cesarini," returned Vargrave, in his blandest accents, "another time we will converse on what has been; believe me, my only object was your happiness, combined, it may be, with my hatred of your rival."

"Liar!" shouted Cesarini, grasping Vargrave's arm with the strength of growing madness, while his burning eyes were fixed upon his tempter's changing countenance. "You, too, loved Florence; you, too, sought her hand; *you* were my real rival!"

"Hush! my friend, hush!" said Vargrave, seeking to shake off the gripe of the maniac, and becoming seriously alarmed; "we are approaching the crowded part of the gardens, we shall be observed."

"And why are men made my foes? Why is my own sister become my persecutor? Why should she give me up to the torturer and the dungeon? Why are serpents and fiends my comrades? Why is there fire in my brain and heart; and why do you go free and enjoy liberty and life? Observed! what care *you* for observation? All men search for *me!*"

"Then why so openly expose yourself to their notice; why — "

"Hear me!" interrupted Cesarini. "When I escaped from

the horrible prison into which I was plunged; when I scented
the fresh air, and bounded over the grass; when I was again
free in limbs and spirit, — a sudden strain of music from a
village came on my ear, and I stopped short, and crouched
down, and held my breath to listen. It ceased; and I thought
I had been with Florence, and I wept bitterly! When I
recovered, memory came back to me distinct and clear; and
I heard a voice say to me, ' Avenge her and thyself! ' From
that hour the voice has been heard again, morning and night!
Lumley Ferrers, I hear it now! it speaks to my heart, it
warms my blood, it nerves my hand! On whom should vengeance fall? Speak to me! "

Lumley strode rapidly on. They were now without the
grove; a gay throng was before them. "All is safe," thought
the Englishman. He turned abruptly and haughtily on
Cesarini, and waved his hand; "Begone, madman!" said he,
in a loud and stern voice, — "begone! vex me no more, or I
give you into custody. Begone, I say! "

Cesarini halted, amazed and awed for the moment; and
then, with a dark scowl and a low cry, threw himself on
Vargrave. The eye and hand of the latter were vigilant
and prepared; he grasped the uplifted arm of the maniac,
and shouted for help. But the madman was now in his full
fury; he hurled Vargrave to the ground with a force for
which the peer was not prepared, and Lumley might never
have risen a living man from that spot, if two soldiers, seated
close by, had not hastened to his assistance. Cesarini was
already kneeling on his breast, and his long bony fingers were
fastening upon the throat of his intended victim. Torn from
his hold, he glared fiercely on his new assailants; and after a
fierce but momentary struggle, wrested himself from their
gripe. Then, turning round to Vargrave, who had with some
effort risen from the ground, he shrieked out, "I shall have
thee yet! " and fled through the trees and disappeared.

CHAPTER II.

AH, who is nigh ?   Come to me, friend or foe !
My parks, my walks, my manors that I had,
Ev'n now forsake me. — *Henry VI.* Part iii.

LORD VARGRAVE, bold as he was by nature, in vain endeavoured to banish from his mind the gloomy impression which
the startling interview with Cesarini had bequeathed. The
face, the voice of the maniac, haunted him, as the shape of
the warning wraith haunts the mountaineer. He returned at
once to his hotel, unable for some hours to collect himself
sufficiently to pay his customary visit to Miss Cameron. Inly
resolving not to hazard a second meeting with the Italian during the rest of his sojourn at Paris by venturing in the streets
on foot, he ordered his carriage towards evening; dined at the
Café de Paris; and then re-entered his carriage to proceed to
Lady Doltimore's house.

"I beg your pardon, my lord," said his servant, as he
closed the carriage-door, "but I forgot to say that, a short
time after you returned this morning, a strange gentleman
asked at the porter's lodge if Mr. Ferrers was not staying at
the hotel. The porter said there was no Mr. Ferrers, but the
gentleman insisted upon it that he had seen Mr. Ferrers
enter. I was in the lodge at the moment, my lord, and I
explained — "

"That Mr. Ferrers and Lord Vargrave are one and the
same? What sort of looking person?"

"Thin and dark, my lord, — evidently a foreigner. When
I said that you were now Lord Vargrave, he stared a moment,
and said very abruptly that he recollected it perfectly, and
then he laughed and walked away."

"Did he not ask to see me?"

"No, my lord; he said he should take another opportunity. He was a strange-looking gentleman, and his clothes were threadbare."

"Ah, some troublesome petitioner. Perhaps a Pole in distress! Remember I am never at home when he calls. Shut the door. To Lady Doltimore's."

Lumley's heart beat as he threw himself back, — he again felt the gripe of the madman at his throat. He saw, at once, that Cesarini had dogged him; he resolved the next morning to change his hotel, and to apply to the police. It was strange how sudden and keen a fear had entered the breast of this callous and resolute man!

On arriving at Lady Doltimore's, he found Caroline alone in the drawing-room. It was a *tête-à-tête* that he by no means desired.

"Lord Vargrave," said Caroline, coldly, "I wished a short conversation with you; and finding you did not come in the morning, I sent you a note an hour ago. Did you receive it?"

"No; I have been from home since six o'clock, — it is now nine."

"Well, then, Vargrave," said Caroline, with a compressed and writhing lip, and turning very pale, "I tremble to tell you that I fear Doltimore suspects. He looked at me sternly this morning, and said, ' You seem unhappy, madam; this marriage of Lord Vargrave's distresses you! ' "

"I warned you how it would be, — your own selfishness will betray and ruin you."

"Do not reproach me, man!" said Lady Doltimore, with great vehemence. "From you at least I have a right to pity, to forbearance, to succour. I will not bear reproach from *you*."

"I reproach you for your own sake, for the faults you commit against yourself; and I must say, Caroline, that after I had generously conquered all selfish feeling, and assisted you to so desirable and even brilliant a position, it is neither just nor high-minded in you to evince so ungracious a reluctance to my taking the only step which can save me from actual ruin. But what does Doltimore suspect? What ground has he for suspicion, beyond that want of command of countenance which it is easy to explain, — and which it is yet easier for a woman and a great lady [here Lumley sneered] to acquire?"

"I know not; it has been put into his head. Paris is so full of slander. But, Vargrave — Lumley — I tremble, I shudder with terror, if ever Doltimore should discover —"

"Pooh! pooh! Our conduct at Paris has been most guarded, most discreet. Doltimore is Self-conceit personified, — and Self-conceit is horn-eyed. I am about to leave Paris, — about to marry, from under your own roof; a little prudence, a little self-control, a smiling face, when you wish us happiness, and so forth, and all is safe. Tush! think of it no more! Fate has cut and shuffled the cards for you; the game is yours, unless you revoke. Pardon my metaphor; it is a favourite one, — I have worn it threadbare; but human life *is* so like a rubber at whist. Where is Evelyn?"

"In her own room. Have you no pity for her?"

"She will be very happy when she is Lady Vargrave; and for the rest, I shall neither be a stern nor a jealous husband. She might not have given the same character to the magnificent Maltravers."

Here Evelyn entered; and Vargrave hastened to press her hand, to whisper tender salutations and compliments, to draw the easy-chair to the fire, to place the footstool, — to lavish the *petits soins* that are so agreeable, when they are the small moralities of love.

Evelyn was more than usually pale, — more than usually abstracted. There was no lustre in her eye, no life in her step; she seemed unconscious of the crisis to which she approached. As the myrrh and hyssop which drugged the malefactors of old into forgetfulness of their doom, so there are griefs which stupefy before their last and crowning consummation!

Vargrave conversed lightly on the weather, the news, the last book. Evelyn answered but in monosyllables; and Caroline, with a hand-screen before her face, preserved an unbroken silence. Thus gloomy and joyless were two of the party, thus gay and animated the third, when the clock on the mantelpiece struck ten; and as the last stroke died, and Evelyn sighed heavily, — for it was an hour nearer to the fatal day, — the door was suddenly thrown open, and pushing aside the servant, two gentlemen entered the room.

Caroline, the first to perceive them, started from her seat with a faint exclamation of surprise. Vargrave turned abruptly, and saw before him the stern countenance of Maltravers.

"My child! my Evelyn!" exclaimed a familiar voice; and Evelyn had already flown into the arms of Aubrey.

The sight of the curate in company with Maltravers explained all at once to Vargrave. He saw that the mask was torn from his face, the prize snatched from his grasp, his falsehood known, his plot counterworked, his villany baffled! He struggled in vain for self-composure; all his resources of courage and craft seemed drained and exhausted. Livid, speechless, almost trembling, he cowered beneath the eyes of Maltravers.

Evelyn, not as yet aware of the presence of her former lover, was the first to break the silence. She lifted her face in alarm from the bosom of the good curate. "My mother — she is well — she lives — what brings you hither?"

"Your mother is well, my child. I have come hither at her earnest request to save you from a marriage with that unworthy man!"

Lord Vargrave smiled a ghastly smile, but made no answer.

"Lord Vargrave," said Maltravers, "you will feel at once that you have no further business under this roof. Let us withdraw, — I have much to thank you for."

"I will not stir!" exclaimed Vargrave, passionately, and stamping on the floor. "Miss Cameron, the guest of Lady Doltimore, whose house and presence you thus rudely profane, is my affianced bride, — affianced with her own consent. Evelyn, beloved Evelyn! mine you are yet; you alone can cancel the bond. Sir, I know not what you have to say, what mystery in your immaculate life to disclose; but unless Lady Doltimore, whom your violence appalls and terrifies, orders me to quit her roof, it is not I, — it is yourself, who are the intruder! Lady Doltimore, with your permission, I will direct your servants to conduct this gentleman to his carriage!"

"Lady Doltimore, pardon me," said Maltravers, coldly; "I will not be urged to any failure of respect to you. My lord, if the most abject cowardice be not added to your other vices, you will not make this room the theatre for our altercation. I invite you, in those terms which no gentleman ever yet refused, to withdraw with me."

The tone and manner of Maltravers exercised a strange control over Vargrave; he endeavoured in vain to keep alive the passion into which he had sought to work himself; his voice faltered, his head sank upon his breast. Between these two personages, none interfered; around them, all present grouped in breathless silence, — Caroline, turning her eyes from one to the other in wonder and dismay; Evelyn, believing all a dream, yet alive only to the thought that, by some merciful interposition of Providence, she should escape the consequences of her own rashness, clinging to Aubrey, with her gaze riveted on Maltravers; and Aubrey, whose gentle character was borne down and silenced by the powerful and tempestuous passions that now met in collision and conflict, withheld by his abhorrence of Vargrave's treachery from his natural desire to propitiate, and yet appalled by the apprehension of bloodshed, that for the first time crossed him.

There was a moment of dead silence, in which Vargrave seemed to be nerving and collecting himself for such course as might be best to pursue, when again the door opened, and the name of Mr. Howard was announced.

Hurried and agitated, the young secretary, scarcely noticing the rest of the party, rushed to Lord Vargrave.

"My lord! a thousand pardons for interrupting you, — business of such importance! I am so fortunate to find you!"

"What is the matter, sir?"

"These letters, my lord; I have so much to say!"

Any interruption, even an earthquake, at that moment must have been welcome to Vargrave. He bent his head,

with a polite smile, linked his arm into his secretary's, and
withdrew to the recess of the farthest window. Not a minute
elapsed before he turned away with a look of scornful exulta-
tion. "Mr. Howard," said he, "go and refresh yourself, and
come to me at twelve o'clock to-night; I shall be at home
then." The secretary bowed, and withdrew.

"Now, sir," said Vargrave, to Maltravers, "I am willing to
leave you in possession of the field. Miss Cameron, it will
be, I fear, impossible for me to entertain any longer the bright
hopes I had once formed; my cruel fate compels me to seek
wealth in any matrimonial engagement. I regret to inform
you that you are no longer the great heiress; the whole of
your capital was placed in the hands of Mr. Douce for the com-
pletion of the purchase of Lisle Court. Mr. Douce is a bankrupt; he has fled to America. This letter is an express from
my lawyer; the house has closed its payments! Perhaps we
may hope to obtain sixpence in the pound. I am a loser also;
the forfeit money bequeathed to me is gone. I know not
whether, as your trustee, I am not accountable for the loss of
your fortune (drawn out on my responsibility); probably so.
But as I have not now a shilling in the world, I doubt whether
Mr. Maltravers will advise you to institute proceedings against
me. Mr. Maltravers, to-morrow, at nine o'clock, I will listen
to what you have to say. I wish you all good-night." He
bowed, seized his hat, and vanished.

"Evelyn," said Aubrey, "can you require to learn more;
do you not already feel you are released from union with a
man without heart and honour?"

"Yes, yes! I am so happy!" cried Evelyn, bursting into
tears. "This hated wealth, — I feel not its loss; I am released from all duty to my benefactor. I am free!"

The last tie that had yet united the guilty Caroline to Vargrave was broken, — a woman forgives sin in her lover, but
never meanness. The degrading, the abject position in which
she had seen one whom she had served as a slave (though, as
yet, all his worst villanies were unknown to her), filled her
with shame, horror, and disgust. She rose abruptly, and
quitted the room. They did not miss her.

Maltravers approached Evelyn; he took her hand, and pressed it to his lips and heart.

"Evelyn," said he, mournfully, "you require an explanation, — to-morrow I will give and seek it. To-night we are both too unnerved for such communications. I can only now feel joy at your escape, and hope that I may still minister to your future happiness."

"But," said Aubrey, "can we believe this new and astounding statement? Can this loss be so irremediable; may we not yet take precaution, and save, at least, some wrecks of this noble fortune?"

"I thank you for recalling me to the world," said Maltravers, eagerly. "I will see to it this instant; and to-morrow, Evelyn, after my interview with you, I will hasten to London, and act in that capacity still left to me, — your guardian, your friend."

He turned away his face, and hurried to the door.

Evelyn clung more closely to Aubrey. "But you will not leave me to-night? You can stay? We can find you accommodation; do not leave me."

"Leave you, my child! no; we have a thousand things to say to each other. I will not," he added in a whisper, turning to Maltravers, "forestall your communications."

CHAPTER III.

ALACK, 't is he. Why, he was met even now
As mad as the vexed sea. — *Lear.*

IN the Rue de la Paix there resided an English lawyer of eminence, with whom Maltravers had had previous dealings; to this gentleman he now drove. He acquainted him with the news he had just heard, respecting the bankruptcy of Mr. Douce; and commissioned him to leave Paris, the first moment he could obtain a passport, and to proceed to London.

At all events, he would arrive there some hours before Maltravers; and those hours were something gained. This done, he drove to the nearest hotel, which chanced to be the Hotel de M——, where, though he knew it not, it so happened that Lord Vargrave himself lodged. As his carriage stopped without, while the porter unclosed the gates, a man, who had been loitering under the lamps, darted forward, and prying into the carriage-window, regarded Maltravers earnestly. The latter, pre-occupied and absorbed, did not notice him; but when the carriage drove into the courtyard it was followed by the stranger, who was muffled in a worn and tattered cloak, and whose movements were unheeded amidst the bustle of the arrival. The porter's wife led the way to a second-floor, just left vacant, and the waiter began to arrange the fire. Maltravers threw himself abstractedly upon the sofa, insensible to all around him, when, lifting his eyes, he saw before him the countenance of Cesarini! The Italian (supposed, perhaps, by the persons of the hotel to be one of the newcomers) was leaning over the back of a chair, supporting his face with his hand, and fixing his eyes with an earnest and sorrowful expression upon the features of his ancient rival. When he perceived that he was recognized, he approached Maltravers, and said in Italian, and in a low voice, "You are the man of all others, whom, save one, I most desired to see. I have much to say to you, and my time is short. Spare me a few minutes."

The tone and manner of Cesarini were so calm and rational that they changed the first impulse of Maltravers, which was that of securing a maniac; while the Italian's emaciated countenance, his squalid garments, the air of penury and want diffused over his whole appearance, irresistibly invited compassion. With all the more anxious and pressing thoughts that weighed upon him, Maltravers could not refuse the conference thus demanded. He dismissed the attendants, and motioned Cesarini to be seated.

The Italian drew near to the fire, which now blazed brightly and cheerily, and, spreading his thin hands to the flame, seemed to enjoy the physical luxury of the warmth. "Cold, cold," he said piteously, as to himself; "Nature is a very bit-

ter protector. But frost and famine are, at least, more merci
ful than slavery and darkness."

At this moment Ernest's servant entered to know if his
master would not take refreshments, for he had scarcely
touched food upon the road. And as he spoke, Cesarini
turned keenly and wistfully round. There was no mistaking
the appeal. Wine and cold meat were ordered: and when
the servant vanished, Cesarini turned to Maltravers with a
strange smile, and said, "You see what the love of liberty
brings men to! They found me plenty in the jail! But I
have read of men who feasted merrily before execution — have
not you? — and my hour is at hand. All this day I have felt
chained by an irresistible destiny to this house. But it was
not you I sought; no matter, in the crisis of our doom all its
agents meet together. It is the last act of a dreary play!"

The Italian turned again to the fire, and bent over it,
muttering to himself.

Maltravers remained silent and thoughtful. Now was the
moment once more to place the maniac under the kindly vigilance of his family, to snatch him from the horrors, perhaps,
of starvation itself, to which his escape condemned him: if
he could detain Cesarini till De Montaigne could arrive!

Agreeably to this thought, he quietly drew towards him
the portfolio which had been laid on the table, and, Cesarini's
back still turned to him, wrote a hasty line to De Montaigne.
When his servant re-entered with the wine and viands, Maltravers followed him out of the room, and bade him see the
note sent immediately. On returning, he found Cesarini
devouring the food before him with all the voracity of
famine. It was a dreadful sight! — the intellect ruined, the
mind darkened, the wild, fierce animal alone left!

When Cesarini had appeased his hunger, he drew near to
Maltravers, and thus accosted him, —

"I must lead you back to the past. I sinned against you
and the dead; but Heaven has avenged you, and me you can
pity and forgive. Maltravers, there is another more guilty
than I, — but proud, prosperous, and great. *His* crime
Heaven has left to the revenge of man! I bound myself

by an oath not to reveal his villany. I cancel the oath now, for the knowledge of it should survive his life and mine. And, mad though they deem me, the mad are prophets, and a solemn conviction, a voice not of earth, tells me that he and I are already in the Shadow of Death."

Here Cesarini, with a calm and precise accuracy of self-possession, — a minuteness of circumstance and detail, that, coming from one whose very eyes betrayed his terrible disease, was infinitely thrilling in its effect, — related the counsels, the persuasions, the stratagems of Lumley. Slowly and distinctly he forced into the heart of Maltravers that sickening record of cold fraud calculating on vehement passion as its tool; and thus he concluded his narration, —

"Now wonder no longer why I have lived till this hour; why I have clung to freedom, through want and hunger, amidst beggars, felons, and outcasts! In that freedom was my last hope, — the hope of revenge!"

Maltravers returned no answer for some moments. At length he said calmly, "Cesarini, there are injuries so great that they defy revenge. Let us alike, since we are alike injured, trust our cause to Him who reads all hearts, and, better than we can do, measures both crime and its excuses. You think that our enemy has not suffered, — that he has gone free. We know not his internal history; prosperity and power are no signs of happiness, they bring no exemption from care. Be soothed and be ruled, Cesarini. Let the stone once more close over the solemn grave. Turn with me to the future; and let us rather seek to be the judges of ourselves, than the executioners of another."

Cesarini listened gloomily, and was about to answer, when —

But here we must return to Lord Vargrave.

CHAPTER IV.

My noble lord,
Your worthy friends do lack you. — *Macbeth.*

He is about it ;
The doors are open. — *Ibid.*

ON quitting Lady Doltimore's house, Lumley drove to his
hotel. His secretary had been the bearer of other communications, with the nature of which he had not yet acquainted
himself; but he saw by the superscriptions that they were of
great importance. Still, however, even in the solitude and
privacy of his own chamber, it was not on the instant that he
could divert his thoughts from the ruin of his fortunes: the
loss not only of Evelyn's property, but his own claims upon
it (for the whole capital had been placed in Douce's hands),
the total wreck of his grand scheme, the triumph he had
afforded to Maltravers! He ground his teeth in impotent
rage, and groaned aloud, as he traversed his room with hasty
and uneven strides. At last he paused and muttered: "Well,
the spider toils on even when its very power of weaving fresh
webs is exhausted; it lies in wait, — it forces itself into the
webs of others. Brave insect, thou art my model! While I
have breath in my body, the world and all its crosses, Fortune and all her malignity, shall not prevail against me!
What man ever yet failed until he himself grew craven, and
sold his soul to the arch fiend, Despair! 'T is but a girl and
a fortune lost, — they were gallantly fought for, that is some
comfort. Now to what is yet left to me!"

The first letter Lumley opened was from Lord Saxingham.
It filled him with dismay. The question at issue had been
formally, but abruptly, decided in the Cabinet against Vargrave and his manœuvres. Some hasty expressions of Lord
Saxingham had been instantly caught at by the premier, and

a resignation, rather hinted at than declared, had been peremptorily accepted. Lord Saxingham and Lumley's adherents in the Government were to a man dismissed; and at the time Lord Saxingham wrote the premier was with the king.

"Curse their folly! — the puppets! the dolts!" exclaimed Lumley, crushing the letter in his hand. "The moment I leave them, they run their heads against the wall. Curse them! curse myself! curse the man who weaves ropes with sand! Nothing — nothing left for me but exile or suicide! Stay, what is this?" His eye fell on the well-known handwriting of the premier. He tore the envelope, impatient to know the worst. His eyes sparkled as he proceeded. The letter was most courteous, most complimentary, most wooing. The minister was a man consummately versed in the arts that increase, as well as those which purge, a party. Saxingham and his friends were imbeciles, incapables, mostly men who had outlived their day. But Lord Vargrave, in the prime of life — versatile, accomplished, vigorous, bitter, unscrupulous — Vargrave was of another mould, Vargrave was to be dreaded; and therefore, if possible, to be retained. His powers of mischief were unquestionably increased by the universal talk of London that he was about soon to wed so wealthy a lady. The minister knew his man. In terms of affected regret, he alluded to the loss the Government would sustain in the services of Lord Saxingham, etc.; he rejoiced that Lord Vargrave's absence from London had prevented his being prematurely mixed up, by false scruples of honour, in secessions which his judgment must condemn. He treated of the question in dispute with the most delicate address, — confessed the reasonableness of Lord Vargrave's former opposition to it; but contended that it was now, if not wise, inevitable. He said nothing of the *justice* of the measure he proposed to adopt, but much on the *expediency*. He concluded by offering to Vargrave, in the most cordial and flattering terms, the very seat in the Cabinet which Lord Saxingham had vacated, with an apology for its inadequacy to his lordship's merits, and a distinct and definite promise of the refusal of the gorgeous viceroyalty of India, which would be vacant next year by the return of the present governor-general.

Unprincipled as Vargrave was, it is not, perhaps, judging him too mildly to say that, had he succeeded in obtaining Evelyn's hand and fortune, he would have shrunk from the baseness he now meditated. To step coldly into the very post of which he, and he alone, had been the cause of depriving his earliest patron and nearest relative; to profit by the betrayal of his own party; to damn himself eternally in the eyes of his ancient friends; to pass down the stream of history as a mercenary apostate, — from all this Vargrave must have shrunk, had he seen one spot of honest ground on which to maintain his footing. But now the waters of the abyss were closing over his head; he would have caught at a straw; how much more consent to be picked up by the vessel of an enemy! All objection, all scruple, vanished at once. And the "barbaric gold" "of Ormus and of Ind" glittered before the greedy eyes of the penniless adventurer! Not a day was now to be lost. How fortunate that a written proposition, from which it was impossible to recede, had been made to him before the failure of his matrimonial projects had become known! Too happy to quit Paris, he would set off on the morrow, and conclude in person the negotiation. Vargrave glanced towards the clock; it was scarcely past eleven. What revolutions are worked in moments! Within an hour he had lost a wife, a noble fortune, changed the politics of his whole life, stepped into a Cabinet office, and was already calculating how much a governor-general of India could lay by in five years! But it was only eleven o'clock. He had put off Mr. Howard's visit till twelve; he wished so much to see him, and learn all the London gossip connected with the recent events. Poor Mr. Douce! Vargrave had already forgotten *his* existence! — he rang his bell hastily. It was some time before his servant answered.

Promptitude and readiness were virtues that Lord Vargrave peremptorily demanded in a servant; and as he paid the best price for the articles — less in wages than in plunder — he was generally sure to obtain them.

"Where the deuce have you been? This is the third time I have rung! you ought to be in the anteroom!"

"I beg your lordship's pardon; but I was helping Mr. Maltravers's valet to find a key which he dropped in the courtyard."

"Mr. Maltravers! Is he at this hotel?"

"Yes, my lord; his rooms are just overhead."

"Humph! Has Mr. Howard engaged a lodging here?"

"No, my lord. He left word that he was gone to his aunt, Lady Jane."

"Ah, Lady Jane — lives at Paris — so she does; Rue Chaussée d'Antin — you know the house? Go immediately — go yourself; don't trust to a messenger — and beg Mr. Howard to return with you. I want to see him instantly."

"Yes, my lord."

The servant went. Lumley was in a mood in which solitude was intolerable. He was greatly excited; and some natural compunctions at the course on which he had decided made him long to escape from thought. So Maltravers was under the same roof! He had promised to give him an interview next day; but next day he wished to be on the road to London. Why not have it over to-night? But could Maltravers meditate any hostile proceedings? Impossible! Whatever his causes of complaint, they were of too delicate and secret a nature for seconds, bullets, and newspaper paragraphs! Vargrave might feel secure that he should not be delayed by any Bois de Boulogne assignation; but it was necessary to *his honour* (!) that he should not seem to shun the man he had deceived and wronged. He would go up to him at once, — a new excitement would distract his thoughts. Agreeably to this resolution, Lord Vargrave quitted his room, and was about to close the outer door, when he recollected that perhaps his servant might not meet with Howard; that the secretary might probably arrive before the time fixed, — it would be as well to leave his door open. He accordingly stopped, and writing upon a piece of paper, "Dear Howard, send up for me the moment you arrive: I shall be with Mr. Maltravers *au second*"—Vargrave wafered the *affiche* to the door, which he then left ajar, and the lamp in the landing-place fell clear and full on the paper.

It was the voice of Vargrave, in the little stone-paven ante-chamber without, inquiring of the servant if Mr. Maltravers was at home, which had startled and interrupted Cesarini as he was about to reply to Ernest. Each recognized that sharp clear voice; each glanced at the other.

"I will not see him," said Maltravers, hastily moving towards the door; "you are not fit to — "

"Meet him? no!" said Cesarini, with a furtive and sinister glance, which a man versed in his disease would have under-stood, but which Maltravers did not even observe; "I will retire into your bedroom; my eyes are heavy. I could sleep."

He opened the inner door as he spoke, and had scarcely reclosed it before Vargrave entered.

"Your servant said you were engaged; but I thought you might see an old friend:" and Vargrave coolly seated himself.

Maltravers drew the bolt across the door that separated them from Cesarini; and the two men, whose characters and lives were so strongly contrasted, were now alone.

"You wished an interview, — an explanation," said Lumley; "I shrink from neither. Let me forestall inquiry and com-plaint. I deceived you knowingly and deliberately, it is quite true, — all stratagems are fair in love and war. The prize was vast! I believed my career depended on it: I could not resist the temptation. I knew that before long you would learn that Evelyn was not your daughter; that the first com-munication between yourself and Lady Vargrave would betray me; but it was worth trying a *coup de main*. You have foiled me, and conquered: be it so; I congratulate you. You are tolerably rich, and the loss of Evelyn's fortune will not vex you as it would have done me."

"Lord Vargrave, it is but poor affectation to treat thus lightly the dark falsehood you conceived, the awful curse you inflicted upon me. Your sight is now so painful to me, it so stirs the passions that I would seek to suppress, that the sooner our interview is terminated the better. I have to

charge you, also, with a crime, — not, perhaps, baser than
the one you so calmly own, but the consequences of which
were more fatal: you understand me?"

"I do not."

"Do not tempt me! do not lie!" said Maltravers, still in a
calm voice, though his passions, naturally so strong, shook
his whole frame. "To your arts I owe the exile of years that
should have been better spent; to those arts Cesarini owes the
wreck of his reason, and Florence Lascelles her early grave!
Ah, you are pale now; your tongue cleaves to your mouth!
And think you these crimes will go forever unrequited; think
you that there is no justice in the thunderbolts of God?"

"Sir," said Vargrave, starting to his feet, "I know not
what you suspect, I care not what you believe! But I am
accountable to man, and that account I am willing to render.
You threatened me in the presence of my ward; you spoke of
cowardice, and hinted at danger. Whatever my faults, want
of courage is not one. Stand by your threats, — I am ready
to brave them!"

"A year, perhaps a short month, ago," replied Maltravers,
"and I would have arrogated justice to my own mortal hand;
nay, this very night, had the hazard of either of our lives
been necessary to save Evelyn from your persecution, I would
have incurred all things for her sake! But that is past; from
me you have nothing to fear. The proofs of your earlier guilt,
with its dreadful results, would alone suffice to warn me from
the solemn responsibility of human vengeance. Great Heaven!
what hand could dare to send a criminal so long hardened, so
black with crime, unatoning, unrepentant, and unprepared,
before the judgment-seat of the ALL JUST? Go, unhappy
man! may life long be spared to you! Awake! awake from
this world, before your feet pass the irrevocable boundary of
the next!"

"I came not here to listen to homilies, and the cant of the
conventicle," said Vargrave, vainly struggling for a haughtiness of mien that his conscience-stricken aspect terribly be-
lied; "not I; but this wrong world is to be blamed, if deeds
that strict morality may not justify, but the effects of which

I, no prophet, could not foresee, were necessary for success in life. I have been but as all other men have been who struggle against fortune to be rich and great: ambition must make use of foul ladders."

"Oh," said Maltravers, earnestly, touched involuntarily, and in spite of his abhorrence of the criminal, by the relenting that this miserable attempt at self-justification seemed to denote, — "oh, be warned, while it is yet time; wrap not yourself in these paltry sophistries; look back to your past career; see to what heights you might have climbed, if — with those rare gifts and energies, with that subtle sagacity and indomitable courage — your ambition had but chosen the straight, not the crooked, path. Pause! many years may yet, in the course of nature, afford you time to retrace your steps, to atone to thousands the injuries you have inflicted on the few. I know not why I thus address you: but something diviner than indignation urges me; something tells me that you are already on the brink of the abyss!"

Lord Vargrave changed colour, nor did he speak for some moments; then raising his head, with a faint smile, he said, "Maltravers, you are a false soothsayer. At this moment my paths, crooked though they be, have led me far towards the summit of my proudest hopes; the straight path would have left me at the foot of the mountain. You yourself are a beacon against the course you advise. Let us contrast each other. You took the straight path, I the crooked. You, my superior in fortune; you, infinitely above me in genius; you, born to command and never to crouch: how do we stand now, each in the prime of life? You, with a barren and profitless reputation; without rank, without power, almost without the hope of power. I — but you know not my new dignity — I, in the Cabinet of England's ministry, vast fortunes opening to my gaze, the proudest station not too high for my reasonable ambition! You, wedding yourself to some grand chimera of an object, aimless when it eludes your grasp. I, swinging, squirrel-like, from scheme to scheme; no matter if one breaks, another is at hand! Some men would have cut their throats in despair, an hour ago, in losing the object of a seven years' chase, — Beauty and Wealth, both! I open a letter, and find success in one quarter to counterbalance failure in another. Bah! bah! each to his *métier*, Maltravers! For you, honour, melancholy, and, if it please you, repentance also! For me, the onward, rushing life, never looking back to the Past, never balancing the stepping-stones to the Future. Let us not envy each other; if you were not Diogenes, you would be Alexander. Adieu! our interview is over. Will you forget and forgive, and shake hands once more? You draw back, you frown! well, perhaps you are right. If we meet again — "

"It will be as strangers."

"No rash vows! you may return to politics, you may want office. I am of your way of thinking now: and — ha! ha! — poor Lumley Ferrers could make you a Lord of the Treasury; smooth travelling and cheap turnpikes on crooked paths, believe me. Farewell!"

On entering the room into which Cesarini had retired, Maltravers found him flown. His servant said that the gentleman had gone away shortly after Lord Vargrave's arrival. Ernest reproached himself bitterly for neglecting to secure the door that conducted to the ante-chamber; but still it was probable that Cesarini would return in the morning.

The messenger who had taken the letter to De Montaigne brought back word that the latter was at his villa, but expected at Paris early the next day. Maltravers hoped to see him before his departure; meanwhile he threw himself on his bed, and despite all the anxieties that yet oppressed him, the fatigues and excitements he had undergone exhausted even the endurance of that iron frame, and he fell into a profound slumber.

CHAPTER V.

By eight to-morrow
Thou shalt be made immortal.

Measure for Measure.

LORD VARGRAVE returned to his apartment to find Mr. Howard, who had but just that instant arrived, warming his white and well-ringed hands by the fire. He conversed with him for half an hour on all the topics on which the secretary could give him information, and then dismissed him once more to the roof of Lady Jane.

As he slowly undressed himself, he saw on his writing-table the note which Lady Doltimore had referred to, and which he had not yet opened. He lazily broke the seal, ran his eye carelessly over its few blotted words of remorse and alarm, and threw it down again with a contemptuous "pshaw!" Thus unequally are the sorrows of a guilty tie felt by the man of the world and the woman of society!

As his servant placed before him his wine and water, Vargrave told him to see early to the preparations for departure, and to call him at nine o'clock.

"Shall I shut that door, my lord?" said the valet, pointing to one that communicated with one of those large closets, or *armoires*, that are common appendages to French bedrooms, and in which wood and sundry other matters are kept.

"No," said Lord Vargrave, petulantly; "you servants are so fond of excluding every breath of air. I should never have a window open, if I did not open it myself. Leave the door as it is, and do not be later than nine to-morrow."

The servant, who slept in a kind of kennel that communicated with the anteroom, did as he was bid; and Vargrave put out his candle, betook himself to bed, and, after drowsily gazing some minutes on the dying embers of the fire, which threw a dim ghastly light over the chamber, fell fast asleep. The clock struck the first hour of morning, and in that house all seemed still.

The next morning, Maltravers was disturbed from his slumber by De Montaigne, who, arriving, as was often his wont, at an early hour from his villa, had found Ernest's note of the previous evening.

Maltravers rose and dressed himself; and while De Montaigne was yet listening to the account which his friend gave of his adventure with Cesarini, and the unhappy man's accusation of his accomplice, Ernest's servant entered the room very abruptly.

"Sir," said he, "I thought you might like to know. What is to be done? The whole hotel is in confusion, Mr. Howard has been sent for, and Lord Doltimore. So very strange, so sudden!"

"What is the matter? Speak plain."

"Lord Vargrave, sir, — poor Lord Vargrave — "

"Lord Vargrave!"

"Yes, sir; the master of the hotel, hearing you knew his lordship, would be so glad if you would come down. Lord Vargrave, sir, is dead, — found dead in his bed!"

Maltravers was rooted to the spot with amaze and horror. Dead! and but last night so full of life and schemes and hope and ambition.

As soon as he recovered himself, he hurried to the spot, and De Montaigne followed. The latter, as they descended the stairs, laid his hand on Ernest's arm and detained him.

"Did you say that Castruccio left the apartment while Vargrave was with you, and almost immediately after his narrative of Vargrave's instigation to his crime?"

"Yes."

The eyes of the friends met; a terrible suspicion possessed both. "No; it is impossible!" exclaimed Maltravers. "How could he obtain entrance, how pass Lord Vargrave's servants? No, no; think of it not!"

They hurried down the stairs; they reached the other door of Vargrave's apartment. The notice to Howard, with the name of Vargrave underscored, was still on the panels. De Montaigne saw and shuddered.

They were in the room by the bedside. A group were collected round; they gave way as the Englishman and his friend approached; and the eyes of Maltravers suddenly rested on the face of Lord Vargrave, which was locked, rigid, and convulsed.

There was a buzz of voices which had ceased at the entrance of Maltravers; it was now renewed. A surgeon had been summoned — the nearest surgeon, — a young Englishman of no great repute or name. He was making inquiries as he bent over the corpse.

"Yes, sir," said Lord Vargrave's servant, "his lordship told me to call him at nine o'clock. I came in at that hour, but his lordship did not move nor answer me. I then looked to see if he were very sound asleep, and I saw that the pillows had got somehow over his face, and his head seemed to lie very low; so I moved the pillows, and I saw that his lordship was dead."

"Sir," said the surgeon, turning to Maltravers, "you were a friend of his lordship, I hear. I have already sent for Mr. Howard and Lord Doltimore. Shall I speak with you a minute?"

Maltravers nodded assent. The surgeon cleared the room of all but himself, De Montaigne, and Maltravers.

"Has that servant lived long with Lord Vargrave?" asked the surgeon.

"I believe so, — yes; I recollect his face. Why?"

"And you think him safe and honest?"

"I don't know; I know nothing of him."

"Look here, sir," — and the surgeon pointed to a slight discoloration on one side the throat of the dead man. "This may be accidental — purely natural; his lordship may have died in a fit; there are no certain marks of outward violence, but murder by suffocation might still — "

"But who besides the servant could gain admission? Was the outer door closed?"

"The servant can take oath that he shut the door before

going to bed, and that no one was with his lordship, or in the rooms, when Lord Vargrave retired to rest. Entrance from the windows is impossible. Mind, sir, I do not think I have any right to suspect any one. His lordship had been in very ill health a short time before; had had, I hear, a rush of blood to the head. Certainly, if the servant be innocent, we can suspect no one else. You had better send for more experienced practitioners."

De Montaigne, who had hitherto said nothing, now looked with a hurried glance around the room: he perceived the closet-door, which was ajar, and rushed to it, as by an involuntary impulse. The closet was large, but a considerable pile of wood, and some lumber of odd chairs and tables, took up a great part of the space. De Montaigne searched behind and amidst this litter with trembling haste, — no trace of secreted murder was visible. He returned to the bedroom with a satisfied and relieved expression of countenance. He then compelled himself to approach the body, from which he had hitherto recoiled.

"Sir," said he, almost harshly, as he turned to the surgeon, "what idle doubts are these? Cannot men die in their beds, of sudden death, no blood to stain their pillows, no loop-hole for crime to pass through, but we must have science itself startling us with silly terrors? As for the servant, I will answer for his innocence; his manner, his voice attest it." The surgeon drew back, abashed and humbled, and began to apologize, to qualify, when Lord Doltimore abruptly entered.

"Good heavens!" said he, "what is this? What do I hear? Is it possible? Dead! So suddenly!" He cast a hurried glance at the body, shivered, and sickened, and threw himself into a chair, as if to recover the shock. When again he removed his hand from his face, he saw lying before him on the table an open note. The character was familiar; his own name struck his eye, — it was the note which Caroline had sent the day before. As no one heeded him, Lord Doltimore read on, and possessed himself of the proof of his wife's guilt unseen.

The surgeon, now turning from De Montaigne, who had

been rating him soundly for the last few moments, addressed himself to Lord Doltimore. "Your lordship," said he, "was, I hear, Lord Vargrave's most intimate friend at Paris."

"I *his* intimate friend!" said Doltimore, colouring highly, and in a disdainful accent. "Sir, you are misinformed." .

"Have you no orders to give, then, my lord?"

"None, sir. My presence here is quite useless. Good-day to you, gentlemen."

"With whom, then, do the last duties rest?" said the surgeon, turning to Maltravers and De Montaigne. "With the late lord's secretary? — I expect him every moment; and here he is, I suppose," — as Mr. Howard, pale, and evidently overcome by his agitation, entered the apartment. Perhaps, of all the human beings whom the ambitious spirit of that senseless clay had drawn around it by the webs of interest, affection, or intrigue, that young man, whom it had never been a temptation to Vargrave to deceive or injure, and who missed only the gracious and familiar patron, mourned most his memory, and defended most his character. The grief of the poor secretary was now indeed overmastering. He sobbed and wept like a child.

When Maltravers retired from the chamber of death, De Montaigne accompanied him; but soon quitting him again, as Ernest bent his way to Evelyn, he quietly rejoined Mr. Howard, who readily grasped at his offers of aid in the last melancholy duties and directions.

CHAPTER VI.

If we do meet again, why, we shall smile. — *Julius Cæsar.*

THE interview with Evelyn was long and painful. It was reserved for Maltravers to break to her the news of the sudden death of Lord Vargrave, which shocked her unspeakably; and this, which made their first topic, removed much con-

straint and deadened much excitement in those which
followed.

Vargrave's death served also to relieve Maltravers from a
most anxious embarrassment. He need no longer fear that
Alice would be degraded in the eyes of Evelyn. Henceforth
the secret that identified the erring Alice Darvil with the
spotless Lady Vargrave was safe, known only to Mrs. Leslie
and to Aubrey. In the course of nature, all chance of its
disclosure must soon die with them; and should Alice at last
become his wife, and should Cleveland suspect (which was not
probable) that Maltravers had returned to his first love, he
knew that he might depend on the inviolable secrecy of his
earliest friend.

The tale that Vargrave had told to Evelyn of his early —
but, according to that tale, guiltless — passion for Alice, he
tacitly confirmed; and he allowed that the recollection of her
virtues, and the intelligence of her sorrows and unextinguish-
able affection, had made him recoil from a marriage with her
supposed daughter. He then proceeded to amaze his young
listener with the account of the mode in which he had discovered her real parentage, of which the banker had left it to
Alice's discretion to inform her, after she had attained the
age of eighteen. And then, simply, but with manly and ill-
controlled emotion, he touched upon the joy of Alice at
beholding him again, upon the endurance and fervour of her
love, upon her revulsion of feeling at learning that, in her
unforgotten lover, she beheld the recent suitor of her adopted
child.

"And now," said Maltravers, in conclusion, "the path to
both of us remains the same. To Alice is our first duty.
The discovery I have made of your real parentage does not
diminish the claims which Alice has on me, does not lessen
the grateful affection that is due to her from yourself. Yes,
Evelyn, we are not the less separated forever. But when I
learned the wilful falsehood which the unhappy man, now
hurried to his last account, to whom your birth was known,
had imposed upon me, — namely, that you were the child of
Alice, — and when I learned also that you had been hurried

into accepting his hand, I trembled at your union with one so false and base. I came hither resolved to frustrate his schemes and to save you from an alliance, the motives of which I foresaw, and to which my own letter, my own desertion, had perhaps urged you. New villanies on the part of this most perverted man came to my ear: but he is dead; let us spare his memory. For you — oh, still let me deem myself your friend, — your more than brother; let me hope now that I have planted no thorn in that breast, and that your affection does not shrink from the cold word of friendship."

"Of all the wonders that you have told me," answered Evelyn, as soon as she could recover the power of words, "my most poignant sorrow is, that I have no rightful claim to give a daughter's love to her whom I shall ever idolize as my mother. Oh, now I see why I thought her affection measured and lukewarm. And have I — I destroyed her joy at seeing you again? But you — you will hasten to console, to reassure her! She loves you still, — she will be happy at last; and that — that thought — oh, that thought compensates for all!"

There was so much warmth and simplicity in Evelyn's artless manner, it was so evident that her love for him had not been of that ardent nature which would at first have superseded every other thought in the anguish of losing him forever, that the scale fell from the eyes of Maltravers, and he saw at once that his own love had blinded him to the true character of hers. He was human; and a sharp pang shot across his breast. He remained silent for some moments; and then resumed, compelling himself as he spoke to fix his eyes steadfastly on hers.

"And now, Evelyn — still may I so call you? — I have a duty to discharge to another. You are loved" — and he smiled, but the smile was sad — "by a younger and more suitable lover than I am. From noble and generous motives he suppressed that love, — he left you to a rival; the rival removed, dare he venture to explain to you his own conduct, and plead his own motives? George Legard — " Maltravers paused. The cheek on which he gazed was tinged with a soft blush, Evelyn's eyes were downcast, there was a slight heaving beneath the robe.

Maltravers suppressed a sigh and continued. He narrated his interview with Legard at Dover; and, passing lightly over what had chanced at Venice, dwelt with generous eloquence on the magnanimity with which his rival's gratitude had been displayed. Evelyn's eyes sparkled, and the smile just visited the rosy lips and vanished again. The worst because it was the least selfish fear of Maltravers was gone, and no vain doubt of Evelyn's too keen regret remained to chill his conscience in obeying its earliest and strongest duties.

"Farewell!" he said, as he rose to depart; "I will at once return to London, and assist in the effort to save your fortune from this general wreck: LIFE calls us back to its cares and business — farewell, Evelyn! Aubrey will, I trust, remain with you still."

"Remain! Can I not return then to my — to her — yes, let me call her *mother* still?"

"Evelyn," said Maltravers, in a very low voice, "spare me, spare her that pain! Are we yet fit to — " He paused; Evelyn comprehended him, and hiding her face with her hands, burst into tears.

When Maltravers left the room, he was met by Aubrey, who, drawing him aside, told him that Lord Doltimore had just informed him that it was not his intention to remain at Paris, and had more than delicately hinted at a wish for the departure of Miss Cameron. In this emergency, Maltravers bethought himself of Madame de Ventadour.

No house in Paris was a more eligible refuge, no friend more zealous; no protector would be more kind, no adviser more sincere. To her then he hastened. He briefly informed her of Vargrave's sudden death; and suggested that for Evelyn to return at once to a sequestered village in England might be a severe trial to spirits already broken; and declared truly, that though his marriage with Evelyn was broken off, her welfare was no less dear to him than heretofore. At his first hint, Valerie, who took a cordial interest in Evelyn for her own sake, ordered her carriage, and drove at once to Lady

ALICE; OR, THE MYSTERIES.

Doltimore's. His lordship was out, her ladyship was ill, in her own room, could see no one, not even her guest. Evelyn in vain sent up to request an interview; and at last, contenting herself with an affectionate note of farewell, accompanied Aubrey to the home of her new hostess.

Gratified at least to know her with one who would be sure to win her affection and soothe her spirits, Maltravers set out on his solitary return to England.

Whatever suspicious circumstances might or might not have attended the death of Lord Vargrave, certain it is that no evidence confirmed and no popular rumour circulated them. His late illness, added to the supposed shock of the loss of the fortune he had anticipated with Miss Cameron, aided by the simultaneous intelligence of the defeat of the party with whom it was believed he had indissolubly entwined his ambition, sufficed to account satisfactorily enough for the melancholy event. De Montaigne, who had been long, though not intimately, acquainted with the deceased, took upon himself all the necessary arrangements, and superintended the funeral; after which ceremony, Howard returned to London; and in Paris, as in the grave, all things are forgotten! But still in De Montaigne's breast there dwelt a horrible fear. As soon as he had learned from Maltravers the charge the maniac brought against Vargrave, there came upon him the recollection of that day when Cesarini had attempted De Montaigne's life, evidently mistaking him in his delirium for another, — and the sullen, cunning, and ferocious character which the insanity had ever afterwards assumed. He had learned from Howard that the outer door had been left ajar when Lord Vargrave was with Maltravers. The writing on the panel, the name of Vargrave, would have struck Castruccio's eye as he descended the stairs; the servant was from home, the apartments deserted; he might have won his way into the bedchamber, concealed himself in the *armoire*, and in the dead of the night, and in the deep and helpless sleep of his victim, have done the deed. What need of weapons — the suffocating pillows would stop speech and life. What so easy as escape, — to pass into the anteroom; to unbolt the door; to descend into the courtyard; to give the signal to the porter in his lodge, who, without seeing him, would pull the *cordon*, and give him egress unobserved?

All this was so possible, so probable.

De Montaigne now withdrew all inquiry for the unfortunate; he trembled at the thought of discovering him, of verifying his awful suspicions, of beholding a murderer in the brother of his wife! But he was not doomed long to entertain fear for Cesarini; he was not fated ever to change suspicion into certainty. A few days after Lord Vargrave's burial, a corpse was drawn from the Seine. Some tablets in the pockets, scrawled over with wild, incoherent verses, gave a clew to the discovery of the dead man's friends: and, exposed at the Morgue, in that bleached and altered clay, De Montaigne recognized the remains of Castruccio Cesarini. "He died and made no sign!"

———◆———

CHAPTER VII.

SINGULA quæque locum teneant sortita.[1] — HORACE : *Ars Poetica.*

MALTRAVERS and the lawyers were enabled to save from the insolvent bank but a very scanty portion of that wealth in which Richard Templeton had rested so much of pride. The title extinct, the fortune gone — so does Fate laugh at our posthumous ambition! Meanwhile Mr. Douce, with considerable plunder, had made his way to America: the bank owed nearly half a million; the purchase money for Lisle Court, which Mr. Douce had been so anxious to get into his clutches, had not sufficed to stave off the ruin, — but a great part of it sufficed to procure competence for himself. How inferior in wit, in acuteness, in stratagem, was Douce to Vargrave; and yet Douce had gulled him like a child! Well said the shrewd

———

[1] "To each lot its appropriate place."

small philosopher of France — "On peut être plus fin qu'un autre, mais pas plus fin que tous les autres."[1]

To Legard, whom Maltravers had again encountered at Dover, the latter related the downfall of Evelyn's fortunes; and Maltravers loved him when he saw that, far from changing his affection, the loss of wealth seemed rather to raise his hopes. They parted; and Legard set out for Paris.

But was Maltravers all the while forgetful of Alice? He had not been twelve hours in London before he committed to a long and truthful letter all his thoughts, his hopes, his admiring and profound gratitude. Again, and with solemn earnestness, he implored her to accept his hand, and to confirm at the altar the tale which had been told to Evelyn. Truly he said that the shock which his first belief in Vargrave's falsehood had occasioned, his passionate determination to subdue all trace of a love then associated with crime and horror, followed so close by his discovery of Alice's enduring faith and affection, had removed the image of Evelyn from the throne it had hitherto held in his desires and thoughts; truly he said that he was now convinced that Evelyn would soon be consoled for his loss by another, with whom she would be happier than with him; truly and solemnly he declared that if Alice rejected him still, if even Alice were no more, his suit to Evelyn never could be renewed, and Alice's memory would usurp the place of all living love!

Her answer came: it pierced him to the heart. It was so humble, so grateful, so tender still. Unknown to herself, love yet coloured every word; but it was love pained, galled, crushed, and trampled on; it was love, proud from its very depth and purity. His offer was refused.

Months passed away. Maltravers yet trusted to time. The curate had returned to Brook-Green, and his letters fed Ernest's hopes and assured his doubts. The more leisure there was left him for reflection, the fainter became those dazzling and rainbow hues in which Evelyn had been robed

[1] One may be more sharp than one's neighbour, but one can't be sharper than all one's neighbours. — ROCHEFOUCAULD.

and surrounded, and the brighter the halo that surrounded his earliest love. The more he pondered on Alice's past history, and the singular beauty of her faithful attachment, the more he was impressed with wonder and admiration, the more anxious to secure to his side one to whom Nature had been so bountiful in all the gifts that make woman the angel and star of life.

Months passed. From Paris the news that Maltravers received confirmed all his expectations, — the suit of Legard had replaced his own. It was then that Maltravers began to consider how far the fortune of Evelyn and her destined husband was such as to preclude all anxiety for their future lot. Fortune is so indeterminate in its gauge and measurement. Money, the most elastic of materials, falls short or exceeds, according to the extent of our wants and desires. With all Legard's good qualities he was constitutionally careless and extravagant; and Evelyn was too inexperienced, and too gentle, perhaps, to correct his tendencies. Maltravers learned that Legard's income was one that required an economy which he feared that, in spite of all his reformation, Legard might not have the self-denial to enforce. After some consideration, he resolved to add secretly to the remains of Evelyn's fortune such a sum as might, being properly secured to herself and children, lessen whatever danger could arise from the possible improvidence of her husband, and guard against the chance of those embarrassments which are among the worst disturbers of domestic peace. He was enabled to effect this generosity unknown to both of them, as if the sum bestowed were collected from the wrecks of Evelyn's own wealth and the profits of the sale of the houses in C——, which of course had not been involved in Douce's bankruptcy. And then if Alice were ever his, her jointure, which had been secured on the property appertaining to the villa at Fulham, would devolve upon Evelyn. Maltravers could never accept what Alice owed to another. Poor Alice! No! not that modest wealth which you had looked upon complacently as one day or other to be his.

Lord Doltimore is travelling in the East, — Lady Dolti-

more, less adventurous, has fixed her residence in Rome.
She has grown thin, and taken to antiquities and rouge.
Her spirits are remarkably high — not an uncommon effect of
laudanum.

———◆———

CHAPTER THE LAST.

ARRIVED at last
Unto the wished haven. — SHAKSPEARE.

IN the August of that eventful year a bridal party were
assembled at the cottage of Lady Vargrave. The ceremony
had just been performed, and Ernest Maltravers had bestowed
upon George Legard the hand of Evelyn Templeton.

If upon the countenance of him who thus officiated as a
father to her he had once wooed as a bride an observant eye
might have noted the trace of mental struggles, it was the
trace of struggles past; and the calm had once more settled
over the silent deeps.   He saw from the casement the carriage
that was to bear away the bride to the home of another, — the
gay faces of the village group, whose intrusion was not forbidden, and to whom that solemn ceremonial was but a joyous pageant; and when he turned once more to those within
the chamber, he felt his hand clasped in Legard's.

"You have been the preserver of my life, you have been
the dispenser of my earthly happiness; all now left to me to
wish for is, that you may receive from Heaven the blessings
you have given to others!"

"Legard, never let her know a sorrow that you can guard
her from; and believe that the husband of Evelyn will be dear
to me as a brother!"

And as a brother blesses some younger and orphan sister
bequeathed and intrusted to a care that should replace a
father's, so Maltravers laid his hand lightly on Evelyn's
golden tresses, and his lips moved in prayer.   He ceased;

he pressed his last kiss upon her forehead, and placed her hand in that of her young husband. There was silence; and when to the ear of Maltravers it was broken, it was by the wheels of the carriage that bore away the wife of George Legard!

The spell was dissolved forever. And there stood before the lonely man the idol of his early youth, Alice, — still, perhaps, as fair, and once young and passionate, as Evelyn; pale, changed, but lovelier than of old, if heavenly patience and holy thought, and the trials that purify and exalt, can shed over human features something more beautiful than bloom.

The good curate alone was present, besides these two survivors of the error and the love that make the rapture and the misery of so many of our kind; and the old man, after contemplating them a moment, stole unperceived away.

"Alice," said Maltravers, and his voice trembled, "hitherto, from motives too pure and too noble for the practical affections and ties of life, you have rejected the hand of the lover of your youth. Here again I implore you to be mine! Give to my conscience the balm of believing that I can repair to you the evils and the sorrows I have brought upon you. Nay, weep not; turn not away. Each of us stands alone; each of us needs the other. In your heart is locked up all my fondest associations, my brightest memories. In you I see the mirror of what I was when the world was new, ere I had found how Pleasure palls upon us, and Ambition deceives! And me, Alice — ah, you love me still! Time and absence have but strengthened the chain that binds us. By the memory of our early love, by the grave of our lost child that, had it lived, would have united its parents, I implore you to be mine!"

"Too generous!" said Alice, almost sinking beneath the emotions that shook that gentle spirit and fragile form, "how can I suffer your *compassion* — for it is but compassion — to deceive yourself? You are of another station than I believed you. How can you raise the child of destitution and guilt to your own rank? And shall I — I — who, Heaven knows! would save you from all regret — bring to you now, when years have so changed and broken the little charm I could ever have possessed, this blighted heart and weary spirit? Oh, no, no!" and Alice paused abruptly, and the tears rolled down her cheeks.

"Be it as you will," said Maltravers, mournfully; "but, at least, ground your refusal upon better motives. Say that now, independent in fortune, and attached to the habits you have formed, you would not hazard your happiness in my keeping, — perhaps you are right. To *my* happiness you would indeed contribute; your sweet voice might charm away many a memory and many a thought of the baffled years that have intervened since we parted; your image might dissipate the solitude which is closing round the Future of a disappointed and anxious life. With you, and with you alone, I might yet find a home, a comforter, a charitable and soothing friend. This you could give to me; and with a heart and a form alike faithful to a love that deserved not so enduring a devotion. But I — what can I bestow on you? Your station is equal to my own; your fortune satisfies your simple wants. 'T is true the exchange is not equal, Alice. Adieu!"

"Cruel!" said Alice, approaching him with timid steps. "If I could — I, so untutored, so unworthy — if I could comfort you in a single care!"

She said no more, but she had said enough; and Maltravers, clasping her to his bosom, felt once more that heart which never, even in thought, had swerved from its early worship, beating against his own!

He drew her gently into the open air. The ripe and mellow noonday of the last month of summer glowed upon the odorous flowers, and the broad sea, that stretched beyond and afar, wore upon its solemn waves a golden and happy smile.

"And ah," murmured Alice, softly, as she looked up from his breast, "I ask not if you have loved others since we parted — man's faith is so different from ours — I only ask if you love me now?"

"More! oh, immeasurably more, than in our youngest days!" cried Maltravers, with fervent passion. "More fondly, more reverently, more trustfully, than I ever loved living being! — even her, in whose youth and innocence I adored the memory of thee! Here have I found that which shames and bankrupts the Ideal! Here have I found a virtue, that, coming at once from God and Nature, has been wiser than all my false philosophy and firmer than all my pride! You, cradled by misfortune, — your childhood reared amidst scenes of fear and vice, which, while they scared back the intellect, had no pollution for the soul, — your very parent your tempter and your foe; you, only not a miracle and an angel by the stain of one soft and unconscious error, — you, alike through the equal trials of poverty and wealth, have been destined to rise above all triumphant; the example of the sublime moral that teaches us with what mysterious beauty and immortal holiness the Creator has endowed our human nature when hallowed by our human affections! You alone suffice to shatter into dust the haughty creeds of the Misanthrope and Pharisee! And your fidelity to my erring self has taught me ever to love, to serve, to compassionate, to respect the community of God's creatures to which — noble and elevated though you are — you yet belong!"

He ceased, overpowered with the rush of his own thoughts. And Alice was too blessed for words. But in the murmur of the sunlit leaves, in the breath of the summer air, in the song of the exulting birds, and the deep and distant music of the heaven-surrounded seas, there went a melodious voice that seemed as if Nature echoed to his words, and blest the reunion of her children.

Maltravers once more entered upon the career so long suspended. He entered with an energy more practical and steadfast than the fitful enthusiasm of former years; and it was noticeable amongst those who knew him well, that while the firmness of his mind was not impaired, the haughtiness of his temper was subdued. No longer despising Man as he is, and no longer exacting from all things the ideal of a visionary standard, he was more fitted to mix in the living World, and to minister usefully to the great objects that refine and elevate our race. His sentiments were, perhaps, less lofty, but his actions were infinitely more excellent, and his theories infinitely more wise.

Stage after stage we have proceeded with him through the MYSTERIES OF LIFE. The Eleusinia are closed, and the crowning libation poured.

And Alice! — Will the world blame us if you are left happy at the last? We are daily banishing from our law-books the statutes that disproportion punishment to crime. Daily we preach the doctrine that we demoralize wherever we strain justice into cruelty. It is time that we should apply to the Social Code the Wisdom we recognize in Legislation! It is time that we should do away with the punishment of death for inadequate offences, even in books; it is time that we should allow the morality of atonement, and permit to Error the right to hope, as the reward of submission to its suffering. Nor let it be thought that the close to Alice's career can offer temptation to the offence of its commencement. Eighteen years of sadness, a youth consumed in silent sorrow over the grave of Joy, have images that throw over these pages a dark and warning shadow that will haunt the young long after they turn from the tale that is about to close! If Alice had died of a broken heart, if her punishment had been more than she could bear, *then*, as in real life, you would have justly condemned my moral; and the human heart, in its pity for the victim, would have lost all recollection of the error. — My tale is done.

THE END.

www.ingramcontent.com/pod-product-compliance
Lightning Source LLC
Chambersburg PA
CBHW020923020726
47495CB00002B/313